Kate Hewitt ha
from drama tea
worker, but writing romance is the best one yet. She also writes women's fiction and all her stories celebrate the healing and redemptive power of love. Kate lives in a tiny village in the English Cotswolds with her husband, five children, and an overly affectionate Golden Retriever.

Lucy Gordon cut her writing teeth on magazine journalism, interviewing many of the world's most interesting men, including Warren Beatty and Roger Moore. Several years ago, while staying in Venice, she met a Venetian who proposed in two days. They have been married ever since. Naturally this has affected her writing, where romantic Italian men tend to feature strongly. Two of her books have won a Romance Writers of America *RITA*® Award. You can visit her website at lucy-gordon.com

Melanie Milburne read her first Mills & Boon at age seventeen in between studying for her final exams. After completing a Masters Degree in Education she decided to write a novel and thus her career as a romance author was born. Melanie is an ambassador for the Australian Childhood Foundation and is a keen dog lover and trainer and enjoys long walks in the Tasmanian bush. In 2015 Melanie won the HOLT Medallion, a prestigious award honouring outstanding literary talent.

Irresistible Italians

January 2023
A Dangerous Deal

February 2023
Securing a Prince

March 2023
A Scandalous Proposition

April 2023
A Price To Pay

May 2023
One Perfect Moment

June 2023
A Holiday Proposal

Irresistible Italians:

A Dangerous Deal

KATE HEWITT

LUCY GORDON

MELANIE MILBURNE

MILLS & BOON

First Published in Great Britain 2023
By Mills & Boon, an imprint of HarperCollins*Publishers,* Ltd
1 London Bridge Street, London, SE1 9GF

www.harpercollins.co.uk

HarperCollins*Publishers*
Macken House, 39/40 Mayor Street Upper,
Dublin 1, D01 C9W8, Ireland

ISBN: 978-0-263-31845-6

This book is produced from independently certified FSC™ paper to ensure responsible forest management.

For more information visit: www.harpercollins.co.uk/green

Printed and Bound in Spain using 100% Renewable electricity at CPI Black Print, Barcelona

THE BRIDE'S AWAKENING

KATE HEWITT

CHAPTER ONE

VITTORIO RALFINO, the Count of Cazlevara, stood on the threshold of San Stefano Castle and searched the milling guests for the woman he intended to be his wife. He wasn't certain what she looked like for, beyond a single small photo, he hadn't seen her in sixteen years. Or if he had seen her, she hadn't made much of an impression. Now he planned to marry her.

Anamaria Viale wasn't readily apparent amidst the tuxedo and evening gown-clad crowd circulating through the candlelit foyer. All he remembered from when he'd seen her at her mother's funeral was a sad, sallow face and too much dark hair. She'd been thirteen years old. The photo in the magazine gave little more information; she had good teeth. Still, her looks—or lack of them—did not interest Vittorio. Anamaria Viale possessed the qualities he was looking for in a wife: loyalty, health and a shared love of this land and its grapes. Her family's vineyard would be an asset to his own; together they would rule an empire and create a dynasty. Nothing else mattered.

Impatiently, he strode into the castle's medieval hall. Shadows danced along the stone walls and he felt the curious stares of neighbours, acquaintances and a few friends. He heard the murmur of speculative whispers travel around the ancient hall in a ripple of suppressed sound and knew he was their subject. He hadn't been back in Veneto for more than a day or two at a time in the last fifteen years. He'd kept away from the place and its memories and regrets. Like a hurt little boy, he'd run away from his past and pain, but he was a man now and he was home for good—to find a wife.

'Cazlevara!' Someone clapped him on the back, thrusting a glass of wine into his hand. His fingers closed around the fragile stem as a matter of instinct and he inhaled the spicy, fruity scent of a bold red. 'You must try this. It's Busato's new red—he's blended his grapes, *Vinifera* and *Molinara*. What do you think?'

Vittorio took a practised sip, swilling the rich liquid in his mouth for a moment before swallowing. 'Good enough,' he pronounced, not wanting to get into a detailed discussion about the merits of mixed grapes, or whether Busato, one of the region's smaller winemakers, was going to give Castle Cazlevara, his own winery—the region's largest and most select—any competition. He wanted to find Anamaria.

'I heard the rumours. You're home then? You're going to make some wine?'

Vittorio glanced at the man who had been speaking to him: Paolo Prefavera, a colleague of his father's. His round cheeks were already rosy with drink and he smiled with the genial bonhomie of an old family friend, although his eyes were shrewd.

'I've always been making wine, Paolo. Castle Cazlevara produces nine hundred thousand bottles a year.'

'While you've been touring the world—'

'It's called marketing.' Vittorio realized he was speaking through his teeth. He smiled. 'But yes, I'm home for good.' Home, so he could rein his grasping brother Bernardo back in, before he squandered the rest of the winery's profits. Home, so he could keep his treacherous mother from taking what was his—and his heir's. At this thought, his forced smile turned genuine, even though his eyes remained hard. 'Have you seen Anamaria

Viale?' Paolo's eyebrows rose and Vittorio stifled a curse. He was too impatient; he knew that. When he made a decision, he wanted it carried out immediately, instantly. He'd decided to marry Anamaria Viale nearly a week ago; it felt like an eternity. He wanted it done; he wanted her vineyard joined to his, he wanted *her* joined to him, in his bed, by his side, being a wife.

Paolo smiled slyly and Vittorio forced himself to smile back. Now there would be whispers, rumours. Gossip. 'I have a question to ask her,' he explained with a shrug, as if it were no matter.

'She was over by the fireplace, last time I saw her.' Paolo gave a small chuckle, more of a guffaw. 'How could you miss her?'

Vittorio didn't understand what Paolo meant until he neared the huge stone fireplace. An alarmingly large stuffed boar's head was mounted above the hearth and a few men were gathered underneath, sipping wine and chatting quietly. At least he thought they were all men. Narrowing his eyes, he realized the tall, strong figure in the centre of the group was actually a woman. Anamaria.

His mouth tightened as he took in his intended wife, dressed in an expensive-looking but essentially shapeless trouser suit. Her long dark hair was held back in a clip and looked as thick and coarse as a horse's tail. She held a glass of wine as most of the castle's guests did; the evening was, after all, a wine-tasting for the province's premier winemakers and guests. She had, Vittorio saw, strong, even features; pretty was not necessarily a word he would use to describe them. There was something too earthy and bold about her, he decided. He preferred the women he took to his bed to be more delicate, fragile even. *Slim.*

Not, he amended, that Anamaria Viale was overweight. Not at all. Big-boned was the word he might have chosen, although his mother would have sneered and called her *grassa*. Fat.

Vittorio's mouth thinned at the thought of his mother. He could hardly wait to see the look on the old bitch's face when he told her he was getting married. Bernardo, her precious favourite, fool that he was, would never inherit. Her plans—the plans she'd cherished since the moment his father's will had been read—would come to nothing.

Vittorio smiled at the thought, little more than a bitter twisting of his mouth, and dismissed his bride's looks as a matter of no importance. He didn't want a beautiful woman; beautiful women, like his mother and his last mistress, were never satisfied, always finding fault. He'd left his mistress in Rio pouting for more time, money, even love. He'd told her he would never set eyes on her again.

Anamaria, he was sure, would take what she was given and be grateful, which was exactly what he wanted. A wife—a humble, grateful wife—the most important accessory a man could ever possess.

Surveying her tall, strong form, Vittorio was quite sure a woman like her was unused to male attention; he anticipated her stammering, blushing pleasure when the Count of Cazlevara singled her out.

He stepped forward, straightening his shoulders, and adopted an easy-going, self-assured smile whose devastating effect he knew well.

'Anamaria.' His voice came out in a low, suggestive hum.

She turned, stiffening in surprise when she saw him. Her eyes widened and a smile dawned on her face, a fragile, tremulous gesture of joy, brightening her whole countenance for the barest of moments. Vittorio smiled back; he almost laughed aloud. This was going to be so easy.

Then she drew herself up—her height making Vittorio appreciate Paulo's comment once more—and raked him with one infuriatingly dismissive glance, that amazed smile turning cool and even—could it be?—contemptuous. He was still registering the change in her expression and mood—his smug satisfaction giving way to an uneasy alarm—when she spoke.

'Hello, Lord Cazlevara.' Her voice was low, husky. Almost, Vittorio thought with a flicker of distaste, like a man's. Although, he noted, there was nothing particularly unpleasing about her features: straight brows and nose, dark grey eyes, the good teeth he'd noticed before. She was not, at least, ugly; rather, she was exceedingly plain. He let his smile deepen to show the dimple in his cheek, determined to win this plain spinster over. A woman like Anamaria would surely appreciate any charm thrown her way.

'Let me be the first to say how lovely you look tonight.'

She raised her eyebrows, the flicker of that cool smile curling her mouth and glinting in her eyes. They had, he saw, gold flecks that made them seem to shimmer. 'You will indeed be the first to say so.'

It took Vittorio a moment to register the mockery; he couldn't believe she was actually making fun of him—as well as of herself. Feeling slightly wrong-footed—and unused to it—Vittorio reached for her hand, intending to raise it to his lips even as he cursed the way he'd phrased his flattery. For flattery it was indeed, and she knew it. She was not stupid, which he supposed was a good thing. She let his lips brush her skin, something darkening her eyes—those gold flecks becoming molten—before she quite deliberately pulled her hand away.

The crowd around them had fallen back, yet Vittorio was conscious of avid stares, intent ears and, even more so, his own mounting annoyance. This first meeting was not going the way he'd anticipated—with him firmly in control.

'To what do I owe such a pleasure?' Anamaria asked. 'I don't believe we've seen each other in well over a decade.' Her voice caught a little, surprising him. He wondered what she was thinking of, or perhaps remembering.

'I'm simply glad to be back home,' Vittorio replied, keeping his voice pitched low and smooth, 'among beautiful women.'

She snorted. She actually snorted. Vittorio revised his opinion; the woman was not like a man, but a horse. 'You have learned honeyed words on your trips abroad,' she said shortly.

'They are far too sweet.' And, with a faintly mocking smile, she turned and walked away from him as if he were of no importance at all. *She* left *him*.

Vittorio stood there in soundless shock, his fury rising. He'd been summarily dismissed, and he, along with the little knot of spectators around him, was conscious of it. He felt the stares, saw a few smug smiles, and knew he'd been put properly in his place, as if he were a naughty schoolboy being disciplined by a mocking schoolmarm. It was a feeling he remembered from childhood, and he did not like it.

Standing there, Vittorio could not escape the glaringly—and embarrassingly—obvious conclusion: as far as opening gambits went, his had been an utter failure.

He'd been planning to ask her to marry him, if not tonight, then certainly in the next few days. When he decided a thing—even to marry—he wanted it done. Completed. Over. He had no time or patience for finer emotions, and frankly he'd considered the wooing of such a woman to be an easy exercise, a mere dispensing of charm, a few carefully chosen compliments.

After reading the article about her—and seeing her photo—he'd assumed she would be grateful for whatever attention she received. She was unmarried and nearing thirty; his proposal would be, he'd thought, a gift. Maybe even a miracle.

Perhaps he had been arrogant, or at least hasty. The wooing and winning of Anamaria Viale would take a little more thought.

Vittorio smiled. He liked challenges. Admittedly, time was of the essence; he was thirty-seven and he needed a wife. An heir. Yet surely he had a week—or two—to entice Anamaria into marriage? He wasn't interested in making the woman fall in love with him, far from it. He simply wanted her to accept what was a very basic business proposition. She was the candidate he'd chosen, the most suitable one he could find, and he wasn't interested in any others. Anamaria Viale would be his.

Still, Vittorio realized, he'd acted like a fool. He was annoyed with himself for thinking a woman—any woman—could be charmed so thoughtlessly. It was a tactical error, and one he would not make again. The next time he met Anamaria Viale, she would smile at him because she couldn't help herself; she would hang on his every word. The next time he met her, it would be on his terms.

Anamaria made sure she didn't look back as she walked away from the Count of Cazlevara. Arrogant ass. Why on earth had he approached her? Although they were virtually neighbours, she hadn't seen him in at least a decade. He hadn't had more than two words for her in the handful of times she *had* seen him, and yet now he'd expressly sought her out at tonight's tasting, had looked for her and given her those ridiculous compliments.

Beautiful women. She was not one of them, and she knew it. She never would be. She'd been told enough. She was too tall, too big-boned, too mannish. Her voice was too loud, her hands and feet too big; everything about her was awkward and unappealing to men like Vittorio, who had models and starlets and bored socialites on his arm. She'd seen the photos in the tabloids, although she pretended not to know. Not even to look. She did, on occasion anyway, because she was curious. And not just curious, but jealous, if she were honest with herself, which Anamaria always tried to be. She was jealous of those tiny, silly slips of women—women she'd gone to school with, women who had no use for her—who could wear the skimpy and sultry clothes she never could, who revelled in their own femininity while she plodded along, clumsy and cloddish. And Vittorio knew it. In the split second before she'd spoken, she'd seen the look in his eyes. Disdain, verging on disgust.

She knew that look; she'd seen it in Roberto's eyes when she'd tried to make him love her. Desire her. He hadn't. She'd seen it in other men's eyes as well; she was not what men thought of—or liked to think of—when they considered a woman. A pretty woman, a desirable one.

She'd become used to it, armoured herself with trouser suits and a practical, no-nonsense attitude, the best weapons a woman like her could have. Yet tonight, from Vittorio—stupidly—that look of disdain had hurt. She'd been so glad to see him, for that split second. Stupidly glad. She'd actually thought he'd remembered—

Why on earth had he approached her with that asinine flattery? Had he been attempting some sort of misguided chivalry, or worse, had he been mocking her? And why had he sought her out so directly in the first place?

He was the Count of Cazlevara—he could have any woman he wanted—and yet he'd entered the party and made straight for her. She only knew that because she'd seen him enter the castle, and felt her heart skip and then completely turn over. Even from afar, he was magnificent; well over six feet, he walked with a lithe grace, his suit of navy silk worn with careless elegance. His eyes—as black as polished onyx—had narrowed and his assessing gaze had swept the hall as if he were looking for someone.

That was all she'd seen before she'd been pulled into another conversation, and now Anamaria wondered if he'd actually been looking for *her*.

Stupid. Fanciful. Wishful thinking, even. Vittorio could have anyone he wanted. Why on earth would he bother with her for a moment?

And yet, for some reason, he *had*.

Anamaria's cheeks burned and she took a hasty sip of wine, barely tasting the superb vintage—she was, ironically, drinking one of Cazlevara's own. It seemed, she acknowledged bleakly, far more likely that he'd been mocking her. Amusing himself with a little easy flattery of a woman who would surely only lap it up gratefully. She knew the type. She'd dealt before with men who treated her with condescending affection, and acted surprised when they were rebuffed. Yet Vittorio hadn't been surprised by her rebuff—he'd been furious.

Anamaria's lips curved into a smile. *Good.*

She knew very little about Vittorio. She knew the facts, of course. He was the richest man in Veneto, as well as a Count. His winery—the region's best—had been run by the Cazlevaras for hundreds of years. In comparison, her own family's three hundred year heritage seemed paltry.

His father had died when he was a teenager; she, along with several thousand others, had been at the memorial service at San Marco in Venice. The funeral had been a quiet family affair at the Cazlevara estate. As soon as he reached his majority, he'd gone travelling—drumming up more business for the winery—and hardly ever came home. He'd been more or less absent—gone—for nearly fifteen years. Anamaria could only imagine that a man like Vittorio needed more entertainment than the rolling hills and ancient vineyards Veneto could provide.

She pictured him now, remembering how he'd looked at her from those gleaming onyx eyes. He was a beautiful man, but in a hard way. Those high, sharp cheekbones seemed almost cruel—at least they did when his eyes were narrowed in such an assessing manner, his mouth pursed in telling disdain before he'd offered her such a false smile.

Yet, even as she considered how she'd seen him only a few moments ago, another memory rose up and swamped her senses. The only real memory she had of Vittorio Cazlevara. The memory that had made her smile when she'd seen him again—smile with hope and even, pathetically, with joy.

It had been at her mother's funeral. November, cold and wet. She'd been thirteen and hadn't grown into her body yet, all awkward angles, her limbs seeming to fly out of their own accord. She'd stood by the graveside, her hand smeared with the clump of muddy dirt she'd been asked to throw on her mother's casket. It had landed with a horrible thunk and she'd let out an inadvertent cry, the sound of a wounded animal.

As the mourners had filed out, Vittorio—he must have been around twenty years old then—had paused near her. It was only later that she'd wondered why he'd come at all; their families were acquaintances, nothing more. She hadn't registered the tall, dark presence for a moment; she'd been too shrouded in her own pall of grief. Then she'd looked up and those eyes—those beautiful eyes, dark with compassion—had met hers. He'd touched her cheek with his thumb, where a tear still sparkled.

'It's all right to be sad, *rondinella*,'—swallow—he'd said, softly enough so only she could hear. 'It's all right to cry.' She'd stared at him dumbly, his thumb still warm against her chilled cheek. He smiled, so sadly. 'But you know where your mother is now, don't you?' She shook her head, not wanting to hear some paltry platitude about how Emily Viale was happy now, watching her daughter from some celestial cloud. He took his thumb, damp with her tears, and touched it to his breastbone. 'In here. *Tua cuore.*' Your heart. And with another sad, fleeting smile, he had moved away.

She'd known then that he'd lost his father a few years before. Even so, she hadn't realized another person could understand her so perfectly. How someone—a stranger—had been able to say exactly the right thing. How later, when she wept scalding tears into her pillow, wept until she felt she'd be sick from it and her mind and body and heart all felt wrung, wasted, she'd remember his words.

It's all right to cry.

He'd helped her to grieve. And when the pain had, if not stopped, then at least lessened, she'd wanted to tell him that. She'd wanted to say thank you, and she supposed she'd wanted to see if he still understood her. Understood her more, even, than before. And she'd wanted to discover if she, perhaps, understood him too. A ridiculous notion, when that passing comment was the only conversation they'd ever really shared.

Over the years, she'd almost—almost—forgotten about Vittorio's words at her mother's graveside. Yet in that second when she'd seen him again, every frail, childish hope had leapt to life within her and she'd thought—she'd actually *believed*—that he remembered. That it had meant something.

Her pathetic foolishness, even if only for a second, annoyed her. She wasn't romantic or a dreamer; any dreams of romance—love, even—she'd once entertained as a child had died out years ago, doused by the hard reality of boarding school, when she'd been a picked-on pigeon among swans. Ana's mouth twisted cynically. Perhaps not a pigeon, but a swallow, a plain and unprepossessing bird, after all.

They'd flickered briefly back to life in her university days, enough so that she had been willing to take a risk with Roberto.

That had been a mistake.

And, just now, the moment Vittorio Ralfino's mouth had tightened in disdain and then uttered words Anamaria knew to be false…the last faint, frail hope she hadn't even known she'd still possessed had flickered out completely. Mockery or lies. She didn't know which. It hardly mattered.

Anamaria took another sip of wine and turned to smile at another winemaker—Busato, a man in his sixties with hair like cotton wool and a smile as kind as that of *Babbo Natale*. As one of the few female winemakers in the room, she appreciated his kindness, as well as his respect. And, she told herself firmly, she would dismiss Vittorio Cazlevara completely from her mind, as he had undoubtedly dismissed her from his. A few words exchanged nearly seventeen years ago hardly mattered now. She wouldn't be surprised if Vittorio didn't remember them; it certainly shouldn't *hurt*. He'd merely been offering her a few pleasantries, scraps tossed from his opulent table, no doubt, and she vowed not to give them a second thought.

A light gleamed in one of the downstairs windows of Villa Rosso as she headed up the curving drive. Her father was waiting for her, as he always did when she went to these events; just a few years ago he would have gone with her, but now he chose to leave such things entirely to her. He claimed she needed her independence, but Anamaria suspected the socialising tired him. He was, by nature, a quiet and studious man.

'Ana?' His voice carried from the study as she entered the villa and slipped off her coat.

'Yes, Papà?'

'Tell me about the tasting. Was everyone there?'

'Everyone important,' she called back, entering the study with a smile, 'except you.'

'Bah, flattery.' Her father sat in a deep leather armchair by the fireplace; a fire crackled in the hearth to ward off the night's chill. A book lay forgotten in his lap and he took off his reading spectacles to look at her, his thin, lined face creasing into a smile. 'You needn't say such things to me.'

'I know,' she replied, sitting across from him and slipping off her shoes, 'and so I should, since I was the subject of a flatterer myself tonight.'

'Oh?' He shut his book and laid it on the side table, next to his spectacles. 'What do you mean?'

She hadn't meant to mention Vittorio. She'd been trying to forget him, after all. Yet somehow he'd slipped right into their conversation before it had even started, and it couldn't even surprise her because, really, hadn't he been in her mind all evening?

'The Count of Cazlevara has returned,' she explained lightly. 'He made an appearance tonight. Did you know he was back?'

'Yes,' Enrico said after a moment and, to Ana's surprise, he sounded both thoughtful and guarded. 'I did.'

'Really?' She raised her eyebrows, tucking her feet under her as she settled deeper into the armchair of worn, butter-soft leather. 'You never told me.' She couldn't quite keep the faint note of reproach from her voice.

Her father hesitated and Ana had the distinct feeling he was hiding something from her. She wondered how she even knew it to be a possibility, when their relationship—especially in the years after her mother had died—had been so close, so open. It hadn't always been that way, God knew, but she'd worked at it and so had he, and yet now…? Was he actually hiding something from her?

She gave a little laugh. 'Well, Papà?'

He shrugged. 'It didn't seem important.'

Ana nodded, accepting, because of course it shouldn't be important. She barely knew Vittorio. That one moment by her mother's graveside shouldn't even count. 'Well, it's late,' she finally said, smiling. 'I'm tired, so I think I shall go to bed.'

Ana scooped up her shoes, letting them dangle from her fingers as she walked slowly from the library through the darkened foyer and up the marble stairs that led to the second floor of the villa. She walked past darkened room after darkened room; the villa had eight bedrooms and only two were ever used. They rarely had guests.

Vittorio's few words had unsettled her, she realized as she entered her room and began to undress for bed. They shouldn't have—what a meaningless conversation it had been! Barely two sentences, yet they reverberated through her mind, her body, their echoes whispering provocatively to her.

She hadn't expected to have such a reaction to the man when she'd barely spared him a thought these last years. Yet the moment he'd entered the castle, she'd been aware of him. Achingly, alarmingly, *agonizingly* aware, her body suddenly springing to life, as if it had been numb or asleep, or even dead.

She slipped on her pyjamas and let her hair out of its restraining clip.

Outside her window, the moon bathed the meadows in silver and she could just make out the shadowy silhouettes in the vineyard that gave Villa Rosso both its name and fortune—*rosso* for the colour of the wine those grapes produced, a rich velvety red that graced many a fine table in Italy and, more recently, abroad.

Ana sat in her window seat, her legs drawn up to her chest, her chin resting on her knees. The wind from the open window stirred her hair and cooled her cheeks—she hadn't realized they'd been heated. Had she been blushing?

And what for? If she had any sort of social life at all, that tiny exchange with Vittorio would have meant less than nothing. Yet the hard fact was that she didn't, and it had. She was twenty-nine years old, staring at her thirtieth birthday in just a few months, without even the breath of hope of a social life beyond the wine-making events and tastings she went to, mostly populated by men twice her age. Not exactly husband material.

And was she even looking for a husband? Ana asked herself sharply. She'd given up that kind of dream years ago, when it had been pathetically, painfully obvious that men were not interested in her. She'd chosen to fill her life with business, friends and family—her father, at least—rather than pursue romance—love—that had, over the years, always seemed to pass her by. She'd *let* it go by, knowing those things were not for her. She'd accepted it…until tonight.

Still, she wished now that Vittorio hadn't come back, wished his absurd flattery—false as it so obviously was—hadn't stirred up her soul, reminded her of secret longings she'd forgotten or repressed. She'd been ignored so long—as a woman—that she'd become invisible, even to herself. She simply didn't think of herself that way any more.

She leaned her head back against the cool stone, closing her eyes as the wind tangled her hair and rattled in the trees outside.

She wanted, she realized with a sharp pang, Vittorio Cazlevara to look at her not with disdain or disgust, but with desire. She wanted him to say the things he'd said to her tonight—and more—and mean them.

She wanted to feel like a woman. For once.

CHAPTER TWO

'SIGNORINA VIALE, YOU have a visitor.'

'I do?' Ana looked up from the vine she'd been inspecting. It was the beginning of the growing season and the vines were covered in tiny unripened fruit, the grapes like perfect, hard little pearls.

'Yes.' Edoardo, one of the office assistants, looked uncomfortable—not to mention incongruous—in his immaculate suit and leather loafers. He must have been annoyed at having to tramp out to the vineyard to find her, but Ana always seemed to forget to bring her mobile. 'It is Signor Ralfino…I mean the Count of Cazlevara.'

'Vittorio…?' Ana bit her lip as she saw Edoardo's surprised look. The name had slipped out before she could stop herself, yet she was hardly on intimate terms with the Count. Why was he here? It had been only three days since she'd last seen him at the wine-tasting event and now he'd come to Villa Rosso, to her home, to find her? She felt a strange prickling along her spine, a sense of ominous yet instinctive foreboding, the way she did before a storm. Even when the sun beat down from a cloudless sky, she could tell when rain was coming. She knew when to cover the grapes from frost. It was one of the things that made her a natural—and talented—winemaker. Yet she had no idea if her instincts were right when it came to men. She'd hardly had enough experience to find out. 'Is he in the office?' she asked, a bit abruptly, and Edoardo nodded.

The sun was hot on her bare head and Ana was suddenly conscious of her attire: dusty trousers and a shirt that stuck to her back. It was what she normally wore on her regular inspection of the Viale vineyards, yet she hardly expected to receive visitors in such clothing…and certainly not Vittorio.

Why was he here?

'Thank you, Edoardo. I'll be with him shortly.' Disconcerted by the sudden heavy thudding of her own heart, Ana turned back to the vines, stared blindly at the clusters of tiny grapes. She waited until she heard him leave, and the rustle of vines as he passed, and then she drew in a long shuddering breath. She unstuck her shirt from her back and brushed a few sweaty strands of hair from her forehead. She was a mess. This was not how she wanted the Count of Cazlevara to see her.

Unfortunately, she had no choice. She could hardly walk the half-kilometre back to the villa to change if Vittorio was already waiting in the winery office.

She'd undoubtedly kept him waiting long enough. Vittorio Cazlevara did not, Ana acknowledged, seem like a patient man. Taking another deep breath, she tried her best to straighten her clothes—how had her shirt become so untucked and with a long streak of dirt on one sleeve?—and, throwing back her shoulders, she headed towards the office.

The long, low building with its creamy stone and terracotta tiles was as much a home to Ana as the villa was. It was a place where she felt confident and in control, queen of her domain, and that knowledge gave her strength as she entered. Here, it didn't matter what she looked like or how she dressed. Here, she was Vittorio's equal.

Vittorio stood by the sofa that was meant for visitors, a coffee table scattered with glossy magazines in front of it. His hands shoved deep in his pockets, he prowled the small space with a restless energy that radiated from his powerful body. He looked like a caged panther, full of contained power, dark and vaguely threatening.

Yet why should she be threatened by him? He was just a man…but what a man. He wore an exquisite suit made of Italian silk, perfectly tailored and hugging his powerful frame—his tall frame, for he had at least four inches on her own five foot eleven. His hair was inky-dark and cut close, emphasizing those hooded onyx eyes, the slashes of his severe brows. He looked up and those knowing eyes fixed on her, making Ana realize she'd been gawping like a schoolgirl. She straightened, managing a small, cool smile.

'Count Cazlevara. An unexpected pleasure.'

'Vittorio, please.' His gaze swept her in an instant, his mouth tightening in what Ana recognized as that now familiar disdain. He didn't even realize how he gave himself away, she thought with a strange little pang of sorrow. Was he going to try some more asinine flattery on her? She braced herself, knowing, no matter what, it would hurt. 'I'm sorry if I've interrupted you,' Vittorio said, and Ana gestured to her dishevelled clothes, even managing a wry smile as if her attire was not humiliating, despite him being dressed with such exquisite care.

'I'm afraid I was not expecting visitors. I was out in the vineyard, as you can see.'

'How are your grapes?'

'Growing.' She turned away from him, surreptitiously tucking in her blouse, which seemed determined on coming untucked at every opportunity. 'The weather has been good, thank God. May I offer you refreshment?'

He paused, and she glanced back at him. His head was cocked, and he was studying her with a thoughtful thoroughness she decided she didn't like. 'Yes, thank you. It is a warm day.'

Did his eyes linger on her heated face, her sticky shirt? Ana willed herself not to flush even more. If even the Count of Cazlevara was going to arrive unannounced, he would have to take her as she was. 'Indeed. Why don't we adjourn to the tasting room? It is more comfortable in there.' Vittorio gave a terse little jerk of his head, and Ana led the way to the room at the back of the winery that was meant for public gatherings.

The room was light and airy, with a vaulted ceiling and large windows that let in the late morning sunshine. A few tables, made from retired oak barrels, were scattered around with high stools. Ana sat down on one of the leather sofas positioned in one corner, meant for a more intimate conversation. She sat down, smoothing her dusty trousers and offering Vittorio another smile, bright and impersonal. Safe. 'How may I help you, Vittorio?' She stumbled only slightly over his Christian name; she wasn't accustomed to using it, even if she had been thinking it to herself.

He didn't reply, instead giving her an answering smile that showed the white flash of his straight, even teeth and said, 'You've done well for yourself these last years, Anamaria. The Viale label has grown in stature—not to mention price.'

'Please call me Ana. And thank you. I've worked hard.'

'Indeed.' He steepled his fingers under his chin, surveying her with that knowing little smile that she now found irritated her. 'And you've stayed at Villa Rosso all these years?'

She gave a little shrug, trying not to be defensive. 'It is my home.'

'You haven't wanted to travel? Go to university? See a bit of the world?'

'I'm happy where I am, Vittorio,' Ana replied, her voice sharpening just a little bit. 'And I did go to university. I took a degree in viticulture at the University of Padua.'

'Of course.' He nodded. 'I forgot.' Ana almost asked him how he would have known such a thing in the first place, but she decided to hold her tongue. 'Your father must be very glad of your dedication and loyalty to Viale Wines—and to him, of course. You've lived with him all these years?'

'Yes.' Ana tilted her head, wondering where these seemingly innocuous comments were coming from. Why did the Count of Cazlevara care what she had been doing these last ten or fifteen years? What interest could he possibly have in Viale Wines? 'I cannot imagine doing anything else,' Ana said simply, for it was the truth. Viale Wines had become her life, her blood. Besides her father and her home, she had little else. Vittorio smiled, seeming pleased by her answer, and an assistant bustled in with a pitcher of iced lemon water and two frosted glasses.

'Thank you,' Ana murmured and, after the assistant had left, she poured two glasses and handed one to Vittorio. 'So,' she said when they'd both sipped silently for a moment, 'you're back at last from your travels abroad. To stay this time?'

'It would seem so. I have, I realize, been gone too long.' His mouth tightened, his eyes looking hard, and for a moment Ana was discomfited, wondering just what had brought him back to Veneto.

'Are you glad to be back?' she asked and his eyes, still hard with some unnamed emotion, met hers.

'Yes.'

Ana nodded. 'Still, it must have been nice to see so many places.' Could she sound more inane? She resisted the urge to wipe her damp palms on her trousers. She wanted to demand to know why he was here, what he wanted from her. This was the second time he'd sought her out, and she could not fathom why he was doing so. Why he would *want* to.

'It was.' He set his glass down on the coffee table with a quiet clink. 'And it was, of course, business.'

'Yes.'

Vittorio still gazed at her in that assessing manner, saying nothing. His silence unnerved her, made her edgy and a little desperate. She wasn't used to feeling so at odds; she'd become accustomed to being in control of her own life, especially here at the winery, her own little kingdom.

'Sometimes business and pleasure mix, however,' he finally said, his words seeming heavy with meaning, and Ana gave a little nod and smile although she hardly knew what he was saying, or why.

'Indeed.' Her nerves now taut and starting to fray, she forced another little laugh and said, 'I must confess, Vittorio, I don't know why you're here. It is good to have you back in Veneto, of course, but if I am to be frank, we've had very little to do with one another.' There. It was said. If she'd been rude, Ana didn't care; his presence, so confident—arrogant—and supremely male, unsettled her. It made her heart jump and her palms sweat and, worst of all, it made some sweet, nameless longing rise up in her like a hungry tide. She swallowed and kept her gaze firmly on him.

He leaned forward to take his glass once more, and the scent of his cologne—something faintly musky—wafted over her. Inadvertently, instinctively, she pressed back against the sofa cushions. He lifted his gaze to meet hers once more, yet she could tell nothing from those onyx eyes. They were as blank as polished marble. 'Actually, Ana, I came to ask you to dinner.'

The words seemed to fall into the stillness of the room, and of her heart. Did he mean a date? she wondered incredulously, even as a sense of sudden fierce pleasure rushed through her. A *date*. When was the last time she'd been on one of those, and with a man like Vittorio Ralfino? She felt her cheeks heat—how easily she gave herself away—and to cover her confusion, she reached for her glass and took a sip.

'I see I've surprised you.'

'Yes.' She pressed the glass against her hot cheek, lifting her gaze to smile wryly at him. 'We have not seen each other in years and, in any case—' She stopped, biting her lip, pulling it between her teeth and nipping it hard enough to draw a drop of blood. She tasted it on her tongue, hard and metallic. Vittorio smiled, his eyes on her mouth, and Ana knew he'd witnessed that traitorous little display of her own uncertainty.

'In any case?' he prompted gently.

She gave a helpless little shrug. 'I'm not exactly the kind of woman—' She stopped again, wishing she had not revealed so much. She didn't know how *not* to; she was terrible at lying, or even dissembling. She could only speak her heart, always had. It had never been dangerous before.

And it had been so long—forever—since a man had asked her out. Since she'd even *hoped* a man might ask her out.

'The kind of woman I take out to dinner?' Vittorio filled in. 'But how would you know what kind of woman I take out to dinner?'

'I don't,' Ana said quickly, too quickly. 'But I know—' She stopped again. There was no way of saving herself or her pride, it seemed. 'I am surprised, that's all,' she finally said, and pressed her lips tightly together to keep from revealing anything more.

Vittorio didn't answer, and Ana couldn't tell a thing from his expression. Surprisingly, she found she was not blushing now; instead, she felt cold and lifeless. This—this feeling of terrible numbness—was why she'd stopped looking for a man, for love. It hurt too much.

She put her glass back down on the table. Memories rushed in to fill the blank spaces in her mind and heart. The cruel laughter of the girls at boarding school, the interminable school dances where she'd clutched a glass of lukewarm punch and tried to make herself invisible. It hadn't been hard to do; no one had wanted to see her anyway.

Stupid schoolgirl memories, yet how they still hurt. How another man's attention—and his disdain—brought it all back.

'I see,' he said finally and, on opening her eyes, Ana felt he saw too much. The last thing she wanted was his pity. 'Actually,'

Vittorio continued, watching her carefully, 'I want to discuss a business proposition with you.' He waited, still watching, and Ana's eyes widened in horror. Now the blush came, firing her body from the roots of her hair to the tips of her toes. She'd made *such* a fool of herself, assuming he was asking her out. And of course he hadn't corrected her, she realized with a vicious little stab of fury. He'd probably enjoyed seeing her squirm, relished her awful confession. *I'm not exactly the kind of woman...* He knew just what she'd meant, and his expression told her he agreed with her. As many had before.

'A business proposition,' she finally repeated, the silence having gone on, awkwardly, for at least a minute. 'Of course.'

'It might not be the kind of business proposition you're expecting,' Vittorio warned with a little smile and Ana tried for an answering laugh, though inwardly she was still writhing with humiliation and remembered pain.

'Now you have me intrigued.'

'Good. Shall we say Friday evening?'

Ana jerked her head in acceptance. 'Very well.' It didn't seem important to pretend she needed to check some schedule, that she might be busy. That she might, in fact, have a *date*. Vittorio would see right through her. He already had.

'I'll pick you up at Villa Rosso.'

'I can meet you—'

'I am a gentleman, Ana,' Vittorio chided her wryly. 'I shall enjoy escorting you somewhere special.'

And where exactly was somewhere special? Ana wondered. And, more alarmingly, what should she wear? Her wardrobe of businesslike trouser suits hardly seemed appropriate for a dinner date...except it wasn't a date, had never been meant to be a date, she reminded herself fiercely. It was simply a business proposition. A trouser suit would have to do. Still, Ana was reluctant to don one. She didn't want to look like a man; she wanted to feel like a woman. She didn't dare ask herself why. For over ten years—since her university days—she'd dressed and acted not purposely like a man, more like a sexless woman. A woman who wasn't interested in fashion, or beauty, or even desire. Certainly not love. It had been safer that way; no expectations or hopes to have dashed, no one—especially herself—to disappoint. There was no earthly reason to change now. There was every reason to keep as she'd been, and stay safe.

On Friday night she stood in front of the full-length mirror in her bedroom, gazing rather ruefully at her reflection. She wore a pair of fitted black trousers with a rather unfortunately boxy jacket; it had looked better on the rack. Her one concession to femininity was the cream silk beaded tank top she wore underneath, and that was completely hidden by the jacket. She piled her hair up on top of her head, wincing a little bit at the strands that insisted on escaping to frame her face and curl with surprising docility along her neck. She couldn't decide if the loose tendrils gave her a look of elegance or dishevelment. She didn't attempt any make-up, as she'd never mastered the art of doing her face without looking like a child who had played in her mother's make-up box.

'There.' She nodded at her reflection, determined to accept what she saw. Wearing a sexy cocktail dress or elegant gown would have been ridiculous, she told herself. She never wore such things—she didn't own such things—and, considering Vittorio's business proposition, there was no reason to start now.

Her father was, as usual, in the study when Ana came downstairs. Most evenings he was content to hole up in the villa with a book or a game of solitaire.

Enrico looked up from his book, raising his eyebrows at her outfit. 'Going out, my dear?'

Ana nodded, suppressing a little pang of guilt. She hadn't told her father about this dinner with Vittorio; she told herself she'd simply forgotten, but she knew that wasn't true. She hadn't wanted him to know, and start reading more into this dinner than there was or ever could be.

'Yes,' she said now, dropping a kiss on the top of his thinning hair. 'Dinner.'

'A date?' Enrico asked, sounding pleased. Ana shook her head and stepped away to look out of the window. Twilight was stealing softly upon the world, cloaking the landscaped gardens in violet.

'No. Just business.'

'Always business,' her father said a bit grumpily, and Ana smiled.

'You know I love it.' And she did love it; the wine, the grapes were in her blood. Her father loved to tell the story about when he had taken her to the vineyards when she was only two years old. He'd hoisted her up to the vines and she'd plucked a perfectly ripe grape, deeply purple and bursting with flavour, and popped it into her mouth. Then, instead of saying how tasty it was, she'd pronounced in a quite grown-up voice, '*Sono pronti.*' They're ready.

'I worry you work too much.'

Ana said nothing, for she knew she had no argument. She did work too much; she had nothing else. In the last few years her father had stepped back from the winery business, as he'd never really wanted to be more than a gentleman vintner, tending the family grapes. Ana wanted more. She dreamed of the day when Viale wines were in every fine restaurant in Europe, and even America. When they were held in reserve for special customers, the bottles dusty and precious. When they rivalled Cazlevara Wines.

Just then she saw headlights pierce the growing darkness, and a navy Porsche swept up the drive. Ana watched from the window, her heart starting to thud with hard, heavy beats as Vittorio stepped from the car. In the lengthening shadows she couldn't see what he wore, yet she could tell he looked magnificent. She felt it in her own shivery response.

The doorbell rang.

'Someone is coming for you?' Enrico asked, his book forgotten in his lap.

'Yes—' Ana started from the study.

'Whoever it is,' Enrico called after her, 'invite him in.'

By the time she reached the door she was breathless and flushed, simply from nerves. Vittorio stood there, hands thrust deep into his pockets, looking as magnificent as Ana knew he would in an immaculately tailored suit of navy silk. His shirt was crisp and white and a tie of aquamarine silk was knotted at the brown column of his throat.

Ana swallowed, her mouth dry, her head empty of thoughts. She could not think of a single thing to say.

'Hello, Ana.' He smiled, a quick flash of white teeth. 'Are you ready?'

Ana nodded, conscious of both how Vittorio had not complimented her—or even commented on—her appearance, and that her father was sitting in the next room, waiting for her to usher in her guest. She swallowed. 'Yes, but would you like to come in for a moment? My father…' She trailed off, hating how hesitant she sounded. 'My father would like to say hello,' she said firmly, and then turned to lead Vittorio to the study without looking back to see if he followed.

Once in the study Ana stepped aside as her father looked up and smiled. He didn't, she realized with a jolt, look very surprised. 'Good evening, Vittorio.'

'Good evening, sir.'

Enrico smiled, pleased by the sign of respect. 'You are going out for dinner?'

'In a manner of speaking. I thought we could eat at Castle Cazlevara.'

Ana looked at him in surprise. Dinner in his own castle? She'd been to the castle once, for a Christmas party when she was a child. She remembered a huge Christmas tree, twenty feet high, in the castle's soaring entrance hall, and eating too many sweets.

Uneasily, Ana realized Vittorio and her father had been talking, and she hadn't heard a word. Now Vittorio turned to her, smiling solicitously. 'We should go.'

'Yes, all right.'

One hand rested lightly on the small of her back—the simple touch seemed to burn—as Vittorio said goodbye to Enrico and then led her out to the softly falling darkness and his waiting car.

Vittorio opened the passenger door for Ana before sliding in the driver's side. She was nervous, he saw, and her clothes were utterly atrocious. He'd been about to compliment her when she'd first opened the door and had just stopped himself from uttering what they both knew would be more unwanted false flattery.

He drummed his fingers against the steering wheel as Ana fastened her seat belt. He felt impatient, as he so often did, and also, strangely, a little uncertain. He didn't like either feeling. He didn't know how best to approach Ana, how to court her, if such a thing could even be done. He doubted he could act convincingly enough. As intelligent and decent a human being as she obviously was, she was not a woman to take to bed. Yet if this marriage was to work—if he were to have an heir—then he would be taking her to bed, and more than once.

Vittorio dwelt rather moodily on that scenario before pushing it aside. He could have chosen another woman, of course; there were plenty of pretty—gorgeous, even—socialites in Italy who would relish becoming the Contessa of Cazlevara. Women he would gladly take to bed but, ironically perhaps, he did not wish to marry them.

Their vineyards did not border his own; they were not dedicated to winemaking, to the region. They were not particularly loyal. They were not, any of them, wife material.

Ana was. When he'd contemplated taking a wife, Ana Viale had ticked every box quite neatly. Experienced in winemaking, running her own vineyard, a dutiful daughter, healthy and relatively young.

And, of course, loyalty. He'd read of her loyalty to her family, and her family's vineyard, in that magazine article. Loyalty was a necessity, an absolute; he would not be betrayed again, not by those closest to him.

No, Anamaria Viale was the wife he wanted. The only wife he wanted.

His hands tightened on the steering wheel as he thought of the other reason—really, the main reason—he wished to marry at all. He needed an heir. God willing, Ana would provide him with one, and would keep his brother—treacherous Bernardo—from ever becoming Count, as his mother had so recently told him she wanted.

The conversation, as it always was with Constantia, the current Countess, had been laced with bitterness on both sides. She'd rung asking for money; had there ever been anything else she wanted from him?

'I don't know why you hoard all your money, Vittorio,' she'd said a bit sulkily. 'Who are you keeping it for?'

He'd been distracted by the business emails on his computer screen, her words penetrating only after a moment. 'What do you mean?'

She'd sighed, the sound impatient and a bit contemptuous; it was a sound he remembered well from childhood, for it had punctuated nearly every conversation he'd had with his mother. 'Only that you are getting on in years, my son,' she had said, and he had heard the mocking note in her voice. 'You're thirty-seven. You are not likely to marry, are you?'

'I don't know,' he'd replied, and she'd laughed softly, the sound making the hair on the nape of his neck prickle.

'But if you don't marry, Vittorio, you can't produce an heir. And then you know what happens, don't you?' She sighed again, the sound different this time, almost sad. 'Bernardo becomes Count.'

He'd frozen then, his hand curled around the receiver, his eyes dark with memory and pain. That was what his mother had always wanted, what his brother had wanted. He'd known it for years, ever since they'd first tried to steal his inheritance from him, his father barely in the grave.

He didn't forget.

And how could he have forgotten the importance of marriage, of children? He'd been so intent on improving Cazlevara Wines, of forgetting the unhappiness he knew waited for him back home. He'd never considered the future, his future. His heirs.

Now he did. He'd considered carefully, chosen his bride as he would a fine wine. Now he just needed to decide when to decant it.

Vittorio drummed his fingers against the steering wheel again and saw Ana slide him a wary glance. How to approach his chosen bride? She sat tensely, one hand clenched around the door handle as if she would escape the speeding car. The suit she wore looked like something pulled out of a convent's charity box and it did nothing for her tall, generous figure. Not that there was something to be done for her figure, but Vittorio imagined that some decent clothes and make-up could go some way to improving his intended bride's appearance.

His mouth twisted. What would Ana think if she knew he planned to marry her—and as soon as possible? Of course, any woman should be thrilled to become part of the Cazlevara dynasty, yet he felt instinctively that Ana Viale might balk. He knew from the other night at San Stefano Castle that she would not be fooled by his attempts to flatter or romance her, and why should she? God knew, the women he usually had on his arm or in his bed did not look or dress or even talk like Ana Viale. Yet he didn't want to marry them. He wanted to marry Ana. It was a matter of expediency, of business.

And that, Vittorio decided, was how he would present the marriage to her. She appreciated plain speaking, and so he would speak as plainly as possible. The thought appealed to him. He wouldn't have to waste time pretending to be attracted to her. Most women would enjoy a little flattery, but he knew now that it would only annoy Ana, perhaps even hurt her.

A tiny twinge of something close to guilt pierced his conscience. Would Ana want some kind of *real* marriage? Was she waiting for love?

With him it was impossible, and she needed to know that from the start. Surely a woman like her was not still holding out for love? She seemed too practical for that, not to mention too plain. Besides, she could always say no.

Except Vittorio would make sure she didn't.

Ana pressed back against the leather seat as the darkened countryside, rolling hills and clusters of oak trees, sped by. She sneaked another glance at Vittorio's rather forbidding profile. He hadn't spoken since they'd got in the car, and he didn't look as if he was up for a chat. His jaw was tight, his eyes narrowed, his hands clenched around the steering wheel. What was he thinking? Ana didn't want to ask. She turned towards the window, tried to still the nerves writhing in her middle. They drove for at least twenty minutes without speaking, and then Ana saw the lights of Castle Cazlevara on a hill in the distance, mere pinpricks in the unrelenting darkness. Vittorio turned into the mile-long private drive that wound its way up the hill to his home.

Ana had seen photos of the castle on postcards, and of course she'd been there the one time. Yet, even so, the sight of the huge medieval castle perched on jutting stone awed and even intimidated her. Its craggy turrets rose towards the darkened sky and an ancient-looking drawbridge was now lowered over the drained moat. At one point the castle had been an imposing fortress, perched high on its hill, surrounded by a deep moat. Now it was simply Vittorio's home.

'So your own home is the "somewhere special"?' she asked lightly, and was rewarded with the flicker of a smile.

'I must admit I find Castle Cazlevara rather special.'

Gazing up at the castle's soaring walls and towers, Ana could only agree. Special, and a bit scary.

Vittorio drove across the drawbridge and parked the car in the castle's inner courtyard, now paved over with slate, providing a perfect backdrop for the Porsche. The building had been updated from the time it had served as a fortress against barbarian invaders—and, if Ana remembered her history, the Pope's own army—although it still retained much of its charm. Though charm was hardly the word, Ana thought as Vittorio came around to open her door before she could even touch the handle. It was darkly impressive, forbiddingly beautiful. Like its owner. Gas-lit torches flickered on either side of the entrance doors as Vittorio led her up the stone stairs.

The huge entryway was filled with dancing shadows, a thick Turkish carpet laid over the ancient stones. Polished mahogany doors led to several large reception rooms, now lost in shadow, but Vittorio forewent these in favour of a small passageway in the back of the main hall. Ana followed him, conscious of the castle all around them, huge, dark and silent.

'Have you ever wanted to build something else?' she asked to Vittorio's back. The narrow corridor was cold and dark. 'A palazzo somewhere, something modern?'

Vittorio stiffened slightly, yet noticeable still to Ana. She was so aware of him: his powerful shoulders and long back, the muscles rippling under the smooth silk of his suit, even the faint musk of him. Aware of his moods, changing like quicksilver, even though he did not look at her or speak. It was strange, being so aware. So *alive*. She wasn't used to it.

'The Counts of Cazlevara have always lived here,' he said simply. 'And their families. Although my mother lives near Milan for much of the year, in a palazzo like you mentioned.' There was a sharp note to his voice, a hint of something dark and even cruel, something Ana couldn't understand. He turned, his eyes gleaming from the light of the sconces positioned intermittently along the stone walls. 'Could you not imagine living in such a place as this?'

In a flash of insight—or perhaps just imagination—Ana *could* see herself living there. She pictured herself in the gracious drawing rooms, presiding over a Christmas party like the one she'd gone to as a child. Overseeing a feast in the ancient dining hall, as if she were the Contessa herself, inviting the citizens of Veneto into her gracious home. Such images caused longing to leap within her. Surprised by its intensity, she pushed the images away; they were absurd, impossible, and surely not what Vittorio meant.

'There is certainly a great deal of history here,' she said, once again to his back.

'Yes. Many centuries. Yet your own family has been in Veneto a long time.'

'Three hundred years,' Ana conceded wryly. 'No more than a day compared to yours.'

'A bit more than a day,' Vittorio said, laughter in his voice. He stopped in front of a polished wooden door which he opened so Ana could enter. 'And now. Dinner.'

Ana took in the cosy room with a mixture of alarm and anticipation. Heavy velvet curtains were drawn at the windows, blocking out the night. A fire crackled in the hearth and sent dancing shadows around the candlelit room. A table for two had been laid in front of the fire, with a rich linen tablecloth and napkins, the finest porcelain and crystal. On a small table to the side, a bottle of red had already been opened to breathe. It was an intimate scene, a romantic scene, a room ready not for business, but seduction.

Ana swallowed. She walked to the table, one hand on the back of a chair. When had she last had a meal like this, shared a meal like this? Never. The idea of what was to come filled her with a dizzying sense of excitement that she told herself she had no right to feel. She shouldn't even want to feel it. Yet still it came, bubbling up inside of her, treacherous and hopeful. This felt like a date. A real date. She cleared her throat. 'This all looks lovely, Vittorio. Somewhere special indeed.'

Vittorio smiled and closed the door behind him. They were completely alone; Ana wondered whether there was anyone else in the castle at all. 'Do you live here alone since you've returned?' she asked.

Vittorio shrugged. 'My brother Bernardo and my mother Constantia are in Milan. They come and go as they please.'

His tone was strange, cold, and yet also almost indifferent. It made Ana wonder if he considered his brother and mother—the only family he had left—as nothing more than interlopers in his own existence. Surely not. Ever since her own mother had died, she'd clung to her father, to the knowledge that he was her closest and only relative, that all they had was each other. Surely Vittorio felt the same?

He pulled back her chair and Ana sat, suppressing a shiver of awareness as he took the heavy linen napkin and spread it across her lap, his thumbs actually brushing her inner thighs. Ana jerked in response to the touch, a flush heating her cheeks, warming her insides. She had never been touched so intimately, and the thought was shaming. He'd just been putting a napkin in her lap.

She supposed it was her lack of experience with men that made her so skittish and uncertain around Vittorio, hyper-aware of everything he did, every sense stirring to life just by being near him. That had to be it; nothing else made sense. This aching awareness of him was just due to her own inexperience. She didn't go on dates and she didn't flirt. She did not know what it felt like to be desired.

And you're not desired now.

This dinner—this room—with all of its seeming expectations was going to her head. It was setting her up, Ana realized, for a huge and humiliating fall. She'd fallen before, she reminded herself, her would-be boyfriend at university had had to spell out the plain truth.

I'm just not attracted to you.

Neither was Vittorio. He wasn't even pretending otherwise. She mustn't forget that, no matter what the trappings now, Vittorio was not interested in her as a woman. This was simply how he did business. It had to be.

And so it would be how she did business as well.

'Wine?' Vittorio asked and held up the bottle. With a little dart of surprised pleasure, Ana realized it was one of Viale's labels. The best, she acknowledged as she nodded and Vittorio poured.

He sat down across from her and raised his glass. Ana raised her own in response. 'To business propositions.'

'Intriguing ones, even,' Ana murmured, and they both drank.

'Delicious,' Vittorio pronounced, and Ana smiled.

'It's a new blend—'

'Yes, I read about it.'

She nearly spluttered in surprise. 'You did?'

'Yes, in the in-flight magazine on my trip home.' Vittorio placed his glass on the table. 'There was a little article about you. Have you seen it?' Ana nodded jerkily. The interview had been short, but she'd been glad—and proud—of the publicity. 'You've done well for yourself, Ana, and for Viale Wines.'

'Thank you.' His words meant more to her than they ought, she knew, but she couldn't keep the fierce pleasure at his praise from firing through her. Ana had worked long and hard to be accepted in the winemaking community, to make Viale Wines the name it was.

A few minutes later a young woman, diminutive and dark-haired, came in with two plates. She set them down, Vittorio murmured his thanks and then she left as quietly as she had come.

Ana glanced down at the paper-thin slices of prosciutto and melon. 'This looks delicious.'

'I'm glad you think so.'

They ate in silence and Ana's nerves grew more and more taut, fraying, ready to break. She wanted to demand answers of Vittorio; she wanted to know just what this business proposition was. She wasn't good at this, had never been good at this; she couldn't banter or flirt, and at the moment even idle chatter seemed beyond her.

It was too much, she thought with a pang. Being here with a devastatingly handsome man—with Vittorio—eating delicious food, drinking wonderful wine, watching the firelight play with shadows on his face—all of it was too much. It made her remember all the things she'd once wanted that she'd long ago accepted she'd never have. A husband. Children. A home of her own. She'd made peace with that, with the lack in her life, because there was so much she had, so much she loved and enjoyed. She'd *thought* she'd made peace with it, but now she felt restless and uncertain and a little bit afraid. She *wanted* again.

She had no idea why Vittorio—Vittorio, of all people, who was so unbearably out of her league—made her feel this way. Made her remember and long for those things. Made her, even now, wonder if his hair felt as crisp as it looked, or if it would be soft in her hands. If she touched his cheek would she feel the flick of stubble against her fingers? Would his lips be soft? Would he taste like her own wine?

Ana nearly choked on a piece of melon, and Vittorio looked

up enquiringly. 'Are you all right?' he asked, all solicitude, and she nodded almost frantically.

'Yes—yes, fine.' She could hardly believe the direction her thoughts had taken, or the effect they were having on her body. Her limbs felt heavy and warm, a deep, pleasurable tingling starting low in her belly and then suddenly, mischievously flaring upwards, making her whole being clench with sudden, unexpected spasms of desire.

She'd never thought to feel this way, had thought—hoped, even—she'd buried such desperate longings. For surely they were desperate. This was *Vittorio*. Vittorio Ralfino, the Count of Cazlevara, and he'd never once looked at her as a woman. He never would.

They ate in near silence, and when they were finished the woman came back to clear the plates and replace them with dishes of homemade ravioli filled with fresh, succulent lobster.

'Have you missed home?' Ana asked in an effort to break the strained silence. Or perhaps it wasn't strained and she only felt it was because her nerves were so fraught, her body still weak with this new desire, desperate for more. Or less. She was torn between the safety of its receding and the need for it to increase. To actually touch. Feel. *Know.*

Vittorio seemed utterly unaware of her dilemma; he sat sprawled in his chair, cradling his glass of wine between his palms.

'Yes,' he replied, taking a sip. 'I shouldn't have stayed away so long.'

Ana was surprised by the regret in his voice. 'Why did you?'

He shrugged. 'It seemed the right thing to do at the time. Or, at least, the easy thing to do.' Vittorio took a bite of ravioli. 'Eat up. These ravioli are made right here at the castle, and the lobster were caught fresh only this morning.'

'Impressive,' Ana murmured, and indeed it was delicious, although she barely enjoyed a mouthful for she felt the tension and the need building inside her, tightening her chest and making it hard even to breathe. She wanted to ask him what she was doing here; she wanted to reach across the table and touch him. The need to touch was fast overriding the need to know. Action would replace words and if she had just one more glass of wine she was afraid she would do just what she was thinking—fantasising—about and actually touch him.

She wondered how Vittorio would react. Would he be stunned? Flattered? Repulsed? It was too dangerous to even imagine a scenario, much less to want it—crave it…

She could stand it no more. She set down her fork and gave Vittorio as direct a look as she could. 'As lovely as this meal is, Vittorio, I feel I have to ask. I must know.' She took a breath and let it out slowly, laying her hand flat on the table so she didn't betray herself and reach out to touch him. 'Just what is this business proposition you are thinking of?'

Vittorio didn't answer for a long moment. He glanced at the wine in his glass, ruby-red, glinting in the candlelight. He smiled almost lazily—making her insides flare with need once more—and then set his glass down on the table.

'Well,' he said with a wry little smile, 'if you must know, it is simply this. I want you to marry me.'

CHAPTER THREE

THE words seemed to ring in the empty air, filling the room, even though the only sound was the crackle of the fire as the logs settled into the grate, scattering a bit of ash across the carpet.

Ana stared, her mind spinning, her mouth dry. Once again, she couldn't think of a single thing to say. She wondered if she'd heard him correctly. Surely she'd imagined the words. Had she wanted him to say such a thing? Was she so ridiculous, pathetic, that she'd *dreamed* it?

Or had he been joking? Common sense returned. Of course he was joking. She let her lips curve into a little smile, although she knew the silence had gone on too long. She reached for her wine. 'Really, Vittorio,' she said, shaking her head a little bit as if she actually shared the joke, 'I want to know why.'

He leaned forward, all lazy languor gone, replaced with a sudden intentness. 'I'm serious, Ana. I want to marry you.'

She shook her head again, unable to believe it. Afraid to believe it. He must be joking, even if it was a terrible joke. A cruel one.

She'd known cruel jokes before. Girls hiding her clothes after gym, so she had to walk through the locker rooms in a scrap of a towel while they giggled and whispered behind their hands. The boy who had asked her to dance when she was fifteen—she'd accepted, incredulously, and he'd laughed and run away. She'd seen the money exchange grubby adolescent hands, and realized he'd only asked her as a bet. And of course the one man she'd let into her life, had wanted to give her body to, only to be told he didn't think of her that way. Roberto had acted affronted, as if she'd misunderstood all the time they'd spent together, the dinners and the late nights studying. Perhaps she had misunderstood; perhaps she was misunderstanding now.

Yet, looking at Vittorio's calm face, his eyes focused intently on hers, Ana slowly realized she hadn't misunderstood. He wasn't joking. He was serious. And yet surely he couldn't be—surely he could not possibly want to marry *her*.

'I told you the proposition was an intriguing one,' he said, and there was laughter in his voice.

'That's one word for it,' Ana managed, and took a healthy draught of wine. It went down the wrong way and for a few seconds her eyes watered as she tried to suppress a most inelegant cough. A smile lurked in Vittorio's eyes, in the upward flick of his mouth and he reached out to touch her shoulder, his hand warm even through the thick cloth of her jacket.

'Just cough, Ana. Better out than in.'

She covered her mouth with her hand, managing a few ladylike coughs before her body took over and she choked and spluttered for several minutes, tears streaming from her eyes, utterly inelegant. Vittorio poured her a glass of water and thrust it into her hands.

'I'm sorry,' she finally managed when she had control over herself once more. She wiped her eyes and took a sip of water.

'Are you all right?' She nodded, and he leaned back in his chair. 'I see I've surprised you.'

'You could say that.' Ana shook her head, still unable to believe Vittorio had actually said what she'd thought he had said. And if he had said it, why? What on earth was he thinking of? None of it made sense. She couldn't even *think*.

'I didn't intend to speak so plainly, so quickly,' Vittorio said, 'but I thought you'd appreciate an honest business proposition.'

Ana blinked, then blinked again. She glanced around the room with its flickering candles and half-drunk glasses of wine, the fire burned down to a few glowing embers; the desire still coiled up inside her, desperate to unfurl. What a fool she was. 'Ah,' she said slowly, 'business.' Marriage must, for a man like Vittorio, determined and ambitious, be a matter of business. 'Of course.' She heard the note of disappointment in her own voice and cringed inside. Why should she feel let down? Everything she'd wanted and felt—that had been in her own head. Her own body. Not Vittorio's. She turned to gaze at him once more, her expression direct and a little flat. 'So just how is marriage a business proposition?'

Vittorio felt the natural vibrancy drain from Ana's body, leaving the room just a little bit colder. Flatter. He'd made a mistake, he realized. Several mistakes. He'd gone about it all wrong, and he'd tried so hard not to. He'd seen her look around the room, watched her take in all the trappings of a romantic evening which he'd laid so carefully. The fire, the wine, the glinting crystal. The intimate atmosphere that wrapped around them so suggestively. It was not, he realized, a setting for business. *Fool.* If he'd been intending to conduct this marriage proposal with a no-nonsense business approach, he should have done it properly, in a proper business setting. Not here, not like this. This room, this meal promised things and feelings he had no intention or desire to give. And Ana knew it. That was why she looked so flat now, so…*disappointed.*

Did she actually want—or even expect—that from him? Had she convinced herself this was a *date*? The thought filled Vittorio with both shame and disgust. He could not, he knew, pretend to be attracted to her. He shouldn't even try. He shouldn't have brought her to this room at all. He needed to stop pretending he was wooing her. Even when he knew he wasn't, he still fell back on old tactics, old ploys that had given him success in the past.

Now was the time for something new.

Vittorio leaned forward. 'Tell me, Ana, do you play cards?'

Ana looked up, arching her eyebrows in surprise. 'Cards…?'

'Yes, cards.' Vittorio smiled easily. 'I thought after dinner we could have a friendly game of cards—and discuss this business proposition.'

She arched her eyebrows higher. 'Are you intending to wager?'

Vittorio shrugged. 'Most business is discussed over some time of sport or leisure—whether it is golf, cards, or something else entirely.'

'How about billiards?'

Vittorio's own eyebrows rose, and Ana felt a fierce little dart of pleasure at his obvious surprise. 'You play billiards?'

'*Stecca*, yes.'

'*Stecca*,' Vittorio repeated. 'As a matter of fact, the castle has a five pins table. My father put it in when he became Count.' He paused. 'I played with him when I was a boy.'

Ana didn't know if she was imagining the brief look of sorrow that flashed across Vittorio's face. She remembered hearing, vaguely, that he'd been very close to his father.

It's all right to be sad, rondinella.

She pushed the memory away and smiled now with bright determination. 'Good. Then you know how to play.'

Vittorio chuckled. 'Yes, I do. And I have to warn you, I'm quite good.'

Ana met his dark gaze with a steely one of her own. 'So am I.'

He led her from the cosy little room with the discarded remains of their meal, down another narrow corridor into the stone heart of the castle and then out again, until he came to a large, airy room in a more recent addition to the castle, with long sash windows that looked out onto a darkened expanse of formal gardens. In the twilit shadows Ana could only just discern the bulky shapes of box hedges and marble fountains. The room looked as if it hadn't been used in years; the billiards table was covered in dust sheets and the air smelled musty.

'I suppose you haven't played in a while,' she said, and Vittorio flashed a quick grin that once more caused her insides to fizz and flare. She did her best to ignore the dizzying sensation, pleasant as it was.

'Not here, anyway.' He pulled the sheet off the table and balled it up, tossing it in a corner, then opened the windows so the fresh, fragrant air wafted in from the gardens. 'The cues are over there. Do you want something to drink?'

Ana felt reckless and a little bit dangerous; she knew why Vittorio had asked her if she played cards, why they were here about to play billiards instead of back in that candlelit room. This was business. *She* was business. He could not have made it plainer. And that was fine; she could handle this. Any disappointment she'd felt—unreasonably so—gave way to a cool determination. 'I'll have a whisky.'

Vittorio gazed at her for a moment, his expression thoughtful and perhaps even pleased, his mouth curling upwards into a little smile before he nodded and went to push a button hidden discreetly by the door. Within minutes another servant—this time a man, some kind of butler—appeared at the doorway, silent and waiting.

'Mario, two whiskies please.'

'Yes, my lord.'

Ana selected her cue and carefully chalked the end. She studied the table with its three balls: two cue balls, one white, one yellow and a red object ball. Vittorio was setting up the castle in the middle of the table: five skittles, four white, one red, made into a cross. The object of the game was simple: you wanted to knock your opponent's ball into the skittles for points, or have it hit the red object ball. Her father liked to say it was a grown-up game of marbles.

'So where did you learn to play *stecca*?' Vittorio asked as he stepped back from the table.

'My father. After my mother died, it was a way for us to spend time together.'

'How touching,' he murmured, and Ana knew he meant it. He sounded almost sad.

'And I suppose your father taught you?' she asked. 'Or did you play with your brother?' She leaned over the table and practised a shot, the cue stick smooth and supple under her hands.

'Just my father.'

Ana stepped back, letting the cue stick rest on the floor. 'Would you like to go first?'

Vittorio widened his eyes in mock horror. 'Would a gentleman ever go first? I think not!'

Ana gave a little laugh and shrugged. 'I just wanted to give you the advantage. I warned you I was good.'

Vittorio threw his head back and let out a loud laugh; the sight of the long brown column of his throat, the muscles working, made something plunge deep inside Ana and then flare up again in need. Suddenly her hands were slippery on the cue stick and her mouth was dry. She was conscious of the way her heart had started beating with slow, deliberate thuds that seemed to rock her whole body. 'And I told you I was good too, as I remember.'

'Then we'll just have to see who is better,' Ana returned pertly, smiling a little bit as if she was relaxed, as if her body wasn't thrumming like a violin Vittorio had just played with a few words and a laugh.

The servant entered quietly with a tray carrying two tumblers, a bottle of Pellegrino and another bottle of very good, very old single malt whisky. Ana swallowed dryly. She'd only said she wanted whisky because she'd known what Vittorio was up to; she'd felt reckless and defiant and whisky seemed like the kind of drink men drank when they were playing a business games of billiards.

She, however, didn't drink it. She had a few sips with her father every now and then, but the thought of taking a whole tumbler with Vittorio made her nervous. She was a notorious lightweight—especially for a winemaker—and she didn't want to make a fool of herself in front of him. Especially not with this desire—so treacherous, so overwhelming, so new—still warring within her, making her feel languorous and anxious at varying turns.

'So,' Vittorio said as he reached for the whisky, 'do you take yours neat or with a little water?'

Water sounded like a good idea, a way to weaken the alcohol. 'Pellegrino, please.'

'As you wish.' He took his neat, Ana saw, accepting her tumbler with numb fingers. Vittorio smiled and raised his glass and she did likewise. They both sipped, and Ana managed not to choke as the whisky—barely diluted by water—burned down her throat.

'Now, please,' Vittorio said, sweeping his arm in an elegant arc. 'Ladies first.'

Ana nodded and set her glass aside. She lined up her first shot, leaning over the table, nervous and shy as Vittorio watched blandly. Focus, she told herself. Focus on the game, focus on the business. Yet that thought—and its following one, *marriage*—made her hands turn shaky and the shot went wide.

Vittorio clicked his tongue. 'Pity.'

He was teasing her, Ana knew, but she ground her teeth anyway. She hated to lose. It was one of the reasons she was so good at *stecca*; she'd spent hours practising so she could best her father at the game, which she hadn't done until she was fifteen. It had been five years of practice and waiting.

She stepped back from the table and took another sip of whisky as Vittorio lined up his shot. 'So why *do* you want to marry me?' she asked, her tone one of casual interest, just as he prepared to shoot. His shot went as wide as her own.

He swung around to face her, his eyes narrowed, and Ana smiled sweetly. 'I think you'd make an appropriate wife.'

'Appropriate. What a romantic word.'

'As I said,' Vittorio said softly, 'this is a matter of business.'

Ana lined up her own shot; before Vittorio could say anything else, she took it, banking his ball and missing the skittle by a centimetre. She'd been a fool to mention romance. 'Indeed. And you see marriage as a matter of business?'

He paused. 'Yes.'

'And what about me is so appropriate?' Ana asked. 'Out of curiosity.' Vittorio took his shot and knocked her ball cleanly into a skittle. Ana stifled a curse.

'Everything.'

She let out an incredulous laugh. 'Really, Vittorio, I am not such a paragon.'

'You are from a well-known, respected family in this region, you have worked hard at your own winery business these last ten years, and you are loyal.'

'And that is what you are looking for in a wife?' Ana asked, her tone sharpening. 'That is quite a list. Did you draw it up yourself?' She took another shot, grateful that this time she knocked his ball into a skittle. They were even, at least in billiards.

Vittorio hesitated for only a fraction of a second. 'I know what I want.'

She had to ask it; she had to know. She kept her voice light, even dismissive. 'You are not interested in love, I suppose?'

'No.' He paused. 'Are you?'

Ana watched as he stilled, his head cocked to one side, his dark eyes narrowed and intent as he waited for her answer. What a strange question, she thought distantly. Weren't most people interested in love?

Yet, even as she asked the question, she knew the answer for herself. She was not—could not—be interested in love, the love of a man, romantic, sexual. She'd tried it once and had felt only failure and shame—both feelings had taken years to forget, and even now she remembered the way they'd roiled through her, Roberto's horrified look…

No. Love—that kind of love—Ana had long ago accepted, was a luxury she could neither afford nor access. Yet did she want it? Crave it? *Need* it? Ana knew the answer to that question as well. No, she did not. The risk was simply too great, and the possibility—the hope—too small. 'No,' she said coolly. She leaned over for her next shot, determined to focus completely on the game. 'I'm not.'

'Good.'

She took the shot and straightened. 'I thought you'd say that.'

'It makes it so much easier.'

'Easier?' she repeated, and heard the sardonic note in her voice. When had she become so cynical? From the moment Vittorio had proposed a marriage of convenience, or before? Long before?

'Some women,' Vittorio said carefully, 'would not accept the idea of a marriage based on common principles—'

'Based on business, you mean.'

'Yes,' Vittorio said after a moment, 'but you must realize that I mean this to be a true marriage.' He paused. 'A *proper* marriage, a marriage in every sense of the word.'

Naïve virgin she may be, but Ana still knew what Vittorio was talking about. She could imagine it all too easily. Or almost. She closed her eyes briefly, but if she wanted to banish the image, she failed. It came back clearly, emblazoned on her brain. An antique four-poster, piled high with pillows and cushions. Vittorio, naked, tangled in sheets. Magnificent. Hers.

Ana turned back to the billiards table. 'So,' she said, blindly lining up a shot, 'you mean sex.' She didn't—couldn't—look at him, even as she kept her voice nonchalant. She missed her shot entirely.

'Yes.' Vittorio sounded completely unmoved. 'I'd like children. Heirs.'

'Is that really why you're marrying?'

He hesitated for only a second. 'The main reason,' he allowed and Ana felt a ripple of disappointment, although she hardly knew why. Of course a man like Vittorio wanted children, would marry for an heir. Heirs. He was a count; he had a title, a castle, a business, all to pass on to his child. A hoped-for son, no doubt. Her son. The thought sliced through her, shocking her, not an altogether unpleasant feeling. Vittorio arched his brows. 'Do you want children, Ana?'

There was something intimate about the question, especially when he spoke in that low, husky tone that made her insides ripple and her toes curl. She'd never expected to have such a fierce, primal reaction to him. It was instinctive and sensual, and it scared her. She turned away.

'Yes, I suppose.'

'You only suppose?'

'I never thought to have children,' she admitted with a bleak honesty that turned her voice a bit ragged. 'I never thought to have the opportunity.'

'Then this marriage suits us both.'

She gave a little instinctive shake of her head. He spoke as if it were agreed, the proverbial done deal. It couldn't be that easy. *She* couldn't be that easy. 'No.'

'Why not?' He'd moved closer to her; she could feel him by her shoulder, the heat and the musk of him.

'We're talking about marriage, Vittorio. A lifetime commitment.'

'So?'

'Such a decision requires some thought.'

'I can assure you I have thought of it a good deal.'

'Well, I haven't.' She turned around, suddenly angry. 'I haven't thought about it at *all*.'

He nodded, annoyingly unperturbed. 'You must have questions.'

She didn't answer. Of course she had questions, but they weren't ones she necessarily wanted to ask. *Why do you want to marry me? What if we hate each other? Do you even desire me at all?*

Why am I so tempted?

She looked up, taking a breath. 'I don't even know what you think of marriage…of a wife. What would you expect of me? How would we…get on…together?' It seemed ridiculous even to ask the questions, for surely she wasn't seriously considering his outrageous proposal. Yet, even so, Ana was curious. She wanted to know the answers.

'We'd get on together quite well, I imagine,' Vittorio replied easily. Ana wanted to scream.

You're not attracted to me, she wanted to shout. *I saw how you looked at me in that first moment—you summed me up and dismissed me! And now you want to marry me?*

She'd convinced herself she could live without love. But desire? Attraction? Could she give her body to a man who looked at her with disdain or, worse, disgust? Could she live with herself, if she did that, day after day?

'Ana, what are you thinking?' Vittorio's voice was gentle, concerned. She almost wanted to tell him, yet she knew she couldn't bear the truth of his confession, or the deception of his denial. She let out a long shuddering breath.

'Surely there are other women who fulfil your criteria,' she said at last.

Vittorio shook his head. 'No. There are few women with your knowledge of wine, Ana, or of this region. And of course your vineyard combined with mine would give us both a legacy for our children. And I appreciate your breeding and class—'

'You make me sound like a horse. I'm as good as, aren't I?' Calm once more, she spoke without rancour, merely stating the rather glum fact.

'Then consider me one as well.'

'A stallion, you mean?' and her mouth quirked upwards with wry amusement in spite of all the hurt and disappointment she felt.

'Of course.' Vittorio matched her smile. 'If I am considering this marriage a business, there is no reason you cannot as well. We are each other's mutual assets.'

Ana bit her lip. He made it sound so easy, so obvious. So natural, as if bartering a marriage over billiards in this day and age was a perfectly normal and acceptable thing to do. Vittorio had already told her he would not love her. Yet, Ana asked herself with bleak honesty, would someone else, *if* she were interested in love, which she'd already told herself she wasn't? Funny how much convincing that took.

She would be thirty years old in just two months. She hadn't had a date of any kind in over five years, and the last one had been appalling, an awkward few hours with a man with whom she'd shared not one point of sympathy. She'd never had a serious boyfriend. She'd never had *sex*. Was Vittorio's offer the best she'd get?

And, Ana acknowledged as she sneaked a glance at him from under her lashes, she could certainly do worse. He'd shed his jacket and tie and undone the top two buttons of his shirt. Under the smooth luxurious fabric, his muscles moved in sinuous elegance. His dark hair gleamed in the dimly lit room like polished ebony. The harsh lines of his jaw and cheek were starkly beautiful… He was beautiful. And he wanted to be her husband.

The thought was incredible. Insane. It couldn't work. It wouldn't. Vittorio would come to his senses, Ana would feel that devastating disappointment once again.

He wouldn't desire her. She'd see it in his eyes, feel it in his body—

And yet. Yet. Even now, she considered it. Even now, her mind raced to find possibilities, solutions. *Hope.* Some part of her wanted to marry Vittorio. Some part of her wanted that life. That, Ana knew, was why she hadn't dismissed him immediately and utterly. It was why she was asking questions, voicing objections as if this absurd and insulting proposal had any merit. Because, to some small suppressed part of her soul, it *did.*

Ana stood up and reached for her cue stick. 'Let's play,' she said, her voice brusque. She didn't want to talk any more. She didn't want to think about any of it. She just wanted to beat the hell out of the Count of Cazlevara.

Vittorio watched as Ana shrugged off her boxy jacket, tossing it onto a chair. She glanced over her shoulder, her eyes dark and smoky with challenge. 'Ready?'

Vittorio felt his insides tighten with a sudden surprising coil of desire. One sharp dart of lust. Without that awful jacket, he could actually see some of Ana's body. She wore a hugging top of creamy beaded silk that pulled taut over her generous breasts as she leaned forward to line up her shot. Vittorio found his gaze fixed first on the back of her neck, where a long tendril of dark hair lay curled against her skin. Her hair wasn't brown, he realized absently, it was myriad colours. Brown and black and red and even gold. His gaze dropped instinctively lower, to her backside. Bent over the billiards table, the fabric of her trousers pulled tightly across her bottom. The realization caused another shaft of lust to slice through him and he found he was gripping his cue stick rather tightly. He'd thought she had a mannish figure because she was tall. Yet, seeing her now, her curves on surprising and provocative display, he realized she wasn't mannish at all.

She still wasn't the kind of woman he normally took to bed, and he would never call her pretty. Even so, that brief stab of lust reassured him, made him realize this could work. He would make it work. Ana was intrigued, interested; she hadn't said no. He'd expected her to say no immediately, a gut reaction. But she hadn't betrayed her own desire—he'd seen it before, at dinner, a flaring in her eyes—as well as, perhaps, her own sense of logic.

When he'd spoken to Enrico about the match, the old man had been surprised but accepting.

'Ana is a practical girl,' he'd said after a moment. 'She will see the advantages.'

Vittorio could see her now, considering those advantages, wondering if the comforts he could give her outweighed the lack of feeling. And yet there would be feeling…affection, respect. He wanted to *like* Ana; he simply didn't want to love her.

And, Vittorio acknowledged with a surprised wryness, he would desire her. Somewhat, at least.

Ana took her shot and then stepped aside so Vittorio could take his. As he passed by her, he inhaled her scent; she wore no perfume and smelled of soap and something else, something impossible to define. Dirt, he realized after a moment and nearly missed his shot. She smelled of sunshine and soil, of the vineyard he'd seen her stride through only days ago, as if she owned the world, or at least all of it that mattered.

It was not a smell he normally associated with a woman.

He straightened, stepping back so Ana could take her shot, making sure to step close enough to her so his elbow brushed her breast, as if by accident, just to see how she reacted. And how *he* reacted. Ana drew her breath in sharply; Vittorio shifted his weight to ease the intensifying ache of need in his groin.

She was untouched, he was sure of it. Untouched and untamed. And, despite the terrible clothes, the complete lack of feminine guile or charm or artifice, at that moment he wanted her. He wanted her, and he wanted to marry her.

He *would*.

* * *

She won. Ana knew she should feel triumph at this victory, yet in the light of everything else she found she felt little at all.

'It seems I must concede the game,' Vittorio said as he replaced his cue stick in the holder. 'Congratulations. You did warn me.'

'So I did.' Ana replaced her cue stick as well. She felt awkward now the game of *stecca* was over; a glance at her watch told her it was nearly midnight. They hadn't spoken of the whole wretched business proposition in over an hour, and she wasn't sure she wanted to bring it up now.

'So,' Vittorio said briskly, 'you'll need a few days to think about my business proposition?'

Vittorio obviously did not share her reluctance. 'A few days?' Ana repeated, her voice rising to something close to a squawk. 'Vittorio, I don't think—'

'Surely you won't dismiss it out of hand?' he countered, cutting off the objection she hadn't even known how to finish. He leaned against the billiards table, smiling, at ease, his powerful forearms folded. 'That is not good business, Ana.'

'Perhaps I don't want my marriage to be business,' she replied a bit stiffly.

Vittorio's gaze dropped to her mouth. She could *feel* his eyes there, on her lips, almost as if he were touching her. She could imagine his finger tracing the outline of her lips even though he hadn't moved. *She* had; she'd parted her lips in a silent yearning invitation. Her body betrayed her again and again. 'I think it could be good between us, Ana,' he said softly. 'Good in so many ways.'

His words thrilled her. They shouldn't—words counted for so little—but they did. They gave her hope, made her wonder if Vittorio could see her as a woman. A woman he wanted not just with his mind, but with his body. Unlike Roberto.

'In fact,' he continued, his voice as soft and sinuous as silk, 'as we have just finished a game where you soundly trounced me, we could shake hands.'

Automatically, Ana stuck out her hand, ignoring the tiny flip-flop of disappointment at his sensible suggestion. This was how she did business, had been doing it for years. In a man's world, she acted like a man. It made sense. It made sense *now*.

'I said we *could*,' Vittorio said, his voice so soft, almost languorous, and yet with a little hint of amusement. 'I didn't say we would.' His eyes glittered, his own mouth parting as hers had, and he leaned forward so when she breathed in she inhaled his musky scent. 'Instead, how about a kiss?'

'A kiss?' Ana repeated blankly as if she didn't understand the word. But oh, she did—already she could imagine it, wanted it, *needed* it: the feel of Vittorio's lips on hers, hard and soft at the same time, his hands on her waist or even— 'That's not how I do business, Vittorio.'

'But this business is a little different, is it not? And we should perhaps make sure we suit. That we are,' he clarified in that soft, dangerous voice, 'in fact attracted to one another.'

Again, his words rippled through her with a frisson of excitement and hope; it was a heady, potent mix. Was he actually saying he could be attracted to her? That he *was*? 'I don't think that's a good idea,' Ana said stubbornly, yet she heard the longing in her own voice. So did Vittorio.

He smiled. Although he hadn't moved—he was still leaning against the billiards table, his arms folded—he exuded a lethal grace and Ana could all too easily imagine him closing the distance between them, taking her into his arms and… For heaven's sake, she'd read too many romance novels. Had too many desperate dreams.

That was just what she *wanted* him to do.

'I think it's a very good idea.'

'You don't want to kiss me,' she said, meaning it as a blunt statement of fact. Yet, even as she said the words she was conscious of how Vittorio looked *now*. There was no lip-curl of disdain, no dismissive flick of the eyes. His eyes were dark, dilated, his cheeks suffused with colour. She felt the answering colour rise up in her own cheeks, flood through her own body.

'Oh, but I do,' he murmured, and Ana realized just how much she wanted him to want to kiss her. And she wanted it too; she'd realized that a long time ago, but now she knew she was going to do it. It had become both a challenge and a craving.

'All right, then,' she said and, smiling a little, her heart thudding sickly, she stepped forward, straight into his arms. She'd been moving too fast and Vittorio's hands came up to steady her, gripping her bare shoulders so she didn't smack straight into his chest. Still, she felt the hard length of his body against hers, every nerve and sinew leaping to life in a way they never had before. This was so new, so intimate, so *wonderful*.

His lips were a millimetre from hers as he whispered, 'I like that when you decide to do something, you do it completely, with your whole heart.'

'Yes, I do,' Ana answered, and kissed him. She wasn't a good kisser. She knew that; she'd had too little experience. She was unschooled, clumsy, her lips hard against his, pressing, not knowing what to do. Feeling a fool.

Then Vittorio opened his mouth, somehow softening his lips—how did he do that? Ana wondered fuzzily—before she stopped thinking at all. His tongue slipped into the warmth of her own mouth, surprising her and causing a deep lightning shaft of pleasure to go right through her belly and down to her toes. Her hands came up of their own accord and bunched on his shirt, pulling him closer so their hips collided and she felt the full evidence of his desire; he hadn't been lying. He *had* wanted to kiss her.

That knowledge thrilled her, consumed her with its wonderful truth. This was not a man who had been left cold by her kiss, by her body. His body had betrayed *him*. Right now, at least, he wanted her. As a woman.

A sense of power and triumph surged through her, making her bold. Her hands slid down the slippery fabric of his shirt to the curve of his backside, pulling him towards her. She heard Vittorio's little inhalation of shock and smiled against his lips. He moaned into her mouth.

His mouth remained on hers, exploring the contours of her tongue and teeth, nipping and sliding, the intimate invasion making Ana's head spin and her breath shorten. She'd never known kissing could be like this. The few chaste pecks and stolen smacks at the end of a date didn't compare, didn't even count—

And then it was over. Vittorio released her and Ana took a stumbling step backwards, her fingers flying to her swollen lips.

'Well…' she managed. Her mind was still fuzzy, her senses still consumed by what had just occurred. Then she looked at Vittorio and saw how smug he seemed. He was smiling as if he'd just proved something, and Ana supposed he had.

'I think that quite settles the matter, wouldn't you say?'

'Nothing's settled,' Ana retorted sharply. She wouldn't have her future decided by a simple kiss—even if there hadn't been anything simple about it at all. It had been amazing and affirming and even transforming, the evidence of Vittorio's desire changing everything—or at least it *could* change everything. 'You said I should have a few days to consider.'

'At least you want to consider it now,' Vittorio replied, and Ana knew nothing she said could take away his smug sense of superiority that he'd been able to kiss her senseless. He looked completely recovered, if he had been shaken by that kiss, which Ana suspected he had not. Not like she had. All right, he'd desired her—for a moment—but perhaps any man would react the same way when a woman threw herself at him, which was essentially what Ana had done.

Except Roberto hadn't. When she'd thrown herself at *him*, desperate to prove herself desirable, he'd remained as still and cold as a statue, as unmoved and emotionless as a block of cold marble. And when she'd finished—pressing herself against him, kissing those slack lips, he'd actually stepped back and said in a voice filled with affront, 'Ana, I never thought of you that way.' A pause, horrible, endless, and then the most damning words of all: 'How could I?'

Still, Ana thought, gazing at Vittorio with barely disguised hunger, was that brief stab of desire—that amazing kiss—enough to base a marriage on? Along with the respect and affection and everything else Vittorio had promised?

'I'll consider it,' she said at last. 'I didn't say I would say yes.'

'Of course.'

Ana touched her lips again, then dropped her hand, knowing how revealing that little gesture was. 'I should go home.'

'I'll have my driver take you.' Vittorio smiled wryly. 'I'm afraid I've drunk a bit too much whisky to handle a car myself, and of course I would never jeopardise your safety.'

Ana nodded in acceptance, and Vittorio pressed the button by the door again. Within seconds a servant appeared. He issued some quick instructions, and then turned back to Ana. 'I'll see you to the door.'

They didn't speak as he led her through several stone corridors back to the huge entryway of the castle. The doors were already open and a driver—in uniform, even at this hour—waited on the front step.

'So this is goodbye,' Ana said a bit unevenly.

Vittorio tucked a tendril of hair behind her ear, his fingers trailing her cheek. That smugness had left his eyes and he looked softer now, if only for a moment. 'For now.'

Ana tried not to react to the touch of his hand. She felt incredibly unsettled, uncertain, unable to believe that the kiss they had just shared was real, that it could possibly mean something. At least to her. She had a horrible sick feeling that Vittorio, inflamed by a bit of whisky, had been acting on his baser instincts, trying to prove that this marriage bargain could actually work.

And he'd almost convinced her that it could.

Too tired to think any more, Ana slipped into the interior of the limo—the Porsche, it seemed, was reserved for Vittorio's exclusive use—and laid her head back against the seat as the driver sped away from Castle Cazlevara back to her home.

Vittorio watched the car disappear down the curving drive with a deep, primal sense of satisfaction. He'd as good as branded her with that kiss; she was his. In a matter of days, weeks at the most, she would be his bride. His wife. He felt sure of it.

He couldn't keep the sense of victory from rushing through him, headier than any wine. He'd set out to acquire a wife and, in a matter of days—a week at the most—he would have one. Mission accomplished.

He imagined the look on his mother's face when he told her he was getting married; he leaped ahead to the moment when he held his son, and saw Bernardo's dreams of becoming Count, of taking control of Cazlevara Wines, crumble to nothing. He pictured his mother looking stunned, lost, and then the image suddenly changed of its own accord and instead he saw her smiling into the face of his child, her grandchild. A baby girl.

Vittorio banished the image almost instantly. It didn't make sense. The only relationship he'd ever had with his mother had been one of, at worst, animosity and, at best, indifference. And he didn't want a girl; he needed sons.

Yet still the image—the idea—needled him, annoyed him, because it made a strange longing rise up in a way he didn't understand, a way that almost felt like sorrow.

Vittorio pushed it aside once more and considered the practicalities instead. Of course, there were risks. With any business proposition, there were risks. Ana might not fall pregnant easily, or they might only have girls. Baby girls, all wrapped in pink—Vittorio dismissed these possibilities, too exultant to dwell on such concerns.

He supposed he should have married long ago and thus secured his position, yet he'd never even considered it. He'd been too intent on avoiding his home, on securing his own future. He'd never thought of his heirs.

He'd run away, Vittorio knew, the actions of a hurt child. Amazing how much power and pain those memories still held. His mother's averted face, the way she'd pushed him down when he'd attempted to clamber on her lap. He'd stopped trying after a while. By the time he was four—when Bernardo had been born—he'd regarded his mother with a certain wariness, the way you would a sleeping tiger in a zoo. Fascinating, beautiful, but ultimately dangerous. And now he was a grown man, nearing forty and he still remembered. He still hurt.

Self-contempt poured through him, dousing his earlier sense of victory. He hated this feeling, as if he was captive to his own past, chained by memories. Surely no man should still lament his childhood? Besides, his hadn't even been very deprived: his father had loved him, had given him every opportunity and privilege. To feel sorry for himself in even the smallest degree was not only absurd, it was abhorrent.

Vittorio straightened his shoulders and pushed the memories back down.

Now he would run away no more. He'd come back to Veneto to finally face his family, his past and make it right in the only way he knew how. By moving on. His first family had failed him, so he would create a second. His own. His wife, his child. *His.*

His face hardening with determination, Vittorio turned back to the dark, empty castle and went inside.

CHAPTER FOUR

VILLA ROSSO was dark as the driver let her out at the front door. Ana tiptoed through the silent downstairs, wanting to avoid her father, even though she was fairly certain he was asleep. Enrico Viale didn't stay up much past ten.

She fell into bed, and then thankfully was fast sleep within minutes. When she awoke, the sun was slanting through the curtains, sending its long golden rays along the floor of her bedroom. Last night filtered back to her through a haze of sleep: the so-called business proposition, the billiards, the whisky, the *kiss*. She had no head for hard liquor at all. If she hadn't had that whisky, she wouldn't have kissed him, wouldn't have let him kiss her. Wouldn't now be wondering about all the possibilities—all the hopes—that kiss had given her, her body awakened to its natural longings, her soul singing with sudden, fierce joy—

Quickly, Ana swung out of bed and dressed. She strode downstairs, determined to put the thoughts and, more importantly, the treacherous desires Vittorio Cazlevara created within her out of her mind completely, at least for a morning. They were too seductive, too dangerous, too *much*.

She stopped short when she saw her father in the dining room, eating toast and kippers. Her English mother, Emily, had insisted on a full English breakfast every day and, sixteen years after her death, Enrico still continued the tradition.

'Good morning!' he called brightly. 'You were out late last night. I waited up until eleven.'

'You shouldn't have.' Almost reluctantly, Ana came into the dining room, dropping her usual kiss on her father's head. She wasn't ready to talk to her father, to ask him how much he knew. She remembered his lack of surprise at Vittorio's return, or the fact that he'd asked her out to dinner. Had he known—could he possibly have imagined—just what the business proposition was? The thought sent something strange and alarming coursing through Ana's blood. She didn't know whether it was fear or joy, or something in between. Had Vittorio asked her father for his *blessing*? How long had he been planning this?

'Come, have some breakfast. The kippers are especially good this morning.'

Ana made a face as she grabbed a roll from the sideboard and poured herself a coffee from the porcelain pot left on the table. 'You know I can't abide kippers.'

'But they're so delicious,' Enrico said with a smile, and ate one.

Ana sat down opposite him, sipping her coffee even though it was too hot. 'I can only stay a moment,' she warned. 'I need to go down to the offices.'

'But Ana! It's Saturday.'

Ana shrugged; she often worked on Saturdays, especially in the busy growing season. 'The grapes don't stop for anyone, Papà.'

'How was your dinner with Vittorio?'

'Interesting.'

'He wanted to discuss business?' Enrico asked in far too neutral a tone.

Ana looked at him directly, daring him to be dishonest. 'Papà, did Vittorio speak to you about this—this business proposition of his?'

Enrico looked down, shredding a kipper onto his plate with the tines of his fork. 'Perhaps,' he said very quietly.

Ana didn't know whether to be disappointed or relieved or, even, strangely flattered. She felt a confusing welter of emotions, so she could only shake her head and ask with genuine curiosity, 'And what did you think of it?'

'I was surprised, at first.' He looked up, smiling wryly, although his eyes were serious. 'As I imagine you were.'

'Completely.' The single word was heartfelt.

'But then I thought about it—and Vittorio showed me the advantages—'

'What advantages?' What could Vittorio have said to convince her father that he should allow his daughter to marry him as a matter of convenience? For surely, Ana knew now, her father was convinced.

'Many, Ana. Stability, security.'

'I have those—'

'Children. Companionship.' He paused and then said softly, 'Happiness.'

'You think Vittorio Cazlevara could make me happy?' Ana asked. She didn't sound sceptical; she felt genuinely curious. She wanted to know. Could he make her happy? Why was she thinking this way? She'd been happy… Yet at that moment Ana couldn't pretend she didn't want more, that she didn't want the things her father had mentioned. Children. A home of her own. To kiss Vittorio again, to taste him…

Some last bastion of common sense must have remained for she burst out suddenly, 'We're talking about *marriage*, Papà.' Her voice broke on the word. 'A life commitment. Not some… some sort of transaction.' Even if Vittorio had presented it as such.

'What is your objection?' Enrico asked, his fingertips pressed together, his head cocked to one side. He'd always been a logical man; some would call him unemotional. Even after the death of his beloved wife, his calm exterior had barely cracked.

Ana remembered the one time he'd truly shown his grief, rocking and keening on Emily's bedroom floor; as a girl, the sudden, uncontrollable display of emotion had shocked her. He'd closed her off from it, slammed the door and then, with a far worse finality, shut himself off from her rather than let his daughter see him in such a state of emotional weakness. The separation at such a crucial time had devastated her.

It had been two years before they'd regained the relationship they'd once had.

Now she knew she couldn't really be surprised that he was approaching the issue of her possible marriage with such a cool head.

Vittorio's arguments would have appealed marvellously to his own sense of checks and balances. Indeed, she shared his sense of logic, prided herself on her lack of feminine fancy. After living with her father as her lone companion for most of her life, the sentimental theatrics of most women were cloying and abhorrent. She didn't, Ana reflected with a wry sorrow, even know how to be a woman.

Yet Vittorio had treated her as one, when he'd kissed her…

Even so. *Marriage…*

'My objection,' she said, 'is the entire idea of marriage as a business proposition. It seems so cold.'

'But surely it doesn't have to be? Better to go into such an enterprise with a clear head, reasonable expectations—'

'I still don't even understand why Vittorio wants to marry me—' Ana said, stopping suddenly, wishing she hadn't betrayed herself. Just like her father, she hated to be vulnerable. She knew what it felt like to be so exposed, so raw, and then so rejected.

'He needs a wife. He must be in his late thirties, you know, and a man starts to think of his future, his children—'

'But why me?' The words came, as unstoppable as the fears

and doubts that motivated them. 'He could have anyone, anyone at all—'

'Why not you, Ana?' Enrico asked gently. 'You would make any man a wonderful wife.'

Ana's mouth twisted. Her father also called her *dolcezza*. Sweet little thing. He was her father, her *papà*; of course he believed such things. That didn't mean *she* believed them, or him. 'Still, there would be no love involved.'

Enrico gave a little shrug. 'In time, it comes.'

She was shredding her roll onto her plate, just as her father had done with his poor little kipper. Her appetite—what little there had been of it—had completely vanished. She looked up at her father and shook her head. 'With Vittorio, I don't think so.' Her throat went tight, and she cursed herself for a fool. She didn't *need* love. She'd convinced herself of that long ago. She didn't even want it, and she couldn't fathom why she'd mentioned it to her father.

Her father remained unfazed. 'Still, affection. Respect. These things count for much, *dolcezza*. More perhaps than you can even imagine now, when love seems so important.'

'Yet you loved Mamma.'

Her father nodded, his face seeming to crumple just a little bit. Even sixteen years on, he still lived for her memory.

'Don't you think I want that kind of love too?' Ana asked, her voice turning raw. Despite what she'd said—what she believed—she needed to know her father's answer.

Enrico didn't speak for a moment. He poured himself another cup of coffee and sipped it thoughtfully. 'That kind of love,' he finally said, 'is not easy. It is not comfortable.'

'I never said I wanted to be comfortable.'

'Comfort,' Enrico told her with a little smile, 'is always underrated by those who have experienced nothing else.'

'Are you saying you weren't…comfortable…with Mamma?'

The idea was a novel one, and one Ana didn't like to consider too closely. She'd always believed her parents to have had the grandest of love matches, adoring each other to the end. A fairy tale, and one she'd clung to in those first dark days of grief. Yet now her father seemed to be implying something else.

'I loved her,' Enrico replied. 'And I was happy. But comfortable, always? No. Your mother was a wonderful woman, Ana, be assured of that. But she was emotional—and I'm the one who is Italian!' He smiled, the curve of his mouth tinged with a little sadness. 'It was not always easy to live with someone who felt things so deeply.' Snatches of memory came to her, swirls of colour and sound. Her mother crying, the cloying scent of a sick room, the murmurs of a doctor as her father shook his head. And then her mother pulling her close, whispering fervently against her hair how she, Ana, would be the only one, the only child. Love, Ana thought, did not protect you from sorrow. Perhaps it only softened the blow.

Enrico put down his coffee cup and gave Ana a level look. 'Be careful to realize what you would be giving up by not marrying Vittorio, Ana.'

Ana drew back, stung. 'What are you saying? That I might as well take the best offer—the only offer—I can get?'

'No, of course I am not saying that,' Enrico said gently. 'But it is a very good offer.'

Ana sipped her coffee, moodily acknowledging the truth of her father's words. She'd only given voice to her own fears—that there would be no other offers. Would she rather live alone, childless, lonely—because, face it, she *was*—than attempt some kind of marriage with Vittorio? She didn't know the answer. She could hardly believe she was actually asking herself the question.

'Vittorio is a good man,' Enrico said quietly.

'How do you know?' Ana challenged. 'He's been away for fifteen years.'

'I knew his father. Vittorio was the apple of Arturo's eye. Arturo was a good man too, but he was hard.' Enrico frowned a little. 'Without mercy.'

'And what if Vittorio is the same?' She remembered the steely glint in his eye and wondered just how well she knew him. Not well at all, was the obvious answer. Certainly not well enough to marry him.

And yet…he *was* a good man. She felt that in her bones, in a certain settling of her soul. She believed her father and, more importantly, she believed Vittorio.

It's all right to be sad, rondinella.

'Vittorio needs a wife to soften him,' Enrico said with a smile.

'I don't want him to be my project,' Ana protested. 'Or for me to be his.' She was so prickly, had been so ever since Vittorio had proposed—if you could call it proposing. The word conjured images of roses and diamond rings and declarations of undying love. Not a cold-blooded contract.

'Of course not,' Enrico agreed, 'but you know, in marriage, you are each other's projects. You don't seek to change each other, but it is hoped that you will affect one another, shape and smooth each other's rough edges.'

Ana made a face. 'You make it sound like two rocks in a stream.'

'But that's exactly it,' Enrico exclaimed. 'Two rocks rubbing along together in the river of life.'

Ana let out a reluctant laugh. 'Now, really, Papà, you are waxing far too philosophical for me. I must get to work.' She rose from the table, kissing him again, and went to get her shoes and coat; a light spring drizzle was falling.

Once at the winery, she immersed herself in what she loved best. Business. *Just like Vittorio*, a sly little voice inside her mind whispered, but Ana pushed it away. She wasn't going to think about Vittorio or marriage or any of it until noon, at least.

In fact, she barely lifted her head from the papers scattered over her desk until Edoardo knocked on her door in the late afternoon. 'A package, Signorina Viale.'

'A package?' Ana blinked him into focus. 'You mean a delivery?'

'Not for the winery,' Edoardo said. 'It is marked personal. For you. It was dropped off—by the Count of Cazlevara.'

Ana stilled, her heart suddenly pounding far too fiercely. Vittorio had been here, had sent her something? Anticipation raced through her, made her dizzy with longing. Somehow she managed to nod stiffly, with apparent unconcern, and raised one hand to beckon him. 'Bring it in, please.'

The box was white, long and narrow and tied with a satin ribbon in pale lavender. Roses, Ana thought. It must be. She felt mingled disappointment and anticipation; roses were beautiful, but when it came to flowers they were expected and a bit, well, ordinary. It didn't take much thought to send a woman roses.

Still, she hadn't received roses or any other flowers in years, so she opened the box with some excitement, only to discover he hadn't sent roses at all.

He'd sent grapes.

She stared at the freshly cut vines with their cluster of new, perfect, pearl-like grapes and then bent her head to breathe in their wonderful earthy scent. There was a stiff little card nestled among the leaves. Ana picked it up and read:

A new hybrid of Vinifera and Rotundifolia, from the Americas, that I thought you'd be interested in.—V.

She flicked the card against her fingers and then, betrayingly, pressed it against her lips. It smelled fresh and faintly pungent, like the grapes. She closed her eyes. This, she realized, was much better than roses, and she had a feeling Vittorio knew it.

Was this his way of romancing her? Or simply convincing her? Showing her the benefits of such business?

Did it even matter? He'd done it; he'd known what she'd like, and Ana found she was pleased.

For the rest of the day Ana immersed herself in work, determined not to think of Vittorio or the spray of grapes that remained on her desk, in plain view. Yet she couldn't quite keep the thoughts—the hopes—from slipping slyly into her mind. She found herself constructing a thousand what-ifs. *What if we married? What if we had a child? What if we actually were happy?*

These thoughts—tempting, dangerous—continued to dance along the fringes of her mind over the next week. She caught herself more than once, chin in hand, lost in a daydream that was vague enough to seem reasonable. Possible. She found she was arguing with herself, listing the reasons why a marriage of convenience was perfectly sensible. Why it was, in fact, a good idea.

She didn't see Vittorio all week, but every day there was something from him: a newspaper article on a new wine, a bar of dark chocolate—how did he know that was her secret indulgence?—a spray of lilacs. Ana accepted each gift, found herself savouring them, even as she knew why he was doing it. It was, undoubtedly, a means to an end, a way of showing her how it could be between them.

I think it could be good between us, Ana... Good in so many ways.

Remembering how it had felt to kiss him—how he'd felt, the evidence of his own arousal—made Ana agree with him. Or, at least, want to agree with him. And want to experience it again.

A week after her dinner with Vittorio, as the day came to a close, the sun starting its orange descent, Ana left the winery office and decided to walk the half-kilometre home along the winding dirt track, her mind still brimming with those seductive what-ifs. A new wealth of possibilities was opening up to her, things she'd never hoped to have. A husband, a child, a home, a life beyond what she'd already made for herself, what she'd been happy to have until Vittorio stirred up these latent desires like a nest of writhing serpents. Ana wondered if they could ever be coaxed to sleep again.

If she said no, could she go back to her life with the endless work days and few evenings out among old men and fellow winemakers? Could she lull to sleep those deep and dangerous desires for a husband, a family, a home—a castle, even—of her own? Could she stop craving another kiss and, more than that, so much more, the feel of another's body against hers, that wonderful spiral of desire uncoiling and rising within her, demanding to be sated?

No, Ana acknowledged, she couldn't, not easily anyway and, even more revealingly, she didn't want to. She wanted to feel Vittorio's lips against hers again. She wanted to know the touch of his hands on her body. She wanted to be married, to live and learn together like the two stones her father had been talking about.

Even if there was no love. She didn't need it.

Stopping suddenly right there in the road, Ana laughed aloud. Was her decision already made? Was she actually going to marry Vittorio?

No. Surely she couldn't make such a monumental decision so quickly, so carelessly. Surely her life was worth more than that.

Yet, even as common sense argued its case, her heart and body were warring against it, lost in a world of wonderful—and sensual—possibility.

Slowly, she started walking again; the sun was low in the sky, sending long lavender rays across the horizon. Villa Rosso appeared in the distance, its windows winking in the sunlight, its long, low stone façade so familiar and dear. If she married Vittorio, she wouldn't live there any more. Her father would be alone. The thought stopped her once more in the road; could she do that? Could she leave her father after all they'd shared and endured together? She knew he would want her to do so; this marriage—should it happen—already had his blessing.

Still, it would be hard, painful even. It made her realize afresh just how enormous a decision she was contemplating.

Could she actually say yes? Was she brave—and foolish—enough to do it?

As she came closer to the house, she saw a familiar navy Porsche parked in the drive. Vittorio's car. He was inside, waiting for her, and the realization made her insides flip right over. She'd *missed* him, she realized incredulously; she'd expected him to come before now.

She'd *wanted* him to come.

At the front step she took a moment to brush the hair away from her face and wipe the dust from her shoes before she opened the door and stepped into the foyer.

It was empty, but she followed the voices into the study, where she checked at the sight of Vittorio and her father in what looked like a cosy tête-à-tête. Enrico looked up and smiled as she entered, and Vittorio stood.

'We were just talking about you,' Enrico said with a little smile and, despite the treacherous beating of her heart, Ana smiled rather coolly back.

'Were you? What a surprise.'

'I came to see if you'd like to have dinner with me,' Vittorio said. He seemed entirely unruffled at being caught gossiping about her with her father.

Ana hesitated. She wanted to have dinner with Vittorio again but suddenly she also felt uncertain, afraid. Of what, she could not even say. She was afraid to rush, to show her own eagerness. She needed time to sort her thoughts and perhaps even to steel her heart. 'I'm not dressed—'

'No matter.'

She glanced down at her grey wool trousers and plain white

blouse—which, aggravatingly, had become untucked. Again. 'Really?'

Vittorio arched his eyebrows, a smile playing around his mouth. 'Really.' And, though he said nothing more, Ana knew he was surmising that she had a wardrobe of similarly unappealing clothes upstairs. At least they were clean and freshly ironed.

Still, she accepted the challenge. Why should she change for Vittorio? Why should she attempt to look pretty—if such a thing could be done—for the sake of this business arrangement? She lifted her chin. 'Fine. Let me just wash my face and hands at least.' He nodded, and Ana walked quickly from the room, trying to ignore the hurt that needled her, the little sink of her heart at his indifference to her clothes, her appearance. She wanted Vittorio to care how she looked. She wanted him to *like* how she looked.

Get over it, her mind told her, the words hard and determined. *If you're going to marry him, this is how it is going to be.*

Her heart sank a little further. She wished it hadn't.

Within just a few minutes they were speeding down the darkening drive, away from Villa Rosso, the windows open to the fragrant evening air.

'Where are we going?' Ana asked as the hair she'd just tidied blew into tangles around her face.

'Venice.'

'Venice!' she nearly yelped. 'I'm not dressed for *that*—'

Vittorio's glance was hooded yet smiling. 'Let me worry about that.'

Ana sat back, wondering just how and why Vittorio was going to worry about her clothes. The idea made her uneasy.

She found out soon enough. Vittorio parked the Porsche at Fusina and they boarded a ferry for the ten-minute ride into the city that allowed no cars. As the worn stone buildings and narrow canals with their sleepy-looking gondolas and ancient arched bridges came into view, Ana felt a frisson of expectation and even hope. What city was more romantic than Venice? And just why was Vittorio taking her here?

After they disembarked, he led her away from the Piazza San Marco, crowded with tourists, to Frezzeria, a narrow street lined with upscale boutiques. Most of them had already closed, but all it took was Vittorio rapping once on the glass door of one for the clerk inside, a chic-looking woman with hair in a tight chignon, wearing a silk blouse and a black pencil skirt, to open the door and kiss him on both cheeks.

A ridiculous, totally unreasonable dart of jealousy stabbed Ana, and fury followed it when the woman swept her assessingly critical gaze over her and said, 'This is the one?'

'Yes.'

She snapped her fingers. 'Come with me.'

Ana turned to Vittorio, her eyes narrowed. 'You talked about me?' she said in an angry undertone, choosing to show anger over the hurt she felt inside, a raw, open wound to the heart. She could only imagine the conversation Vittorio must have had with this woman, talking about her hopeless clothes, her terrible taste, how pathetic and *ugly* she was…

She tasted bile, swallowed. What a fool she'd been.

'She's here to help you, Ana,' Vittorio murmured. 'Go with her.'

Ana could see racks of gorgeous-looking clothes—a rainbow of silks and satins—in the back of the boutique. They beckoned to her, surprisingly, because she'd never been a girly kind of woman. She'd avoided all things feminine, mostly out of necessity. She didn't want to look ridiculous. Yet the enticement of the clothes was no match for the hurt—and fury—she felt now.

'Perhaps I don't want help,' she snapped. 'Did you ever consider that?'

Vittorio remained unfazed. 'Is that true?' he asked calmly, so clearly confident of the answer. Humiliatingly, his gaze raked over her, more eloquent than anything he could have said. Ana's cheeks burned.

The woman appeared once more in the doorway, her lips pursed in impatience. She was holding a gown over one arm, frothy with lace. Ana had never seen anything so beautiful. She could not imagine wearing such a thing, or what she would look like in it. It could not possibly be her size.

'Ana,' Vittorio murmured, 'you will look beautiful in these clothes. Surely you want to look beautiful?'

'Perhaps I just want to be myself,' Ana said quietly. She didn't add that she was afraid she *wouldn't* look beautiful in those clothes, or that she wished he thought she looked beautiful already. It was too difficult to explain, too absurd even to feel. She didn't want Vittorio to want to change her, even if she was willing to be changed. Stupid, unreasonable, perhaps, but true. She shook her head and pushed past him to the door. 'I'm sorry, Vittorio, but I'm not going to be your Cinderella project.'

Vittorio stifled a curse as he called back to Feliciana before following Ana out into the street. He'd thought she would appreciate the clothes, the opportunity to look, for once, like a woman. He'd thought he was giving her a *gift*. Instead, she acted offended. Would he ever understand women? Vittorio wondered in annoyed exasperation. He'd *thought* he understood women; he was certainly good with them. Allow them unlimited access to clothes and jewels and they'd love you for ever—or think they did.

Not that he wanted Ana's love, but her gratitude would have been appreciated at this point. He gazed at her, her arms wrapped around herself, her hair blowing in the breeze off the canal, and wondered if he'd ever understand her. He'd thought it would be simple, easy. He'd thought her an open book, to be read—and discarded—at his own leisure. The realization that she was far more complicated, that he'd managed to dismiss her before even getting to know her, was both annoying and shaming.

'I think perhaps you should take me home.'

'We have reservations at one of the finest restaurants in Venice,' Vittorio said, his voice clipped, his teeth gritted. 'That's why I brought you to this boutique—so you could be dressed appropriately, preferably in a dress!'

'If you want to marry me,' Ana replied evenly, 'then you need to accept me as I am. I won't change for you, Vittorio.'

'Not even your clothes?' He couldn't keep the caustic note out of his voice. The woman was impossible. And, damnation, she was blinking back tears. He hadn't meant to make her cry; the last thing he needed now was *tears*. He'd hurt her, and his annoyance and shame deepened, cutting him. Hurting *him*. 'Ana—'

She shook her head, half-talking to herself. 'I don't know why I ever thought—hoped, even—that this could work. You don't know me at all. We're *strangers*—'

'Of course I don't know you!' he snapped. Impatience bit at him, the swamping sense of his own failure overtook him. He'd lost control of the situation, and he had no idea how it had happened. When she'd come into the villa this evening and he'd seen how her eyes had lit at the sight of him, he'd felt so confident. So sure that she was going to marry him, that she'd already said yes in her mind, if not her heart. Hearts need not be involved.

Yet, even as Vittorio reminded himself of this, he realized how impossible a situation this truly was. He wanted to be kind to Ana; he wanted affection and respect to bud and grow. He wanted her loyalty; he just didn't want her to fall in love with him.

Yet there seemed no danger of that right now.

'I thought,' he finally said, 'this could be an opportunity for us to get to know one another.'

'After you've changed me.'

'After I bought you a dress!' Vittorio exploded. 'Most women would have been thrilled—'

'Well, I'm not most women,' Ana snapped. Her cheeks glowed with colour and her eyes were a steely grey. She looked, Vittorio thought with a flash of surprise, magnificent. Like a woman warrior, Boadicea, magnificent in her self-righteous anger, and all that vengeful fury was directed at him. 'And *most* women I know,' she spat, 'wouldn't entertain your business proposition for a single minute!' With that, her eyes still shooting angry sparks at him, she turned on her heel and stormed down Frezzeria towards the Piazza.

This time Vittorio cursed aloud.

Standing alone, crowds of tourists pushing past her, Ana wondered if she should have gone back with that stick-thin saleswoman and tried on those gorgeous clothes. In one part of her mind—the part that still managed to remain cool and logical—she knew Vittorio had been trying to please her. Surprise her with a gift. It would have been the kind thing—the sensible thing—to accept it and go back into that dressing room. Part of her had even wanted to.

And part of her had been afraid to, and another part had wished Vittorio didn't want to improve her. No matter what her father had said about smoothing stones and that ridiculous river of life, she didn't want Vittorio to improve her. She wouldn't be his little project.

And if he was thinking of marrying her—if she was actually still considering marrying him—then she knew he needed to accept that. Accept *her*.

She'd only walked a few metres before Vittorio caught up, grabbing her by the arm none too gently. 'How are you planning on returning home?' he asked, his voice coldly furious and, angry again, Ana shrugged off his arm.

'Fortunately, there are such things as water taxis.'

'Ana—' Vittorio stopped helplessly and Ana knew he was utterly bewildered by her behaviour. Well, that made two of them. She stopped walking, her head bowed.

'I know you think you meant well,' she began, only to stop when Vittorio laughed dryly.

'Oh, dear,' he said. 'I've *really* botched it then, haven't I?'

She looked up, trying to smile. 'I just—' She took a breath, trying to explain without making herself utterly vulnerable. It was impossible. 'I don't wear dresses for a reason, Vittorio. It's not simply that I have appalling taste in clothes.' He looked so surprised, she almost laughed. 'Is that what you thought? That I don't know a designer gown from a bin bag?'

'I didn't—' he began, and now she did laugh. She'd never expected to see the Count of Cazlevara so discomfited.

'I'm a full-figured five foot eleven,' she said flatly. 'Designer gowns generally don't run in my size.'

Surprise flashed briefly in Vittorio's eyes. 'I think,' he said quietly, 'you are selling yourself a bit short.'

'I prefer not to sell myself at all,' she returned rather tartly.

Someone tapped her on the shoulder and Ana turned. 'Would you mind moving? I'm trying to get a snap of San Marco,' a camera-toting tourist explained and, muttering an oath, Vittorio took Ana by the arm once more and led her away from the crowded piazza.

'We can't have a conversation here—let's go to dinner, as I originally suggested.'

'But I'm not dressed appropriately—'

Vittorio gave her an arch look. 'And whose fault is that?'

'Yours,' she replied but, instead of sounding accusing, her voice came out pert, almost as if she were flirting. Except, Ana thought, she didn't know how to flirt. Yet Vittorio was smiling a little and so was she. 'If you'd let me change,' she continued in that same pert voice, 'instead of trying to turn a sow's ear into a—'

'Don't.' Suddenly, surprisingly, his hand came up to cover her mouth. Ana could taste the salt on his skin. 'Don't insult yourself, Ana.' His expression had softened, his mouth curved in something close to a smile, except it was too serious and even sad. She tried to speak, her lips moving against his fingers, but he wouldn't let her. 'I'm taking you to dinner,' he stated, 'no matter what you're wearing. Anyone who is with the Count of Cazlevara doesn't need to worry about clothes.' He smiled and his thumb caressed the fullness of her lower lip, the simple touch sending shockwaves of pleasure down into her belly. 'You'll find that's one of the advantages of becoming a Countess,' he said, and dropped his hand.

CHAPTER FIVE

ONCE seated at the best table at the Met, one of Venice's finest restaurants, Ana took in the glamorous couples all around them, the women all in designer gowns like the one she could have worn, and she felt another shaft of regret that she'd spurned Vittorio's generous offer of a dress. Even if it had been the safe—and even the right—thing to do.

Still, Vittorio seemed utterly unperturbed by the difference between her own attire and that of every other woman in the room. He gazed down at the menu, tapping it with one finger. 'The mussels are particularly good.'

'I'll keep that in mind.' Now that she was here, seated across from Vittorio, contemplating actually *marrying* him...Ana swallowed. Her throat felt bone-dry. She felt as if she were poised to jump off a cliff and she had no idea what waited underneath her, water or rocks, life or death.

They chose from the menu—Ana decided on chicken over fish—and Vittorio ordered the wine, a local vintage, of course, although not one of either of theirs. 'Always good to consider the competition,' he said with a smile, and Ana nodded. She did the same when she dined out, which admittedly wasn't all that often.

When their first courses arrived and the wine had been poured,

Ana gave Vittorio as direct a look as she could and said, 'I have some questions.'

Vittorio took a sip of wine. 'Very well.'

Nerves made her hands slippery around her wine glass and her voice came out a little breathless. 'What would you expect of…of a wife?'

Vittorio's expression was annoyingly inscrutable. He took another sip of wine, cocking his head to regard Ana thoughtfully. 'I'd expect my wife to be a life partner,' he said finally. 'In every sense.'

The answer, so simple, so honest, made Ana feel even more breathless and her cheeks heated. She looked down. 'Without knowing me, that's quite a big gamble.' She looked up at him again, searching for some clue to his emotions, trying to discover just why he had, over all women, chosen her in this surely coveted role.

'It's not,' Vittorio said after a moment, 'as big a gamble as you think.'

'What do you mean?'

He shrugged. 'I'm not about to embark on one of my life's major decisions without any knowledge at all, Ana. I did some research.'

'Research?' she practically spluttered. 'On me?'

'Of course.' He smiled, amused by her outrage. 'And you can research me if you like. As I said, we are each other's best assets.' He sat back, still smiling, and Ana found she was annoyed at his smug confidence. He was so very sure that any research she did would show him to advantage and, annoyingly, she was quite sure of it too.

'What did you learn?' she finally asked, her voice stiff with dignity.

'That you are a hard worker. That you are healthy—'

'You accessed my medical records?' Ana squawked, wondering how he had managed to do *that*, and Vittorio gave a negligent shrug. Nothing, apparently, was beyond the power—or the pale—for the Count of Cazlevara.

'Now I really feel like a horse,' she muttered. 'Would you like to see my teeth as well?'

'I see them when you speak,' Vittorio replied with a little smile. 'They're very nice.'

Ana just shook her head. Was there any aspect of her life—her body—that he had not researched and inspected? Should she be honoured that she'd passed all these nameless tests? She wasn't. She was furious and, worse, she felt horribly vulnerable, as if Vittorio had spied on her when she was naked. At least he seemed to have liked what he'd seen.

'I also learned,' Vittorio continued blandly, 'that you are passionate about wine and this region. That you are a good friend to those who know you. And, most importantly, that you are loyal.'

She looked up in curiosity and surprise, remembering how he'd spoken of loyalty the other night. 'And loyalty is so important to you?'

'It is,' Vittorio said and his voice, though still low and modulated, seemed suddenly to vibrate with intensity, 'paramount.'

Ana stared, trying to digest this new bit of information. Loyalty was surely so important mainly to those who had once been betrayed. What had happened to Vittorio? 'Are you speaking of fidelity?' she asked.

'No, although of course I would expect you to be faithful to me and our marriage vows. I speak of another kind of loyalty. I would expect you to stand by me and the decisions I make, never to take another's position against me.' His dark eyes caught and held hers. 'Can you do that, Ana? It will not always be easy.'

The conversation that had started so matter-of-fact had suddenly become emotional, intense. Dark. 'If you mean will I never question you—'

His hand slashed through the air. 'I'm not asking for blind

obedience. I want a wife, not a lapdog. But you must realize that, because of my position and my wealth, there are those who seek to discredit me. They would even enlist your aid, attract your sympathy by the foulest and most devious motives. Can you—will you—be loyal to me against those enemies?'

Ana suppressed a shiver. She wanted to make a joke of it, tell Vittorio to stop being so melodramatic, yet she had the terrible feeling that he was deadly serious. 'Vittorio—'

'I mean all that I say, Ana,' he said quietly. He reached across the table to encircle her wrist with his hand, his fingers pressing against her bare skin. Nerves jumped at the touch. 'I can tell you think I exaggerate, that I am seeing shadows where there is only light. But I will tell you that the quality that attracted me to you most of all was your sense of loyalty. You've lived with your father for nearly ten years, ever since you returned from university. You've helped him and taken care of him in a way that is gentle and beautiful. Of course, he is your father and he commands your loyalty because of his role. I will ask you now—do you think you can give such allegiance to me?'

'If I were married to you,' Ana said slowly, 'then, yes.'

Vittorio released her wrist and sat back with a deeply satisfied smile. 'Then I know all I need to know. Now it is your turn to ask questions of me.'

'All right,' Ana said, still a bit shaken by the intensity of their exchange. 'If we were married, I would still expect to work for Viale Wines. Would that be acceptable to you?'

Vittorio lifted a shoulder in assent. 'Of course. Naturally, I would expect our children to take the reins of both the Cazlevara and Viale labels. Truly, an empire.'

Ana nodded slowly. *Children.* Under the table, she pressed a hand against her middle. 'And my father,' she said after a moment. 'Of course, he would still live at Villa Rosso, but I would want to see him often, and invite him to be with us whenever possible.'

'Naturally.'

A bubble of sudden nervous laughter escaped her and she shook her head. 'This is so crazy.'

'It seems so, I agree, but actually it makes wonderful sense.'

And she was a sensible person, which was why she was considering it all. Because it was so logical. It just didn't feel that way at the moment. It didn't feel logical when he kissed her.

It felt wonderful.

'I'm scared,' she whispered, her voice so low she didn't know if Vittorio had heard her. She didn't know if she wanted him to.

In fact, she thought he hadn't heard her, for he didn't reply; then she felt his hand on hers, his fingers warm on her skin, curling around her own fingers, squeezing slightly. She took a deep breath and let it out in a shuddering sigh. 'I never thought I'd marry, you know.'

'Why not?' Vittorio asked, his voice as quiet as hers.

Ana shrugged, not wanting to explain. Vittorio squeezed her fingers again, and she felt a lump at the back of her throat. 'What if we end up hating each other?'

'I have too much faith in both of us for that.'

'But we might—' she persisted, her mind coming up with every possibility, every consideration, now that she was actually at the moment of decision. Now that she was ready to jump.

'All good business decisions require a certain amount of risk, Ana. They also take courage and determination.' He smiled and released her hand to take a sip of wine. 'I recently closed a deal with several major hotels in Brazil. South America has never imported much Italian wine, and some would have said I was wasting time and money going there.' He leaned forward. 'But, when I went there, I did so knowing I would do anything to make it succeed. Once the decision is made, all it requires is a certain amount of persistence and follow-through.'

What clinical terms, Ana thought. Although she knew Vittorio meant them to be comforting, she found a certain coldness settling inside her instead. 'This really is…business.'

'Of course.' He glanced at her sharply. 'I told you last week, I'm not interested in love. You agreed with me. If you were not telling the truth—'

'I was.' Ana swallowed. 'Why?' she whispered. When Vittorio simply looked nonplussed, she continued, her voice only a bit ragged, 'Why do you not want to fall in love?'

He didn't answer for a long moment. 'Love,' Vittorio finally said, his voice flat, 'is a destructive emotion.'

'It doesn't have to be—'

'Invariably, because we are all imperfect people, it becomes so. Trust me, Ana, I have seen it happen.' He swivelled his glass between his palms. 'Time and time again.'

'You've been in love, then?' Ana asked, her voice small, far too small and sad. Vittorio shook his head and she felt an absurd leap of relief.

'No. Because I have never wanted to be. But don't think that a loveless marriage must therefore be joyless. We will have affection, respect—'

'You sound like you've been speaking to my father.'

'He is a wise man.'

'He loved my mother,' Ana countered a bit defiantly.

'And yet he recommends you marry me?' There was only the faintest questioning lilt to Vittorio's voice and he smiled, leaning back once more, utterly confident. He arched an eyebrow. 'Why are you not interested in love, then?'

'I was in love once,' Ana said after a moment. She saw shock ripple across Vittorio's features before it was replaced by his usual bland composure. She wondered at her own answer. She didn't think she'd actually *loved* Roberto, but he had hurt her. 'I decided not to experience it again.'

'This man—he hurt you?'

'Yes. He...he decided he...' She faltered, not wanting to spell it out. *I never thought of you that way. How could I?* She'd left Roberto utterly cold, and Ana felt cold herself just remembering it. At least Vittorio desired her, to some degree. She could not deceive herself that he felt even an ounce of the overwhelming attraction she experienced with him, but at least he felt *something*. He wouldn't have kissed her otherwise. He wouldn't have responded to her own clumsy kiss.

That, at least, was something. Something small, pathetically so, perhaps, but it was more than Ana had ever had with a man before.

'We need not discuss it,' Vittorio said, covering her hand briefly with his own. Ana heard a hardness in his voice and his eyes flashed darkly. 'That man is in the past. We are forging something new, something good.'

'You sound so sure.'

'I am.' Ana just shook her head, still too overwhelmed by the speed with which these negotiations had been conducted. 'Why is it so difficult?' Vittorio asked. His voice remained bland, reasonable, yet Ana thought she heard the bite of impatience underneath. He'd made up his mind ages ago; he'd decided he wanted a wife and so he immediately went out and acquired one. For Vittorio, without the complications of any emotions, it was easy. Simple. 'There is no one else now,' he asked sharply, 'is there?'

She looked up, surprised. 'You know there isn't.'

'Then surely I am the best candidate.'

'If I even want a candidate,' she returned, her tone sharpening too. 'Perhaps living alone would be better.'

Vittorio's lips twisted wryly. 'Ouch.'

Ana's own mouth curved in a reluctant smile; even now he could make her laugh. 'What's your favourite colour?' she asked suddenly, and Vittorio raised his brows.

'Blue.'

'Do you like to read?'

'Paperback thrillers, my secret weakness.' He leaned back, seeming to enjoy this little exchange. Ana searched her mind for more questions; she should have dozens, hundreds, yet in the face of Vittorio's sexy little smile her mind was blanking horribly.

'Do you like dogs?'

'Yes, but not cats.'

'What food do you like?'

'Seafood. Chocolate. I keep a bar of dark chocolate in the kitchen freezer for my own personal use.' He was still smiling that incredible little smile that melted Ana's insides like that bar of dark chocolate left out in the sun.

'What food could your mother never get you to eat?'

His smile faltered for the merest of seconds, barely more than a flash, yet Ana saw it. Felt it. 'Broccoli.' He loosened his collar with one finger. 'Now I'm almost embarrassed.'

'For not liking broccoli?' Ana returned, smiling too. 'Surely you have more secrets than that.'

Vittorio's lips twitched even as his eyes darkened. 'A few.'

She thought about asking other questions. *What makes your expression change like that, darkening as if the sun has disappeared? What memories are you hiding? How many lovers have you had? Why do you think love is destructive?* She swallowed, forcing them away, knowing that now was not the time. 'Tell me something about you that I'd never guess.'

'I play the trombone.'

She laughed aloud, the sound incredulous and merry. 'Really?'

Vittorio nodded solemnly. 'You had to take music lessons at school, and the trombone was the only instrument left in the music cupboard.'

'Were you any good?'

'Awful. I sounded like a dying sheep. My music teacher begged me to stop eventually, and I played football instead, thank God.'

Ana pressed her lips together against another laugh, and shook her head a little bit. *Don't make me fall in love with you.* She pushed the thought aside. 'If you could go anywhere or do anything, what would it be?'

His little smile widened into something almost feral, his eyes glinting in the candlelight. 'Marry you.'

Her heart leaped and she shook her head. 'Be serious.'

'I am.'

'Only because I tick the right boxes.'

'I have a lot of boxes.'

'Just when did you decide I was such a suitable candidate?' Ana asked. She looked up to see Vittorio tilt his head and narrow his eyes; it was a look she was becoming used to. It meant he was thinking carefully about what to say…and what he thought she wanted to hear.

'Does it matter?'

'I'm curious.'

He gave a tiny shrug. 'I've already told you, I first read about you in the in-flight magazine. It was a short article, but it piqued my interest.'

'Enough to dig into my background?' Ana guessed, and Vittorio's mouth tightened. He gestured to the waiter to take their plates, and the man scurried forward.

'I don't particularly like your tone or your choice of words,' he said calmly. 'I've been honest from the beginning.'

'That's true.' Yet, for some reason, his honesty hurt all the more. 'It's just so…cold-blooded.'

'Funny,' Vittorio said, taking a sip of wine, 'I thought you said you weren't a romantic.'

'I'm not,' Ana said quickly. She wondered whether she was lying. Had she actually been waiting for her knight in shining armour all this time? Was she really such a lovelorn fool?

No. She would not allow herself the weakness.

'Then what is the trouble?'

'It is a big decision, Vittorio,' Ana replied, a hint of sharpness to her tone. 'As you said before. I don't make such decisions lightly.' She took a breath. If he wanted businesslike, then that was what he would get. 'What about a pre-nuptial agreement?'

Vittorio arched his eyebrows. 'Are you worried I'll take your fortune?' he asked dryly, for the Viale wealth was a fraction of his.

'No, but I thought you might have that concern.'

Vittorio's mouth hardened into a thin line. 'Divorce is not an option.'

Ana swallowed. 'What if you meet someone else?'

'I won't.' The steely glint in those dark eyes kept Ana from even asking the question about whether she would.

'Children?' she finally managed. Vittorio regarded her coolly, waiting. 'You said you needed an heir. How many?'

'Several, if God wills it.' He paused. 'You intimated you wanted children. Will that be a problem?'

'No.' The ache for a baby had only started recently, her biological clock finally having begun its relentless tick. Yet right now she couldn't think of babies, only how they were made.

Her and Vittorio. Her mind danced with images and her body ached with longing. She'd never realized how much desire she could feel, how it caused a sweet, sweet pain to lance through her and leave her breathless with wanting. The knowledge that Vittorio surely did not share it, or at least feel it as she did, that he could talk about the consummation of their marriage—the joining of their bodies—without so much as a flicker of emotion or longing made Ana ache, not just with desire, but with disappointment.

She wished he desired her the way she desired him, a wonderful consuming ache that longed only to be sated. Yes, she knew she could stir him to sensuality, but surely any man—well, *almost* any man—would have such a response.

Was it enough?

'Ana, what are you thinking?' Vittorio asked. His voice was gentle, and Ana saw a wary compassion in his eyes.

'I'm thinking I don't want to marry a man who doesn't find me attractive,' she said flatly. The words seemed to lie heavily between them, unable to be unsaid. Vittorio's face was blank, but Ana sensed his withdrawal, as if he'd actually recoiled from the brutal honesty of her words.

'I think you are being too harsh.'

The fact that he did not deny it completely made her heart sink a little. 'Am I?' she asked, and heard the hurt in her own voice.

'You felt the evidence of my desire for you the other night,' Vittorio told her in a low voice. A smile lurked in his eyes. 'Didn't you?'

Ana flushed. 'Yes, but—'

'Admittedly, you are different from the other women I've… known. But that doesn't mean I can't find you attractive.'

Having drunk enough whisky and given the right inducements, Ana silently added. 'Have you had many lovers?' she asked impulsively, and almost laughed at Vittorio's expression of utter surprise.

'Enough,' he said after a moment. 'But there is no point raking over either of our pasts, Ana. As I said before, we should look now to the future. Our future.'

Ana tossed her napkin on the table, suddenly restless, needing to move. 'I've finished. Shall we? The last boat back to Fusina leaves before midnight.'

'So it does.' Vittorio raised one hand with easy grace to signal for the bill, and within minutes they were winding their way through the tables and then outside, the spring air slightly damp, the heady scent of flowers mixing with the faint whiff of stagnant water from one of the canals, an aroma that belonged purely to Venice. 'Shall we walk?' Vittorio asked, taking her arm; it fitted snugly into his and her side collided not unpleasantly with his hip. She could feel the hard contours of his leg against hers.

The piazza outside San Marco had emptied of tourists and now only a few people lingered over half-drunk glasses of wine at the pavement cafés; Ana saw a couple entwined in the shadows by one of the pillars of the ancient church. She found herself hurrying, needing to move, to get somewhere. Her thoughts—her hopes, her fears—were too much to deal with.

They didn't speak as they made their way back to the ferry and, even once aboard the boat, they both stood at the rail, silently watching the lights of Venice disappear into the darkness and fog.

Ana knew she should have a thousand questions to ask, a dozen different points to clarify. Her mind buzzed with thoughts, concerns flitting in and out of her scattered brain.

'I don't want my children to be raised by some nanny,' she blurted and Vittorio glanced sideways at her, his hands still curved around the railing of the ferry.

'Of course not.'

'And I refuse to send them to boarding school.' Her two years at a girls' school near Florence had been some of the darkest days she'd ever known. Even now, she suppressed a shudder at the memory. Vittorio's expression didn't even flicker, although she sensed a tension rippling from him, like a current in the air.

'On that point we are of one accord. I did not enjoy boarding school particularly, and I am presuming you didn't either.'

'No.' She licked her lips; her mouth was suddenly impossibly dry. 'You can't expect to change me.' Vittorio simply arched an eyebrow and waited. 'With make-up and clothes and such. If you wanted that kind of woman, Vittorio, you should have asked someone else.' She met his bland gaze defiantly, daring him to tell her—what? That she needed a little polish? That her shapeless trouser suits—expensive as they were—would have to go? That she wasn't beautiful or glamorous enough for him? Or was that simply what *she* thought?

'There would be little point in attempting to change you,' he finally said, 'when I have asked you to marry me as you are.' Ana nodded jerkily, and then he continued. 'However, you will be the Countess of Cazlevara. I expect you to act—and dress—according to your station.'

'What does that mean exactly?'

Vittorio shrugged. 'You are an intelligent adult woman, Ana. I'll leave such decisions to you.'

Ana nodded, accepting, and they didn't speak until they were off the boat and back in Vittorio's Porsche, speeding through the darkness. A heavy fog rested over the hills above Treviso, lending an eerie glow to the road, the car's headlights barely penetrating the swirling mist. The air was chilly and damp and Ana's mind flitted immediately to the vineyards, the grapes still young and fragile. She didn't think it was cold enough to be concerned and she leaned her head back against the seat, suddenly overwhelmingly exhausted.

Vittorio turned into Villa Rosso's sweeping drive, parking the car in front of the villa's front doors and killing the engine. The world seemed impossibly silent, and Ana felt as if she could nearly fall asleep right there in the car.

'Go to bed, *rondinella*,' Vittorio said softly. His thumb skimmed her cheek, pressed lightly on her chin. 'Sleep on it awhile.'

Ana's eyes fluttered open, his words penetrating her fogged mind slowly. 'What did you say?' she asked in a whisper.

Vittorio's mouth curved in a small smile, yet Ana saw a shadow of sorrow in his eyes, lit only by the lights of the villa and the moon, which had escaped from the clouds that longed to hide it from view. 'I told you to sleep. And preferably in a bed, I think.'

'Yes, but—' Ana swallowed and struggled to a more upright position. 'What did you call me?'

'*Rondinella*.' His smile deepened, as did the sorrow in his eyes. 'You think I don't remember?'

Ana stared at him, her eyes wide, thoughts and realizations tumbling through her now-clear mind. He remembered. Suddenly she was back at her mother's graveside, her hand still caked with mud, tears drying on her cheeks. Suddenly she was looking at the only person who had shown her true compassion; even her own father had been too dazed by grief to deal with his daughter. And suddenly the answer was obvious.

'I don't need to sleep on it,' she said, her words no more than a breath of sound.

Hope lit Vittorio's eyes, replacing the sorrow. His smile seemed genuine now and he touched her cheek again with his thumb. 'You don't?'

'No.' She reached up to clasp his hand with her own, her fingers curling around his. 'The answer is yes, Vittorio. I'll marry you.'

CHAPTER SIX

EVERYTHING happened quickly after that. It was as if her acceptance had set off a chain reaction of events, spurring Vittorio into purposeful action that left Ana breathless and a little uncertain. It was all happening so *fast*.

The morning after she'd accepted his proposal—his proposition—he came to the winery offices. Seeing him there, looking official and elegant in his dark grey suit, the only colour the crimson silk of his tie, Ana was reminded just how businesslike this marriage really was. Vittorio hardly seemed the same man who had caressed her cheek and called her swallow only the evening before. The memory of his touch still lingered in her mind, tingled her nerve-endings.

'I thought we should go over some details,' Vittorio said now. 'If you have time?'

Ana braced her hands on her desk, nodding with swift purpose, an attempt to match Vittorio's own brisk determination. 'Of course.' He paused, and Ana moved from behind the desk. 'Why don't we adjourn to the wine-tasting room? I'll order coffee.'

He smiled then, seeming pleased with her suggestion. Just another business meeting, Ana thought a bit sourly, even as she reprimanded herself that she had no right to be resentful of Vittorio's businesslike attitude. She was meant to share it.

Once they were seated on the leather sofas in the wine-tasting room, a tray of coffee on the table between them, Vittorio took out a paper that, to Ana, looked like a laundry list. He withdrew a pair of wire-rimmed spectacles and perched them on the end of his nose, making an unexpected bubble of laughter rise up her throat and escape in a gurgle of sound. 'I didn't know you wore specs.'

He arched his eyebrows, smiling ruefully. 'I started needing them when I turned thirty-five, alas.'

'Is that in your medical file?' Ana couldn't help but quip. 'I should have a full report, you know.'

'I'll have it sent to you immediately,' Vittorio returned, and Ana realized she didn't know if he was joking or not. To cover her confusion she busied herself with preparing the coffee.

'I realize I don't know how old you are,' she commented lightly. 'At my mother's funeral, you were—what? Twenty?'

'Twenty-one.'

The mood suddenly turned sober, dark with memories. Ana gazed at him over the rim of her coffee cup. 'Your father died when you were around my age then, didn't he?'

'Yes. I was fourteen.'

'A heart attack, wasn't it? Sudden.'

Vittorio nodded. 'Yes, as was your mother's death, if I remember correctly. A car accident?'

Ana nodded. 'A drunk driver. A boy no more than seventeen.' She shook her head in sorrowful memory. 'He lost his life as well.'

'I always felt like the death of a parent skewed the world somehow,' Vittorio said after a moment. 'No matter how happy you are, nothing seems quite right after that.' Ana nodded jerkily; he'd expressed it perfectly. He understood. Vittorio looked away, sipping his coffee before he cleared his throat and consulted his list. 'I thought we could have a quiet ceremony in the chapel at Castle Cazlevara. Unless you object?'

'No, of course not. That sounds...fine.'

'If you envisioned something else—'

'No.' She'd stopped dreaming of any kind of wedding years ago. The thought of a huge spectacle now seemed like an affront, a travesty, considering the true nature of their marriage. The thought was an uncomfortable one. 'A quiet ceremony will be fine,' she said a bit flatly, and Vittorio frowned.

'As long as you are sure.' He turned back to his list, a frown still wrinkling his forehead, drawing those strong, straight brows closer together. 'As for dates, I thought in two weeks' time.'

Ana nearly spluttered her mouthful of coffee. 'Two *weeks*!'

'Three, then, at the most. There is no reason to wait, is there?'

'No, I suppose not,' Ana agreed reluctantly. 'Still, won't it seem…odd? People might talk.'

'I am not interested in gossip. In any case, the sooner we marry, the sooner we become…used to one another.' He gave her the glimmer of a smile. 'Of course, we can wait—a while—before we consummate the marriage. I want you to feel comfortable.'

Ana blushed. She couldn't help it. Despite his tone of cool, clinical detachment, she could imagine that consummation so vividly. Wonderfully. And she didn't want to wait. She took another sip of coffee, hiding her face from Vittorio's knowing gaze. She wasn't about to admit as much, not when Vittorio was all too content to delay the event.

'Thank you for that sensitivity,' she murmured after a moment, and Vittorio nodded and returned to his list.

'I thought a small wedding, but do let me know if there is anyone in particular you would like to invite.'

'I'll have to think about it.'

'I realize if we invited only some of the local winemakers, others will be insulted at not being included,' Vittorio continued. 'So I thought not to invite any… We'll have a party at the castle a few days after the wedding. Everyone can come then.'

'All right.' Ana wished she could contribute something more

coherent to this conversation other than her mindless murmured agreements. Yet she couldn't; her mind was spinning with these new developments, realizations. Implications.

In a short while—as little as two weeks—they could be married. *Would* be married. Her hand trembled and she put the coffee cup back in its saucer with an inelegant clatter.

'We will need witnesses, of course, for the ceremony,' Vittorio said, reaching for his own cup. If he noticed Ana's agitation, he did not remark on it. 'Is there a woman friend in particular you would like to stand witness?'

'Yes, a friend from university.' Paola was still her best friend, although they saw each other infrequently ever since her friend had married a Sicilian. She'd moved south and had babies. Ana had moved home, caring for her father and the winery. 'She'll be surprised,' Ana said a bit wryly. She could only imagine Paola's shock when she told her she was getting married, and so suddenly. 'And what about you? Who will you have as your witness?'

'I thought your father.'

'My father!' Ana couldn't keep the surprise from her voice; she didn't even try. 'But…'

'He is a good man.'

'What about your brother?'

'No.' Vittorio's voice was flat and when his gaze met Ana's his eyes looked hard, even unfriendly. 'We are not close.'

There was a world of knowledge in that statement, Ana knew, a lifetime of memory and perhaps regret. She longed to ask why—what—but she knew now was not the time. 'Very well.'

Vittorio finished his coffee and folded his list back into his breast pocket. 'I assume I can leave the details of your dress and flowers to you?' he asked. His eyebrow arched, a hint of a smile around his mouth, he added, 'You will wear a dress?'

Ana managed a smile back. 'Yes. For my own wedding, I think I can manage a dress.'

'Good. Then I'll leave you to work now. I thought you could come to dinner this Friday, at the castle. You will need to meet my family.' Again that hardness, that darkness.

Ana nodded. 'Yes, of course.'

And then he was gone. He rose from the table, shook her hand and left the office as if it had just been another business meeting, which, Ana recognized, of course it had.

That evening, over dinner, she told her father. She could have told him that morning, but something had held her back. Perhaps it was her own reluctance to admit she'd done something that seemed so foolhardy, so desperate. Yet, now the wedding was a mere fortnight away, she could hardly keep such news from her father, especially if Vittorio intended for him to stand as witness.

'I said yes to Vittorio, Papà,' Ana said as they finished the soup course. Her voice came out sounding rather flat.

Enrico lowered his spoon, his eyes widening in surprise, a smile blooming across his dear wrinkled face. 'But Ana! *Dolcezza!* That is wonderful.'

'I hope it will be,' Ana allowed, and Enrico nodded in understanding.

'You are nervous? Afraid?'

'A bit.'

'He is a good man.'

'I'm glad you think so.'

Enrico cocked his head. 'You aren't sure?'

Ana considered this. 'I would hardly marry a bad man, Papà.' Vittorio was a good man, she knew. Honourable, just, moral. She thought of that hardness in his eyes and voice when he spoke of his family. He was a good man, but was he a gentle man? Then she remembered the whisper of his thumb on her cheek, the soft words of comfort. *It's all right…rondinella.*

She didn't know what to think. What to believe or even to hope for.

'I am happy for you,' Enrico said, reaching over to cover her hand with his own. 'For you both. When is the wedding?'

Ana swallowed. 'In two weeks.'

Enrico raised his eyebrows. 'Good,' he said after a moment. 'No need to waste time. I will telephone Aunt Iris today. Perhaps she can come from England.'

Ana nodded jerkily. She'd only met her aunt a handful of times; she'd disapproved of her sister marrying an Italian and living so far away. When Emily had died, she'd withdrawn even more. 'I hope she'll come,' Ana said, meaning it. Perhaps her wedding could go some way towards healing such family rifts.

Even when at work in the winery on Monday she found her thoughts were too hopelessly scattered to concentrate on much of anything. She jumped at the littlest sound, half-expecting, hoping even, to see Vittorio again. He did not make an appearance.

In the middle of a task or phone call she would catch herself staring into space, her mind leaping ahead...*I'll be the Countess of Cazlevara. What will people say? When will Vittorio want to—?*

She forced her mind back to her work, even as a lump of something—half dread, half excitement—lodged in her middle and made it impossible to eat or even to swallow more than a sip of water. She was a seething mass of nerves, wondering just what insane foolishness she'd agreed to, longing to possess the cool business sense Vittorio had credited her with. She couldn't summon it for the life of her.

On Thursday evening, as she headed back to the villa, she compiled a list in her head of all the things she needed to do. Tell the winery staff. Ring Paola. Find an outfit—a dress?—for her dinner with Vittorio and his family tomorrow.

The downstairs of the villa was quiet and dark when Ana entered.

'Papà?' she called, and there was no answer. She headed upstairs, pausing in the doorway of one of the guest bedrooms they never used. Her father, she saw, was seated on the floor, his head bowed. Ana felt a lurch of alarm. 'Papa?' she asked gently. 'Are you all right?'

He looked up, blinking once or twice, and smiled brightly. 'Yes. Fine. I was just looking through some old things.'

Ana stepped into the room, now lost in the gloom of late afternoon. 'What old things?' she asked.

'Of your mother's…' The words trailed off in a sigh. Enrico looked down at his lap, which was covered by a heap of crumpled white satin. 'She would be so pleased to know you were getting married. I like to think that she does know, somehow. Somewhere.'

'Yes.' Ana couldn't help but remember Vittorio's words: *tua cuore*. 'What's that on your lap?'

'Your mother's wedding dress. Have I never shown it to you?'

Ana shook her head. 'In photographs…'

Enrico held it up, shaking it out as he smiled tremulously. 'I know it's probably out-of-date,' he began, his voice hesitant. 'And it needs to be professionally cleaned and most likely altered, but…'

'But?' Ana prompted. She felt moved by her father's obvious emotion—unusual as it was—but it saddened her too. This enduring love was something she'd agreed never to know.

'It would give this old man great joy for you to wear your mother's gown on your wedding day,' Enrico said, and Ana's heart sank a little bit.

'You're not an old man, Papà,' she protested, even as she scanned his face, noticing how thin and white his hair was, the new deeper grooves on the sides of his mouth. He'd been forty when he'd married; he was just past seventy now. It seemed impossible, and her heart lurched as she reached for the gown. 'Let me see.' She shook the dress out, admiring the rich white satin even as she recognized the style—over thirty years old—was far from flattering for her own fuller figure. The round neckline was bedecked with heavy lace and the skirt had three tiers of ruffles. Not only would she look like a meringue in it, she would look like a very large meringue. She'd look *awful*. Ana turned back to her father; tears shimmered in his eyes. She smiled. 'I'd be honoured to wear it, Papà.'

The next day Ana stood outside Castle Cazlevara. The torches guttered in a chilly spring breeze and lights twinkled from within. Even before she stepped out of her car—she'd insisted on driving herself—a liveried footman threw open the double doors and welcomed her inside.

'Signorina Viale, welcome. The Count and his mother, the Countess, are in the drawing room awaiting your arrival.'

Ana swallowed past the dryness in her mouth; her heart had begun to thump so loudly she could feel it in her ears. She straightened, her hands running down the silvery-grey wide-legged trousers she wore. She'd taken great pains over her outfit, and yet now she wondered if it was as plain as the other trouser suits she donned as armour. Only yesterday she'd taken the ferry to Venice, had even ventured down Frezzeria to the chic boutique Vittorio had led her to just the other night. She'd stood in front of the window like a child in front of a sweet shop; twice she'd almost gone in. But the stick-thin sales associate with her black pencil skirt and crisp white blouse looked so svelte and elegant and forbidding that after twenty minutes Ana had crept away. The thought of trying on such beautiful clothes—of looking at herself in such beautiful clothes—in front of such a woman was too intimidating. Too terrifying.

So she'd scoured her closet, finding a pair of trousers she'd never worn; the fabric shimmered as she moved and even though it was still a pair of trousers, the legs were wide enough to almost pass for a skirt. She chose the beaded top she'd worn the last time she'd come to the castle and she'd pulled back her hair loosely so a few loose tendrils framed her face, softening the effect. She'd even put on a little lipstick.

Now as she made her way to the drawing room, she wondered if Vittorio would notice. If he would care. And, if he did, would she be glad? She couldn't decide if she would feel more of a fool if he did notice or if he didn't.

All these thoughts flew from her head as she stood in the doorway of the drawing room and a slim, petite blonde—the kind of woman who made Ana feel like an ungainly giant—swivelled to face her. Constantia Ralfino, the Countess of Cazlevara. Soon to be the *Dowager* Countess.

The moment seemed suspended in time as they both stood there, the Countess taking in Ana with one arctic sweep of her eyes. Ana quailed under that gaze; she felt herself shrivel inside, for Constantia Cazlevara was looking at her as so many people had looked at her, beginning with most of the girls at the boarding school her father had sent her to after her mother had died.

It was a look of assessment and then disdain, followed swiftly by dismissal. It was a look that hurt now, more than it should, because it made Ana feel like a gawky thirteen-year-old again, awkward and still stricken with grief.

'So,' Constantia said coolly. She lifted her chin and met Ana's humble gaze directly. 'This is your bride.' Her tone was most likely meant to be neutral, but Ana heard contempt. She lifted her chin as well.

'Yes. We met many years ago, my lady. Of course, I am pleased to make your acquaintance once more.'

'Indeed.' Constantia did not make any move to take Ana's proffered hand, and after a moment she dropped it. Constantia turned to Vittorio, who was watching them both in tight-lipped silence. 'Aren't you going to introduce us, Vittorio?'

'Ana seems to have accomplished the introductions better than I ever could,' he said in a clipped voice. 'However, if you must.' He waved one hand between the pair of them. 'Mother, this is Ana Viale, one of the region's most promising winemakers, daughter of our neighbour Enrico Viale, and my intended bride.' His lips, once pursed so tightly, now curved in a smile that still managed to seem unpleasant. 'Ana, this is my mother, Constantia.'

The tension almost made the air shiver; Ana imagined she could hear it crackle. Constantia shot her son a look of barely veiled resentment before she turned back to Ana. 'So was it love at first sight, my dear?'

Ana couldn't tell if the older woman was baiting her or genuinely interested in knowing. She glanced at Vittorio, wondering what to say. How to dissemble. Did he want people to know just how convenient their marriage was meant to be? Or was he intending to deceive everyone into thinking they were in love? Such a charade would be exhausting and ultimately pointless, Ana was sure.

Before she could frame an answer, Vittorio cut in. 'Love at first sight? What a question, Mother. Ana and I both know there is no such thing. Now, dinner is served and I don't enjoy eating it cold. Let's withdraw to the dining room.' He strode from the room, pausing only to offer Ana his arm, which she accepted awkwardly, her elbow crooked in his, her strides made awkwardly longer than normal in order to match his.

Dinner was, of course, interminable. Vittorio and Constantia both spoke with that chilly politeness that managed to be worse than outright barbs or even insults. Ana felt her whole body tense and she had the beginnings of a terrible headache. It was impossible to know what to say, how to act. Vittorio gave her no clues.

A thousand questions and, worse, doubts, whirled in her head, demanding answers. What was the source of the antipathy between Vittorio and his mother? How could two people in the same family seem to dislike each other so much? And how could she possibly fit into this unhappy picture? The thought of living in Castle Cazlevara with Constantia's continual scorn and disdain was unendurable. An hour into the evening, Ana was just beginning to realize how much she'd agreed to when she'd accepted Vittorio's proposal. Not just a marriage, but a family. Not just a business proposition, but a lifestyle. A *life*.

She felt fraught with nerves, sick with dread by the time the miserable meal came to an end. There had been some sort of conversation, she supposed, desultory remarks that still managed to be pointed, poised to wound. Ana had contributed very little; she'd eaten less, merely toying with her food.

Constantia rose from the table in one graceful movement. She was a slender slip of a woman, still strikingly beautiful despite the wrinkles that lined her face like a piece of parchment that had been crumpled up and smoothed out again. 'I'm afraid I'm too weary from my journey to stay for coffee,' she said, offering Ana a cool little smile. 'I do hope you'll forgive me, my dear.'

'Of course,' Ana murmured. She was relieved to be able to avoid any further awkwardness with her future mother-in-law—if she was even going to marry Vittorio. A single evening had cast everything into terrible doubt.

'Well, then.' She turned to Vittorio, her haughty expression seeming to turn sad, the cool little smile softening into something that looked weary and lost. Before Ana could even register what that look meant, it had cleared, leaving Constantia distant and regal once more, and with one last haughty look she swept from the room and left Vittorio and Ana suspended in a tense and uneasy silence.

'Vittorio—' Ana began, the word bursting from her. She stopped, unable to continue, afraid to frame the thoughts pounding through her head.

'What is it, Ana?' His tone was sharp, his look assessing. Knowing. 'You're not having second thoughts already?' he asked, his voice soft now and yet still faintly menacing. He rose from the table, coming around to help Ana from her chair. His hands slid down her bare shoulders in what was surely no more than a pretext to touch her; she shivered noticeably. 'Cold feet, *rondinella*?' he whispered and she shook her head, sudden pain lancing through her.

'Don't call me that.'

'Why not?'

'Because—' She pressed her lips together. It would sound foolish—pathetic, even—to admit the endearment was special. That it *meant* something. Yet still she couldn't stand Vittorio using it now, when his expression was so forbidding, his voice faintly mocking. When there suddenly seemed so much she didn't know about him, so much she was afraid of.

'Because why?' Vittorio asked. He'd trailed his hand down Ana's bare arm so now their fingertips were touching. Smiling faintly, he laced his fingers with her own and drew her from the table, out into the foyer with its flickering torches, the ancient stones dancing with shadows. 'We are about to be married, after all.'

Ana let him lead her. His touch was mesmerizing, her thoughts and even doubts seeming to fly from her head as she followed him slowly, knowing each step was taking her closer to danger. Danger, and yet such exquisite danger it was. All she could think or feel was his fingers on her skin. Wanting more. Needing more.

'I don't—' she began, and then simply shook her head, at a loss for words. Feeling was too much, taking over every sense.

'You don't…?' Vittorio prompted. She thought she heard laughter in his voice; he *knew*. He knew how much his simple touch affected her, reduced her. He used it as a weapon. His fingers still laced with hers, he pulled her towards him. She came, unresisting, until their bodies collided and she had to tilt back her head to look up into his face, his onyx eyes glittering as he gazed down at her. 'Don't be afraid, Ana,' he murmured, his lips inches from hers.

Her own lips parted instinctively, yet also in anticipation. *Hope.* Even so, she summoned one last protest; it was both an attack and a defence. 'There's so much I don't know about you, Vittorio.'

'Mmm.' Vittorio's fingers trailed up and down her arm, playing her skin like an instrument, his lips now a scant inch from hers so his breath feathered her face. She knew what he was doing. He was distracting her, keeping her from asking the questions whose answers she needed to know, whose answers, she realized fuzzily, might keep her from marrying him. And, even as she knew this, she couldn't help her overwhelming response to his touch, blocking out all rational thought, all sense of reason.

And so another damning thought followed on the heels of the first: that *nothing* could keep her from marrying Vittorio, from possessing him, or having him possess her. She knew that as, with his free hand, he cupped her cheek and brought her face closer to his, their lips now no more than a breath apart.

He was going to kiss her. She needed him to kiss her, craved it, knew that her body and mind and soul could not be satisfied until she'd felt his lips on hers once more. Later, she knew, she would be humbled and perhaps ashamed by her own helpless desire. For now, it remained only an unstoppable force, an overwhelming hunger. So much so, in fact, that in barely a breath of sound, she whispered, *begged*, 'Kiss me.'

Vittorio's mouth curved in a smile tinged with triumph. Ana didn't care. She didn't care if she was humiliating herself, if Vittorio would gloat in his sensual power over her. She *couldn't* care, because the need was too strong. 'Kiss me,' she said again, and then, because still he just smiled, she closed the gap between their lips herself, her eyes closing in blissful relief as their mouths connected and her whole body flooded with both satisfaction and yet more need.

Her hands found their way to his hair, fisting in its softness, her body pressing against the full length of his. She let her mouth move slowly over his, let her tongue slide against his lips, knowing she was inexpert, clumsy even, and not caring because it felt so good. She lost herself in that kiss, sank into it like she would a big feather bed, revelling in its softness, its wonder and pleasure, until she realized—slowly—that Vittorio had not moved, had not responded at all. Dimly, distantly, she became aware that his body was rigid against hers, his hands only loosely on her shoulders, his lips unresponsive and even slack under hers.

Desire had swamped her senses, flooded her reason, and yet Vittorio barely seemed affected at all.

In a sickening flash she remembered how she'd kissed Roberto—just as clumsily, no doubt—and how he had not moved either. He had remained still, enduring her touch, relieved when it was over. He'd felt disgust, not desire. And—oh, please, no—was Vittorio the same? She took a stumbling step backwards, shame pouring through her, scalding her senses, making her eager for escape.

Yet Vittorio would not let her flee. His hands came up to encircle her arms and he pulled her towards him as he deepened the kiss and made it his own. His hands moved to her hips, rocking her so their bodies collided in the most intimate way, and her lips curved in a triumphant, incredulous smile when she heard his sharp intake of breath and felt the evidence of his arousal.

Yet if Ana felt she was in control—even for a second—she soon realized she was sorely mistaken. Vittorio had taken command, pulling her into even closer contact, keeping her there, trapped between his powerful thighs. His mouth, at first so still and unresponsive under hers, now moved with deliberate, languorous ease, travelling from her lips to the sensitive skin under her ear so she was the one gasping aloud, and then to the intimate curve of her neck, and finally to the vee between her breasts.

Ana threw her head back, her eyes clenched shut, her breath coming in audible moans. She'd never been touched so intimately, so *much*. Her head spun and her body felt as if every nerve-ending had blazed to life; it almost hurt to feel this much, to know such pleasure.

She'd never known that *anything* could be like this.

Then Vittorio stepped away, leaving Ana reeling and gasping, the aftershocks of exquisite sensation still rocking her, and he smiled rather coolly. 'See, Ana?' he said, reaching behind her to open the front door of the castle; a cool breeze blew over her heated body. 'I think you know me well enough.'

Vittorio waited until Ana was safely in her car, making her way down the curving drive, before he let out a long, low shudder.

He had not expected that. He'd been planning to seduce Ana, to sweep away her doubts with a kiss—or two. Instead, *she'd* kissed *him*. He'd been shocked by her audacity as well as his response. For, in that kiss, he'd realized that Ana was more than this thing he wanted, this possession he meant to acquire, his goal achieved. *Wife.*

She was a person, a being with hopes and needs and oh, yes, desires—and, even as he'd sent his little gifts and said the right words and kissed her, he'd somehow managed to forget this fact. Had he ever really known it?

Why he should realize that when she'd been kissing him, pressing against him, stirring him to a sudden desperate lust, he had no idea. He wished he hadn't realized; it was easier not to know, or at least to pretend not to know.

To hold someone's happiness in your hand, to take responsibility for her life—

It was monumental. Frightening, too.

'Why, Vittorio?'

Vittorio stilled, his mother's accusing voice ringing in his ears. He turned slowly, his gaze sweeping over her in one dismissive glance. She stood poised on the bottom step of the ornate marble staircase—a nineteenth-century addition to the castle—her eyes blazing blue fire and her mouth twisted into a contemptuous sneer. It was an expression he'd become accustomed to.

'Why what, Mother?' he asked, his words holding only a veneer of icy politeness.

'Why are you marrying that poor girl?'

Vittorio's eyes narrowed. 'I don't appreciate the way you refer to my bride. There is nothing poor about Ana.'

Constantia let out a crow of disbelieving laughter. 'Come, Vittorio! I know the women you've taken to your bed. I've seen them in the tabloids. They would eat Anamaria Viale alive.'

He just kept himself from flinching. 'They will never have the opportunity.'

'No?' Constantia took a step towards him, incredulity lacing the single word. 'You think not? And how will you manage that, my son? Will you keep your precious wife locked away in a glass case? Because, I assure you, that is not a pleasant place to be.'

'I have no intention of putting Ana anywhere,' Vittorio said flatly, 'that she does not wish to be.'

'She loves you,' Constantia said after a moment. Her voice was quiet. 'Or at least she could.'

Vittorio's jaw tightened. 'That is no concern of yours, Mother.'

'Isn't it?' Constantia lifted her chin, her expression challenging and obdurate. 'Do you know how it feels to love someone and never have them love you back? Do you know what that can drive you to think, to *do*?' Her voice rang out, raw and ragged, and Vittorio narrowed his eyes. Her words—her tone—made no sense to him; was her obvious distress another ploy?

'What are you talking about?'

Constantia pressed her lips together and shook her head. 'Why are you going to marry her, Vittorio? Is it simply to spite me?'

'You give yourself too much credit.'

'You had no interest in marriage until I spoke of it.'

Vittorio lifted one shoulder in a careless shrug. 'You simply reminded me to do my duty as Count of Cazlevara and CEO of Cazlevara Wines,' he said. 'It is my duty to provide an heir.'

'So Bernardo cannot take your place,' she finished flatly.

Vittorio's eyes narrowed. She didn't even hide her true ambition, but then she never had. 'Every man wants a son.'

'Why her?' Constantia demanded. 'Why marry a woman you could not love?'

'I'm not interested in love, Mother.'

'Just like your father, then,' she spat, and again Vittorio felt a confused lurch of unease which he forced himself to dismiss.

'I'm finished with this conversation,' he said shortly and he turned away, walking quickly from the room. It was only later, when he was preparing for bed, that he remembered and reflected on his mother's words. She'd called Ana a woman he could not love, as if such a thing—to love Ana—was an impossibility.

His hands stilling on the buttons of his shirt, Vittorio wondered if his mother spoke the truth. He'd never *wanted* to love, that was true; was he even capable of it?

CHAPTER SEVEN

TODAY was her wedding day. Ana stared at her reflection in her bedroom mirror and grimaced. She looked awful. Although she couldn't regret the decision to wear her mother's wedding gown, neither could she suppress the natural longing to look better in it.

The gown had been professionally cleaned and altered, but it was still befrilled and belaced to within an inch of its life—and hers. The thought of Vittorio seeing her looking like Little Bo Beep from a bad pantomime made her cringe. Sighing, she stroked the rich satin—no matter what the style, the dress was of the highest quality—and forced such negative thoughts from her mind. Today was her wedding day. She wanted to enjoy it.

Yet other negative thoughts—the doubts and fears that had dogged her since her dinner with Vittorio and Constantia—crept in and gnawed at her already struggling sense of happiness.

She'd seen Vittorio many times in the last fortnight; he'd made a point of stopping by the winery office, whether it was for a simple hello, or to show her a magazine article on the latest growing techniques, or to stroll through the Viale vineyards with her, the sun blazing benevolently down on them as they walked. Ana appreciated his attempts to make their relationship at least appear normal and pleasant, yet she couldn't quite stop the creeping doubt that, even though she enjoyed them, the visits seemed a little…*perfunctory*. Another item ticked off on her husband-to-be's to-do list. He'd acquired his bride; now he was maintaining her.

She knew she shouldn't begrudge Vittorio the time he spent with her, and she shouldn't expect more. She shouldn't even *want* more. She'd agreed to a business-minded marriage, she reminded herself, not nearly for the first time. She had to stick to her side of the bargain.

Someone tapped on the door and then a dark curly head peeked round the frame. 'Are you ready?' Paola asked. Ever since Ana had told her friend about her upcoming wedding, Paola had been wonderfully supportive. Ana had not yet told her the truth of her marriage. 'The car is here to take you to the castle.'

Ana nodded. 'Yes, I just need my veil.'

Smiling, Paola reached for the gossamer-thin veil of webbed lace and settled it on Ana's head. She wore her hair up in a chignon, clusters of curls at the corners of her brow. 'You look…' Paola began, and Ana smiled wryly.

'Terrible.'

Paola smiled back at Ana, their eyes meeting in the mirror. 'I wasn't going to say that.'

'The dress doesn't suit me in the least.'

Paola gave a little shrug. 'I think it's wonderful you're wearing your mother's gown and anyone with any sense will think the same, no matter what it looks like. Anyway,' she continued robustly as she twitched the veil so the lace flowed down Ana's back, 'I think a bride could wear a bin bag and it wouldn't matter at all. When you're in love, you glow. No one looks better than a bride on her wedding day.'

'You think so?' Ana asked, her voice pitched just a little too shrill. She didn't glow, and it was no wonder. She wasn't in love. She looked, in fact, rather pasty.

Paola laid a hand on Ana's shoulder. 'Is everything all right, Ana? I know we haven't been in touch in a while, but—' she paused, chewing her lip '—you seem so nervous. Everyone has cold feet, of course. I was nearly sick the morning of my own wedding, do you remember? But…are you sure this is what you want?' She softened the question with a smile, adding, 'It's my duty as your bridesmaid and witness to ask that, you know.'

'I know.' Ana made herself smile back, despite the nerves that were fluttering rather madly in her stomach and threatening to make their way up her throat. 'Yes, Paola, this is what I want.' No matter how nervous she was now, Ana knew she couldn't go back to her old life, her old ways. She couldn't walk out on Vittorio, and what marriage to him would—could—mean. She let out her breath slowly. 'If I seem particularly nervous, it's because this marriage isn't—isn't really a normal marriage.'

Paola frowned. 'What are you talking about?'

'Vittorio and I only agreed to get married a fortnight ago,' Ana explained in a rush. She felt better for admitting the truth she hadn't been brave enough to reveal since Paola's arrival two days ago. 'We're not in love, not even close. It's a marriage…of convenience.'

'Convenience?' Paola echoed. She gave a disbelieving laugh. 'Just what is convenient about marriage?'

Ana tried for a laugh as well; the sound came out shaky. 'Vittorio and I have common goals. We're both ambitious and we have similar ideas about…things…' She trailed off, realizing how absurd she sounded. She didn't even know if she believed half of what she said. From the look in Paola's narrowed eyes, neither did her friend.

'Ana, are you really sure—'

A knock sounded at the door and the muffled voice of her father could be heard from behind it. 'Ana, *dolcezza*, are you ready? The car is here and if we are to be on time…'

Ana took a deep breath. Her wedding day was here; the moment had arrived. In less than an hour she would be married to Vittorio, she would be the Countess of Cazlevara. A thousand thoughts and memories flitted through her dazed mind: the moment when she'd learned her mother had died, and her whole world fell away. Her father's refusal even to see her, hiding his grief behind locked doors, insisting she attend boarding school. The hellish days at that school, alone, grief-stricken, awkward and miserable, teased and ignored. Then, later, her years at university, slowly learning how to be confident, what it would take to be successful, only to have her frail self-esteem obliterated by that awful moment in Roberto's arms. The nights spent gazing out of her window, wondering if life would ever offer more, if love could be found. The decision to stop looking for love and enjoy what she already had, to live for what life offered her rather than seeking more, always more… All of it, every second, it seemed then, had led up to this moment and her decision to marry Vittorio.

And then new, fresh memories raced through her: the gentle touch of Vittorio's hand on her cheek, both when she was thirteen and when she was nearly thirty. The feel of his lips on hers, his hands on her body, so deft, so desirable. The kindnesses he'd shown her in the last fortnight—calculated, perhaps—whether it was a spray of new grapes or the offer of a new gown. The tension with his mother, the hope they both had for the future.

And then, to her surprise, as the memories faded and she blinked the room back into focus, she realized she was no longer afraid. Her nerves had fled and in their place a new, serene determination had emerged. She smiled at Paola.

'This is what I want, Paola. I am sure.' Turning, Ana called to her father, 'Papà! I'm ready.'

As she opened the door, Enrico blinked tears from his eyes as he saw her in her mother's gown. 'Oh, *dolcezza! Magnifica!*'

Ana smiled.

She didn't quite manage a smile as she saw Vittorio's expression when she came down the aisle of the chapel attached to Castle Cazlevara. Only a dozen guests were scattered among the dark wood pews, a few relatives and friends. Paola, Vittorio and her father all stood at the front as Ana walked down the aisle alone in her mother's ruffled gown.

Vittorio, for a single second, looked horrified. Then his expression smoothed out as if an iron had been applied to it and he gave her the barest flicker of a smile; his eyes remained dark. Ana remembered what she'd once said about her own fashion sense and knew Vittorio was doubting her now. He was probably wondering just what kind of woman he was marrying, when she came down the aisle in a gown thirty years out of date, a gown that made her look like a melting meringue.

Ana lifted her chin and found her smile.

The ceremony only lasted a few minutes, or so it seemed, for, after a blur of words and motions, Vittorio was sliding the heavy band of antique gold on her finger and then his lips, cool and somehow remote, were pressing her cheek in the chastest of kisses. Even so, Ana's blood stirred and desire leapt low in her belly.

Vittorio stepped away.

Ana heard a spattering of applause from the paltry crowd as if from a great distance, and then Vittorio was leading her down the aisle, away from the chapel and towards the great hall of the castle where their wedding feast would be held.

She sneaked a glance at his profile; his jaw was tight, his gaze staring straight ahead. Ana realized afresh just how much of a stranger her husband was.

Her husband. The thought was incredible, bizarre, ridiculous.

Exciting. She swallowed past the fear and remembered her earlier certainty, tried to feel it again.

A servant opened the doors to the great hall, the long table now laid for a meal for twenty. Vittorio turned to her.

'A small wedding reception, and then we can retire. I'm sure you're tired.' He spoke with a careful politeness that managed to make Ana feel even more awkward and strange. She nodded jerkily.

'Thank you.'

Vittorio nodded back, and Ana wondered if this kind of stilted conversation was what she had to look forward to for the rest of her life.

What had she just done? What had she agreed to?

Like the ceremony, the wedding reception passed in a blur that still managed to make Ana both uncomfortable and exhausted. It wasn't a normal marriage, and people seemed to sense that, so it wasn't a normal wedding reception either. Her friends regarded her a bit quizzically; everyone she'd told had been utterly surprised by her abrupt engagement, although too polite perhaps to show it. Even her Aunt Iris, a distant stranger, scrutinized her with pursed lips and narrowed eyes, as if she suspected that something was amiss. Vittorio's brother, Bernardo, shook her hand; his fingers were cold against hers and his smile didn't reach his eyes. Constantia didn't speak to her at all.

Ana did her best to chat and smile with those who did want to talk to her; she ate a few mouthfuls of the delicious *cicchetti*, meatballs and fried crab, as well as one of the region's specialities, a lobster risotto. And of course there was wine: a rich red wine with the pasta, and crisp white wine with the fish, and prosecco with lemon sorbet for dessert.

By the time the plates had been cleared, Ana felt both exhausted and a bit dizzy. She saw Vittorio signal to a servant, and then moments later felt someone's hand on her shoulder. She turned and saw Paola smiling at her.

'Come, the wedding feast is nearly over. I'll help you out of your dress.'

'Out of…?' Ana repeated blankly, her mind fuzzy from the food and wine. Of course; the wedding was over, it was now her wedding night.

Vittorio had been vague about what he expected—what he *wanted*—from their first night together as husband and wife. He'd mentioned that he would give her time; there was no need to consummate their marriage on the very first night.

Yet what did he want? What did she want?

She knew the answer to the second question: *him.*

Ana let Paola lead her away from the reception, up to an unfamiliar corridor—she'd never even been upstairs before—and finally to a bedroom suite. Ana took in the massive stone fireplace, a fire already laid, the huge four poster bed piled high with velvet and satin pillows and the dimmed lighting. It was a room for seduction. It was a room for love.

'How did you know where to go?' she asked Paola, who had already closed the door and was reaching for the back of Ana's dress, and the thirty-six buttons that went from the nape of her neck to the small of her back.

'One of the servants showed me. Vittorio has a timetable, apparently. It's all very organized, isn't it?'

'That's a good thing,' Ana replied. She couldn't help but feel just a little defensive; she heard a note of censure in her friend's voice.

'So,' Paola asked as she finished with the buttons and the dress sank around Ana's ankles in a pool of satin, 'just how convenient is this marriage, anyway?' She gestured towards the room with its candlelight and pillows with a wry smile.

'Not that convenient, I suppose.' Ana smiled, felt the leap of anticipation in her belly, the tightening of her muscles and nerves in heady expectation. She was ready. She *wanted* this. So terribly, dangerously much.

'Do you love him, Ana?' Paola asked quietly. Ana stepped out of her dress, standing in just a thin slip, and reached for the pins that held her hair in its fussy chignon. Her back remained to Paola.

'No,' she said after a moment, 'but that's all right.'

'Is it?'

Ana turned around. 'I know you married for love, Paola, but that doesn't mean it's the only way. Vittorio and I want to be happy together, and I think we will be.' Brave words. She'd believed them once, when she'd accepted his proposal, when she'd agreed with all of his logical points. It had made *sense*.

Yet, looking at that bed piled high with pillows and flickering with candlelit shadows, there was nothing sensible about it.

'I almost forgot,' Paola said. 'Your husband left this for you.' She gestured to a plain white box, wrapped with a ribbon of ivory silk.

'Oh?' Ana reached for it; the ribbon fell away with a slither and she opened the box. Inside was the most exquisite nightdress she'd ever seen; the silk was whisper-thin and delicately scalloped lace embroidered the edges. It was held up by two gauzy ribbons, to be tied at each shoulder.

'It's gorgeous,' Paola breathed, and Ana could only nod. Then she caught sight of the tag, and her heart sank straight down to her feet.

'It's also three sizes too big.'

'Men are terrible with things like that—' Paola said quickly, too quickly.

Ana nodded, tossing the gorgeous gown back into its box. 'Of course. It doesn't matter.' Yet it did. She felt hurt, ridiculously near tears, horribly vulnerable, and suddenly she wanted—needed—to be alone. 'I'm fine, Paola. Vittorio will most likely arrive soon. You can leave me.'

'Ana—'

'I'm fine,' she said again, more firmly, and then she gave her friend a quick kiss on the cheek. 'Thank you for all you've done, and for coming to be my bridesmaid. I know how sudden it all was—'

'That doesn't matter.' Paola hugged her tightly for a moment before releasing her and stepping back. 'Are you sure you'll be all right? I can wait—'

'No, I'd like a few moments alone.' Ana smiled, straightening her spine, throwing her shoulders back. When she spoke, her voice came out firm. 'Don't worry about me, Paola. I'll be fine.' If she kept saying it, perhaps she would believe it.

When she was alone, Ana spared that gown one more accusing glance and then she moved around the room, pacing, anxiety taking the place of her earlier resolve. She told herself it hardly mattered that the gown was three sizes too big, yet no matter how many times she repeated the words, a desperate litany, she couldn't believe it.

She felt that it did matter. She felt that Vittorio must secretly think she was plain and overweight and he couldn't possibly desire her at all, unless fortified with a great deal of very good whisky. Each thought, each realization, was like a direct hit to her self-confidence, a dagger wound to her heart.

An hour passed in agonizing slowness. She wanted him to come; she didn't want him to come. She wanted to confront him; she wanted to hide. She was annoyed with herself and her own absurd indecision. For ten years she'd been in control of things—of the winery, of her life, of her own emotions. Admittedly, it hadn't been a very exciting life, but she'd been purposeful and determined and *happy*.

Now she felt completely lost, adrift in the bewildering sea of her emotions. It was a sensation she did not enjoy at all.

When a light knock sounded on the door, Ana was almost relieved. Anything at that point was better than waiting. She'd found a thick terry cloth dressing gown in the wardrobe and she'd thrown it on, belting it tightly around her waist so she was covered nearly from her neck to her ankles.

'Where have you been?' she demanded before she'd even laid eyes on him properly; too late, she realized she sounded rather shrewish.

'I thought you'd appreciate a bit of time alone,' Vittorio replied mildly.

Ana swallowed all the hurt and disappointment and nodded stiffly. 'Yes, well. Thank you.'

'Apparently I thought wrong?' he asked, moving past her into the bedroom.

'I just wondered where you were.'

Standing in the middle of the sumptuous bedroom, Vittorio looked utterly in his element. He'd removed his tie and jacket and the top two buttons of his crisp white shirt were undone. His hair was a little rumpled, and Ana could see the shadow of stubble on his strong jaw. He looked unbearably sexy and suddenly, despite everything, she felt faint with longing. She sagged against the door.

Vittorio held up a bottle he was carrying. 'I brought you a wedding present.'

'Oh?' Ana glanced at it. 'Whisky,' she said a bit flatly, and tried to smile. 'Thank you.'

'You did express a preference for it,' Vittorio replied in that same mild voice that Ana wasn't sure she liked. It was so damn unemotional, and here she was, feeling utterly fraught.

'Actually,' she told him, 'I lied.' She enjoyed the look of surprise on his face, his jaw slackening for a second. 'I don't really like whisky. That is, I haven't tried it very much.'

'Really.'

'Really.' Ana strode across the room and plucked the bottle from Vittorio's hand. 'I only said that because I could see how intent you were on manufacturing some kind of businesslike atmosphere, and it seemed like a bottle of whisky would help that.'

'Or we could have just had coffee,' Vittorio replied with the flicker of a smile.

'Coffee over billiards?' Ana arched an eyebrow. 'I don't think so. Anyway, since you brought it, why don't we have a glass now?'

'I thought you said you didn't like it.'

'Oh, didn't I tell you?' Ana gave him a wicked little smile. 'I've developed a taste for it, after all.'

Vittorio paused; Ana could see he was trying to gauge her mood, to decide what was the best—the most efficient and effective—thing to do now. Well, she was tired of that kind of attitude. Just like the last time they'd drunk whisky together, she felt reckless and defiant and even a little dangerous; it was not a pleasant feeling but it made her feel *alive*. She raised the bottle. 'Are there any glasses around?'

'I'm sure I can find some,' Vittorio murmured and moved past her to the en suite bathroom. He returned with two water tumblers and handed them over. 'No ice, I'm afraid.'

'That's all right. I've found I prefer it straight.'

'As do I,' he murmured. He was standing close to her so his breath tickled her ear, making her want to shiver. She just barely suppressed the urge and unscrewed the bottle, pouring two rather large whiskies. She handed Vittorio one of the glasses.

'Cento anni di salute e felicità,' he said with a wry twist to his mouth; it was the traditional wedding toast. A hundred years of health and happiness.

Ana nodded jerkily, and they drank at the same time.

In the aftermath of the alcohol her eyes burned and watered. She just barely kept herself from choking.

'All right?' Vittorio asked, putting his glass aside, and Ana smiled defiantly.

'Never better.'

For a second, his expression flickered. 'Ana—'

'Thank you for the gown, by the way. It's gorgeous.'

'Gown?' Vittorio repeated a bit warily and Ana smiled, the curve of her mouth forced and overbright.

'This.' She reached for the box with its rather large scrap of silk. 'Am I meant to wear it tonight? Because I'm afraid it's a bit too big.' She gave a little laugh. 'I'm not actually as large as you think I am, I suppose.'

Vittorio took the gown without speaking, shook it out and gazed at it with a rather clinical eye. 'I see. It is a beautiful gown, Ana, but I'm afraid I didn't give it to you. I've learned my lesson with you where clothes are concerned.'

Now Ana's jaw slackened, the wind leaking right out of her self-righteous sails. 'You didn't send it?'

'No. But I can guess who did.'

'Who?'

'My mother. To send you a gown several sizes too big—this is the kind of thing she would do. Her little attempt to wound. It stings, *si*?' His eyes hardened. 'Trust me, I know.'

Suddenly the gown didn't matter at all. 'Vittorio—what has happened between you and your mother? And your brother too? Why are you all so—so terrible to one another? So cold.'

Vittorio was silent for a moment, before he shook his head. 'It is past, Ana, past and forgotten. There is nothing you need to know.'

'But it isn't really forgotten, is it? I can tell by the way you talk about it, even now—'

'It's late—' he cut her off '—and you need your sleep. I'll see you in the morning.'

Disappointment opened up inside her, a vast looming pit. She wanted to ask him to stay, but she knew she wouldn't. Couldn't begin their marriage this way, with her begging for him, for his touch. Yet why was he leaving? Was this his so-called sensitivity or merely his indifference? 'All right,' she whispered, her voice catching on the words.

He reached out with one hand and touched her cheek, his

thumb finding that secret place where a tear had once sparkled. Ana closed her eyes and nearly swayed where she stood. 'It will be all right, *rondinella*,' he murmured. 'I know this is hard now—awkward too, for both of us, but it will be all right.'

Ana swallowed and nodded, her throat too tight to speak. She didn't open her eyes for a moment and, when she did, Vittorio had already gone.

Alone in the hallway, Vittorio cursed under his breath. Of course his mother would seek to discredit him with Ana from the first moment of their marriage. Of course she would find ways to weaken the tenuous link he'd forged with his bride. And, if Constantia stayed here, she would continue to poison Ana's mind and pare away her self-confidence.

Yet he knew he would not ask his mother to leave. He'd never asked her to leave. He'd been the one to leave, all those years ago; he'd felt like an interloper in his own home, unwanted and undesired, and it had been easier simply to walk away.

Vittorio thought of the disappointment he'd seen in Ana's eyes. She'd wanted him to stay; she'd even wanted him to make love to her. And he'd wanted it, too; his body even now stirred to lust. Yet he'd balked, like a shy virgin! The thought almost made him laugh in exasperation at his own reticience. All too easily he could imagine taking her in his arms, unwrapping her from that thick, bulky robe like a parcel from its paper.

Yet she wasn't merely a parcel, a thing, this wife of his, and it was this uncomfortable new knowledge that kept him from staying. From consummating their marriage, for surely that was all it would be. A consummation, a soulless act, and he was—suddenly, stupidly too—afraid of hurting her.

Vittorio cursed aloud. Now was not the time to develop some kind of stupid sensitivity. He stopped, almost turned around, even if just to prove a point to himself. Then he remembered the way Ana's grey eyes, so wide and luminous and somehow soft, had darkened with disappointment when he'd said he was leaving, how her breath had shortened when he'd touched her cheek and, furious with himself, at a loss for what he should do now, he kept on walking.

CHAPTER EIGHT

THE next few days were some of the most depressing Ana had ever known, simply by reason of their utter sameness. Except for the fact that she drove back to Castle Cazlevara every night after work, Ana would not know she was married. Her days had not changed at all; after an impersonal breakfast with Vittorio, she left for the winery offices, spent the day there and returned to the castle for another impersonal and often silent meal.

Vittorio seemed to have retreated into himself; they hardly talked, and the little gifts he'd showered her with before their marriage had stopped completely. Ana couldn't tell if Vittorio was simply satisfied now he'd married her, or if he actually regretted the deed. As far as periods of adjustment went, theirs was an utter failure. There was no adjusting; there was only enduring.

Ana saw Constantia and Bernardo on occasion; they were currently residing at the castle, although they seemed to avoid both her and Vittorio. Bernardo ate out, and Constantia took her meals in her rooms. It was, Ana reflected, an unhappy household, shrouded in its own misery.

After three days of this, Ana could take it no longer. She found Vittorio at the breakfast table, reading the newspaper and drinking his espresso. He barely glanced up when she entered.

'You'd think,' Ana said, hearing the acid in her own voice, 'that we'd been married three decades rather than three days.'

She saw Vittorio's fingers tense and then he lowered the newspaper. 'What do you mean, Ana?' he asked in that careful, mild voice he seemed to save just for her. It was so neutral, so *irritating*, for it made Ana feel as if he was dealing with a child or a puppy that needed training.

'I mean,' she retorted, as Giulia, the morning maid, came bustling forth with her own latte, 'that for the last three days—the only three days we've been married—you have been ignoring me. Are you regretting your decision, Vittorio? Because of course you know we can still get the marriage annulled.'

The only change in Vittorio's expression was a tightening of his lips and a flaring of his nostrils. 'I have no wish to annul this marriage.'

'You have no wish to act as if you were married, either.'

Vittorio folded his paper and dropped it on the table. He picked up his tiny cup of espresso and took a sip, studying Ana from over its rim. 'I wanted to give you time,' he finally said quietly. 'I thought…to rush into things might be difficult.'

'To feel like I don't belong—that we're not even married—is difficult too,' Ana countered. His words had comforted her, given her hope, but she wasn't about to give up any ground quite yet.

Vittorio nodded slowly. 'Very well. I was drawing up the guest list for the party I mentioned earlier. I thought we could have it on Friday, in two days' time. If you have anyone you'd like to add to the list, just tell me, or email me the particulars.' He paused before adding only a bit acerbically, 'Perhaps when we announce to the world we are married, you will feel it yourself.'

Or, Ana thought a bit savagely as Vittorio rose and took his leave, perhaps she would feel married when Vittorio treated her like a wife, a proper wife, a wife in every sense of the word as he'd told her he would.

Alone in the dining room, she drummed her fingers on the burnished mahogany table top and moodily sipped her latte. All around her the castle was quiet; even though Giulia was undoubtedly hovering just outside the door, Ana could hear nothing. She felt very alone.

I didn't think it would be like this.

Annoyed with herself, Ana pushed the traitorous thought aside and rose from the table. The dining room, like many other rooms in the castle, had been refurbished some time in the last century and now possessed long elegant windows overlooking the terraced gardens that led down to the drained moat. Under a fragile blue sky, it was austerely beautiful, yet it hardly felt like home. And she still couldn't see or hear another living soul.

Without even realizing she was doing it, Ana brushed at the corner of her eye and her fingertip came away damp. She was crying. She never cried, not since her mother had died. Even during those miserable years at boarding school, that first seeming rejection of her father and, later, Roberto's worse rejection, she'd always choked her sorrow down and soldiered on so it remained a hot lump in her chest, pushing it further and further down until she couldn't feel it at all. Almost.

Now she felt it deeply, all the sorrow and anger and fear, rising up in a red tide of emotion she didn't have the time or energy to deal with.

She'd accepted that Vittorio didn't love her. She'd been prepared that he might not desire her the way she desired him. She hadn't counted on the fact that he'd actually avoid her.

How was this meant to make her life easier?

'Has Vittorio left you alone?'

Ana whirled around at the sound of her mother-in-law's clipped voice. The ageing beauty stood framed in the doorway of the dining room, poised as ever to make an entrance. Ana forced a small smile. She really didn't feel like dealing with Constantia just now.

'He went to work, and I'm off in a moment too,' she said, trying to sound cheerful even as she attempted some kind of regretful look that she wouldn't be able to spend breakfast with her mother-in-law. 'We're both very busy.'

'Of course you are.' Constantia glided into the room, followed by Giulia, who brought a separate tray of espresso and rolls. The Dowager Countess clearly deserved special service. 'Tell me, Anamaria,' Constantia asked as she sat down and neatly broke a roll in half, 'how is marriage suiting you?' She glanced up, her eyes narrowed only slightly, so Ana couldn't tell if her mother-in-law knew just what kind of marriage she and Vittorio had, or if she genuinely wanted to know the answer to that thorny question. Constantia never gave anything away.

Ana's mouth widened into a bright false smile. 'Wonderfully.'

Constantia nodded thoughtfully and nibbled a piece of her roll. 'Vittorio is so much like his father. A hard man to be married to.'

In a flash Ana remembered her own father's assessment of Arturo Cazlevara: *Arturo was a good man too, but he was hard. Without mercy.*

She glanced at Constantia, now composedly sipping her espresso, with genuine curiosity. 'What do you mean?'

Constantia shrugged one shoulder. 'Surely you know what I mean? Vittorio isn't…affectionate. Emotional.' She paused, and when she spoke her voice sounded almost ragged. 'He will never love you.'

Something sharp lanced through Ana; she didn't know whether it was fear or pain. Perhaps both. She turned back to the window. 'I don't expect him to love me,' she said quietly.

'You may have convinced yourself of that once, my dear,' Constantia said. 'But can you continue to do so? For years?'

There was too much knowledge, too much sorrowful experience in the older woman's voice for Ana not to ask. 'Is that what happened to you?' Ana turned around; for a moment Constantia looked vulnerable, and her fingers shook a little bit as she replaced her cup in its saucer.

'Yes, it is. I loved Arturo Cazlevara from the time I was a little girl. We were neighbours, you know, just like Vittorio and you are—were. Everyone approved of the marriage, everyone thought it was a great match. Arturo never said he didn't love me, of course. And on the surface he was considerate, kind. Just like Vittorio, *si*? Yet here—' Constantia lightly touched her breastbone '—here, I knew.'

Tua cuore. Sudden tears stung Ana's eyes and she blinked them away. She was *not* going to cry. 'Consideration and kindness,' she said after a moment, 'count for much.'

Constantia laughed once, the sound sharp with cynicism. 'Oh, you think so? Because I happen to believe those agreeable sentiments make you feel like a puppy that has been patted on the head and told to go and lie down and stop bothering anyone anymore. Not a nice feeling all these years, you know? To feel like a dog.' She paused, and something hardened in both her face and voice. 'You would be amazed to know the things you can be driven to, the things you do even though you hate them—hate yourself—when you feel like that.' She drained her espresso and rose from the table, giving Ana one last cool smile. The haughty set of her shoulders and the arrogant tilt of her chin made Ana think Constantia regretted her moment of honesty. 'Perhaps it is different for you, Ana.'

'It *is* different,' Ana replied with sudden force. 'I don't love Vittorio either.'

Constantia's smile was pitying. 'Don't you?' she said, and walked from the room.

Constantia's words echoed through Ana's mind all morning as she tried to focus on work. She couldn't. She argued endlessly with herself, trying to convince herself that she didn't love Vittorio, she didn't love the way his eyes gleamed when he was amused, the way they softened when he spoke quietly, the broad set of his shoulders, the feel of his lips—

Of course, those were all physical attributes. You couldn't love someone based on how they *looked.* Yet Ana knew there was more to Vittorio than his dark good looks. When she was in his presence, she felt alive. Amazed. As if anything could happen, good or bad, and the good would be wonderful and even the bad would be all right because she still would be with him. She wanted to know more about him, not just to feel his body against hers, but his heart against hers also. She wanted to see him smile, just for her. To have him whisper something just meant for her.

She wanted him to love her. She wanted to love him.

She wanted love.

'No!' The word burst out of her, bounced around the walls of her empty room. 'No,' she said again, a whisper, a plea. She couldn't want love. She couldn't, because Vittorio would never give it. She thought of Constantia, her face a map of the disappointments life had given her. Ana didn't know all the history between Constantia and Vittorio, or Constantia and her own husband, but she knew—it was plain to see—that the woman was bitter, angry, and perhaps even in despair. She didn't want that. Yet, if she wanted Vittorio's love—which she was still trying to convince herself she didn't—it seemed like only a matter of time until she was like Constantia, unfulfilled and unhappy, pacing the rooms of Castle Cazlevara and cursing other people's joy.

That afternoon Ana left work early—a rare occurrence—and drove to the Mestre train station that crossed the lagoon into Venice. As she rode over the Ponte della Libertà—the Bridge of Liberty—Ana wondered what she was doing…and why. Why had she summoned all her courage and rung the boutique Vittorio had taken her to before their marriage, why had she made an appointment with the pencil-thin Feliciana to be fitted for several outfits, including a gown for the party on Friday night?

Ana told herself it was because she needed some new clothes, now that she was the Countess. Part of her arrangement with Vittorio was that she would dress appropriately to her station, as he'd said. Naturally, it made sense to visit the boutique he'd chosen above all others for this purpose.

Yet, no matter how many times Ana told herself this—mustering all her logic, her common sense—her heart told her otherwise. She was doing this—dressing this way—because she wanted Vittorio to see her differently. She wanted him to see her as a wife, and not just any wife, but a wife he could love.

The thought terrified her.

'Contessa Cazlevara!' Feliciana started forward the minute Ana entered the narrow confines of the upscale boutique. Ana smiled and allowed herself to be air-kissed, even though she felt awkward and cloddish and, well, *huge* in this place. Feliciana had to be a good eight inches shorter than her, at the very least.

'I've put some things aside for you,' Feliciana said, leading her to a private salon in the back of the boutique, 'that I think will suit you very well.'

'Really?' Ana couldn't keep the scepticism from her voice. Feliciana had only glimpsed her once before; how on earth could she know what suited her? And a little mocking voice asked, how could *anything* suit her?

Ana commanded that voice to be silent. Yet other voices rose to take its place: the locker room taunts of the girls at boarding school, the boys who had ignored or teased her, the helpless sigh of the matron who had shaken her head and said, 'At least you're strong.' And then, most damning of all, Roberto's utter rejection. *How could I?*

Over the years she'd avoided places like this, dresses like these, for a reason. And now, standing in the centre of a brightly lit, mirrored dressing room while Feliciana bustled over with an armful of frocks, she felt horribly exposed and vulnerable.

'Now, first I thought, a gown for the party, *si*?' Feliciana smiled. 'Most important.'

'Yes, I suppose,' Ana murmured, looking dubiously at a white lace gown she'd glimpsed on her last visit to the boutique. It now hung over Feliciana's arm, exquisite and fragile.

'A formal occasion, is it not? I thought we'd try this.' Feliciana held up the gown.

Ana shook her head. 'I don't think…'

'You'll see,' Feliciana said firmly. She gestured to Ana's trouser suit with a tiny grimace of distaste. 'Now, you hide yourself in these clothes, as if you are ashamed.'

Ana flushed. 'I'm just not—'

'But you *are*,' Feliciana interjected. She smiled, laying a hand on Ana's arm. 'It is not my job to make women look awkward or ugly, *si*? I know what I am doing. Right now, you walk with your shoulders stooped, your head bowed as if you are trying not to be tall.'

'I don't—' Ana protested.

'You are tall,' Feliciana said firmly. 'With a beautiful full figure. And don't you know many women long to be so tall? You are strikingly beautiful, but I know you don't think you are.' She let go of Ana's shoulders and gestured to the lace confection of a dress. 'In this, you will see.' She smiled again, softly. 'Trust me.'

So Ana did. She took the dress and let Feliciana take her trouser suit, slipping into the lacy sheath with some foreboding and also a building excitement. The dress fitted like a second skin, hugging her hips, the dip of her waist and the swell of her breasts. Its plunging neckline was made respectable by the handmade Burano lace edging it, and the material ended in a frothy swirl around her ankles. Ana sucked her stomach in as Feliciana did up the hidden zipper in the back, but there was no need as the dress fitted perfectly. They *did* make gowns like this in her size.

Ana didn't dare look in the mirror. She wasn't afraid, precisely, but neither did she want to be disappointed.

'Uno minuto…' Feliciana muttered, surveying her, her hands on her hips. She reached out and tugged the clip from Ana's hair; it cascaded down her back in a dark swirl. 'Ah…*perfectto*!'

Perfect? Her? Ana almost shook her head, but Feliciana steered her towards the mirror. 'Look. You've never seen yourself in something like this before, have you?'

No, she hadn't. Ana knew that the minute she gazed at her reflection, because for a second at least she couldn't believe she was staring at herself. She was staring at a stranger, a woman—a gorgeous, confident, sexy woman. She shook her head.

'No…'

Feliciana clucked in dismay. 'You don't like it?'

'No.' A bubble of laughter erupted, escaping through her lips as Ana turned around. 'I don't like it. I love it.'

Feliciana grinned. '*Buon*. Because I have at least six other gowns I want you to try.'

By the time Ana left the boutique, she'd purchased four gowns, several skirts and tops, three pairs of shoes, including a pair of silver stilettos that she'd balked at until Feliciana had told her sternly, 'Your husband must be almost five inches taller than you. You can wear heels.'

She'd never worn heels in her life. She'd probably fall on her face. Ana giggled; she wasn't used to making such a girlish sound. Yet right now she felt girlish, feminine and frivolous and *fun*. She'd enjoyed this afternoon and, best of all, she couldn't *wait* until Vittorio saw her in the lace gown on Friday night.

Yet, when Friday night actually came and she stood at the top of the sweeping staircase that led down to the castle's foyer and its waiting master, Ana didn't feel so confident. So *fun*. She felt sick with nerves, with a queasy fear that Vittorio wouldn't like how she looked or, worse, that he wouldn't even care how she looked. They'd barely seen each other outside meals and Ana spent her nights alone. She was a wife in name only, and she longed to change that tonight.

From the top of the stairs she could see him waiting at the bottom, could feel his impatience. He wore a perfectly cut suit of grey silk and he rested one long tapered hand on the banister railing.

'Ana?' he called up, a bit sharply. 'Are you ready? The guests will be here very soon.'

'Yes,' she called, her own voice wavering a little. 'I'm ready.'

Vittorio heard Ana coming down the stairs behind him, but he didn't turn around right away. He needed to steel himself, he realized, for however his wife might look. So far he had not been impressed with her clothes; her wedding dress had been an unmitigated disaster. She'd told him she knew the difference between a designer gown and a bin bag, but Vittorio had yet to be convinced. Not, he reflected, that he'd taken Ana's dress sense into consideration when he'd chosen her as his bride.

Why *had* he chosen her as his bride? Vittorio wondered rather moodily. All the businesslike reasons about merging wineries and knowing the region seemed utterly absurd to base a marriage on. Of course, when his mother had spoken to him about heirs, his logical mind had not thought about a *marriage*; it had simply fastened on the one necessity: wife. Object. Then he'd seen the vulnerability in Ana's eyes, had felt her softness against him, had breathed in the earthy scent of her desire and known that *wife* and *object* were not two words ever to string together.

Ana was a person, and not just a person, but his *wife*. His beloved. The person he should protect and cherish above all others. The person, he realized bleakly, he was meant to love. And he had no idea what to do with her.

It was why he'd avoided her since their wedding; why he still had not come to her bed. He'd thought he could live with a business arrangement. That was what he had wanted. Yet now, bizarrely, he found the cold-blooded terms of their arrangement to be...distasteful. Yet he didn't love Ana, didn't know if he was even capable of such an emotion. He hadn't loved anyone in years. His entire adult life had been focused on *not* loving, on building Cazlevara Wines, maintaining his reputation and influence as Count, trying to forget the fractured family he'd left behind. The women he'd involved himself with hadn't even come close to touching his heart.

Yet *Ana*...Ana with her blunt way of speaking and her soft grey eyes, her brash confidence and her lurking vulnerability, her tall, lush figure and her earthy scent...Ana somehow slipped inside the defences he'd erected around himself, his heart. He'd prided himself on being logical, sensible, perhaps even cold. Yet now he wouldn't even go to his wife's bed for fear of—what? Hurting her?

He'd told his bride very plainly that he never intended to love her. Love, he had said, was a destructive emotion. And perhaps that was what made him afraid now; he was afraid that his love would destroy Ana, would ruin their marriage.

His love was destructive.

'Vittorio...?' He felt Ana's hand on his sleeve, her voice no more than an uncertain whisper. She must have been standing there for some moments, waiting for him to notice her while he was lost in his gloomy reflections. Vittorio turned around.

'Good even—' He stopped, the words dried in his mouth, his head suddenly, completely empty of thoughts. The woman in front of him was stunning, a vision of ethereal loveliness in white lace. No, he realized distantly, she wasn't ethereal. She was earthy and real and so very beautiful. And she was his wife. 'You look...' he began and, though she tried to disguise it, he saw Ana's face fall, the disappointment shadowing her eyes and making her shoulders slump just a fraction. He let himself touch her, holding her by the shoulders. Her skin was warm and golden. The dress clung to her figure; he'd never realized how perfectly she was proportioned, the swell of her breasts and the curve of her hips. He'd once considered her mannish; the thought was now laughable. He'd never seen a more feminine woman. 'You look amazing,' he said, his voice low, heartfelt, and Ana smiled.

She had the most amazing smile. He'd noticed her teeth before, straight and white, as one might notice a piece of workmanship. Now he saw the way the smile transformed her face, softened the angles and made joy dance in her eyes in golden glints.

Amazing. His wife was amazing.

'Thank you,' she said, her voice just as heartfelt, and Vittorio did the only thing he could do… He kissed her. As he drew her close, he was conscious of her generous curves fitting so snugly against his own body, amazed at the way her length lined up to his. How had he ever stooped to kiss a shorter woman before? His back ached just to think of it.

And Ana's lips… They were soft and warm and as generous as the rest of her, open and giving and so very sweet. Vittorio had meant only to kiss her briefly—something between a peck and a brush—but once he tasted her he found he couldn't get enough. The kiss went on and on, her arms snaking up around his shoulders, her body pressing against his—she'd never been shy—until someone behind him cleared his throat in a pointed manner.

'Pardon me for breaking up this rather touching scene,' Bernardo drawled, 'but the guests are starting to arrive.'

'Good.' Vittorio stepped away from Ana, his arm still around her waist. She *fitted* against him, nestled near him in a way that was neither cloying nor coy. It was, he knew, as genuine as the rest of her was.

Bernardo eyed Ana with obvious surprise. 'You cleaned up rather well.'

'Bernardo,' Vittorio said sharply, 'that is no way to speak to my wife the Countess.'

Bernardo turned back to Vittorio, his eyebrows raised. 'Isn't it what you were thinking?' he countered. Vittorio pressed his lips together; he didn't want to argue with his brother now. He wouldn't spoil this evening for Ana. Bernardo turned to Ana and made a little bow. 'Forgive me, Ana. I meant no insult. You look very beautiful.'

Vittorio said nothing. This was how his brother always acted; he'd deliver the sting with one hand and the sweetness with the other. It made it impossible to fight him, or at least to win. Vittorio had learned this long ago, when his parents had drawn the battle lines. Constantia got Bernardo and his father took him. They had been his parents' most potent weapons. It had, Vittorio reflected, been a long drawn-out war.

'No offence taken, Bernardo,' Ana said, smiling. 'I was thinking the same thing myself.'

Bernardo gave her an answering flicker of a smile and bowed again. Vittorio squeezed Ana's waist and the first guests came towards them before he could thank his wife for being so gracious.

Ana moved through the party in a haze of happiness. She never wanted to forget the look on Vittorio's face when he'd turned around and seen her. She'd expected the disbelief, of course, but not the joy. He'd been *happy* to see her. He'd wanted her by his side. And when he'd kissed her… Every secret hope and latent need had risen up inside her on newly formed wings, and she hadn't suppressed them or forced them back to the ground. For years she'd refused to entertain such dreams, knowing they could only lead to disappointment, yet when Vittorio had looked at her, she'd felt like the woman she'd always longed to be. The woman she was meant to be. It was a wonderful feeling.

She stayed by Vittorio's side for most of the party. He wanted her there, kept his arm around her, her hip pressed against his. She laughed and chatted and listened and nodded, but none of it really penetrated. The need—the desire—was building within her slowly, a force rising up and needing to be reckoned with. To be satisfied.

Tonight, she told herself. *Tonight, he will come to me.* As the evening wore on, her certainty—and her happiness—only grew.

Vittorio had been so proud, so happy to have Ana by his side. He'd drifted through the party in a haze, on a cloud. He couldn't wait to get Ana alone, to touch her—

Yet now she'd gone to see her father off and, alone, he felt strangely flat, indifferent to all he'd achieved. He wanted her to come back to him and yet, even so, he didn't go in search of her. He didn't even know what he would say.

He thought of how Enrico Viale had stopped him in the middle of the party, one hand on his sleeve. 'She looked beautiful, our Ana, *si*?' the older man had said, pride shining in his eyes. Vittorio had been about to agree when he realized Enrico was not talking about how Ana looked tonight. 'It was her mother's wedding dress, you know. I asked her to wear it.'

Vittorio had been left speechless, amazed and humbled by Ana's selflessness, by her loyalty. And he'd demanded that same loyalty of her for *him*? When he didn't even know what to do with her, how to treat her, how to *love* her?

Love. But he didn't *want* love.

As the last guests trickled outside, the cars heading down the castle's steep drive in a steady stream of light, Vittorio wondered what on earth he'd been trying to accomplish by setting out to acquire a wife like so much baggage. What had been the point, to take another being into his care, another life into his hands? Who was meant to notice, to know?

Who cared?

Of course, most of his neighbours and fellow winemakers

were curious about the Count of Cazlevara's sudden return and even more sudden marriage. He'd felt their implicit approval that he'd returned to where he belonged, was now taking his rightful place, esteemed winemaker and leader of the community.

Yet he hadn't been trying to gain *their* approval. At that moment, their approval hardly mattered at all.

'So, Vittorio. A success.'

Vittorio turned slowly around; his mother stood in the doorway of the drawing room. She looked coldly elegant in a cream satin sheath dress, her expression unsmiling. This was the person whose approval he'd been trying to gain, Vittorio realized, and how absurd that was, considering his mother had not had a moment of interest or affection for him since he was four. When his brother had been born.

He was jealous, Vittorio realized, incredulous and yet still somehow unsurprised by this. All these years, his desire to return to his home and show his brother and mother his success, his self-sufficiency—it had just been jealousy. Petty, pathetic jealousy.

He turned back to the window. The last cars had disappeared down the darkened drive. 'So it appears.'

'You're not pleased?' she asked, moving into the room. He heard a caustic note in her voice that still made his shoulders tense and the vulnerable space between them prickle.

Go away, Vittorio. Leave me alone.

At that moment he felt like that confused child who had tugged his mother's sleeve, desperate to show her a drawing, receive a hug. She'd turned away, time and time again, forever averting both her face and her heart. When she'd welcomed Bernardo, adored and doted on and spoiled him utterly, it seemed obvious. She simply preferred his brother to him.

Vittorio made an impatient sound of disgust; he was disgusted with himself. Why was he remembering these silly, childish moments now? He'd lived with his mother's rejection for most of his life. He'd learned not to care. He'd steeled himself against it, against the treachery she'd committed when his father had died—

Except obviously he hadn't, for the emotions were still present, raked up and raw, and they made him angry. What kind of man was still hurt by his *mother*? It was ridiculous, pathetic, shaming.

'On the contrary, Mother. I am very pleased.' His voice was bland with just a hint of sharpness; it was the tone he always reserved for her.

She gave an answering little laugh, just as sharp. 'Oh, Vittorio. Nothing is ever enough, is it? You're just like your father.' The words were meant to be an accusation, a condemnation.

'I'll take that as a compliment.'

His mother's lip curled in a sneer. 'Of course you will.'

Impatient with all her veiled little barbs, Vittorio shrugged. 'Where's Ana?'

Constantia arched her eyebrows in challenge. 'Why do you care?'

His temper finally frayed. 'Because she is my *wife*.' And he wanted to know where she was, he wanted to see her now, to feel her smile, her sweetness—

'A wife you won't love.'

Vittorio stiffened. 'That is no concern of—'

'Isn't it?' She stepped closer and he saw the anger in her eyes, as well as something else. Something that looked strangely like sorrow. It was unfamiliar. He was used to his mother angry, but sad—?

'You don't know what it is like to love someone, Vittorio, who will never love you back—'

He laughed in disbelief; he couldn't help it. 'Don't I?'

Constantia looked utterly nonplussed. 'No—'

He shook his head, too weary to explain. 'Do you know where Ana is?'

'You will bring heartache to that girl. You will destroy her—'

Vittorio tensed, steeling himself once more, but this time he couldn't. *Love is a destructive emotion.* The thought of bringing such pain and misery to Ana made his head bow, his shoulders shake. 'Why do you care?' he asked in a low, savage voice.

'She is a good woman, Vittorio.'

'Too good for me, obviously.'

Constantia sighed impatiently. 'I have made many mistakes with you, I know. I have many regrets. But this marriage—it can only lead to more despair. And surely our family has had enough unhappiness?'

She was pleading with him, as if their family's misery was his fault? Vittorio turned around, his body rigid with rage. 'On that point we agree, Mother. Yet it seems odd that the instrument of so much unhappiness should then seek to end it.'

Constantia blinked as if she'd been struck. 'I know you blame me—'

'Blame you?' Vittorio repeated silkily. 'Are you referring to your attempt to take my inheritance, my father only *hours* in the grave? Your desperate desire to drag the family into the law courts and give my brother my title?'

Constantia straightened and met his hostile gaze directly. 'Yes, Vittorio, I am referring to that. God knows you will never let me forget it.'

'One hardly forgets the dagger thrust between one's shoulders,' Vittorio returned, every word encased in ice. He still remembered how he had reeled with shock; he'd come back from his father's funeral, devastated by grief, only to find that in his absence his mother had met a solicitor and attempted to overturn the contents of his father's will, disinheriting him completely and giving everything to Bernardo. All the childhood slights had led to that one brutal moment, when he'd understood with stark clarity that his mother didn't just dislike him, she *despised* him. She'd do anything to keep him from inheriting what was rightfully his.

He would never forget. He couldn't.

'No,' Constantia agreed softly, her eyes glittering, 'one does not forget. And I will tell you, Vittorio, that for a woman to be denied love—by her own husband—is not a dagger between the shoulders, but one straight to the heart. For your wife's sake, if not my own, do not hurt her.'

'Such pretty words,' Vittorio scoffed. The rage had left him, making him feel only weary. 'You have come to care for my wife then, Mother?'

'I know how she feels,' Constantia said bleakly and, with one last shake of her head, she left the room.

Her words rang in his ears, and yet Vittorio still made himself dismiss them. *I know how she feels.* Was his mother implying she'd loved his father? To Vittorio's young eyes, his parents had agreed on a polite marriage of convenience. Just like the one he'd meant to have. Yet his parents' marriage had descended into anger and even hatred, and at the thought of that happening to him—to Ana—Vittorio swore aloud. All the old feelings, hurt memories, had been raked up tonight and Vittorio knew why.

Ana.

Somehow she'd affected him, touched him in a way he had never been touched. Made him open and exposed and, more than that, she made him want. Made him need.

Love.

He swore again.

'Vittorio?'

He whirled around. Ana stood in the doorway, her face nearly as white as her lace gown.

'How much did you hear?' he asked, his tone brusque, brutal.

Ana flinched. 'Enough. Too much.'

'I told you my family's history was not worth repeating,' Vittorio replied with a shrug. He moved to the drinks table and poured himself a whisky.

'Don't—' Ana said inadvertently and he turned around, one eyebrow arched.

'I'm having a *drink*, Ana,' he said, the words a taunt. 'Whisky. Your favourite. Don't you want to join me?'

'No. Vittorio, I want to talk.'

He took a healthy swallow and let the alcohol burn straight to his gut. 'Go ahead.'

Ana flinched again. Vittorio knew he was being callous, even cruel, but he couldn't help it. The exchange with his mother, the emerging feelings for Ana—it all left him feeling so exposed. Vulnerable.

Afraid.

He hated it.

Turning away from her, he kept his voice a bored drawl. 'So what do you want to talk about?'

Ana watched her husband as he gazed out of the window, affecting an air of bored indifference, yet she knew better now. He was hurting. She didn't understand everything he'd referred to in his conversation with Constantia, didn't know the source of all the pain, but she did know her marriage had no chance if Vittorio was going to remain mired in his painful past.

'Tell me what went wrong,' she said quietly.

Vittorio must not have been expecting that, for he bowed his head suddenly, his fingers clenched around his whisky glass.

'Everything,' he finally said in a low voice. 'Everything went wrong.'

Cautiously Ana approached him, laid a hand on his shoulder. 'Oh, Vittorio—'

He jerked away. 'Don't pity me. I could not stand that.'

'I just want to understand—'

'It's simple, Ana.' He turned to face her, his expression hard and implacable once more. 'My mother didn't love me. What a sad story, eh? Pathetic, no? A thirty-seven-year-old man whingeing on about his mean *mamma*.'

'There's more to it than that,' Ana said quietly.

'Oh, a few trite details.' He gave a negligent shrug and drained his glass. 'You see, my parents hated each other. Perhaps there was once love or at least affection, but not so I could remember. By the time Bernardo came along, the battle lines were drawn. I belonged to my father and Bernardo was my mother's.'

'What do you mean?'

'Simple. My father had no time or patience for Bernardo, and my mother had none for me. They used us like weapons. And my father was a good man, he trained me well—'

'But he was a hard man,' Ana interjected, remembering.

Vittorio glanced at her sharply. 'Who told you that?'

'My father. He said Arturo was a good man, but without mercy.'

Vittorio let out a little breath of sound; Ana wasn't sure if it was a laugh or something else. Perhaps even a sob. 'Perhaps that is true. But he knew I was to inherit, and he wanted to train me up for the role—'

Ana could just imagine what that must have felt like, especially if Bernardo was not receiving the same harsh treatment. 'And Bernardo?' she asked softly.

'My mother lavished all her love on him. He was like a spoilt poodle.'

Ana flinched at the contempt in his voice. Surely being spoiled was just as bad as being disciplined, just in a different way. 'It sounds like both of you had difficult childhoods.'

'Both of us?' Vittorio repeated in disbelief, then shrugged. 'Maybe.' He sounded bored, and Ana clung to her belief that it was merely a cover for the true, deeper emotions he was too afraid to expose.

She knew all about being vulnerable. Physically and emotionally. Even wearing this dress—opening herself to scorn—made her feel exposed, as exposed as Vittorio did raking through his unhappy childhood. No one liked to talk about such dark memories, admit how they hurt.

'What happened when your father died?' Ana asked.

'My mother did what she'd undoubtedly been planning to do ever since Bernardo was born. She went to court to have his will overturned—and Bernardo made heir.'

Ana gasped. Even though she'd suspected as much, it still surprised her. Why would Constantia do such a vindictive thing? Yet, even as she asked the question, Ana thought she knew the answer. Hadn't Constantia explained it herself? *You would be amazed to know the things you can be driven to…when you feel like that.* And then, her words tonight: *You're just like your father.* Had she transferred all the bitterness and anger she'd felt towards her husband to her son? It seemed perfectly possible, and unbearably sad.

'Oh, Vittorio,' Ana whispered. 'I am sorry.'

'Well, don't be,' he replied, his voice turning harsh again. 'She didn't have a prayer of succeeding. My father was too smart for that. Perhaps he suspected what she was up to, what she could be capable of. His will remained intact, and Bernardo didn't inherit a single *lira*.'

Ana gasped again. 'Not…anything?'

'No, and rightly so. He would have squandered it all.'

'But then,' Ana said slowly, realization dawning, 'he lives here only on your sufferance. Doesn't he work at the winery?'

Vittorio shrugged. 'I let him work as the assistant manager.'

'You let him,' Ana repeated. 'As an assistant.'

'Are you saying it is not enough?' Vittorio demanded raggedly. 'This brother who would have taken everything from me? Do you think he would have been so merciful?'

Ana shook her head. 'But if your mother attempted all this with the will when your father died, you were only—'

'Fourteen.'

'And Bernardo was a child—nine or ten at the most—'

'Ten,' Vittorio confirmed flatly. Anger sparked in his eyes; his face had become hard again, a stranger's. 'Are you taking his side, Ana? Don't you remember what I told you, what I warned you about?'

His tone was so dangerous, so icy, that Ana could only blink in confusion, her mind whirling with all these revelations. 'What—?'

Vittorio closed the space between them, circling her wrist with his hands, drawing her to him. The movement was not one of seduction, but possession, and Ana came up hard against his chest. 'Loyalty, Ana. I told you those closest to me would try to discredit me. You swore you would be loyal to me—'

She could hardly believe he was bringing up loyalty now. This was his *family.* 'Vittorio, I am simply trying to understand—'

'Maybe I don't want you to understand,' Vittorio said harshly. 'Maybe if you understood—' He stopped, shaking his head, a look of what almost seemed like fear flashing across his face before he muttered an oath and then, with a sudden groan, claimed her mouth in a kiss.

It wasn't a kiss, Ana thought distantly, so much as a brand. He was punishing her for her curiosity and reminding her of her vow. And, in that kiss she felt all his anger, his hurt and even his fear. And despite her own answering anger—that he would kiss her this way—she felt the traitorous flicker of her own desire and she pressed against him, let her hands tangle in his hair, wanting to change this angry embrace into something healing and *good*—

'No!' With a bellow of disgust, Vittorio pushed her away. Ana stumbled and reached out to steady herself; both of them were gasping as if they'd run a race. And lost.

'Vittorio—'

'No,' he said again. He raked a hand through his hair, let out a ragged sob. 'Not like this. God help me, I never wanted this.'

'But—'

'I told you,' he said in a low voice, 'love is a destructive emotion.'

Ana shook her head, wanting to deny what he said, wanting to fight—and wondering if he was actually telling her, in a terribly twisted way, that he loved her.

Was this love? This confusion and sorrow and pain?

No wonder they'd both agreed to live without it.

'It doesn't have to be destructive,' Ana said quietly but, his back now to her, Vittorio just shook his head.

'With me,' he said in a voice so low Ana strained to hear, 'it is.' He let out a shuddering sigh. 'Leave me, Ana. Just leave me.'

Ana stood there uncertainly, knowing to slink away now was surely the worst thing to do. 'No,' she said finally. 'I don't want to.'

Vittorio swung around, incredulous. 'What—'

'We're married, Vittorio. I'm not going to run away like some frightened child.' He flinched, and she raised her chin. 'And I'm not going to sleep alone tonight, either. I'm your wife and I belong in your bed.'

Vittorio's disbelief turned to disdain. *'Now—'*

She stepped closer to him, reached out with one hand to touch his lapel. 'Just hold me, Vittorio.' She saw his mouth tremble and she touched his lips. 'And let me hold you. And maybe, together, for a few moments, we can forget all this bitterness and pain.'

Vittorio shook his head slowly and Ana's heart sank. She'd thought she'd reached him, managed to get past the barrier he'd constructed to keep her—and anyone important—out. She could not bear his rejection now, not when she'd made herself so vulnerable, so exposed—just as he had—

Then, to her amazement and joy, he slowly reached for her hand, lacing his fingers tightly with hers, and silently, accepting, he led her from the darkened room.

CHAPTER NINE

ANA woke to sunlight. Even better, warming her deep inside, she woke with Vittorio's arm around her, her head nestled against his shoulder. She breathed in the scent of his skin, loving it, loving him.

Yes, she loved him. It seemed so obvious, so simple, in the clean, healing light of day. Yes, love was confusing and scary and full of sorrow and pain; it was *love*. Opening your heart and your body and even your soul to another person. Risking everything, your own health and happiness and well-being. And yet gaining so much.

Maybe.

She pulled away from Vittorio a little so she could look at him; he remained asleep, his features softened, almost gentle in repose. She touched the dark stubble on his chin, felt her heart twist painfully. Yes, love hurt.

This love hurt—for, if she loved him, she had no idea if he loved her.

Love is a destructive emotion.

She was starting to understand why he believed such a thing. Constantia's love for her husband had been destructive, her unhappiness and despair leading her to unhealthy relationships with both of her sons. And, as the one who felt unloved by his mother—and harshly loved, no doubt, by his father—Ana could almost understand why Vittorio wanted no more of it.

My love wouldn't be destructive. My love would heal you.

She touched his cheek, let her fingers feather over his eyebrow. He stirred and she stilled, holding her breath, not wanting him to wake up and ruin this moment. She was afraid when he opened his eyes the distance would be back, the cold, logical man who had insisted on a marriage of convenience, a marriage without love.

And she had agreed. She had, somehow, managed to convince herself that that was the kind of marriage, the kind of life, she wanted. Lying there, half in his arms, Ana knew it was not and never had been. She'd accepted such a poor bargain simply because she was afraid she'd find nothing else—and because it had been a bargain with Vittorio.

A life with Vittorio.

When had she started loving him? The seeds had surely been sown long ago, when he had touched her cheek and called her swallow. Such a small moment, yet in it she'd seen his gentleness, his tender heart, and she hoped—prayed—that she could see them again now. Soon.

She wouldn't let Vittorio push her away or keep their marriage as coldly convenient—and safe—as he wanted it to be.

Ana eased herself out of Vittorio's embrace, wondering just how she could accomplish such a herculean task. She'd agreed to a loveless marriage, very clearly. How could she now change the terms and expect Vittorio to agree?

Lying there in a pool of sunlight, still warmed by Vittorio's touch, the answer was obvious. By having him fall in love with her.

And Ana thought she knew just how to begin.

Vittorio awoke slowly, stretching languorously, feeling more relaxed and rested than he had in months. Years. He blinked at the sunlight streaming in through the windows and then shifted his weight, suddenly, surprisingly, *alarmingly* conscious of the empty space by him in the bed.

Ana was gone.

It shouldn't bother him—hurt him—for, God knew, he was used to sleeping alone. Even when he was involved with a woman, he left her bed—or made her leave his—well before dawn. It had been his standard practice, and he neither questioned it nor chose to change it.

Now, however, he realized how alone he felt. How lonely.

'Good morning, sleepy-head.'

Vittorio turned, his body relaxing once more at the sight of Ana in the doorway of his bedroom, wearing nothing but his shirt from last night. He could see the shadowy vee of her breasts disappearing between the buttons, the shirt tails just skimming her thighs. She looked wonderfully feminine, incredibly sexy. Vittorio felt his own desire stir and wondered how—and why—he'd kept himself from his wife's bed for so long.

'Where did you go?' he asked, shifting over so she could sit on the bed.

'To the loo.' She gave a little laugh. 'I drank quite a bit of champagne last night. Dutch courage, I suppose.'

'Were you nervous?' He found he was curious to hear what she said, to know what she thought. About everything.

Ana shrugged. 'A bit.' She paused. 'You can't say that our marriage is usual, or normal, and I don't want people…saying things.'

'What kinds of things?'

She gave another shrug, the movement inherently defensive. 'Unkind things.'

Vittorio nodded, realizing for the first time how their marriage bargain might reflect on her, as if she wasn't good enough—or attractive enough—for a proper marriage. For love.

I'm not interested in love.

What he was interested in, Vittorio decided, was getting his wife into bed as quickly as possible, and then taking his own sweet time in making love to her. Whatever the guests from the party might think, their marriage would certainly be wonderfully normal in at least one respect.

'I know it's Saturday,' Ana said, rising from the bed before Vittorio could even make a move towards her, 'but it was quite cool last night and I wanted to go to the vineyards and check—'

'We have managers for that, Ana.'

She gave a low throaty chuckle that had Vittorio nearly leaping out of bed and dragging her back to it with him. Had she ever laughed like that before? Surely he would have noticed—

'Oh, Vittorio. I don't leave such things to managers. You might, with your million bottles a year—'

'Nine hundred thousand.'

Her eyebrows arched and laughter lurked in her eyes, turning them to silver. 'Oh, pardon me. Well, considering that Viale only has two hundred and fifty—'

'What does it matter?' Vittorio asked, trying not to sound as impatient as he felt. His wife was wearing his shirt and he was half-naked in his own bed; their marriage was still unconsummated nearly a week after the wedding. Why the hell were they talking about wine production?

'It matters to me,' Ana said, a smile still curving that amazingly generous mouth. Vittorio wondered if she knew how she was teasing him. Seducing him. He'd thought she was insecure, unaware of her own charms, but at the moment his wife looked completely sexy, sensual and as if she knew it. Vittorio felt as if he'd received a very hard blow to the head.

Or to the heart.

Either way, he was reeling.

'It's a beautiful day—' he started again, meaning to end the sentence with *to spend in bed.*

Ana's smile widened. 'Exactly. And I wanted you to show me the Cazlevara vineyards, or at least some of them. It's too nice to be inside.'

Enough, Vittorio thought. Enough talking. He smiled, a sleepy, sensual smile that left no room for Ana to misunderstand. 'Oh, I think we could be inside for a little longer.' Her eyes widened and she hesitated, clearly uncertain. Vittorio extended a hand. 'Come here, Ana.'

'What—' she began and nibbled her lower lip, which was just about the most seductive thing Vittorio had ever seen. He groaned aloud.

'Come *here*.'

She came slowly, hesitantly, perching on the edge of the bed so her shirt rode even higher on her thighs. God give him patience, Vittorio thought, averting his eyes. 'What is it?' she asked, and he heard the uncertainty and even fear in her voice. His wife, Vittorio realized, didn't think he desired her.

He smiled and reached out to brush a strand of silky hair away from her eyes, his fingers skimming the curve of her ear. 'Don't you think,' he murmured, 'we've waited long enough to truly become man and wife?'

Ana's breath hitched. 'Yes, but—'

'But what?'

Again she nibbled her lip. 'You seemed content to wait.'

'Only because I didn't want to hurt you.' Vittorio paused, the moment turning emotional, scaring him. Even now he shied away from the truth of his own feelings. 'I wanted to give you time.'

A smile lurked in Ana's eyes, in the generous curve of her mouth. 'And now you feel you've given me enough time?'

'Oh, yes.' He reached out to stroke her leg; he couldn't help himself, her skin looked so silky. And it felt silky, too. Vittorio suppressed a shudder. 'Do you feel you've had enough time?'

'Oh, yes,' Ana said, and he chuckled at her fervent reply.

'Good.'

Ana sat there in shock, unable to believe Vittorio was saying these things, touching her this way, his fingers skimming and stroking her thigh, sending little shocks of pleasure through her body. His other hand tangled in her hair and he drew her to him, his lips fastening on hers with hungry need; as he kissed her he let out a low groan of relief and satisfaction, and Ana felt another deeper shock: that he seemed so attracted to her, wanted her so, that he couldn't help but touch her, right here in the middle of the morning, in the sunshine, without her having done anything at all. She'd meant to seduce him, to wear a sexy nightdress and have champagne—but this was so much better. So much more real.

'Ana…' Vittorio murmured, his lips now on her ear, her jaw, her neck, 'Ana, you're going on about grapes and vineyards and all I can think about is…this…'

And then it was all Ana could think about too, for Vittorio claimed her lips in a kiss so consuming, so fulfilling, she felt replete and satisfied—as if this kiss could actually be enough—instead of the endless craving she normally felt when they touched.

Vittorio pulled away, just a little bit, but it was enough to make Ana realize that actually she wasn't satisfied at all. She wanted more…and more…and oh, please, a little more than that.

She must have made her need and frustration known, for he chuckled and traced a circle on her tummy with his tongue, making Ana moan aloud, the sound utterly foreign to her. She could hardly believe she was making these sounds, feeling these things.

So *much*.

Vittorio's mouth hovered over her skin. 'I'm going to take my time,' he promised her, and then did just that, while Ana closed her eyes in both surprise and pleasure.

Yet Ana wasn't willing to be a passive recipient, as wonderful as it was. As Vittorio teased her with his mouth and hands, she finally could take no more and flipped him over on his back, straddling his powerful thighs. Vittorio looked so surprised, she laughed aloud.

'You seem to be wearing too many clothes,' she remarked in a husky murmur, and Vittorio nodded.

'I completely agree.'

'Let's do something about that, then.'

'Absolutely.'

She tugged at his pyjama shirt and bottoms, laughing a little bit as buttons snagged and caught, but soon enough he was naked, and Ana pushed back on her elbow to take in his magnificent body, sleek and powerful, all for her. She ran one hand down the taut muscles of his chest.

'I've been wanting to do that for a while,' she admitted a bit shyly, for now that they were both naked, his arousal hard against her thigh, she felt a little uncertain. A little afraid.

'There's a lot I've been wanting to do,' Vittorio admitted, his voice low and a little ragged. 'And I can't take much more waiting, Ana—' True to his word, Vittorio rolled her onto her back, his hands and lips finding her secret sensitive places once again, until Ana found that waiting was the last thing she could think of doing. The wanting took over.

When he finally entered her, filling her up to the very brim with his own self, and with the knowledge of their bodies, fused, joined as *one*, Ana felt no more than a flicker of pain and then the wonderful, consuming certainty that this was the very heart of their marriage, the very best thing that could have ever happened, that they could have ever shared.

Afterwards, as they lay in the warm glow of the sun, their limbs still entangled, she wondered how she'd lived so long without knowing what sex was about. What love was about. For surely the two were utterly entwined, as entwined as her body was now with Vittorio's. She couldn't imagine loving a man she hadn't felt in her own body, and neither could she imagine sharing this with anyone but a man she loved—and that man was Vittorio.

Vittorio ran his hand down her stomach and across the curve of her hip. 'Ana, if I'd known—' he said softly, and she turned to him.

'Known?'

'Known you were a virgin,' he explained. 'I would have—' he smiled ruefully '—I would have taken *more* time, I suppose.'

'You didn't know I was a virgin?' Ana couldn't keep the amusement from her voice. 'Goodness, Vittorio, I thought it was rather obvious.'

'Obvious to you, perhaps,' Vittorio returned. 'But you mentioned a relationship—a man—'

'It never got that far,' Ana replied. The hurt she usually felt when she remembered Roberto's rejection seemed distant, like an emotion she knew intellectually but had never truly felt. It hardly mattered now.

'I'm sorry he hurt you,' Vittorio murmured.

'It's long past,' Ana told him. She pressed her lips to his shoulder; his skin was warm. 'I've completely forgotten it.' She kissed the hollow of his throat, because now that he was truly hers she just couldn't help herself.

It was several hours later when they finally rose from that bed. Ana was sweetly sore all over, her body awakened in every sinew and sense. 'Now the vineyard,' she said and, still lounging among the pillows, Vittorio threw his head back and laughed.

'The vineyard will always be your first love,' he said, his words giving Ana a tiny pang. She wanted to say, *You're my first love*, but she found she could not. The words stuck in her throat, clogged by fear. Instead, she reached for her clothes.

'Absolutely.'

An hour later Ana followed Vittorio from the estate office to one of Cazlevara's finest vineyards. Since Vittorio owned a much bigger operation than she, he had hectares of vines all over Veneto, but the one closest to the castle—on the original estate—was still reserved for the label's most prized grapes.

The sun beat down hot on her head and her shirt was already sticking to her back as Ana walked between the grape plants in their neatly staked rows. She wished she'd worn a hat, or make-up. Instead, without thinking, she'd donned dusty trousers and an old shapeless button-down shirt, her standard field clothes. Hardly an outfit to impress her husband. And just why did she want to impress him? Ana wondered. The answer was painfully clear. Because she still felt a little uncertain, a little worried.

Because she loved him, and she didn't know if he loved her.

If she'd had any sense, she would have worn one of Feliciana's carefully selected outfits—something sexy and slimming—and asked Vittorio to take her to Venice or Verona, even one of the sleepy little villages nestled in one of the region's valleys, somewhere where they could laugh and chat over antipasti and a jug of wine.

She should not have taken him to his work place and donned her own well-worn work clothes to do it! What had she been thinking? Yet, even as she ranted at herself, Ana knew the answers. She loved the vineyards. She loved the grapes, the earth, the sun. The rich scent of soil and growing things, of life itself.

It was the place she loved most of all, and she'd wanted to share it with Vittorio.

Yet, as perspiration beaded on her brow and her boots became covered in a thin film of dust, she wondered if sharing a meal might have been the better choice. She stopped to touch a vine, its cluster of *Nebbiolo* grapes so perfectly proportioned. The grapes were young, firm and dusky, and this breed wouldn't be harvested until October. She bent to inhale the grapes' scent, closing her eyes in sensual pleasure at the beauty of the day: the wind ruffling her hair, the sun on her face, the earthy aroma all around her.

After a few seconds she opened her eyes, conscious of Vittorio's gaze on her. His expression was inscrutable, save for the faintest flicker of a smile curling his mouth.

'I like the smell,' she said, a bit self-consciously. 'I always did. When I was little, my mother found me curled under the bushes asleep.'

Vittorio had, Ana thought, a very funny look on his face now. Almost as if he were in pain. 'You looked like you were enjoying yourself very much,' he said. His voice sounded strangely strangled.

'It was a safe place for me,' Ana acknowledged. 'And, more than that—a bit of heaven.'

'A bit of heaven,' Vittorio repeated. He was standing surprisingly awkwardly, his hands jammed into the front pockets of his trousers, and his voice still sounded—odd.

'Vittorio?' Ana asked uncertainly. 'Are you all right—?'

'Ana.' He cut her off, smiling now, her name coming out in what sounded like a rush of relief. 'Come here.'

Ana didn't know what he meant. They were standing a foot apart; where was she meant to *go*?

Then Vittorio took his hands out of his pockets and, in one effortless movement, he pulled her towards him and buried his head in her hair, breathing in deeply.

'It's the smell of your hair *I* love,' he murmured. His hand had gone under the heavy mass of her hair to her neck. 'I want you,' Vittorio confessed raggedly, 'so much. Come back to the castle with me. Make love to me, Ana.'

Love. Ana couldn't keep the smile from her voice. 'Again?'

'You think once—or twice—is enough?'

She could hardly believe he wanted her so much. It shook her to her very bones, the heart of herself. 'No, definitely not,' she murmured.

'Come back—'

'No.'

Vittorio's face fell in such a comical manner that Ana would have laughed if she wasn't half-quivering with her own reawakened desire. 'Not at the castle, Vittorio. Here.'

He stared down at the dusty ground. 'Here?' he repeated dubiously.

'Yes,' Ana said firmly, tugging on his hand, 'here.' Here, where he'd found her desirable—sexy—even in her work clothes and wind-tangled hair. Here, where she'd felt safe and heaven-bound all at once, and wanted to again, in Vittorio's arms. Here, because among the grapes and the soil she was her real self, not the woman who wore fancy dresses and high heels and tried to seduce her husband with tricks she couldn't begin to execute with any skill or ease.

Here.

And Vittorio accepted that—or perhaps he couldn't wait any longer—for he spread his blazer, an expensive silk one that was soon covered in dust—on the ground and then lay Ana on it, her hair fanning out around her in a dark silken wave.

Vittorio touched her almost reverently, a look of awe on his face Ana had never expected to see. To know. The ground was hard and bumpy; pebbles dug into her back and the dust was gritty on her skin, but Ana didn't care. She revelled in it, in this. In him.

Vittorio reached for the buttons of her old shirt. 'I never thought white cotton could be so…inflaming,' he murmured, and bent his head to the flesh he'd exposed.

And, as Ana's hand clutched at his hair, she realized she had no idea that she could *feel* so inflamed, as if the very fires of passion were burning her up, turning her craving to liquid heat.

'Vittorio…'

'We may be lying in a field like some farm hand and his dairymaid,' Vittorio murmured against her skin—somehow, all her clothes had been removed, 'but I'm not going to have you like that, with your skirts rucked up around your waist, over in a few pathetic seconds.'

'No, indeed, since I'm not wearing any clothes.'

And, as he smiled against her skin, Ana found she had no thoughts or words left at all. Later, as they lay entangled in a sleepy haze of satisfaction, she murmured, 'We're going to have the most interesting sunburn.'

'Not if I can help it.' In one fluid movement, Vittorio rose from the dusty ground, Ana in his arms. She squealed; she *never* squealed, and yet somehow that ridiculously girlish sound came out of her mouth. Vittorio grinned. 'Put your clothes on, wife,' he said, depositing her on the ground. 'We have a perfectly good bed at home, and I intend to use it…all day.'

'All day?' Ana repeated, still squealing, and then she hurried to yank her clothes back on.

The next few weeks passed in a haze of happiness Ana had never dreamed or even hoped to feel. Although they never spoke of love, her uncertainty melted away in the light of Vittorio's presence and affection, and she hardly thought they needed to. Why speak of love when their bodies communicated far more eloquently and pleasurably? The days were still taken up with work; Ana found herself smiling at the most ridiculous moments, while signing a form or reading a purchasing order. Sometimes, spontaneously, she even laughed aloud.

Vittorio seemed just as happy. His happiness made her happy; his countenance was light, a smile ready on his lips, those onyx eyes lightened to a pewter grey, glinting with humour and love—surely love, for Ana had little doubt that he loved her.

How could he not, when they spent night after night together, not just in passion but in quiet moments afterwards, talking and touching in a way that melted both her body and heart?

He told her bits of his childhood, the hard memories which she'd guessed at, as well as some of the good times: playing *stecca* with his father, going to Rome on a school trip when he was fifteen and getting outrageously drunk.

'It's fortunate I was not expelled.'

'Why weren't you?'

'I told you, I played the trombone,' he replied with a wicked little smile. 'They needed me in the orchestra.'

And Ana told him things she'd never told anyone else, confessed the dark days after her mother's death.

'My father was overwhelmed with grief. He refused to see me for days—locked himself in her bedroom.'

'It's so hard to believe.' Vittorio let his fingers drift through her hair, along her cheek. 'He is so close to you now.'

'It took work,' Ana replied frankly. 'In fact, a week after she died, he sent me to boarding school—he thought it would be easier. For him, I suppose.' It was good, if still hard, to speak of it; bringing light to the dark memories. 'Those two years were the worst of my life.'

Vittorio pressed his lips against the curve of her shoulder. 'I'm sorry.'

'It doesn't matter now.' And it didn't, because in Vittorio's arms she didn't feel big and mannish and awkward; she felt beautiful and sexy and loved.

Loved.

No, she had no doubt at all that Vittorio loved her, no sense that there was anything but happiness—that bit of heaven—ahead of them, shining and pure, stretching to a limitless horizon.

CHAPTER TEN

SIX weeks after their wedding, Vittorio came to see Ana at the Viale offices. She looked up from her desk, smiling in pleased surprise as he appeared in the doorway.

'I didn't expect to see you here,' she said, rising to embrace him. Vittorio kissed her with a distracted air, his face troubled before relaxing into a smile that still didn't reach his eyes.

'I have to go to Brazil again. There has been trouble with some of the merchants there.'

'What kind of trouble?' Ana asked, her smile turning to a frown. Her heart had already sunk a bit at the thought: *Brazil*.

Vittorio gave a little shrug. 'It's not worrisome, but important enough that I should go soothe a few ruffled feathers, murmur encouragement in the right ears.'

'You're good at that,' Ana teased, but Vittorio missed the joke entirely.

'I came here because I am leaving this afternoon, before you return. If I take the private jet to Rio, I can return within a week.'

'A week!' Disappointment swamped her. It seemed like a horribly long time.

'Yes, this is business,' Vittorio said a bit sharply, and his tone as well as his words were like ice water drenching her spirit. Her happiness.

Business. Was Vittorio actually reminding her that business was what their marriage was all about? *Just* business? Ana swallowed dryly. 'Yes, of course.'

'I'll ring you,' he said, pressing a quick kiss against her cold cheek, and then he was gone.

Ana stood in the middle of the office for a few moments, listening to the sounds around her: Vittorio slamming the front door of the building, the purr of the Porsche's engine starting up again, the murmur of voices from other offices. And, the loudest sound of all, the sick thudding of her own frightened heart.

Had she been deceiving herself these last few weeks? Lost in a haze of happiness, mistaking lust for love? Ana moved back to her desk and sat down hard in her chair, her head falling into her hands. She couldn't believe how unsure she felt, how afraid. Her serene certainty that Vittorio loved her had been swept away by one careless remark.

Clearly she hadn't been so certain after all.

The castle felt lonely and quiet when she returned that evening, its endless rooms lost in shadow. Ana told the cook she'd have something in her room rather than face the elegant dining room alone; Constantia had returned to Milan last week and Bernardo, as he so often was, appeared to be out. She didn't want to see anyone.

Marco, the cook, however, looked surprised. 'Ah, but I've made dinner! For two—it is all prepared.'

'For two?' Ana repeated, hope leaping absurdly inside her. Had Vittorio come back? But of course not; he was halfway to South America by now.

'Yes, Signor Bernardo wishes to dine with you.'

Ana felt a finger of foreboding trail along her spine, then shrugged the shivery sensation away. Whatever had passed between Bernardo and Vittorio was long ago, and didn't concern her. Perhaps getting to know her husband's younger brother would go some way in helping to heal his family's rift. Despite the happiness of the last few weeks, Ana knew Vittorio was still snared by the dark memories of his childhood. She saw it when he didn't think anyone was looking, a moment alone lost in sorrowful thought, the shadow of grief in his eyes.

'All right,' she told Marco. 'Thank you.'

As Ana entered the dining room, the setting rays of the sun sending long golden beams of light across the elegant room, she saw the table set cosily for two at one end and Bernardo standing by the window. He started forward as soon as he saw her.

'Ana! Thank you for joining me.'

'Of course, Bernardo. I am happy to dine with you.' Yet, as he took her hands and pressed his cheek against hers in a brotherly embrace, Ana couldn't shake the feeling that Bernardo had an agenda for this meal.

She stepped back, surveying him as he moved to the table to pull out her chair. He was a slighter, paler version of Vittorio, still handsome, with the same dark hair and eyes, yet he lacked his brother's strength and vitality. If they stood next to each other, there could be no doubt as to who was the more dynamic, charismatic and frankly attractive brother. How could Bernardo fail to be jealous?

'Thank you,' she murmured, and sat in the chair Bernardo had drawn for her. He sat opposite and reached for the bottle of red he'd left breathing on a side table.

'One of the vineyard's own?' Ana asked as she watched the rich ruby liquid being poured into her glass.

'In a way. I've been experimenting a bit with mixed grapes.' His expression turned wary, guarded. 'Vittorio doesn't know.'

Ana took a sip of wine. 'But this is delicious.' It was rich and velvety, with a hidden aroma of fruit and spice. She set the glass down and gave Bernardo a frank look. 'Why doesn't Vittorio know you've been experimenting with hybrids? Especially as the result is so pleasing.'

Bernardo gave her a faint smile and took a sip from his own glass. 'Surely you've seen by now that Vittorio and I…' He paused, cocking his head thoughtfully. 'We are not like normal brothers.'

'Of course I've noticed that,' Ana returned. 'In fact,' she added, a bit sharply, 'I even wondered if he would want us to dine like this together, alone.'

'He wouldn't. Not because he thinks it is inappropriate, but because he is afraid I will whisper poison in your ear.'

Ana gestured to her glass. 'Is this poison?' She asked the question lightly, yet Benardo regarded her with grave eyes.

'It is, as far as Vittorio is concerned. He is not interested in anything I have to do with Cazlevara Wines.'

Ana felt a stab of pity. 'Why? Is it simply because of what happened so long ago, when your father died?' Bernardo looked surprised and Ana said quickly, 'I know Constantia tried to take his inheritance, and make you Count. Vittorio told me. Yet that happened so long ago, and you were only a boy—'

'That was merely the beginning,' Bernardo replied. 'I suppose he told you what our childhood was like? We were forced to take sides, Vittorio and I. At first we resisted it. We resented our parents drawing us into their battles. But after time…' He shrugged and spread his hands. 'I admit, I was not a sensible boy. My mother's attention went to my head. When she so clearly preferred me to Vittorio—and my own father did not have so much as a glance for me—well, I flaunted it. I rubbed Vittorio's nose in it. Special presents, trips…these things turn a boy's head. They turned mine.' His mouth twisted in a bitter smile of regret. 'Vittorio saw it all, and said nothing. That only made me angrier. He had my papà's attention and praise, all of it, and I wanted to make him jealous.'

'And of course he was,' Ana cut in. 'Nothing can take the place of a mother's love.'

'Or a father's. I don't know which of us got the better bargain. Vittorio was my father's favourite, but he didn't get spoiled and cosseted like I did. He was whipped into shape.' He held up a hand. 'Not literally. But my father was a hard taskmaster. I remember one time he called Vittorio out of bed—he must have been ten or so, home from boarding school. I was but six at the time. It wasn't even dawn, but my father saw that Vittorio had done poorly on a maths exam. He sat him down at the dining room table and made him write the exam all over again. He didn't stop until every problem was correct. Vittorio worked for hours. He didn't even have breakfast.' Bernardo made a face. 'I remember because I smacked my lips and slurped my juice and he didn't even look up, though he must have been hungry.' Bernardo shook his head, his mouth twisting in a grimace. 'I am not proud of how I behaved over the years, Ana. I freely admit that.'

Ana let out a sorrowful little sigh. It was such a sad, pointless story. Why had Constantia rejected Vittorio so utterly? Couldn't she see how her behaviour had affected him, how her love could have softened her husband's harsh treatment? She'd been so blinded by her own misery, Ana supposed. Arturo's lack of love for his wife had been the rotten seed of it all.

The food had been served, but she found she had no appetite. 'And when your father died? What happened then?'

Bernardo steepled his fingers under his chin. 'By that time the lines were well and truly drawn. Vittorio hated both my mother and me, or at least acted as if he did. He was only fourteen, and he had not one word of kindness for either of us. Oh, he was polite enough, icily respectful, and it drove my mother mad. I suppose Vittorio was so like our father—and my father had never had a true moment of empathy or love for my mother. He was polite, courteous, solicitous even, but there was no love behind it. He was a cold man.'

'Even so, why did your mother try to have the will overturned and disinherit Vittorio? Simply because you were her favourite?' Ana heard the accusation in her own voice. What could justify such cruel, callous behaviour?

Bernardo shrugged. 'Who knows? She has told me she did it because she thought if Vittorio became Count, he would be too hard a man, like my father was. She said she could not bear to see Vittorio become like Arturo.' He smiled sadly. 'I rather thought she believed she was saving him—from himself.'

Ana raised her eyebrows. 'He certainly didn't view it that way.'

'It made things worse, of course,' Bernardo agreed. 'The plan failed, and Vittorio's enmity was cemented. Over the years we have had nothing to say to one another and—' he paused, his gaze sliding from hers '—I have not always acted in a way I could be proud of.' He turned back to face her resolutely. 'And so it continues even now, as you've undoubtedly seen. Which is why I am here.'

Ana met his gaze levelly. 'You have something to ask me.'

'Yes.' Bernardo took a breath and gestured to the wine he'd poured, glinting in their crystal goblets. 'You have tasted my own vintage, Ana, and as an experienced vintner you know it is good. Vittorio is determined never to let me have any control or authority in Cazlevara Wines. God knows, I can understand it. I have not proven myself worthy. I have done things I regret, even as a grown man. But I cannot live like this, under my brother's thumb. Everything is a grudging favour from him. It wears me down to nothing. And to know he would never market this vintage simply because it is mine—'

'Surely Vittorio wouldn't be so unreasonable,' Ana interjected. 'He is a man of business, after all.' How well she knew it.

'When it comes to me and my mother, he is blind,' Bernardo stated flatly. 'Blind and bitter, and I can hardly blame him.'

'So what are you asking of me?'

'You've done some experimenting with hybrids, yes?'

'A little—'

'If you passed this wine off as your own creation, he would accept it.'

'And I would take the credit?'

Bernardo lifted one shoulder in a tiny shrug. 'That does not matter so much to me. It cannot.'

Ana stared at Vittorio's brother, saw the weary resignation on his pale face. She had no doubt that he'd been petted and spoiled as a child, and he'd made his brother's life miserable—more miserable than it already was—well into young adulthood. Yet now she saw a man who was over thirty and resigned never to prove himself, never to have the satisfaction of excelling in a job he was created to do. The injustice and sorrow of it twisted her heart.

'I will not take credit for your own hard work, Bernardo.' He nodded slowly, accepting, his mouth pulled downwards. 'This wine is excellent, and you deserve to be known as its creator.' Ana took a breath. 'So you can either market it under the Viale label or, as I'm sure would be much more satisfying, under the Cazlevara one. This bitter feud between you and Vittorio must end. Perhaps, if he sees how well you have done, he will be convinced.'

Bernardo leaned forward. 'What do you suggest?'

'Why don't you prepare to market the vintage? Vittorio has given me authority over the vineyards while he is gone.' Ana knew her authority was more perfunctory than anything else; he hardly expected her to change things, or implement strategies such as the one she was suggesting. 'I can arrange a meeting with some merchants in Milan. Start there, and see what happens. By the time Vittorio comes home, God willing, you will have something to show him.' And, Ana added silently, God willing, Vittorio wouldn't be too angry with her. God willing, this feud would finally end and their marriage could continue, grow, work. If he loved her—and she was desperate now to believe he did—his anger would not rule the day.

His love would.

Hope had lit Bernardo's eyes, erasing the resigned lines from his face. He looked younger, happier already. 'What you are doing is dangerous, Ana. Vittorio might be furious. In fact, I know he will be.'

'This feud must end,' Ana said firmly. 'It is the only way forward for any of us. I am not biased by childhood slights the way he is. And I'm sure,' she added with more confidence than she felt, 'my husband will see reason once I have spoken to him.'

It had been a long, hard week, courting the South American merchants. They wanted to rely on their own wines; they were dubious of a European import. Yet, finally, with honeyed words and persuasive arguments, meetings and dinners and tastings, Vittorio had convinced them.

Now he was home and eager—desperate—to see Ana. As his limo pulled up to the castle, Vittorio nearly laughed at himself. He was acting like a besotted boy. He *was* besotted, utterly in love with his wife, and it had taken a week apart to realize just what he was feeling.

Love.

He loved Ana, and he'd felt it in every agonising second he'd spent apart from her, when he'd kept looking for her, even though he knew she was thousands of miles away. He'd felt it when he'd reached for her at night, and both his body and heart had ached when his arms remained empty. It didn't even surprise him, this new-found love; it simply felt too right. He felt completed, whole, and he hadn't realized how much he'd been missing—in and of himself—until he knew that sense of fulfilment, of rightness, caused by loving Ana.

He knew she loved him. He knew it, he'd seen it in her eyes and felt it in her body, yet it still filled him with wonder and incredulous joy. How could he have been so blind to think he didn't want this, didn't need it? Now he could not imagine life without it, without Ana. The very thought left him cold and despairing. But now he didn't despair; now he felt hope. Wonderful, miraculous hope. And he couldn't wait to tell Ana.

The castle was quiet as he entered; it was four o'clock in the afternoon and he had no doubt Ana was at her own office. He thought of surprising her there; he'd make love to her right on her own desk. His mouth widened into a grin at the thought of it. First, he would check in at the Cazlevara office and then…Ana. He could hardly wait.

He was just sorting through the post left by his secretary when his vineyard manager knocked on the door.

Vittorio barely glanced up. 'Yes, Antonio? Everything went well while I was gone?' He tossed another letter aside, only to pause when he realized his manager had not spoken. He glanced up, saw the man twisting his hands together, looking uncertain. Afraid, even. Vittorio's eyes narrowed. 'Antonio? Has something happened?'

'It's Bernardo, Lord Ralfino…Bernardo and the Contessa.'

Vittorio stilled. He felt as if his blood had turned to ice water; the sense of coldness gave him a chilling clarity, a freezing resolve. He'd been expecting this, he realized. He wasn't surprised. 'Has my mother been plotting again?' he asked levelly. 'Now that I am married, she seeks to disinherit and discredit me once more?'

Antonio shook his head, looking wretched. 'Not the Dowager Contessa, my lord. Your wife.'

For a moment Vittorio couldn't speak. Couldn't think. The words made no sense. What his manager was saying was impossible, ridiculous—

Vittorio drew a breath. 'Are you saying my wife is acting with Bernardo?'

'She told me not to ring you,' Antonio confessed unhappily.

'What?' Vittorio could barely process it. His wife had been attempting to deceive him? To scheme against him? The shock left him senseless, reeling, nearly gasping in pain.

'I know you do not wish Bernardo to—well, I knew you'd want this approved,' Antonio continued, 'but since she said—and you'd given her authority—'

Vittorio laid one hand flat on his desk, bracing himself. He would not jump to conclusions. He would *not*. He kept the rage and fear down, suppressing it, even though it fermented and bubbled, threatened to boil over and burn them all. He would not let it. He would listen to Antonio, he would hear Ana's side of the story. He would be fair. 'What has happened, Antonio?'

'Bernardo went to Milan,' the manager confessed. 'He is marketing his own label. I didn't know of it until yesterday, but the Contessa approved it, arranged the meeting—'

'His own label?' Vittorio repeated blankly. Was his brother actually trying to take over the family winery, to make it his own? And Ana was *helping* him? Had they been planning this—this *takeover*—together while he was gone? Or even before? He could hardly make sense of it, his heart cried out its innate, desperate rejection of such lies, even as his mind coolly reminded him that this was exactly how he'd felt returning from his father's funeral, hoping—desperately hoping—that now his father was dead his mother might turn to him, if not with open arms, then at least with a smile.

She'd turned her back instead. Something had died in Vittorio then, that last frail hope he'd never realized he'd still clung to. The desire for love. The hope it would find him. He'd lost it then, or thought he had, only to find the desire and the hope—the need for love—inside him, latent, and with Ana it had begun to grow, young and fragile, seeking her healing light.

Now he felt as if it had been felled at its tender root. His heart had become a barren wasteland, frozen and unyielding. He turned back to Antonio. 'Thank you for telling me. I will deal with it now.'

'I would have rung you, but since the Contessa was meant to be in charge—'

'I completely understand. Do not think of it again.' Vittorio dismissed the man with a nod, then turned to stare blindly out of the window. Rows upon rows of neat growing grapes stretched to the horizon, Cazlevara's fortune, his family's life blood. He'd made love to Ana out there, among those vines. He'd held in her arms and loved her.

Loved her.

And now she'd betrayed him. He tried to stay reasonable, to keep the anger and hurt and oh, yes, the fear from consuming him, but they rose up in a red tide of feeling until he couldn't think any more. He could only feel.

He felt the hurt and the pain and the sorrow, the *agony* of his mother and brother's rejection, over and over again. Day after day of trying to please his father, only to strive more and more; nothing he'd ever done was enough. And then when his father had died, torn between despair and relief, he'd wanted to turn to his mother, thinking that now she would accept him, love him even, only to realize she'd rejected him utterly.

And now. This. Ana had somehow been working against him with his brother, waiting until he was gone to use the authority he'd given her on *trust* to discredit him. This, he acknowledged, was the worst betrayal of all.

'Lord Cazlevara is here to see you, Signorina Vi—Lady Cazlevara.'

Ana half-rose from the desk, smiling at Edoardo. 'You don't need to stand on ceremony, Edoardo. Send him in!' Yet, even as a smile of hope and welcome—how she'd missed him!—was spreading across her face, another part of Ana was registering the look of wariness on her assistant's face and wondering why he seemed so uncomfortable.

'Good afternoon, Ana.'

'Vittorio!' The word burst from Ana's lips and, despite his rather chilly greeting, she couldn't keep from smiling, from walking towards him, her arms outstretched, needing his touch, his kiss—

Vittorio didn't move. Ana dropped her arms, realization

settling coldly inside her. He'd heard about Bernardo, obviously. He knew what she'd done. And he hadn't liked it.

'You're angry,' she stated, and Vittorio arched one eyebrow.

'Angry? No. Curious, perhaps.' He spoke with arctic politeness that froze Ana's insides. She hadn't heard that voice in such a long time; she'd forgotten just how cold it was. How cold it made her feel. Vittorio leaned against the door frame, hands in his pockets, and waited.

Ana took a breath. She'd been preparing for this conversation, had known that Vittorio, on some level, would not be pleased. He'd try to distance himself; that was how he stayed safe. She *knew* that, yet she'd trusted what she felt for him—and what she believed and hoped he felt for her—that their love would make him see reason. She'd told herself so hundreds of times over the last week, yet now that the time had come and Vittorio was standing here looking so icy and indifferent, all the calm explanations she'd come up with seemed to have vanished, leaving her with nothing but a growing sense of panic, a swamping fear. She didn't want her husband looking at her this way, talking to her as if she were a stranger he didn't really like. She couldn't bear it. 'Vittorio,' she finally said, and heard the plea in her voice even though her words sounded firm, 'Bernardo showed me the vintage he's created. He's been working with hybrids—you didn't know—'

'Funny, I thought I knew everything that happened in my company. And, as I recollect, my brother was assistant manager, not head vintner. Or did you give him a promotion in my absence?' He spoke pleasantly, yet Ana heard and felt the terrible coldness underneath. It crept into her bones and wound its icy way around her heart. She felt like shivering, shuddering, crying out.

This was what Constantia had lived with day in, day out. This was what Vittorio had been to her, a man who refused to be reached, whose heart was enclosed in walls of ice. No wonder the woman had gone half-mad. She already felt perilously close to the edge of reason after just a few minutes under his freezing stare.

'No, I didn't give him a promotion,' Ana replied as levelly as she could. 'I wouldn't presume to do such a thing—'

'Wouldn't you?'

Ana forced herself to ignore the sneering question. 'But I did allow him to market his own wine. He's in Milan right now, talking to some merchants about it. I thought we could put it in the catalogue this autumn—'

'Oh, you did, did you?' Vittorio took a step into the room, his pleasant mask dropped so Ana saw the icy rage underneath. 'You didn't waste much time, did you, Ana?' he asked, fairly spitting the words. 'The moment I'd gone, you were plotting and planning behind my back.'

Ana quelled beneath the verbal attack. Did he think so little of her? 'It wasn't a plot, Vittorio,' she insisted, 'though I can understand why you might think that way. But I am not your mother, and Bernardo has changed—'

Vittorio gave a sharp laugh. 'Nothing has changed. Don't you think I have a reason for keeping him on as short a leash as I do?'

Ana struggled to keep her calm. 'Vittorio, your brother was ten when your mother tried to disinherit you—'

'And he was twenty when he tried to sabotage the winery and discredit me to my customers, and twenty-five when he embezzeled a hundred thousand euros. Don't you think I know my own brother?'

Ana stared at him in shock, her mouth dropping open before she had the sense to snap it shut. Realization trickled icily though her. 'I didn't know those things,' she finally said quietly. Vittorio gave another disbelieving laugh and she thought of Bernardo's words: *I have done things I regret, even as a grown man.* She almost felt like laughing hysterically, despite the panic and the fear. Perhaps she should have asked Bernardo to clarify what he'd meant. Perhaps she shouldn't have leapt in so rashly, thinking she could heal old wounds, hurts that had never scarred over, just festered and bled—

Still, Ana knew there was more going on here, more at risk than Vittorio's sour relationship with his brother. There was his relationship with *her*, a fundamental issue of trust and love. She had to ask crucial questions, and now she was afraid of their answers.

'I really didn't know everything he'd done,' she said, trying to keep her voice steady. 'Still, I believe Bernardo has changed. If you just give him a chance—'

'So he's convinced you,' Vittorio stated quietly. He turned away so she couldn't see his face. 'He's turned you from me.'

Ana suddenly felt near to tears. Vittorio's voice sounded so final, so *sad*. 'Vittorio, it's not like that! I just wanted to give Bernardo a chance, not only for his sake, but for *ours*.'

'Ours,' Vittorio repeated, the word dripping sarcasm.

'Yes, ours, because your hatred of him poisons everything! Poisons—' She stopped, not wanting to expose herself so utterly and admit she loved him. 'And he could be a credit to you,' she continued quietly. 'He rang me from Milan this morning, and the meetings went well. He's not trying to take some kind of control—'

'So he says.'

'This bitterness must end,' Ana stated. Her voice trembled and she forced herself to go on, to say the words she'd shied away from. The truth was the only thing that had the power to heal. 'It poisons you, and it poisons our love.'

She felt as if she'd laid down a live wire; the room crackled with uncontained energy. *Love.* She'd said it, admitted to that most dangerous forbidden feeling.

Vittorio turned around; his eyes were like two pools of black ice. 'Love?' he enquired silkily. 'What are you talking about, Ana?'

Ana blinked, forcing back the tears. She would be strong

now, even if that strength meant being more vulnerable than she ever had before. 'I love you, Vittorio. I gave Bernardo a chance for love of you—'

'Just like my mother took my inheritance, claiming she did it out of love for me?' Vittorio mocked.

'Is that what she said?'

'Or something like it. I found it rather hard to believe.'

Yet Ana didn't. She could see Constantia's twisted reasoning now, understand how she might do anything—*anything*—to keep Vittorio from becoming the cold, hard man his father had been, and had wanted to make him. Yet, right now before her eyes, he was changing, hardening, the last weeks of love and gentleness falling away as if they'd never been, leaving her with a man she didn't like or even know.

'It's true, Vittorio. I don't doubt Bernardo has hurt you, as has Constantia, but this cannot go on. You are all poisoned by it—all three of you. I thought if Bernardo proved himself to you, you could see each other as equals. Forgive each other and learn to—'

'Oh, Ana, this is all sounding very cosy,' Vittorio drawled. 'And completely unrealistic. I didn't marry you to play therapist to my family. I married you to be loyal to *me*.'

Ana blinked. 'And does that loyalty mean blind obedience? I can't take any decisions for myself? You didn't want a lapdog, you said. You rather touchingly referred to our marriage as one of *partnership*—'

'A business partnership,' Vittorio corrected. 'That is what I meant.'

Ana swallowed, struggling to stay reasonable, as if her heart and soul hadn't been shredded to pathetic pieces as they spoke. 'Yet you do not want me to have any concern with your business—'

'I do not want you to use your influence to put my brother's concerns forward!' Vittorio cut her off, his voice rising to a near-shout before he lowered it again to no more than a dark whisper. 'You have betrayed me, Ana.'

'I love you,' Ana returned. Her voice shook; so did her body. 'Vittorio, I *love* you—'

He shook his head in flat dismissal. 'That wasn't part of our bargain.'

She searched his face, looking for any trace of compassion or even regret. Every line, every angle was hard and implacable. He had become a stranger, a terrible stranger. 'I know it wasn't,' she said quietly. 'But I fell in love with you anyway, with the man you…you seemed to be. Yet now—' she took a breath '—you are so cold to me. Vittorio, do you not love me at all?'

A muscle jerked in Vittorio's cheek and he didn't answer. He gazed down at her, his eyes hard and unrelenting, and suddenly Ana could stand it no more. She'd felt this exposed only once before in her life, when she'd flung herself at Roberto, hoping he would take her into his arms and admit he was attracted to her, to make his love physical as well as emotional. She'd been rejected then, utterly, or so she'd thought. Yet that moment was nothing—*nothing*—compared to this. Now Vittorio was rejecting her emotionally; he was rejecting her heart rather than her body and it hurt so much more.

It hurt unbearably.

'I see you don't,' she said quietly and, when Vittorio still didn't answer, Ana did the only thing she could think of doing, the only option left to her. She fled.

In a numb state of grief—the same kind of frozen despair she'd felt when her mother had died—Ana walked away from her office. She didn't think about where she was going until she found herself on the dirt road back to Villa Rosso, its mellow stone and terracotta tiles gleaming in the afternoon sun.

She was going home.

The villa was quiet when she entered, her footsteps falling softly on the tiled floor of the foyer. She headed for the stairs but heard her father's voice call out from his study.

'Hello? Is someone there?'

'It's me, Papà.' Ana paused on the stairs; her father came to the hall. He took one look at her face—Ana could only imagine how terrible she looked—and gasped aloud.

'Ana! What has happened?'

Ana gave a sad little smile. She felt as if her whole body were breaking, her soul rent into pieces. 'I discovered you were right, Papà. Love isn't very comfortable, after all.'

Enrico's face twisted in sorrow, but Ana knew she could not bear even his sympathy now. She just shook her head and walked with heavy steps upstairs, to the room she had not slept in since she'd got married.

Married. Vittorio was her husband, yet she hardly knew what that meant any more.

She spent the night alone, lying on her bed, watching the moon rise and then descend once more. She didn't sleep. She found herself reliving the joy of the last few weeks, now made all the sweeter by its brevity. Vittorio kissing her, taking her in his arms. Laughing as they played *stecca* again; he'd won that time. Talking about the vineyards, and grapes, and wine, gesturing with their hands, shared enthusiasm in their voices. The way he touched her casually, a hand on hers, when they were reading in bed, simply because he wanted to feel her next to him. And then later, the way he touched her so her body cried out in pleasure. So many memories, so many wonderful, sweet, *terrible* memories, because she was afraid they were all she'd ever have.

Was their marriage actually over? She could hardly believe he had rejected her so utterly; she thought of trying to see him again and then knew she couldn't. She couldn't face that hard, blank face again. She couldn't face the feeling of being so raw, so exposed and rejected again. Not by Vittorio, not by the man—the only man—she'd ever love.

She pressed her face into her pillow and willed the tears to come; crying would bring relief of a sort. They didn't. Some things, Ana knew, were too deep for tears.

Enrico knocked on her door in the morning, begging her to take a bit of breakfast. 'Ana, have some toast at least,' he called, his voice sounding thin and frail. 'I told the cook not to make kippers. I know they put you off.'

Ana couldn't even summon a smile. 'Don't trouble yourself, Papà. I'm not hungry. I just need to be alone for a little while.'

She needed to be alone to grieve the ending of her marriage, for surely that was what this was. Vittorio had not come to see her and Ana dreaded some horrible letter, a cold official ending to their marriage. Although, she reminded herself, he'd said divorce was not an option.

Yet the alternative—the cold convenient marriage she'd once agreed to—would be so much worse, for affection and respect had been obliterated. All that was left was duty.

Funny, Ana thought distantly as she lay on her bed, watching the sun rise in the sky, still in her clothes from the day before, how she had once convinced herself she could accept such a thing. A loveless marriage, a business arrangement. She'd deceived herself. Love wasn't comfortable but it was everything.

In the early evening, Enrico knocked again. *'Dolcezza—'*

'I'm still not hungry,' Ana called.

'You don't need to eat,' her father called back, 'but your husband is here, and he wants to see you.'

Ana stilled. Her hands clenched into fists on her bed covers. 'I can't see him, Papà,' she said, her voice no more than a choked whisper.

'Please, Ana. He is desperate for you.'

'Desperate?' She said the word disbelievingly, yet still laced with damning hope.

'Desperate, *rondinella*.' Vittorio's voice, no more than a husky whisper, made Ana freeze. Distantly, she heard her father's footsteps patter down the hall and, after a moment, her heart beating with hard, heavy thuds, she went to open the door. Vittorio stood there, ushaven, his hair rumpled, still wearing his clothes from yesterday. His eyes remained grave as he gave her a small uncertain smile.

'You look as awful as I do,' Ana said.

Vittorio touched her cheek. 'You have not been crying, at least.' His own eyes looked red.

'Some things are too deep for tears,' Ana told him and he stepped into the room. She leaned against the door, her arms crossed, unwilling to relax her guard. Afraid to hope.

'Oh, Ana.' Vittorio shook his head, his voice choking a little bit. 'I made you so unhappy.'

'Yes, you did,' Ana agreed, and was amazed at how level her voice sounded, as if she wasn't affected at all. As if she wasn't dying inside.

'I was so angry,' Vittorio said quietly. 'And it blinded me. All I could see—feel—was betrayal.'

'I know.'

His smile was touched with sorrow. 'It's not an excuse, is it?'

'No.'

'Just a reason.' He sighed again. 'I have a lot to learn, I suppose, if you will consent to be my teacher.'

Ana shook her head. 'I don't want to be your teacher, Vittorio. I want to be your wife. And that means you need to trust me.'

'I know,' Vittorio said in a low voice. 'I know I should have, but I couldn't *think*—'

'It doesn't even matter.' Ana cut him off, her voice tight. 'I realize the bargain we made doesn't work for me, Vittorio. I can't...I can't accept our marriage on your terms.'

'What?' He looked shocked. 'What are you talking about?'

She swallowed, her voice raw. 'I need more from you than your trust. I need your love.'

He stared at her, slack-jawed, and Ana braced herself for his refusal. His rejection. It never came.

'I do love you, Ana,' Vittorio said, his voice a throb of intensity. 'And it has terrified me. That's why I acted like I did yesterday. Not another excuse—just the truth. I am sorry. So sorry. Please forgive me.'

Ana could hardly believe what he'd said. 'You love me?' she repeated, and he offered her a tremulous smile.

'Utterly. Unbearably. I spent the most wretched night last night, and for love of you—I thought I'd just gone and thrown out the most wonderful thing that's ever happened to me, and for what? My own pride?'

She shook her head. Hope bubbled up inside her, an everlasting well of joy. 'I shouldn't have acted without you, but I thought…I thought to help heal the past—'

'And you have,' Vittorio said. 'Already, it has begun. When you walked out of that office I realized you might actually be walking away from me for ever, and I was letting you go. I was devastated, in agony, and I knew I could not let my pride keep you from me. I spoke to Bernardo, and to my mother.' He took a breath, offering her a wry smile. 'It was not easy or comfortable for any of us. We have all committed wrongs against each other and there is still much to do, to say and to forgive. Yet we have begun. You have helped us, Ana. You are the best thing to have come into my life.'

Ana's throat ached with unshed tears and suppressed emotion. 'And you are the best thing in mine.' Still, she felt the fear lurking in the dark corners of her heart. It seemed so hard to believe, too wonderful to be true. To last. 'Yesterday you were so cold, so hard to me—'

Vittorio reached for her fingers and pressed them against his lips. 'I do not want to be a hard man,' he confessed, his voice a ragged whisper, his eyes glinting with unshed tears of his own.

'God knows, I don't. Yet, when I am afraid, I find that is how I become, for it is what I learned as a boy.'

'I know it is,' Ana whispered, remembering what both Constantia and Bernardo had told her. They'd helped her understand Vittorio, and she was grateful to them for that.

'It is no excuse,' Vittorio replied resolutely. 'And yet you have changed me, Ana. I am so grateful for that. I realized just how much you've changed me when you left me yesterday. I do not want to be that man any more. With you, I am not him.'

He touched her cheek, resting his forehead against hers. 'Can you forgive me, *rondinella*, for those moments when I became him again? Can you forgive me, and believe in the man I am trying to become?'

Ana thought of the man who had comforted her as a grieving child so many years ago; she remembered his many kindnesses over the last few months. She recalled the wonder and joy she'd felt in his arms. 'You are that man, Vittorio. You always have been.'

He kissed her then sweetly, so very sweetly, a kiss that was healing and hope together. 'Only because of you, Ana. Only because of you.'

She laughed, a tremulous, muffled sound, for the knowledge that Vittorio loved her—that this was *real*—was too wonderful, too overwhelming. She trusted it now; she believed in it, and it was good.

It was amazing.

Vittorio touched her cheek; it came away damp. 'It's all right to cry, *rondinella*,' he whispered and Ana laughed again, entwining his fingers with her own as she kissed him once more.

'For joy,' she said. 'This time for joy.'

EXPECTING THE FELLANI HEIR

LUCY GORDON

CHAPTER ONE

AFTERWARDS ELLIE ALWAYS remembered the day when things really started to happen, when the sky glowed, the universe trembled to its foundations and nothing was ever the same again.

It began gloomily, a cold February morning with the traffic in a jam, delaying her as she drove to work. Drumming her fingers against the steering wheel, she drew in sharp breaths of exasperation.

The world would call her a successful woman, a highly qualified lawyer employed by one of London's most notable legal practices. To be late for work should have been beneath her. But it was happening.

When she finally arrived, Rita, her young secretary, greeted her with agitation.

'The boss has been asking about you every minute.'

The boss was Alex Dallon, founder and head of Dallon Ltd. He was an efficient, demanding man, and it was no small achievement that Ellie had earned his favour.

'Is he annoyed because I'm late?' Ellie asked.

'A bit. Signor Fellani called to say he was coming in this morning and Mr Dallon doesn't have time to see him.'

'I wasn't aware that Signor Fellani had an appointment.'

'No, but you know him. He just announces he's coming.'

'And we all have to jump to it,' Ellie groaned.

'I wouldn't mind jumping for him,' Rita declared longingly. 'He's gorgeous!'

'That's not the point,' Ellie told her, severely but kindly. 'Looks aren't everything.'

'His are,' Rita sighed.

'No man's are,' Ellie said firmly.

Rita's response was a cynical look that Ellie understood. She knew exactly how she appeared to her secretary. Rita was a pretty, vivacious young woman with an eager interest in finding 'the one'. Ellie was a successful, efficient woman in her late thirties, with no husband or lover. Rita would clearly see that as a fate to avoid. To her, a man as attractive as Leonizio Fellani was not merely a client, but a dream to sigh over.

Ellie could understand how naïve Rita could fall for him. He was a man nobody could overlook, in his early thirties, with black hair and dark eyes that drew instant attention. He had a tall, athletic build and moved with a masculine grace that drew many eyes towards him. His face, she conceded, was handsome, although too often marred by tension.

Just once she had seen him smile, and there had been a glimpse of the kinder man he might have been. But it was over in a moment as the unyielding side of his nature took over again.

She herself ignored male attractions. There had been moments in her past when she had weakened, which was how she thought of it. But things hadn't worked out and she'd gathered her defences again.

Her appearance disappointed her. Her face was pleasant but not strikingly pretty. She possessed only one outstanding feature. Her hair. If she wore it long it could appear lush and wildly wavy. But she chose to scrape it back, tying the length into a bun at the back.

Businesslike, she often thought, regarding herself sadly in the mirror. *Nobody is going to sigh over those looks.*

She tended to judge herself severely. Many women would have envied her slender figure, but she considered herself too thin and overly angular. It was her nature to be realistic about her own lack of conventional attractions. Unlike Rita, she would never sigh over a handsome man like Signor Fellani.

He was an important client, wealthy, Italian, strong-minded. Curiosity had inspired Ellie to look up his name and she'd discovered that Leonizio meant 'lion-like'. It suited his commanding ways, she reckoned.

He had made a fortune manufacturing shoes. His luxurious, elegant products sold all over the world, especially in the UK. Just across the road from Ellie's office was a large store that sold them in great numbers.

His base was in Rome, but he employed this London firm to handle the divorce from his English wife. Alex Dallon liked Ellie to deal with this client often because her grandmother had been Italian and she had a basic knowledge of the language. Not that she ever needed to use it. Signor Fellani's command of English was like everything else about him: precise and efficient.

'Has there been any more mail from his wife's lawyers?' Ellie asked. 'The last I heard was that she was refusing to budge about custody of their baby.'

'But since she's left him and the child hasn't been born yet, she's bound to get custody,' Rita pointed out.

'I'm not looking forward to telling him that. Anything significant in the mail?'

'Not that I've seen so far, but I haven't opened them all yet. I'll check.'

She vanished and Ellie went to her desk. Taking out the Fellani file, she glanced quickly through the papers, reminding herself of the details.

Three years earlier, Signor Fellani had made a whirlwind marriage with Harriet Barker, an Englishwoman he'd met while she was on holiday in his native city, Rome. But after the initial excitement died the marriage had suffered. When Harriet finally discovered that she was pregnant she had left him, coming back to England.

He'd followed her, insisting that she return to him, and, when she refused, he'd demanded joint custody of the unborn child. This she also refused.

Harriet must be a woman of great courage, Ellie thought. Leonizio was an autocrat, a man who demanded obedience and knew how to get it. In their few meetings he had treated her with cool courtesy, but she had always sensed an underlying steeliness. To the wife who was defying him he might be terrifying, but perhaps that was why she was so determined to escape him.

Rita appeared in the doorway, holding out a letter.

'He's going to create merry hell when he reads this,' she said.

Ellie read it with mounting dismay. It was from Harriet's lawyers.

> *Your client must understand that he has no rights over this child, because it is not his. His wife left him because she had found another partner and become pregnant. Now a DNA test has proved that the child she is carrying is not her husband's.*
>
> *She is anxious to conclude the divorce as soon as possible so that she can marry the child's father before the birth.*
>
> *Please persuade Signor Fellani to see sense.*

A copy of the paperwork for the DNA test was enclosed. There was no doubt that the baby had been fathered by the other man.

'Oh, heavens!' she sighed. 'What a dreadful thing to have to tell him.'

'Especially today,' Rita said.

'Why, what's different about today?'

'It's Valentine's Day. The day for lovers, when they celebrate the joy of their love.'

'Oh, no!' Ellie groaned. 'I'd forgotten the date. You're right. But he's Italian. Perhaps they don't celebrate Valentine's Day in Italy. I hope not because that would really rub it in.'

A noise from outside made her glance through the window. She saw a taxi draw up, and Signor Fellani get out. She went to wait for him in her office, longing for this soon to be over.

A few moments later he appeared at her door, his face stern and purposeful.

'I'm sorry to spring this meeting on you without warning,' he said, 'but something has happened that changes everything.'

Did that mean he already knew?

'I went to see Harriet yesterday evening,' he continued. 'I believed we could talk things over properly; find a way to make a future together for the sake of our child. But she wasn't there. She's gone, and not left an address. Why? Why pick this moment to run away from me?'

So he didn't know, Ellie realised, her heart sinking. The next few minutes were going to be terrible.

'She obviously doesn't feel able to talk,' she said. 'Perhaps you should just accept that it's over.'

'Over between her and me, but not between me and my child,' he retorted swiftly.

She hesitated, dismayed at the disaster that was heading their way. Sensing her unease, he spoke more quietly.

'You probably think I'm being unreasonable about this; pursuing a woman who doesn't want me. Why don't I just let her go? But it's not that simple. I can let *her* go, but not the baby. There's a connection there that nothing can break, and if she thinks she's going to make me a stranger to my own child, she's wrong. I'll never let that happen.'

Ellie wanted to cry out, to make him stop at all costs. Never before had this hard man revealed his feelings so frankly, and her heart ached at the thought of how she was about to hurt him.

'I need you to find her,' he said. 'Her lawyers won't tell me where she is but you can get it out of them.'

'I'm afraid it wouldn't help,' she said heavily.

'Of course it would help. They tell you, you tell me, and I go to see her and make her stop this nonsense.'

'No!' Ellie clenched her fists. 'It isn't nonsense. I'm sorry, I hate to tell you this, but I have to.'

'Tell me what?'

She took a deep breath and forced herself to say, 'The baby isn't yours.'

Silence. She wondered if he'd actually heard her.

'What did you say?' he asked at last.

'She's carrying another man's child. I only found out myself just now. It's all in this letter.'

She handed him the letter from his wife's lawyer, and tried to read his expression as he read it. But his face was blank. At last he gave a snort.

'So this is her latest trick. Does she think to fool me?'

'It's not a trick. She had a DNA test done and that proves it.'

'A DNA test? But surely they can't be done before the child is born? It's too dangerous.'

'That was true once. But recently new techniques have been developed, and it can be done safely while a baby is still in the womb.'

'But they'd have needed to compare the child's DNA with mine. I haven't given a sample so they can't have.'

'They got a sample from the other man in her life and compared it with that,' Ellie said. 'The result was positive. I'm afraid there's no doubt he's the father. You'll find it here.'

He took the paper she held out. Ellie tensed, waiting for the storm to break. This man couldn't tolerate being defied, and the discovery of his soon-to-be ex-wife's treachery would provoke an explosion of temper.

But nothing happened. A terrible stillness had descended on him as he stared at the message that meant devastation to all his hopes. The colour drained from his face, leaving it with a greyish pallor that might have belonged to a dead man.

At last he spoke in a toneless voice. 'Can I believe the test?'

'I know the lab that did it,' she said. 'They are completely reliable. I'm afraid it's true.'

Suddenly he turned away and slammed his fist down on the desk.

'Fool!' he raged. *'Fool!'*

Her temper rose. 'So you think I'm a fool for telling you what you don't want to know?'

'Not you,' he snapped. '*Me!* To be taken in by that woman and her cheap tricks—I must be the biggest fool in creation.'

Her anger faded. His self-blame took her by surprise.

His back was still turned to her, but the angle of the window caught his face. It was only a faint reflection, but she managed to see that he had closed his eyes.

He was more easily hurt than she'd suspected. And his way of coping was to retreat deep inside himself.

But perhaps a little sympathy could still reach him. Gently she touched his arm.

'I know this is hard for you,' she began.

'Nothing I can't cope with,' he said firmly, drawing

away from her. 'It's time I was going. You know where I'm staying?'

'Yes.' She named the hotel.

'Send my bill there and I'll go as soon as it's paid. Sorry to have troubled you.'

He gave her a brief nod and departed, leaving her feeling snubbed. One brief expression of sympathy had been enough to make him flee her. But then, she reflected, he hadn't become a successful businessman by allowing people to get close. For his wife he'd made an exception, and it had been a shattering mistake.

Ellie got back to work, setting out his bill then working out a response to the lawyer's letter. It took her a few minutes to write a conventional reply, but when she read it through she couldn't be satisfied. Something told her that Signor Fellani would dislike the restrained wording.

Yet is there any way to phrase this that wouldn't annoy him? she wondered. *He seems to spend his whole life on the verge of a furious temper. Still, I suppose I can hardly blame him now.*

She rephrased the letter and considered it critically.

I should have done this while he was here, she mused. *Then I could have got his agreement to it. Perhaps I'd better go and see him now, and get this settled.*

She went to find Rita.

'I have to leave. I need to talk to Signor Fellani again. My goodness! Look at the weather.'

'Snowing fit to bust,' Rita agreed, glancing out of the window. 'I don't envy you driving in that.'

'Nor do I. But it has to be done.'

She hurried outside to where her car was parked, and turned onto the route that led to the hotel. It was about a mile away, and the last hundred yards took her along the River Thames. Driving slowly because of the snow, she glanced at the pavement, and tensed at what she saw.

He was there by the wall, staring out over the river. A pause in the traffic gave her time to study him as he stood, wrapped in some private world, oblivious to his surroundings, unaware of the snow engulfing him.

She found a space to park, then hurried across the road to Leonizio.

'Signore!' she called. 'I was on my way to your hotel. It's lucky I happened to notice you here.'

He regarded her, and she had a strange sensation that he didn't recognise her through the snow.

'It's me,' she said. 'Your lawyer. We have business to discuss. My car's waiting over there.'

'Then we'd better go before you catch your death of cold.'

'Or you catch yours,' she retorted. 'You're soaking.'

'Don't bother about me. Let's go.'

She led him across the road to where two cars were parked, one shabby, one new and clearly expensive. He headed for the shabby one.

'Not that one,' Ellie called, opening the door of the luxury vehicle. 'Over here.'

'This?' he demanded in disbelief. 'This is yours?'

Obviously he felt that the decrepit little wreck was more her style, she thought, trying not to be offended.

'I like to own a nice car,' she said coolly. 'Get in.'

He did so, and sat in silence while she took the wheel and drove to the hotel. As she pulled into the car park he said, 'You're shivering. You got wet.'

'I'll be all right when I get home. But first I must come in and show you the letter I wrote to your wife's lawyer.'

The Handrin Hotel was famed for its luxury, and as she entered it she could understand why. The man who could afford to stay here was hugely successful.

They took the elevator up to his opulent suite on the top

floor. Now she could see him more clearly and was even more dismayed by his condition.

'I'm not the only one who's wet,' she said. 'You were standing too long in that snow. Your hair's soaking. Better dry it at once, and change your clothes.'

'Giving me orders?' he asked wryly.

'Protecting your interests, which is what I'm employed to do. Now get going.'

He vanished, reappearing ten minutes later in dry clothes. He handed her a towel and with relief she undid her hair, letting it fall about her shoulders so that she could dry it. When he joined her on the sofa she handed him the bill, and the letter she planned to write to his wife's lawyer.

'I suppose I'll have to agree to it,' he said at last. 'It doesn't say what I really think, but it might be better not to say that too frankly.'

'You'd really like to commit murder, wouldn't you?' she said.

He regarded her with wry appreciation.

'A woman who understands me. You're perfectly right, but don't worry. I'm not going to do anything stupid. You won't have to defend me in court.'

His grin contained a rare glimpse of real humour which she gladly returned, enjoying the sensation of suddenly connecting with him in both thoughts and feelings.

'I'm glad,' she said. 'I'm not sure I'd be up to that task.'

'Oh, I think you'd be up to anything you set your mind to. Can I offer you a drink?'

Ellie knew she should refuse; she should get this meeting over and done with as quickly as possible. But she still had to get his agreement to send the letter. And she was freezing. A hot drink would be very welcome.

'I'd love a cup of tea, please.'

He called Room Service and placed an order. While

they waited she watched while he read through the papers again.

'How do you feel about the answer I planned to send to your wife's lawyer?' she said.

'It's a damned sight too polite. But you haven't sent it yet?'

'No. I thought we should talk first.'

'And what are you going to advise me to do?'

'Go ahead with the divorce as quickly as possible.'

'So that she can marry the father and make the child legitimate? Her lawyer said that in his letter, didn't he? And he told you to persuade me to 'see sense'.

'I wish he hadn't said that—'

'But that's how lawyers think,' he said bitterly. 'Let my treacherous wife have her way, no matter what it does to me. That's seeing sense, isn't it?'

'Don't be unfair. I don't see everything like that.'

'I think you do. After all, you're a lawyer.'

'Yours, not hers. If things were different we could try to make *her* see sense, but she's pregnant by another man and there's nothing to be done about it. The best advice I can offer you is to put her into the past and move on with your life.'

Before he could answer, the doorbell rang and he went to collect the delivery of tea and cakes. He laid the tray on a table near the sofa, sat down beside her and poured tea for her.

'Thank you,' she said. 'I needed this.'

She sipped the hot tea, feeling better at once.

'How come you were standing by the river?' she asked. 'Did the taxi drop you there?'

'I didn't take a taxi. I walked all the way. And don't say it.'

'Say what?'

'*In this weather? Are you mad?* That's what you're thinking. It's written all over your face.'

'Then I don't need to say it. But you've had a terrible shock. You were bound to go a bit crazy.'

'Like I said before, I was a fool.'

'Don't blame yourself,' she said gently. 'You loved her—'

'Which makes me an even bigger fool,' he growled.

'Perhaps. But it's easy to believe someone if your heart longs to trust them.'

He looked at her with sudden curiosity. 'You talk as though you really know.'

She shrugged. 'I've had my share of relationship traumas.'

'Tell me,' he said quietly.

Her disastrous emotional life wasn't something she usually talked about, but with this man everything was different. The blow that had struck him down meant that he would understand her as nobody else understood. It was strange to realise that, but everything in the world was becoming different.

'Romance hasn't been a large part of my life,' she said.

'I guess your career comes first. Your car tells me that.'

It was true. The purchase of the glamorous vehicle had been one of her most delightful experiences.

'But there has been something, hasn't there?' he said. 'The path I'm treading is one you've travelled yourself.'

'Yes. There was a time when I thought things were going to be different. I allowed myself to have feelings for him and I thought he—well, it just didn't work out.'

'Didn't he love you?'

'I thought so. We seemed good together, but then he met this other woman—she was a great beauty. Long blonde hair, voluptuous figure—I didn't stand a chance.'

'And that was all he cared about? Looks?'

'So it seemed. Isn't that what all men care about?'

'Some. Not all.' He gave a brief cynical laugh. 'Some of us can see beyond looks to the person beneath: cold and self-centred or warm and kindly. Didn't this man see your warmer side? I can see it.'

'He didn't think it mattered, unless he could make use of it.'

She made a wry face. 'You said I'd travelled this road before you, and you were right. I don't normally talk about it, but at least now you know that this isn't just a lawyer "seeing sense". I really do have some idea of what you're going through. I know what it's like to be lied to, and to wonder afterwards how I could have been so naïve as not to see through it. But if you don't want to see through it—' She sighed.

'Yes,' he said heavily. 'If you don't want to face the truth, there's a great temptation to ignore it. You have to beware of that in business, and I suppose it's true of life as well.'

It was the last thing she had expected him to admit, but something about him had changed. He was speaking with a self-awareness that made him seem more pleasant. It was almost like talking to a different man, a kindly one who felt for her own pain as well as his own.

'I know this is all very hard for you,' she said.

He shrugged. 'I'll get through it.' But suddenly his voice changed, became weary. 'Oh, hell, who am I kidding? Can I call this managing? What she's done has destroyed the world. I wanted to be a father, to have someone who was really mine. My parents died when I was a child. I was adopted by an uncle and aunt who treated me properly but—well, we were never really close. I believed my wife and I were close, but that proved to be an illusion.

'Now I realise she was already sleeping with another man, but I never thought of it. Then, suddenly she was gone, demanding a divorce on the grounds that we were incompatible. I found out afterwards that she'd set spies on me to see if I had other women. But I hadn't. I'd been boringly faithful, which must really have disappointed her.'

'It certainly weakened her case,' Ellie agreed.

He gave a grunt of mirthless laughter.

'And she dumps this news on me on Valentine's Day. She could hardly have timed it more cynically.'

'Do you celebrate Valentine's Day in Italy?'

'A little. Not as much as you do in England, but enough to make me see the irony. The great day for lovers, except that it's smothered in snow, both physically and—well, there's more than one kind of snow.'

'Yes, it couldn't have worked out worse, could it?' she said sadly. 'I don't suppose she thought of that—'

'Of course not. She never thinks of anything except what suits her. But her pregnancy made it all different. The world changed. For the first time ever there was somebody who would be mine, connected to me in a way that nothing and nobody could deny. I told her that I couldn't let her go. She made a dash for it and came to England because she must have thought divorce would be easier, since we married over here.

'I followed her, determined to keep her, and if not her then at least my child. But now I learn that the baby's not even mine—'

'And I'm afraid it isn't,' Ellie murmured.

A tremor went through him. 'Then I have nothing.'

The way he said 'nothing' made her want to reach out to him.

'You think that now,' she said gently, 'but you'll come through it. There's always something else in life.'

'Only if you want something else. What I want is my child. Mine and only mine.'

He spoke like a man used to bending the world to his

will. But there was a blank despair in his face, as though even he knew that he couldn't control this situation.

She guessed that such helplessness was alien to him, and he was finding it frustrating. He was used to giving orders, demanding total subservience, which was why this left him at a loss. Ironically, the strength he was used to wielding had undermined him now. She felt a surge of pity for him.

'There are other things to care about,' she urged. 'You'll find them.'

But he shook his head. 'Nothing,' he said softly. 'Nothing.'

She gingerly placed a comforting hand on his shoulder. 'What will you do now?' she asked.

He sighed.

'Accept reality in a way I've never had to before.' He frowned. 'I'm good at arranging things the way I want, or at least persuading myself that I've done so.' He made a wry face. 'Meet the biggest self-deceiver in the world.'

'No, you're strong. And you'll be strong now.'

'Why are you so sure? You don't know me.'

'Do you know yourself?'

'I guess not,' he sighed. 'Oh, heavens!'

He dropped his head into his hands. Touched, Ellie drew him closer, enfolding him in both arms, her instinct to offer comfort to him overwhelming. He raised his head so that their eyes met, hers gentle and tender, his full of confusion and despair.

'That must be how it seems now,' she said gently. 'But your life isn't over. You'll meet someone who'll love you and give you a child. And the two of you will be united in that child for ever.'

'You make it sound so easy,' he whispered.

'When the time comes it will be easy,' she promised.

'For other men perhaps. Not for me. I said I didn't know

myself, but I do know a few things. I know I can come across as overbearing, so that even if I like a woman she recoils from me.'

His words caused a pain in her heart. Driven by an impulse she barely understood, she took his face in her hands.

'I'm not afraid of you,' she said softly. 'Life is treating you cruelly, not the other way around.'

'How do I stand up to life and fight it back? And if I win, how will I know?'

'You might never know. Sometimes the fight goes on for ever. But you don't give in. There's always something to fight for.'

A new look came into his eyes and he leaned forward until his mouth almost met hers.

'Yes, there's always something to fight for,' he whispered.

The soft touch of his lips sent a tremor through her, then another, with such power and intensity that she had no choice but to return the caress. And then again, responding helplessly to the sweet excitement of the feeling.

'Ellie,' he murmured.

'Yes—yes—'

She could not have explained what she was saying 'yes' to. She only knew that the desire to continue doing this had taken possession of her.

She felt his arms going around her tentatively, as though leaving the next move up to her. She returned the embrace, moving her mouth softly against his.

'Yes,' she repeated. 'Yes.'

Then his arms became stronger, his embrace more desperate, and she felt herself drawn into a new world.

CHAPTER TWO

THE FLIGHT FROM London to Rome took two and a half hours. Ellie spent the time gazing out of the window, trying to escape the thoughts that haunted her. But in her heart she knew there was no escape.

She had thought of herself as sensible, controlled and disciplined. These were the characteristics that had enabled her to keep command of her life. Years of watching the aching unhappiness that had destroyed her parents' marriage had made her overcautious. Feelings were dangerous things to be kept to herself.

Yet Leonizio had destroyed her caution without even knowing he was doing it. He was a hard man, protected from the world. That was how she saw him, how he preferred to be seen. But suddenly there had been a crack in his armour, giving her a glimpse of the pain concealed within.

Even more surprising had been the sympathy he'd shown for her own troubles. It was the last thing she'd expected from him, and it had softened her heart, making her reach out to him even more intensely.

The result had been devastating. She had meant only to offer him comfort. Yet the touch of his lips had sent desire and emotion blazing through her, destroying common sense, destroying caution, destroying everything but the need to travel this road to the end.

Night after night the memories returned as she lay alone. The sudden cool air on her skin as he'd stripped away her clothes and laid his lips against her breasts; the fierce yearning for him to touch her more—then more—and more. Finally the great moment when he had taken her completely, and everything in her had rejoiced.

It was something she would never forget: the fierce pleasure, unlike anything she had ever known before, the blazing satisfaction as they both climaxed. The feeling of empty desolation as they'd parted, each avoiding the other's eyes.

When her mind cleared she was shocked at herself for having given in to her feelings without caution. But how could she have thought about it in advance when it had sprung on her out of nowhere, like a storm from a calamitous sky?

And if I'd seen it coming I wouldn't have let it happen, she mused. *Would that have been better?*

She found that a hard question to answer. Would it really have been better not to discover the fierce pleasure of his lovemaking?

And could she have turned away from Leonizio when everything in her had flamed with need of him?

When it was over there had been the dizzying sensation of seeing her own reflection, her locks cascading about her shoulders. It was like meeting another person and trying to believe that it was herself.

Silently she'd addressed the woman in the mirror.

I guess you're my other self. A different me, and yet the same me. I've never met you before, and I'm not sure I want you to hang around. You've already got me into trouble.

To make certain of it, she pulled her hair back again, fixing it tightly as before.

Now stay away, she told her other self, now fading into the mists.

If Leonizio noticed that she had changed selves he didn't mention it. He'd paid his bill and they bade each other a polite farewell.

He'd soon returned to Italy and after that they had communicated only formally. He had abandoned his claim on his wife's child and the divorce was moving to a speedy conclusion. That was the end, she told herself. Leonizio no longer needed her professional services and each could forget that the other existed,

Eight weeks had passed since she'd last seen him. She'd spent the intervening time telling herself that it had been a fantasy. Nothing had really happened.

But, with shattering impact, she had discovered that she was wrong. She'd been reckless to sleep with him, but they had used protection. Only it must have failed. It had to have failed. She was carrying his child.

To make her troubles worse, she desperately needed someone with whom she could share the news. But she was alone. Both her parents had died several years before, and there were no other family members that she was close enough to confide in.

Suddenly her life had become a desert. She was thirty-eight, and pregnant by a man four years younger than herself. Who else could she tell but her baby's father? However hard it would be to manage, they must have one more meeting so that she could reveal the news that changed the world.

By good luck some papers arrived that required his signature.

'Best not entrust these to the post,' she'd said to Dallon. 'I'll hand deliver them.'

'There's no need for you to go all the way to Italy to be

a messenger,' he'd protested. 'There's a firm I can use to deliver this stuff.'

'I think it would help if I was with him when he signs, in case he raises any problems.'

'Fair enough.' He'd given her a friendly grin. 'You weren't planning on doing some sightseeing in Rome as well?'

'Well, it's my grandmother's city and I've always longed to see it.'

'Ah, I see. Get a sneaky holiday under the guise of duty. Very clever.'

He'd winked kindly. 'All right, I'll fall for it. You're due for a break.'

She'd smiled and let the matter go. Anything was better than having him suspect her real reason for going to Rome.

She'd emailed Leonizio that she would bring the papers and set off at once, without waiting for his reply. There was a flight due to leave that same day.

She landed in Rome in the evening, too late to go to his office, so she made for the Piazza Navona.

It was among the most prosperous places in the great city. Here, Leonizio's business centre was located, with his apartment two streets away. Checking into a nearby hotel, Ellie asked herself for the hundredth time whether she was doing the right thing in coming here. But these days most of her own actions confused her.

I was mad to come, she mused. *I should have sent someone else. I was also mad to go into his arms, but it all happened so fast I couldn't think. I have to see him. I have to tell him everything myself.*

Briefly, she considered letting her hair hang loose, but all her defensive instincts rose against it for fear that he would get the wrong idea.

'I don't want him thinking that other me is still around. He must have no doubt who he's dealing with now.'

From their correspondence she knew his private address. As the light faded she slipped out of the hotel and made her way to the nearby street where he lived. There was an elegant block of apartments, with lights in almost every window. She looked up, wondering if she might see him.

Several minutes passed while she tried to pluck up the courage to ring the bell. But she couldn't manage it, and had almost decided to retreat when the sight of him at a window made her draw in a sharp breath. He pushed it open, leaning out, while she stood, tense and undecided. She was just beginning to back into the shadows when he looked down.

His face was in shadow but there was no mistaking the shock that pervaded his whole body.

'Ellie? *Ellie?*'

'Yes, it's me,' she called back.

'Wait there.'

He was with her in a moment, ushering her inside and towards the elevator, which took them up to the second floor. Once they were inside his apartment she walked ahead a few steps, then turned and saw him standing by the door, regarding her curiously.

'I couldn't believe it was really you down there,' he said.

He approached and put his hands on her shoulders.

'Let me look at you,' he said. 'It *is* you, isn't it?'

'Can you doubt it?'

'Maybe. You look like a woman I once knew—just for a short time.'

A very short time, she thought. *And we didn't know each other, except in one particular sense.*

Aloud, she said, 'Nobody stays the same for ever.'

'That's true. So tell me, has the divorce hit a new problem at the last minute?'

'No, you have nothing to worry about. Harriet has

signed all the papers so far, and we've fixed a date for her to sign the rest. There are some more forms for you to sign, and then it will be pretty much over. I've brought a few of them with me.'

'Instead of just putting them in the mail? Thank you so much.'

'Things can get lost in the mail,' she said. She was prevaricating as the crucial moment neared, but she knew she must soon summon up her courage.

'Here they are,' she said, drawing out the papers.

He seized them eagerly. Watching his face, she saw it flooded with relief tinged by a hint of sadness.

'It's nearly over,' he murmured. 'I'll soon be free of her. But I'll also be free of the child who should have been mine, and that's a freedom I never wanted.'

'But soon you'll have the final documents, and then you can make a new life.'

'That's what I tell myself, but I keep thinking of that little boy. Even though he isn't born yet, I loved him so much. But the love must stop.'

'And now you think you have nobody to love,' she said gently.

'That's one way of putting it.'

'But it isn't true. I came to see you because—' She paused. Now that the moment had arrived she was suddenly nervous.

'I needed to see you,' she said slowly. 'There's something I have to tell you.' She took a deep breath. 'I'm pregnant.'

She wasn't sure what reaction she'd expected, but not the total silence that greeted her. At last he managed to speak in a voice so low that it was almost inaudible.

'What—did you say?'

'I'm pregnant. That night we were together—there was a consequence.'

He drew in a sharp breath. 'Are you telling me that—?'

'That I'm carrying your baby.'

'But we used protection. How can that be? You're sure? Quite certain?'

'I promise I'm not trying to trick you. You're the father. It has to be you because there's nobody else it could be. I don't know how but the condom must have become damaged. I swear I didn't plan this…'

'I wasn't accusing you of—I only meant—are you sure you're pregnant?'

'There's no doubt of it. I did a test. It was positive.'

Suddenly the tension drained from his face. Now there was only a blazing smile.

'Yes!' he cried. *'Yes!'*

He tightened his grip and drew her forward against him in a hug so fierce that she gasped.

'Sorry,' he said, loosening his clasp. 'I must be careful of you now.'

'It's all right,' she said. 'I'm not delicate.'

'Yes, you are. You're frail and vulnerable and I must do everything to look after you and our child.'

He led her to the sofa and nudged her gently until she sat down.

'How long have you been sure?' he asked.

'A couple of weeks.'

'And you waited this long to tell me?'

'I've been trying to get my head around it.'

'Is that all?' he asked quietly.

She felt she understood his true meaning and said, 'Look, I told you, you're the father. There are simply no other candidates. There's nobody else. You have to believe me.'

'I do believe you. You told me before that your relationships tended to be unsuccessful. It sounds like a lonely life.'

'Yes,' she said thoughtfully. 'It has been.'

'But not any more. When we're married you'll have me to care for you.'

'Wait!' She stopped him. 'Did you say "married"?'

'Of course. Why do you look so surprised? Did you think I wouldn't want to marry you?'

'To be honest, I never even considered it.'

'But you must have been thinking of the future when you came here to tell me. What did you expect would happen?'

'I thought you'd be pleased. You want a child. I can give you one.'

'And I can give you a lot—a good life with everything you want.'

'But I'd lose my career, which I enjoy. I'd lose my country. We barely know each other but you expect me to move into a new world with you—'

'And our child.'

'Our child will live with me in England. But I'll put your name on the birth certificate and you can see him or her whenever you like.'

It was sad to see how the eagerness drained from his face, replaced by something that might have been despair. He dropped his head into his hands, staying there for a long moment while she thought she saw a tremor go through him.

'It's too soon to make a decision,' he said at last.

Tact prevented her from pointing out that she'd already made her decision. Clearly he didn't regard it as final until it suited him.

'I'm going back to the hotel,' she said.

'I'll drive you.'

'No need. It's only a couple of streets away. Just a short walk.'

'But you must be careful about getting tired now. My car's just below.'

'Signor Fellani—'

'Don't you think you could call me Leonizio—under the circumstances?'

'Yes, I suppose so.'

'Let's go.'

He put his arm protectively around her. She gave in, letting him take her downstairs, into the car and back to the hotel, where he escorted her up to her room.

'I'll collect you tomorrow morning,' he said. 'We have a lot to talk about.' He grew tense suddenly. 'You will be here, won't you?'

'I've arranged to have several days off, so I don't have to dash back.'

'Fine. I'll collect you tomorrow morning.'

For a moment she thought he might kiss her, but something made him back off, bid her farewell with a nod and retreat down the corridor until he was out of sight. With any other man she would have felt that he'd fled for safety, but with Leonizio that was impossible.

Wasn't it?

After the traumatic events of the day it was good to be alone. She needed to think. Or perhaps just to feel. She went to bed early, hoping to sleep at once, but sleep wouldn't come.

She had a strange feeling of being transported back to the past, when she had been a child, watching the misery of her parents' life together. They had married only because Janet, her mother, was pregnant. Ellie recalled an atmosphere of hostility between two people who didn't belong together, even with a shared child.

'I should have known it could never work,' Janet had once told her bitterly. 'But our families were thrilled at the thought of a grandchild, and determined to make sure of it. So they pressured us into marriage.'

'Didn't you love Dad?' Ellie had once asked. 'I thought that sometimes there seemed to be love—'

'Oh, yes, sometimes. He was a handsome man and all the girls were wild for him. They envied me being his wife, but he only married me because he was backed into a corner. After a while I started to have feelings for him, and I thought I could make him return them. But it didn't work. Why should he bother to court me when he already had me there to do his bidding? You have to keep a man wanting, and if you can't do that he'll take advantage of it.'

Thinking back now, Ellie remembered that the only happiness had come from her grandmother, Lelia, who was Italian. She had married an Englishman, given up her country to live with him in England, and been left stranded by his death. When her son, Ellie's father, married she'd moved in with him and his wife.

Ellie had been close to her grandmother. Lelia had enjoyed nothing better than regaling her with tales of Italy, and teaching her some of the language. It had been a severe loss when she died.

Without her kindly presence Ellie's parents had grown more hostile to each other, until their inevitable divorce.

'Will you be all right on your own?' Ellie had ventured to ask her mother.

'I won't be on my own. I've got you.'

'But—you know what I mean.'

'You mean without a husband? I'll actually be better off without him. Better no man at all than the wrong man. Better no relationship than a bad one.'

Life was hard. Her father paid them as little as he could get away with, and Janet took a job with low wages. Determined to have a successful career, Ellie had buried herself in schoolwork, coming top of the class. In this she was encouraged by her mother, who told her time and again that independence was the surest road to freedom.

'Have your own career, your own life,' she'd urged. 'Never be completely dependent on a man.'

Ellie had heeded the lesson, took a law degree at university and qualified as a solicitor with flying colours. Alex Dallon was eager to employ her. She was a success.

The firm specialised in divorce cases. In the years she had worked there she'd witnessed every kind of break-up for every kind of reason. She'd soon realised that wretchedly unhappy marriages were more common than she'd thought. Men and women swore eternal love and fidelity, then turned on each other in a miasma of hate and mistrust. She wondered if love was ever successful.

Her own experiences gave her no cause for comfort. There were men attracted by her wit and her lively personality. But the attraction soon died when they were faced with an intelligence often sharper than their own, and an efficiency that tolerated no nonsense.

Finally there had been the man she'd described to Leonizio, briefly interested in her but then leaving her for a woman of more conventional charms.

Besides, how could Leonizio want marriage after the disaster that was his last one? His divorce wasn't even through. He'd be mad to even entertain the idea of getting involved again so soon.

No, whatever the solution was for her situation with Leonizio, it certainly wasn't marriage. They were both adults. She felt sure that they could come up with a solution for sharing their child that would suit them both.

Reassured that her sensible side had returned, she turned over and drifted off to sleep.

Next morning she went downstairs to eat breakfast in the restaurant. Her table was by the window, looking out on the street. After a while she saw a familiar figure appear, heading for the hotel entrance. She hurried out into the lobby, waving to Leonizio, and he followed her back into the restaurant.

'Did you sleep well?' he asked as they sipped coffee.

'Not really. Too much to mull over. You?'

'Same with me. Have you done any more thinking about what we discussed yesterday?'

'We agreed to be good parents, friendly for our child's sake.'

'That isn't what I meant. I proposed marriage. You were going to consider it.'

'I gave you my answer last night.'

He didn't reply at once, seeming sunk in thought. At last he said, 'We're still virtually strangers. It can't work like that. At least let's spend some time getting to know each other. You might find I'm not the monster you think me.'

'Or I might find you're worse,' she said in a teasing voice.

'I'll just have to take that risk. I want you to stay with me. You'll find the spare room very comfortable. My housekeeper will take care of you.'

'But—I'm not sure. It might be better if I stayed in the hotel.'

'The more time we spend together the better it will be.'

'But I don't think—'

She stopped as she saw a young man approaching their table. He handed Leonizio a piece of paper, saying, *'Ecco la ricevuta, signore.'*

Ellie frowned, recognising just one word. *Ricevuta* meant receipt.

'Receipt?' she asked when the man had gone.

'I've paid your bill here. I called them last night and paid over the phone. There's no reason why the cost should fall on you.'

It sounded fine and generous, but something about it made her uneasy.

'Last night?' she queried. 'Why? My bill won't need to be paid until I check out.'

'Actually—you already have.'

'What? You mean you—?'

'I told them you would be leaving this morning.'

'Oh, really? And the little matter of consulting me slipped your mind. So this is your way of showing me that you're not a monster?'

'I just want you to stay with me. Ellie, you're important to me—both of you. I couldn't let you go.'

'You mean you couldn't let me do what I want if it conflicts with what you want.'

'It'll help us get to know each other really well so that we can plan out a future that's good for all of us. Isn't that what we both want?'

Ellie regarded him with her head on one side. 'So that's how you do it.'

'Do what?'

'Conduct your business. Nobody else stands a chance, do they? You get the better of the other guy by doing something outrageous that he can't fight. Then you put on an innocent look and say, "Isn't that what we both want?" And he gives in. Or so you hope. And that way you get everyone so scared of you that they can't fight back.'

'Are you scared of me, Ellie? Strange that I never noticed. You're not afraid of anyone.'

'True. And in my own way I too can be fearsome. I keep my worst side hidden until it leaps out and catches you unprepared. So be very careful.'

'I'll bear your warning in mind. As for persuading you to stay with me—I guess I used the wrong method. Perhaps I should try another way.'

'Such as what?'

'I could beg you.' He assumed a slightly theatrical air. 'Please, Ellie, do this for me. *Please.* Stay with me for the next couple of days, at least until we can agree on the best way to move forward with this situation.'

Ellie had to concede that he had a point. They did need to sort things out. And maybe a venue more private than a busy hotel was a better place to plan their future. 'I will stay with you, but only for a few days. And I won't be sharing your bed.'

He nodded, giving her an unexpectedly warm smile. 'Whatever you want, Ellie. I only want to make this work. When you're ready we'll go up and collect your things.'

'Let's go,' she said.

Be realistic, she told herself. *He changed tactics and got his own way again. And he thinks he always will. But he's got another think coming.*

Upstairs, she packed quickly, then let him carry her bags down to the car. A few minutes and they had reached his home. As they approached the front door, a window opened high above them and a young woman looked out, smiling and waving down to them. Leonizio waved back.

The front door was already open as they approached. The young woman stood there, smiling.

'Mamma indisposta,' she said. *'Non puo venire oggi.'*

Ellie just managed to understand this as, 'Mamma is unwell. She can't come today.'

'Better speak English,' Leonizio said. 'Ellie, this is Corina. Her mother is my housekeeper.'

'But today she has a bad headache,' Corina said. 'So I came instead. I must go now, or my husband will be cross.' She smiled at Ellie. 'But first I show you your room.'

The room was large and luxurious, dominated by a double bed.

'The *signore* left before I arrived,' Corina said, 'but he

left a note saying everything in this room was to be perfect for you.'

'How kind of him,' Ellie said politely.

So he'd left those instructions before she had agreed to come here, she thought. Just as he'd checked her out of the hotel without asking her. Those were his methods, and she would have to be always on her guard.

Corina helped her unpack, then went out to Leonizio, who paid her and showed her out.

'Let's have some coffee,' he said to Ellie.

He made good coffee, and they sat together in the kitchen.

'We can make our arrangements,' he said. 'You can tell me how you want things to be.'

'Is that meant to be a joke? How I want things? After the way you've controlled me today. You ordered the room to be fixed before I'd even agreed to come.' She gave a brief laugh. 'Suppose you hadn't been able to get me here? You'd have looked foolish in front of Corina.'

'It wouldn't have done my dignity any good,' he agreed. 'And you'd have enjoyed that. I'm going to have to beware of you.'

'As long as you realise that.'

Before he could reply the telephone rang. He answered it, spoke tersely in rapid-fire Italian and hung up.

'I've got to go to my office for a couple of hours. Why not come with me and let me show you around?'

'Thank you but there's no need. I won't escape. I promise.'

He made a wry face. 'I wasn't exactly thinking that—oh, hell, yes, I was.'

'I wonder what your employees would think if they saw how easily you get into a panic.'

'Only with you. You're the scariest person I know.'

'Then I'll just have to stick around for the pleasure of scaring you.'

He smiled suddenly, but his smile was quickly replaced by a frown. 'I have to be going. I'll be back as soon as I can.'

He departed quickly, leaving her to lean from the window, watching him until he vanished. She had a good view of the neighbourhood, with its expensive shops and elegant roads.

So many roads, she thought. And no way of seeing where they all led.

CHAPTER THREE

LEFT ALONE, ELLIE explored the luxurious apartment. Her own room was large with a double bed, extensive wardrobes and bulky drawers. Putting her things away, she couldn't help noticing how plain and dull they looked in these glamorous surroundings.

If I was in search of a rich husband I'd jump at his offer, she thought wryly. *But I'm looking for something else in a husband. Something Leonizio can't give me. Not that he'll ever understand that. He's got money and why should a wife ask for anything else? That's how he sees it.*

She switched on the television and sat watching a news channel, discovering that her understanding of Italian was better than she'd thought.

I could do with something to read, she mused after a couple of hours. *That looks like a newsagent just over the road. Let's see if they've got any English papers.*

Hurrying downstairs, she crossed the road to the shop, which turned out to be a delightful place, full of foreign publications. By the time she left she had an armful of papers.

But a shock awaited her when she arrived back at Leonizio's apartment. As she reached the front door she could hear him inside, shouting, 'Where are you? *Where are you?*'

There was something in his voice that hadn't been there

before. It was no longer the cry of a bully demanding obedience, but the misery of a man in despair. She thought she could guess the reason. Once before he had gone home to find his wife vanished, taking with her the unborn child on which he pinned his hopes. Now he was reliving that moment, fearing that he was deserted again, seeing his world collapse and everything he valued snatched from him.

'Where are you?' came the frantic cry again.

Unable to bear it any longer, she opened the door. At the same moment he strode out so quickly that he collided with her, forcing her to cling to him to avoid falling. He tightened his grip and they stood for a moment, locked in each other's arms.

'So there you are,' he snapped.

'Yes, I'm here.'

'Come in,' he said, still holding onto her as he led her inside. His arms about her were tight, as though he feared to release her.

He saw her onto the sofa, then stood back and regarded her uneasily.

'Did I hurt you?' he growled.

'Not at all. But there was no need for you to get worked up. I just slipped out for a moment to buy a few things over the road. I'm here now.'

He sat down beside her.

'You should have left a note saying where you'd gone.' He spoke calmly but his face was tense.

'Yes, perhaps I should have done that,' she said, 'but I knew I'd only be away for a couple of minutes, and I thought I'd be back here before you returned. I'm sorry. I really am.'

She spoke gently, regretting the distress she'd caused him. When he didn't answer she reached out to put a hand on his shoulder.

'Finding the place empty made you think I'd deserted you, taking your baby, as Harriet did.'

His shoulders sagged. 'You're right,' he said heavily.

'But I promised to stay, and I'll keep that promise. So stop worrying, Leonizio. It's not going to happen again. If you need to go out, just go. I'll always be here when you get back. Word of honour.'

He turned, looking her in the eyes as though he couldn't quite believe what he heard.

'Really? You mean that?'

'When I give a promise I keep it. You have to trust me, Leonizio.'

'I do trust you. Completely.'

'But you're still afraid I might betray you as she did.'

'No. You're not like her.'

'Then relax.'

He smiled and squeezed her hand.

'Actually, I need to go out again for a little while,' he said. 'Why don't you rest, and when I return I'll take you out for dinner? We can start to get to know each other.'

'That would be lovely, Leonizio,' she said.

He seemed to relax but she knew the pain and fear she had heard in his voice had been real. It was there in his heart, and she would always remember it.

'Go out,' she said. 'And stop worrying.'

'I'll try.'

He departed, giving her a brief glance before he left.

She was glad to be alone again that afternoon. Since her arrival in Rome, everything that had happened had disconcerted her. Leonizio's reaction had only underlined how little she knew him.

But something else disturbed her even more. It was the memory of their collision in the corridor, the way his arms had enfolded her. She knew he'd been protecting her from a fall, but the sensation of being held against his body had been shattering, recalling another time.

That night still lived in her heart, her mind and her senses. She, who had never before even considered a one-night stand, had gone willingly into this one, letting it tempt her as though it was the most natural and the most desirable thing in the world.

She had come to Rome because Leonizio had the right to know about his child, yet she was still determined to stay in control of herself and the situation. Perhaps it was going to be harder than she had thought, but she was strong. Whatever disagreements they might have, she would be the winner. On that she was determined.

She prepared for the evening ahead with a shower, followed by an inspection of her clothes. She had nothing glamorous, but a simple green dress gave her an air of quiet elegance.

She hesitated briefly over her hair, finally deciding to wear it pulled back, sending a silent message that tonight her controlled self was the one in command.

When she heard Leonizio's key in the lock she positioned herself so that he could see her as soon as he entered, and was rewarded by the look of relief that dawned in his eyes as soon as he saw her.

'Let's go,' he said.

His car was waiting below, with a smartly dressed chauffeur in attendance. He opened a rear door, bowing to Ellie.

'Take us to the Venere,' Leonizio told him.

Ellie gave him a quick startled glance.

'Is that the Venere Hotel, near the Colosseum?' she asked.

'Yes. It's got a fine restaurant. You know it?'

'I've heard of it,' she said.

Lelia, her Italian grandmother, had worked in the

Venere and had described it as one of the most luxurious places in Rome. It would be fascinating to see it now, Ellie thought.

She understood its reputation as soon as they arrived. The building looked as though it had once been a palace. Inside, a waiter greeted them and led them to a table by the window, from which she could see the Colosseum, the huge amphitheatre built nearly two thousand years ago.

'It's eerie,' she mused. 'Once people crowded there for the pleasure of seeing victims fed to the lions. Now the tourists go because it's beautiful and fascinating. And maybe we've all got somebody we'd like to see fed to the lions.'

'You wouldn't be aiming that at me, would you?' he queried.

'I'm not sure,' she said. 'I'll let you know when I've decided.'

'Well, I can't say I haven't been warned.'

'Right. I can be a real pain in the neck. You'll probably be glad to be rid of me.'

'Forget it. There's no way you'll escape.'

She gave him a teasing smile. 'Surely you don't want a woman who's a pestiferous nuisance?'

He returned the smile. 'I might. They can often be the most fun.'

He held out his hand and she shook it. 'As long as we understand each other,' she said.

'Perhaps we always did.'

'No, I don't think we ever did.'

While he was considering this a waiter approached with a menu, which he gave to Ellie.

'Need any help?' Leonizio asked.

'I can manage the Italian but I'll need you to explain the food to me. What's *Coda all Vaccinara?*'

'Stewed oxtail in tomato sauce,' Leonizio told her.

'It sounds nice. I'd like to have some.'

'May I suggest the Frascati wine to go with it, *signorina*?' the waiter said.

'No,' Leonizio said at once. 'Sparkling water for the lady. No alcohol.'

'And for you, *signore*?'

'I'll have the Frascati.'

When the waiter had retired, Leonizio said, 'I know you can't drink wine while you're pregnant.'

She didn't reply and after a moment he demanded, 'Why are you glaring at me?'

'I'm not.'

'Yes, you are. You'd like to thump me.'

'That's very perceptive of you. All right, the way you made that decision without consulting me makes me think a good thump might be satisfying.'

'You do me an injustice. I paid you the compliment of assuming that you would already have made the sensible decision. You're such an efficient, businesslike person that—'

'All right, all right. You can stop there. You always know what to say, don't you?'

He gave her a cheerful grin. 'Luckily for me, yes. With some combatants it's a useful skill.'

'Is that what we are? Combatants?'

'Not all the time. But it's something that's going to crop up now and then.'

'Now and then. I suppose that's true.'

'And while we can have an evening out like this, we can relax together and find a way to solve the problem.'

His tone was friendly, but a man working at a business arrangement might have spoken in just this way, she thought.

'How are you feeling now?' he asked.

'Fine. That rest did me good. Now I'm in the mood to enjoy myself.'

'You're all right after what I put you through?'

'You mean when you got so upset because I wasn't there? I'm sorry for the whole thing. It must have been terrible for you, feeling like you were reliving the past.'

He nodded. 'It was exactly the same. I came home one day and she'd gone. She didn't leave a note. I was left to wonder until an email arrived the next day.

'Yes. Coming back to an empty house is something I don't cope with very well.' He gave a brief self-mocking laugh. 'I remember telling you that we should discover things about each other. Well, that's something you've discovered. Perhaps you should take warning.'

'I've already had plenty to warn me, and there's nothing I can't cope with. Beware. This lioness has claws.'

'Well, I know that. They left a few scratches on me when we were together.'

She drew a sharp breath. His words brought back the memory of the time she had spent in his arms, overcome by a physical excitement she'd never known before. Bereft of all self-control, she had clutched him in a fever of desire that it shocked her to remember now.

'I'm sorry,' she said hastily. 'I didn't mean to hurt you.'

'Don't apologise. It was an accident. The world seemed to change that night, as though we'd become different people.'

'Yes, that's true. I no longer really know what to think about anything.'

'Is that why you refuse to marry me?'

'I haven't actually refused. I just can't take it for granted, the way you did. I don't like being given orders.'

'That's not what I did.'

'But it is. You just assumed I'd jump at the chance to marry you. How arrogant is that?'

She gave a brief laugh. 'I once looked up your name and found that Leonizio means 'lion-like'. That says it all about you. The lion rules the plains, and Leonizio thinks he can rule wherever he likes.'

Briefly she wondered if she was wise to risk offending him, but his smile contained only wry amusement.

'Except for the lioness,' he said. 'She could stand up to him better than anyone else.'

She nodded. 'As long as he understands that.'

'He understands completely. And he knows he'll have to be cleverer than usual to achieve victory.'

'But he doesn't really doubt that he'll be the winner, does he?'

'Tact prevents me answering that.' He raised his glass. 'Here's to victory—for both of us.'

She raised her own glass and they clinked.

'As long as we each understand what victory means,' he said. 'You know what it means to me but—' He paused.

'You just can't understand why I don't jump at the chance to marry you, can you?' she said.

'I'm not the conceited oaf that makes me sound. As a person I may not be likeable. I understand that.'

'Is that what your wife said?'

'She said plenty about me. None of it good, in the end.'

'In my experience, marriage ends badly. My parents divorced. You're about to be divorced. It's par for the course, it seems. Can you blame me for refusing you?'

'Yes, but don't forget that not all marriages need end that way. Ours would be different. We would be entering it with our eyes wide open. What do I have to offer to persuade you?'

'You don't understand. It's what I'd lose. My country, my career, my freedom, my independence. I'm not ready to rush into it.'

'Not even to benefit our child?'

'But does marriage always benefit the child?' she asked. 'My parents were married and the unhappiness filled the air. I need to know—this is going to sound crazy to you—but I need to know that we can be friends.'

'I don't think it's crazy at all. It makes sense.' He gave a contented nod. 'We've got a while to get to know each other, and hopefully like each other.'

'Yes,' she said eagerly. 'That's the luckiest thing that can happen to a child, that its parents can be best friends.'

'You think that's luckier than if the parents love each other?'

'It can be. Friendship doesn't have so many ups and downs, so many dramas and crises. I can remember coming home from school wondering if my parents were speaking to each other today. When I got the lead in the school play they each came to a different performance. It would have been lovely if they'd come together and we'd had an evening as a happy family, but—' she shrugged '—that's how it was.'

Suddenly they were surrounded by applause. A man had appeared, bearing a guitar. He bowed to the guests at the tables who were applauding his entrance, and began to sing. Ellie listened with pleasure as he made his way between the tables, coming close until she could see him clearly. Noticing that she was delighted, Leonizio signalled to the man. He approached them, carolling cheerfully, until Leonizio held out a generous tip. He bowed and departed. When he finished his performance she clapped eagerly.

'That was lovely,' she said. 'It's such a nice, cheeky song.'

'You understood it?' Leonizio asked, astonished. 'But he was singing in Roman dialect. I know you understand some Italian, but dialect?'

'My grandmother used to sing it to me when I was a little girl. She came from Rome; she was born and spent her early years in Trastevere and she told me so much about it that I longed to see it. I loved my grandmother so much. I used to call her Nonna when I knew that was what Italians called their grandmothers. Now I'm here I feel wonderfully close to her.'

'Tell me about her.'

'She's the reason I'd heard of the Venere. Years ago she worked here as a chambermaid.'

'Here? In this very building?'

'Yes. Then she met an Englishman who was a guest, and they fell in love. He took her back to England with him. They married and had a son, my father. Sadly, my grandfather didn't live very long. Nonna mostly brought up my father on her own. When he married my mother she lived with them, looking after me.

'So you're nearly as much Italian as English?'

'In some ways. My mother didn't really like my grandmother very much. She said Nonna was a bad influence on me. She was very cross one day when she found her playing me some music. It was opera and my mother said it was way above my head.'

'And was it?'

'No, I like opera because of its terrific tunes. That's all.'

'So if I want to take you to an opera that would be a mark in my favour?'

'It would be lovely.'

'You're so knowledgeable that I'm sure you know about the Caracalla Baths.'

'They were a kind of spa built by the Emperor Caracalla nearly two thousand years ago. There's very little left standing, but what's left is used as a theatre for open-air performances.'

'Right. They open every summer, but this year they're doing a special run in April. We'll get the programme and you can take your pick.'

'That's lovely. Oh, how I wish I had Nonna here now so that she could see me becoming her real granddaughter after all this time. She died many years ago, and I miss her so much.'

'You're going to enjoy Rome, I promise you.'

Of course he wanted her to enjoy Rome, because it would make it easier for him to persuade her to stay and marry him. A slightly cynical voice whispered this in her mind, but she refused to let it worry her. Leonizio was handsome and attentive and part of her simply wanted to relax and be with him.

A sudden loud noise announced the arrival of a crowd. The waiter dashed around, trying to find room for them all. Ellie closed her eyes, trying to shut out the commotion. These days she tired easily.

'Perhaps we should go,' Leonizio said wryly, looking at her. 'It's time you were getting some rest.'

'Giving me orders again?'

'Yes.' He said it with a smile that made the word humorous.

'In that case I'd better obey,' she chuckled.

A few minutes' drive brought them home. He saw her to her bedroom door.

'Is there anything I can do for you?'

'No, thank you. I have all I need.'

'Go to bed, then.'

For a moment he seemed on the verge of kissing her, but he only opened the door and indicated for her to go in.

'Goodnight,' he said softly. 'Sleep well.'

'And you.'

She slipped inside and closed the door.

Now she could go to bed and try to come to terms with everything that was happening to her. It was hard because so many things in her mind seemed to direct her two ways. Some were troublesome, others suggested the hope of happiness if only she could understand many ideas. Still trying to get clear, she faded into sleep.

Suddenly she found herself in a new place, one where there were no boundaries, no definite positions. Here there was only mist and sensation, leading her forward into an unknown world.

But she realised that it wasn't completely unknown. She had been here once before in another life, another universe, one that was still offering intriguing possibilities. She could feel again the sweetness that had tempted her, the touch so different from anything she had known.

But there was also the apprehension at the way she was losing control. Deep inside her a nervous voice was crying out.

'What am I doing? Do I dare do this? Am I just a little mad? Or am I turning into somebody else—somebody I don't know? I mustn't do this…not now—not this time—'

Even as she spoke, she gasped with the tremor of remembered sensation that possessed her.

Be strong, whispered the warning voice. *Stay in control. You lost control that time and you're paying for it. You know that.*

'Yes, I do. And I mustn't—*no*—*no*!'

Then everything changed. There was a pounding on her door. The next moment Leonizio was there, leaning over her, taking her in his arms.

'Ellie,' he said hoarsely. 'Ellie! Wake up!'

The sound of his voice startled her awake. Gradually her breathing slowed and the world came back into focus. She found that she was clinging to him.

'Wake up,' he said again.

'It's all right… I'm awake now.'

'You must have had a nightmare.'

Her mind and senses were spinning. 'A nightmare—yes—no—I'm not sure—'

'You sounded as though you were suffering something

terrible. I could hear you right out in the corridor, and I just had to come in and see if I could help.'

'Thank you but I'm all right. It was just a dream.'

The sight of this room was bringing reality back, but the dream was still there. It would always be there, she realised. As long as she lived.

His arms were around her and she could feel his hands stroking her hair, which flowed loose again. It was a sweet sensation and she yielded to the temptation to rest her head on his shoulder, enjoying the soft caresses.

But suddenly the pleasure stopped. He snatched back his hands and rose from the bed. He turned away to the door, but there he stopped, standing with his back to her. She waited for him to turn around but something seemed to be constraining him.

'What is it?' she asked. 'What's wrong?'

'When you were asleep you were crying out, *No—no.* Why was that?'

'I can't remember,' she said evasively.

'Tell me the truth, Ellie. That time we spent together—' a shudder went through him '—I've always thought you enjoyed it as much as I did.'

'I did. It was beautiful.'

'Yes, it was. I can remember when you were in my arms—feeling that I wanted you more than I've ever wanted any—' He paused, full of tension and self-doubt.

'I felt like that too,' she assured him.

He turned back and came closer, though still keeping a slight distance between them.

'But just now,' he said uneasily, 'I heard you crying, *No—no*!'

'I didn't say no that day. If I had you'd have stopped.' She reached up to take his hands, drawing him down to sit on the bed. 'You would have stopped,' she repeated gently. 'You're a good man. Much kinder than you like people to know. But *I* know.'

'I would never have done anything against your will, I swear it. But hearing you cry out tonight scared me—made me wonder—'

'Don't. There's no need to wonder. It was all lovely.'

'Truly? You embraced me of your own free will?'

'Absolutely. I wanted you. Couldn't you feel that?'

'Yes. At the time it felt so wonderful to be together.'

'At the time? But not afterwards?'

'Afterwards you seemed to turn against me. You couldn't get away from me fast enough.'

'That's not how I—' She sighed. 'I guess we misunderstood each other.'

'There's a lot about that day that I didn't understand, but things look different now. I wanted you then and now I want you for always.'

But did he want her, or only the child she carried? If only that thought would go away and leave her in peace.

'I guess we have lots to talk about,' she said. 'You speak of marriage but you know nothing about me except that I'm pregnant.'

'What else do I need to know?'

'I'm thirty-eight.'

'Why should that matter?'

'It makes me four years older than you, and it gives me a slightly greater chance of miscarrying. You might simply find yourself stuck with an older wife who can't give you a child. I could be very bad news for you.'

'Stop it, Ellie. Stop trying to put me off. I want you, and I want you to want me.'

'It's not that simple.'

'Then we'll make it simple.'

'How?'

'Like this,' he said, taking her into his arms.

The kiss he gave her wasn't passionate but gentle and comforting, filling her with happiness.

'We belong together,' he said. 'And one day you'll see that.'

'Perhaps,' she whispered.

'There's no perhaps about it. You're mine.' His words might sound demanding, but his tone was gentle.

'So I'm yours,' she said. 'That's an order, is it?'

He rose and went to the door, pausing to look back at her.

'It could be.' He smiled. 'But I guess I'll have to be patient.'

Then he departed, leaving her full of confusion.

She closed her eyes, trying to make sense of the crowd of impressions and memories that converged on her. But it was impossible. She needed more time to come to terms with Leonizio. The authoritative man she had known at first had seduced her by letting her glimpse his vulnerability.

The discovery that she was pregnant had brought his commandeering side back to the surface. But his other side had been there again in his plea to be reassured that he hadn't behaved badly.

He has good qualities, she mused. A woman who wasn't careful could even be tricked into falling in love with him.

But I'm going to be careful, she promised herself. *Oh, yes, I am.*

CHAPTER FOUR

NEXT MORNING LEONIZIO waited for Ellie to join him at breakfast, but time passed with no sign of her. At last he knocked on her door. When this produced no response he opened it quietly and went inside.

She lay still and silent in her bed, her luscious hair spread over the pillow. Her head was turned in his direction, enabling him to see her gentle, relaxed expression. Last night she had been wretchedly agitated by whatever she had dreamed, but now peace seemed to have come over her, as though she had slipped into a kinder world.

How long would she stay in that world? And was he the demon who would destroy her peace? He was reluctant to think so.

He left the room quietly and breakfasted alone, trying to come to terms with the different signals coming from every direction.

She was a woman to confuse any man. From the first moment of knowing her he'd felt at ease with her serious mind, her businesslike efficiency, so appropriate in a lawyer.

But that had changed in a few stunning hours. Her understanding of his pain over his lost child, the sympathy he had sensed in her, these had drawn from him a reaction that had surprised even himself. He was a man who allowed few people to see inside his mind, and even fewer inside his heart. Life was safer with defences in position.

But she had seen beyond the defences, reaching out to touch him in a place where he badly needed to be touched.

The instinct to draw her closer had overcome him without warning. His arms had tightened, and their lovemaking had been just what he'd longed for.

But afterwards she'd seemed reluctant to meet his gaze, and their parting had been inevitable.

Memories of their lovemaking were still vivid. She had brought him wonderful news, but somehow she seemed to be the lawyer again. Instinctively, he had assumed that she wanted marriage, but the cool way she'd discounted it had told him much that he didn't want to know. Already she had planned the future she wanted: a life in England, her career, his place in their child's life limited to occasional visits.

As they'd dined together her manner had been pleasant but behind it he sensed her laying down the law in a way that aroused his opposition. Years of wealth and success had accustomed him to women seeking his attention and goodwill. A woman who rejected all he had to offer despite carrying his child was a new, stunning discovery.

By the end of the evening he understood how fiercely determined she was to do things her way, and summoned in himself an equal determination not to let her get away with it.

She was right. They were combatants. He would do whatever he could to win her to his point of view, but he would always be wary of her.

But there was another surprise for him: her nightmare, the way she had clung to him, his stab of pleasure at comforting her. These had knocked him back, weakening his resolve. And the sight of her sleeping this morning had touched his heart, weakening him further.

He checked the clock. Her office would be opening about now, and it was time to get everything sorted. Ellie must marry him. On that he was determined. He picked up the phone and dialled the number of her office.

Ellie awoke to find the room already light. For a few moments she allowed herself to stretch out and relish her comfortable surroundings. At last she slipped out of bed and opened the bedroom door a crack, looking out into the corridor. On the far side was another open door, from behind which she could hear Leonizio's voice.

'I want no more delays. Get the divorce papers ready... Yes, I know it's not what I said before but I've considered the matter. Get it done, fast.'

There was the sound of a telephone being slammed down.

She closed the door and stood quietly considering what she had heard. Leonizio was intent on finalising his divorce quickly. Last night she'd told him he was close, but that wasn't enough for him. He wanted to be free to marry her and secure his child as soon as possible.

She showered, dressed and went out to meet him, expecting to find him in the grim mood suggested by his phone call. But he gave her a friendly smile.

'Did you sleep well? How do you feel this morning?'

'Fine, thank you.' She touched her stomach. 'We're both in good health.'

'Sit down while I get you some breakfast. Then we can make our plans. Today you're a tourist and I'm your guide.' He poured her coffee. 'That is, if you want to do that.'

'Oh, yes, I've always been fascinated by Rome. All that power—emperors who are famous even today. Tiberius, Caligula, Julius Caesar, Augustus, Nero, all conquering their neighbours.'

'Including your country,' Leonizio observed lightly.

'Right. You invaded Britain and ruled us for nearly four hundred years. But then we got rid of you and that was that.' She raised the coffee cup in comical salute. 'Here's to telling the Romans to push off.'

He raised his own cup. 'Here's to pushing off for a while but coming back later.'

'If we let you,' she teased.

'Yes, we'll have to see who wins that one.'

They shared a laugh and clinked cups.

'Your emperors didn't just go to war,' she mused. 'They used to murder each other. But actually—oh, thank you.'

She broke off as he set a dish before her.

'There's more right next to you,' he said. 'Yes, I think you'll enjoy the grandeur of Rome.'

She had been about to say that she was equally fascinated by another part of the city: Trastevere, the impoverished part where her grandmother had lived. But perhaps that could wait.

'Anywhere you want to start?' he asked.

'Yes, the Trevi Fountain. I've always thought it looked lovely.'

'We'll go as soon as you've finished breakfast,' Leonizio said.

When they were ready to leave, his driver was waiting. A few minutes brought them to the Trevi district, where a building almost as big as a palace rose up. In front of it was a huge pool into which water flowed, and standing just above the pool was the statue of Neptune, the Roman god of fresh water and the sea. Splendid, handsome and nearly naked, he seemed to symbolise power and authority.

Crowds had gathered around the edge of the water, including a few market stalls. One elderly woman, selling flowers, waved some of them hopefully. Leonizio purchased a small bouquet and gave it to Ellie, who received it with pleasure. It was lovely to be treated like this, even if she did know that his behaviour was calculated to win her over and gain his own way.

At the edge of the water she paused, reached into her bag for coins, and flung them into the air.

'Not like that,' Leonizio said. 'The proper way is to stand with your back to the fountain and toss the coin over your right shoulder.'

'But it might not go in properly.'

'Then you must toss another coin, to be sure. And perhaps a third.'

'Here we go.' She tossed three coins over her shoulder, but Leonizio shook his head.

'Not all together. One at a time. Do it again.'

'All right. One—two—three.'

From behind them came a cackle. Turning, Ellie saw the flower seller, convulsed with laughter.

'Never trust a man,' she said. 'He tells you to throw coins but he doesn't tell you the secret code.'

'What secret code?' Ellie asked.

'It's the legend of Trevi. One coin will bring you back to Rome. Two coins will make you fall in love with a Roman man. Three coins will make you marry him.' She cackled again. 'But perhaps you're already in love with him, and scheming to fix the wedding.'

'No such thing,' Ellie announced. 'I've never been in love in my life, and I hope I never will be. As for scheming to marry—not a chance.'

The old woman sent a crow of amusement up to the heavens.

'But he fooled you!' she cried.

A naughty imp seemed to take over Ellie's mind, making her say teasingly, 'He fools everybody. That's how he's got so many wives. They toss three coins and they all have to marry him.'

Cheers and laughter from the crowd. Leonizio regarded

her wryly, partly amused, partly disconcerted at having the joke turned back on him.

'I think we should go,' he said, drawing her away.

She let him lead her to a small café in a side street.

'Very clever,' he said when they were seated. 'But did you really have to make a fool of me?'

'What about the fool you made of me? Tricking me like that.'

'Well, I've got to get you to marry me somehow, haven't I?' he said cheerfully. 'And if I have to invoke Neptune's help—that's what I'll do.'

She laughed. 'That's your code of life, isn't it? Get your own way at all costs, no matter what you have to do.'

'Are you saying your code isn't the same?'

She considered a moment before admitting, 'Exactly the same. Of course, I don't have a lot of practice—'

'You astonish me.'

'But I'm learning from you.'

'Yes, you got your revenge today, didn't you?'

'I made sure of it. Besides, where's the harm in a bit of fun?'

'No harm at all, especially if you take the other guy by surprise.'

'And it did take you by surprise, didn't it? You're not used to people fighting back.'

'I'm getting used to it with you. You obviously relished every moment.'

'I do enjoy a laugh.'

'So you think our marriage is just a joke.'

'What marriage? We're not married and who knows if we ever will be? I think it's a joke that you thought you only had to snap your fingers and I'd jump to obey. And you didn't tell me about the danger of tossing three coins.'

'Seriously, do you think I really believe that mad legend?'

'I'm not sure what I really think. This city is so different to everywhere else that I could believe impossible things. Besides which—' she regarded him ironically '—some people have a gift for making things happen. You have to be wary of them.'

'You do me an injustice. If I had anything like the power you seem to think, you would already have my ring on your finger. But I have no power at all, which is why you can keep me dancing to your tune.'

'You?' she echoed, astonished. 'You, dancing to my tune? Never.'

'I want you, Ellie, but you act like that is a crime.'

No, she thought, laying her hand gently over her stomach. *It's not me you want. If you did, everything would be different.*

'Have you really decided against me so completely?' he said. 'What have I done that offends you? Or is it that?' He indicated her stomach. 'Was that unforgivable of me?'

'Don't be melodramatic. I just haven't decided and I don't like you trying to make my decisions for me.'

'No, you like to be the one telling me what to do. Does it occur to you how alike we are? That could make a very happy marriage.'

'What, with each of us giving orders?' she demanded. 'That's not a happy marriage, it's a recipe for disaster.'

'Is that what went wrong with your parents' marriage?'

'That was a big part of it. But they didn't have the best start. They only married because they were expecting me. It wasn't what either wanted but they went ahead with it to please their parents, and were miserable together for years as a result. So, believe me, I know that isn't a good reason.'

'But wasn't there any affection between them?'

'If there was it didn't last. The air was always sharp and hostile. They made their mistakes. I'm not about to repeat them.'

Ellie stopped suddenly, her skin paling visibly as she gasped and clutched her stomach.

'What is it?' he asked urgently.

'Nothing— I just feel a bit—ooh—'

'You're nauseous, aren't you? Keep still and take deep breaths. Does it happen often?'

'Too often. I hate it. I thought pregnancy sickness only happened in the mornings.'

'It can happen any time, and it's actually something to be glad of.'

'You're kidding me.'

'No, it means that you have a lot of pregnancy hormones, and that's good news. They nourish the baby until your placenta has grown big enough to take over the job.'

She stared. 'You sound like a doctor. Have you studied medicine?'

'No, I've just trodden this path before.'

Of course he had, with his wife. Ellie could have cursed herself for her momentary forgetfulness.

'Did Harriet have a lot of sickness?' she asked.

'Plenty. She really suffered. I went to the doctor with her because I wanted to understand what she was going through, so that I could help her with the pregnancy.' He gave a wry grunt. 'There's a laugh if ever there was one.'

'It means you were a kind, considerate husband. That's not at all funny.'

'It is if I was helping her care for another man's child,' he said with a touch of wry bitterness. 'That's the biggest laugh of all time. But enough of this. You're the one who matters now.'

You mean my baby is the one that matters, she mused silently. But she suppressed the thought. Leonizio's concern was pleasant, whatever his motives.

'Let's go home,' he said. 'You need to rest.'

Taking out his cell phone, he called his driver, to summon him. A few minutes later they were on the road.

'Deep breaths,' he reminded her. 'We'll be there soon.'

In a few minutes they had reached his home. He supported her into her room, easing her down onto the bed.

'What can I get you?'

'Just a little water,' she gasped.

She drank the water he brought her, then lay down and drifted into a contented sleep. Dreams seemed to come and go. Once she had the sensation of opening her eyes to find Leonizio looking down at her anxiously. But then the mist descended again, and he vanished.

When she finally awoke the sickness had gone and she felt much better. She rose and left the room, finding him in the kitchen, cooking.

'Better?' he asked.

'Everything's fine.'

'Then you need a good meal. It'll be ready in a moment.'

She guessed this was what he had done for Harriet, caring for her when she felt poorly, feeding her to ensure she recovered properly. But he'd acted out of love for his wife, which meant Harriet had been fortunate.

How could she have betrayed a man who so loved and protected her? Ellie wondered.

But she knew the answer. It was because she hadn't returned his love.

How could she not return it? How could any woman be indifferent to such adoration?

'Are you all right?' Leonizio's voice broke into her consciousness.

'I—what did you say?'

'You had a strange look on your face—as though you were lost in a lovely dream. Or perhaps a troublesome dream.'

'A little bit of both,' she murmured.

'Care to tell me?'

'It wouldn't interest you,' she said hastily. 'You're right about supper. I'm hungry.'

She would have said anything to get him off the subject.

'Let's eat.' He led her to the table.

The light meal was delicious. As she tucked in he handed her a newspaper.

'Look at this. It lists the opera performances at the Caracalla Baths. Take your choice.'

'Lovely.'

Eagerly she scanned the paper and found one of her favourite operas being shown the following evening.

'The Barber of Seville,' she said.

'Let's hope it isn't sold out.'

He took out his mobile phone, embarked on a short conversation and gave her the thumbs-up sign.

'We're in luck,' he said. 'I think we got the last two tickets going.'

'Lovely. I'm looking forward to this.'

'There is one thing. They were very expensive seats, so you'll have to dress up to the nines. Give it everything you've got. Your most luxurious dress, your best jewellery.'

'But I haven't got anything like that with me,' she said, alarmed. 'I just came out for a quick visit with casual clothes.'

'Then we'll have to get you something suitable. There's a shop just around the corner where they sell very nice dresses. We'll go there tomorrow.'

'How much do I owe you for my ticket?'

He gave her a wry, teasing look. 'Never ask me anything like that again. It insults me, and I take terrible revenge.'

'I'll just have to risk that. You can't pay for my ticket.'

'I can if I say so. Now, be quiet, finish eating and go to bed.'

She gave a comical salute. 'Yes, sir.'

He saw her into bed, pulled the duvet up over her and kissed her cheek.

'Goodnight,' he said.

'Goodnight.'

She was glad to be alone to brood over the day's events, and the confusion they inspired in her. They had the advantage of a shared sense of humour, which enabled them to fight their battles without bitterness. Thus far, things looked hopeful, if only she could keep her feelings under control. His feelings were for the baby, not herself, and the worst thing that could happen to her would be to fall in love with him. That was something she would never allow to happen.

Finally feeling safe and content, she fell asleep.

The next morning Leonizio took her to the shop, whose window featured a dress more luxurious than she had ever dreamed of wearing. It was made of deep red satin, tight-fitting to emphasise her perfect figure. She tried it on and was left breathless with delight at the sight of herself.

'Like it?' Leonizio asked in a casual tone that suggested no real interest.

'Yes, I love it. Will it make me look suitable?'

'Hmm.' He seemed to consider the matter. 'I guess it will.'

'Then I'll— *What?*'

The exclamation of horror was torn from her as she saw the price tag.

'Oh, I've been so stupid!' she cried. 'I should have checked that sooner. I can't afford that much.'

'You don't have to,' Leonizio said. 'I've already paid for it.'

'But—you can't have.'

Leonizio inclined his head towards a staff member standing nearby. The young woman held up her hand, revealing that it was full of notes.

'You've already paid?' Ellie said, aghast. 'But suppose I hadn't liked it?'

'Then you could have chosen something else.'

Except that he had already made his own choice, she thought. It looked like an act of generosity but actually she was being steered to do his bidding.

'Leonizio, I can't let you buy my clothes. We're not—'

'It's too soon to say what we are and what we're not. Just now you look perfect in that dress, and it's what you ought to wear.'

'Thank you,' she said in a voice that gave nothing away.

They were still playing a game, she thought. He was charming, yet she knew it was chiefly a way of overcoming her refusal.

But I can play as cunning a game as you, she thought. *Beware.*

When they returned to the apartment she donned the dress again, studying herself with satisfaction as she thought of the evening ahead. When it was time to leave, he came to find her.

'You look splendid,' he said. 'You'll do me credit.'

'And that's what matters, of course,' she said lightly.

'It matters more than you think. My business is well known in Rome, and so am I. I have a reputation to keep up.'

'And a woman who looked too ordinary would take you down a peg?'

'Exactly. I can't be seen with a lady who doesn't wear glamorous clothes and expensive jewels.'

'Then you'll have to ditch me. I have no expensive jewels.'

'Luckily, I anticipated that and took precautions.' He reached into his pocket. 'Turn around.'

She did so, and gasped as he came close behind her, raising his hands to fit a glittering diamond necklace about her neck. Ignorant as she was about jewellery, she could tell that it was worth a fortune.

'Whatever is that?' she asked breathlessly.

'My proof to the world that they needn't have doubts about me,' he said cheerfully.

She turned and saw him laughing in a way that made her heart leap.

'You're right,' she said. 'We'll flaunt it tonight and tomorrow you can take it back to the shop.'

'Hey, you're up to every trick,' he said admiringly.

'Sure I am. I could probably teach you a few.'

'Here's another one. We won't be taking this necklace back. Once I've given it you, it's yours.'

'But—'

'No buts. It's yours. My gift to you.'

'But I can't let you give me something like this.'

'Let me? Did I ask your permission?'

'You never ask my permission for any of your crazy ideas.'

'Certainly not,' he said cheerfully. 'You'd refuse, just for the pleasure of being difficult.'

'Of course. Because that's the kind of maddening woman I am.' She challenged him humorously, 'And you actually want to marry me? Are you out of your mind?'

'Probably. I've always enjoyed a challenge. And something tells me you're the biggest challenge I've ever faced. Now, stop arguing. Take the necklace and wear it for the sake of my reputation.'

She wasn't fooled. Behind his talk of reputation he'd performed a cunning manoeuvre to make her accept a luxurious gift. It was beautiful and generous. It was also a way of asserting ownership.

He stood beside her, facing the mirror.

'Will we look good together?' he asked.

Anyone would look good with such a handsome man, she thought. But she only shrugged and said lightly, 'I guess we'll pass.'

'That's all it takes. Let's go.'

CHAPTER FIVE

THE CARACALLA BATHS were unlike any other opera house in the world. The ruins of the original building provided the open-air stage, with sides marked by two vast columns. Facing it was a huge array of seats, climbing high.

'I can hardly get my head round this,' Ellie laughed as she looked around. 'Here we are to enjoy ourselves, but I looked up the Emperor Caracalla and apparently he was one of the most horrifying men who ever ruled Rome. He murdered his brother, murdered his wife and daughter, murdered anyone else who got in his way.'

'It's what emperors did two thousand years ago,' Leonizio said with a grin. 'But in the end someone murdered him.'

'Oh, that's all right then,' she chuckled. 'Fair's fair.'

She soon realised what Leonizio had meant about needing to maintain a reputation. Heads turned at the sight of him, and as he led her towards the seats nearest the stage they were greeted many times, sometimes eagerly, always respectfully. Leonizio introduced Ellie as 'a friend visiting from England'.

'Aha! Doing business in England now?' teased one man.

'But of course,' Ellie said. 'Why else would I be here?'

'It might be something to do with his weakness for a pretty face,' joked another man.

'No, no,' she assured him. 'Strictly business.'

Cheers and laughter. The murmur went around that Leonizio's latest 'friend' was shrewd and funny.

'You're a success,' Leonizio told her as he showed her to her seat. 'Strictly business, eh? Who knows?'

'Nobody. It's too soon to know.'

When everyone in the audience was settled the conductor appeared, bowed and raised his hands to conduct the overture and for the next couple of hours there was no need to talk as both Ellie and Leonizio were swept up with the drama and romance unfolding on stage—their own drama temporarily forgotten.

The performance came to a triumphant end. Smiling, the cast bowed, the audience rose and began to leave.

'Let's have a snack before we go,' he suggested.

She agreed and they headed to the theatre's bar.

'An interesting evening,' he said ironically. 'Even after watching that performance, are you still determined that you are against marriage?'

'I don't believe it's a guarantee of a happy ending.'

'True. If a couple are dazzled by unrealistic dreams they're asking for trouble. But if they're not—if their eyes are open and their thoughts realistic, they can be a success.'

'But what kind of success?'

'You said it yourself when you told my associate that we were strictly business.'

For a moment she was too taken aback to speak. Then she said, 'You think we could have a successful business relationship?'

'We each have something to offer. We arrange the terms, shake hands, and if we trust each other to keep our word it can be a successful arrangement.'

'And just what are the terms?'

'I want our child. You are carrying our baby. In return

I'll provide you with a life of comfort. Whatever you want will be yours.'

'Including your fidelity?'

'If you include that in the terms.'

She considered her answer for a moment before saying casually, 'I might include a certain level of affection in the terms. But I don't think you could manage that.'

'On the contrary. My gratitude for what you have given me would ensure my warmth of feeling.'

But that's not the kind of feeling I would want, she thought. *And no life of comfort would console me for the loss.*

But there was no way she could speak such thoughts to this cool, detached man.

Assuming her most businesslike tone, she said, 'Now let me declare my terms. You can take your proper place as the child's father. Your name will be on the birth certificate, you may visit us whenever you like and establish a relationship. I promise I'll never try to shut you out, but there will be no marriage and we will not live together.'

'Meaning that we'll live in separate countries,' he declared. 'What kind of an arrangement is that?'

'The only kind I will agree to.'

He leaned back and regarded her shrewdly.

'You're a very astute businesswoman. You know you've got the power on your side and you don't concede a single point.'

'But I've conceded a lot. You'll be a real father, part of our child's life.'

'At a distance. If only you knew how much I—' He checked himself and said quickly, 'Time we were going.'

'No, finish what you were saying. If I knew how much you—?'

'It's late. You're tired. Let's go.'

She understood. He'd been on the verge of revealing

the depth of his inner feelings, and he wasn't a man who did that easily. Now he wanted to escape her.

She was beginning to feel sleepy and it was pleasant to let him escort her home and to her door.

'Goodnight,' he said. 'Tomorrow we'll have another chance to talk.'

'Yes,' she murmured. 'There's still a lot to say. And we never know what may happen next.'

He placed his hands gently on her shoulders. 'Sleep well,' he said. 'And if you need anything, call me.'

He backed out, closing the door firmly. He felt a sudden need to be free of her, and the unsettling effect she could have on him.

There was a mysterious quality in Ellie that tempted him to venture into dangerous territory. He'd discovered that on the day they'd first got to know each other, when something about her had lured him out of his protective shell, to make love.

Since then there had been other moments when his defensiveness had faded, alerting him to danger. Tonight he'd hovered on the brink of telling her how much pain he suffered from the feeling of being excluded.

It had been something he'd known all his life, first with the family that reared him, then with the wife who had cheated on him. With the hope of a child he'd cherished a new dream: someone who belonged to him in a way that couldn't be denied. The disillusion had been an experience that made him think of hell.

He confided in nobody. That was weakness, and weakness was something he despised. But with Ellie he was tempted to yield and it alarmed him.

He stood for a while, gazing at the door that he had shut between them. Then he went back to the main room, opened the drinks cabinet and poured himself a large whisky.

* * *

He was up before her next morning, greeting her politely, making the coffee.

'You must tell me where you want to go today,' he said. 'The Colosseum, the Pantheon, more fountains?'

'It sounds wonderful. Rome is so beautiful, so grand and glorious…' Ellie paused.

'But it's not enough for you,' Leonizio ventured.

'No, if anything it's too much for me. I was hoping to see the other Rome—not the one where the emperors ruled, but where the poorer people lived.'

'Of course; you told me that your grandmother came from Trastevere. Is that where you want to see?'

'I'd love to. But I'm not sure that you'd enjoy it.'

'You mean I'd stick out like a sore thumb?'

'No, of course not.'

He gave a wry smile. 'I think you do. When your grandmother lived in Trastevere it was a much poorer district. But now the tourists have discovered it, it's not really poor. Just lively and colourful.'

'Yes, I remember her saying that was beginning to happen.'

'Let's go to the car and we can head there first.'

'Oh, no,' she said quickly. 'I'd like to walk. We're not that far away. Trastevere is just the other side of the river, and we can get there over a footbridge.'

'The Ponte Sisto,' Leonizio murmured.

'Yes, Nonna used to say it was the loveliest way to cross the river. And the bridge isn't far from here.'

He regarded her curiously. 'You've really studied Rome, haven't you?'

'One part of it, because that's the part I've always heard about. It felt like another home, and I always promised myself I'd come here one day. I promised Nonna too, and it makes me sad that she isn't with me.'

'We'll make a good day of it,' he assured her.

'Look,' she said uneasily, 'you really don't need to come. I've studied the route. I can find my way.'

'You think you can but you'd get lost and who knows what would happen to you? The fact is you're afraid I'll spoil it, just by being there. Don't worry. I know when to back off.'

She didn't try to argue further. He was right. She was afraid that his presence would spoil everything. How could this wealthy man, so used to luxury, ever appreciate the special pleasures of Trastevere?

But she understood that he wouldn't let her out of his sight, lest some harm come to the unborn child around whom his world now revolved.

A few minutes' walk brought them to the footbridge that would take them over the Tiber River. Walking across it slowly, Ellie was able to enjoy the sight of a great hill on one side and St Peter's Basilica on the other. But at last she saw something that drove everything else out of her mind. There ahead were the tightly woven cobbled streets of Trastevere.

Soon they had left the bridge and were walking through the streets. With cobblestones underfoot and laundry hanging overhead, it was so different from the neighbourhood they had left that it might have been a new world.

Ellie walked slowly, stopping to look inside a shop or glance upwards at the flowers that seemed to decorate every balcony. Leonizio waited for her patiently, content to let her take her pleasure in her own way. He thought wryly of other women he had entertained in Rome, flaunting the glamorous city to impress them.

But Ellie was different. He had the strange sensation that very little impressed her.

Suddenly she paused, alerted by something she had seen attached to a wall.

'What is it?' Leonizio asked.

'There—just there. The name—I can barely read it—'

He leaned close and read the name of the street.

'That's it?' she gasped. 'That's really it?'

'Yes. Does it mean something?'

'It's where Nonna used to live.'

'In one of these tiny little houses?'

'Yes. And the café must be at the end of the street. Oh, I do hope it's still there.'

'What's its name?'

'I don't know. But it was something to do with clowns.'

'Let's go.'

He took her hand and led her until they came to a place where the narrow road expanded into a square, full of shops and cafés. Although it was still before noon the place was full of life. The shops were open, the cafés had tables out on the pavements. Music and laughter floated through the air.

'Oh, it's lovely,' Ellie breathed. 'But can you see any clowns?'

'I think so,' Leonizio said. 'Over there.' He pointed to a café on the corner with a notice that read, 'Casa dei Pagliacci'.

'Is your Italian good enough for that?'

'Oh, yes!' she cried in delight. 'It means Home of the Clowns.'

He took her hand. 'Let's go.'

As soon as they entered she knew she was going to love this place. Clowns were everywhere. Pictures of them covered the walls, and the waiters were all colourfully dressed as clowns.

The place was crowded, with just one unoccupied table, which they approached quickly. A waiter danced up to them, showed them a menu and bounced away.

'It's like nowhere I've ever been before,' she breathed.

They were just enjoying a light lunch when suddenly there was the sound of cheering. A musician dressed as a clown appeared, bearing a guitar, and began to play. He was joined by another clown, who did a little dance and sang a cheeky ballad. The crowd applauded and he bowed theatrically, travelling around the tables, gesturing to everyone and accepting their gifts.

The first clown went on singing, bowing elaborately when the crowd applauded. Ellie clapped excitedly and the clown approached her, performing theatrically, evidently enjoying her contribution. When they had finished everyone applauded and the clown gazed at her.

'Do you know this song?' he asked.

'My grandmother used to sing it,' Ellie said. 'She came from here.'

'From here? From Trastevere?'

'She lived nearby and she knew this very café. She had friends here.'

'What was her name?'

'Lelia Basini.'

The clown stared in amazement. 'Lelia? You are Lelia's granddaughter? Oh, yes, you must be. Your face is so like hers.'

Now she could see him more closely, and realised that beneath the clown's make-up he was an old man.

'Sit down and talk to us,' Leonizio invited. 'What is your name?'

'I am called Marco. And it is a pleasure to meet Lelia's granddaughter. Is Lelia still alive?'

'Sadly no. It's a long time since she was here,' Ellie said. 'Did you really know her?'

'Oh, yes. I was a waiter here in those days. There were many young men who courted her, and she flirted with us all, but not seriously. She fell in love with another man and went to England. We had only the pictures she left us as memories.'

'Pictures?'

'We all had our photographs taken with her, so that we could keep and treasure them.'

'You have photographs of her?' Ellie breathed. 'Are any of them here? Can I see them?'

'I'll go and find out.'

He returned a few minutes later with a large folder that he laid on the table before Ellie.

'These pictures belong to my great friend, Paolo. He also knew your grandmother well,' he said. 'He doesn't keep them at home in case his wife finds them.'

'After so many years?' Leonizio queried.

'Yes, indeed,' Marco agreed. 'He was very much under Lelia's spell.'

'I can see why,' Leonizio observed.

The girl in the pictures was no beauty but she had a charm and personality that glowed even through the old black-and-white photographs. She laughed, she met the eyes of the men she was with. She was an enchantress.

'Do you recognise her?' Leonizio asked.

'I remember her as a lot older, but yes, it's the same face. And something about her smile never changed over the years.'

'And you are very like her,' Marco said. He addressed Leonizio. '*Signore*, you are a lucky man.'

'Believe me, I know it.'

'Was she happy in England?' Marco asked.

'Oh, yes, my grandparents were happily married.'

'I'm glad she was happy,' Marco said, adding theatrically, 'No man here was happy without her. Ah, but I must leave you.'

He made as if to gather up the pictures, but Ellie fended him off.

'Let me look at them a little longer,' she begged.

When he'd gone she went through the pictures again, entranced by this new view of Lelia.

'I don't believe this is happening,' she said in a daze.

'We were right to come here,' Leonizio said. 'You're a different person in these surroundings.'

'Different? How?'

'You're more relaxed, as though you felt at home here in a way you haven't before.'

'I hoped it would be a nice day,' she said happily, 'but I couldn't have hoped for anything like this. I have the strangest feeling that Nonna is here somewhere; like a ghost haunting me.'

'Not a ghost,' Leonizio said gently. 'She really is with you, here—' he touched her forehead '—and here.' He laid his hand over her breast. 'She's still in your mind and your heart, and I think she always will be.'

It was true, she realised. But what surprised her most was that Leonizio had been able to see it.

She realised that her knowledge of him was limited. His mind and his feelings went deeper than she had understood.

'Just a moment,' he said. 'I've thought of something.'

He rose and left her, heading for the door through which Marco had disappeared. Ellie barely noticed him go. She had found one picture that seemed to speak to her more than any other.

In it Lelia sat alone, smiling at the camera, her gaze full of a kind of cheeky charm that Ellie remembered well from her childhood.

'Oh, how I miss you,' she murmured. 'We understood each other. If only—'

She stopped as she saw Leonizio approaching her with Marco.

'He says you can have any of the pictures you like,' Leonizio said. 'Just take your pick.'

'You mean—?'

'Whatever you want,' Marco said.

Her heart leapt with happiness. 'Can I take this one?' she said, holding up the picture that had entranced her.

Marco nodded. 'You are welcome to keep it,' he said.

He backed away, but not before Ellie had noticed him reaching out to take something from Leonizio's hand. She couldn't see exactly what passed between them, but she reckoned she knew. Astonished, she looked up at Leonizio as Marco left them.

'Did you pay him?' she gasped.

'Just a little. I could see what those pictures meant to you. I thought you should have at least one.' He added wryly, 'Of course I did it without consulting you, which doubtless condemns me as a bully. You might want to take some revenge.'

'And how would I do that?' she said, smiling.

'It's up to you. I suppose you could thump me.'

'Mmm. I'm sure I could think of something more interesting. In the meantime, I'll just say thank you. It's a lovely thing to have.'

She gazed at the photograph, eyes shining with pleasure. Leonizio regarded her, fascinated. He thought of something else he'd given her, the luxurious diamond necklace. He'd offered costly gifts to women before and they had seized on them as the natural spoils from a rich man. But this woman cared nothing for expensive jewels. She had even tried to reject the diamonds. It was a memento of her grandmother that made her happy.

This was his chance to get closer to her, Leonizio realised. Ellie had let her guard down around him for the first time since arriving in Italy. When they got home they could talk more freely than before, and everything would be different. By the end of the day she might even have agreed to marry him.

'Perhaps we should go home now,' he said. 'You're looking tired.'

'Yes, let's go.'

'And this time we're taking a taxi. No arguments.'

'All right. Whatever you say.'

He grinned. 'Now you've got me really worried. When you speak in that submissive way I wonder what you're planning. I guess I'll have to wait and see.'

She chuckled but made no reply in words. He paid the bill, adding a substantial tip to reflect his pleasure in the way the lunch had turned out, and led her out.

In the taxi she leaned back, sighing with pleasure. 'That was lovely,' she said.

'Yes, wasn't it? But the day doesn't have to end now. We could go somewhere else this evening.'

'Actually, Leonizio, I'm rather worn out. If you don't mind, I would like to rest up this afternoon and evening. And I should really check in with the office. I'm sure that my work is really piling up back in London. But thank you for taking me there.'

Back at his apartment, she touched his arm gently and went into her room, leaving him standing there, reflecting on how wrong he'd been to think they could have an affectionate talk.

It was true, he thought wryly, that the day had aroused her warmer feelings.

But not for him.

CHAPTER SIX

THE NEXT MORNING Leonizio was already up, making the coffee. He greeted Ellie with a smile when she wandered into the kitchen.

'Did you have a good night?'

'A lovely night. I felt Nonna and I were back together, talking as we used to.'

'Did she say anything interesting?'

'Oh, yes. She's so wise. She helps me see everything differently. I want to remember seeing her street, the house she once lived in and going to that café. It was such a happy day. Did it seem that way to you? Or isn't Trastevere your kind of place?'

'What makes you think that? Why shouldn't it be?'

'Well, since you made your fortune don't you live a more high society life?'

'You think I'm too lofty? You couldn't be more wrong. Trastevere is very much my kind of place, and I know it well. My uncle owned a little shop there, and he made such a success of it that he managed to buy another shop. I used to earn pocket money being his messenger boy.' He grinned. 'And not just him. A lot of the other shops used me to run errands—for a price. Those were good times. I had a lot of friends there.

'In fact I still have friends who live there. Taking you

there yesterday made me realise how long it's been since I've seen some of them. In fact I quite fancy looking up some of my old friends.' A thought seemed to strike him. 'Do you fancy coming with me?'

'Oh, yes, I'd love to.'

'We'll go tonight then. Do you want to do some more exploring this afternoon?'

'I'd like to see the Pantheon.'

'That's where we'll go.'

After the Pantheon they took a stroll through the streets. Ellie found Rome so beautiful that just wandering about was a pleasure. Escorting her, Leonizio was alert for anything that might interest her.

'Over there you'll see— Ellie? Ellie—where are you?'

Looking around, he saw that he had completely lost her attention. She had moved away and was gazing ecstatically into a shop window at a collection of shoes.

'I've heard that Italian shoes are lovely,' she said. 'And these really are. Especially those.' She indicated a pair in the centre of the display. 'I'm going in to try them on. Hey, let me go.'

Leonizio had put his arm about her waist, holding her back.

'Don't move,' he said, smiling. 'You're not going in there.'

'Why? Is something wrong with those shoes?'

'No, the pair you're looking at are Fellani shoes.'

'Fellani? Yours? Really?'

'From our latest range. Come to the factory and see.'

She agreed, eager to see the factory, which she felt would tell her so much about him.

In half an hour they had reached a large building near the edge of the city. Looking at the windows, Ellie saw faces which lit up at the sight of him.

Inside, there were machines everywhere, making buzzing noises. A young man came to meet them.

'My assistant, Francesco,' Leonizio said.

He introduced them, explaining that Ellie was a lawyer, and a friend. On his instructions, Francesco fetched a collection of shoes, which Leonizio proceeded to fit on her feet. The ones she liked best were the ones she had seen in the shop, but they were too small.

'I'm afraid we don't have a larger size here at the moment,' Francesco said.

'Then we'll make a pair specially,' Leonizio said.

They proceeded to examine Ellie's feet.

'I hadn't expected this,' she said when Francesco had left them. 'How much do I owe you?'

'Owe me? You surely don't think I'm going to charge you? You're a special guest.'

'But the shoes look expensive and I sort of forced this on you,' she said, embarrassed.

'Do you really think you could force anything on me against my will?'

'Well, if you put it that way—I guess I couldn't. But I'm honoured. A pair made especially for me. Wow!'

'You're not just an ordinary customer.'

His voice was warm and she wondered if she'd only imagined that his glance fell on her stomach.

But of course, she thought. It was her pregnancy that made her special. He had never pretended otherwise. But still his care of her was heart-warming.

When it was settled that the shoes would be delivered next day they left to finish the journey to Trastevere.

As they went through the streets Ellie recognised some of the places they had passed the day before. Leonizio stopped outside a little shop.

'This was the first one my uncle owned,' he said. 'He made a success out of it but it took all his energy.'

The shop was tiny and narrow, selling everything at low prices.

'Did you ever work for him in here?' she asked.

'Yes, for hours. And I promised myself I'd escape and make a different life.'

'You certainly did that,' she laughed. 'Is there anyone who hasn't heard of the powerful Leonizio Fellani?'

He grinned. 'I hope not. Of course, some of them disapprove of me.'

'Naturally. If you've got the better of them they'll curse you, but that just means you're a success.'

'Ellie, you have the soul of a true businesswoman.'

'So I should hope,' she said cheerfully. 'Life's more fun that way.'

'Hey, Leonizio!'

The cry made Ellie look round at the man waving and making his way towards them.

'Ottimo per vedere di nuovo.'

Ellie just recognised the words as 'Great to see you again.' Leonizio greeted him, introduced her and said, 'Speak English for my friend. Ellie, this is Nico.'

'It is a pleasure to meet you,' Nico said, taking her hand. 'In fact it's always a pleasure to meet one of Leonizio's lovely ladies.'

'Be careful,' Leonizio warned.

'Don't worry,' Ellie said. 'I doubt he could tell me anything I haven't already worked out. And I am only your lawyer.' She faced him, smiling. 'Aren't I?'

Leonizio's face betrayed his confusion. 'Whatever you say.'

'Ah, then all is well!' Nico exclaimed in relief. 'Now let me take you for a coffee.'

'I don't think—' Leonizio began.

'That's a lovely idea,' Ellie said. 'I could just do with a coffee.'

As they left the shop Leonizio whispered in her ear, 'You're enjoying this, aren't you?'

'More than you'll ever imagine,' she agreed.

There was a small café next door. When they were settled, Nico ordered for them before saying, 'Hey, look who's over there!'

Another man was waving to them from the far side of the room. He too seemed familiar with Leonizio, signalling him to come over.

'Go and say hello,' Nico said. 'After all, you owe them.'

Leonizio glowered at him but went across to the couple, both of whom embraced him heartily.

'He owes them?' Ellie queried.

'Yes, but not money,' Nico chuckled. 'A favour. Something to do with a young lady. It was several years ago. In those days Leonizio was a *libertino*, a rather wild young man.'

'You mean wild where women are concerned?' Ellie queried. 'Libertine is an English word too.'

'Ah, yes. He often created trouble for himself, and they gave him an alibi for—well, I don't know the details. It was before he got married and became middle-aged.'

'Middle-aged? He's only thirty-four.'

'On the outside. Inside, he's grim and ferocious and years older than he actually is.'

'I see what you mean. So he has quite a history?'

'They say he had his pick of all the girls in Rome, and sometimes he seemed to pick them all. And they picked him. But then he fell in love with this English lady and became a different man—at least for a while. I heard a rumour that he was divorcing her for infidelity.'

'That's true.'

'Then he must have turned into a different man again. Who can say who he is now?'

She nodded, but did not reply. Nico had struck a nerve.

Who could say who Leonizio was now? Perhaps he didn't even know himself.

'Have you known him long?' she asked.

'I used to work in the shop when his uncle owned it. I hated that man. So did most people. Cold, hard, indifferent to everyone but himself. When Leonizio inherited it I worked for him, which was much more pleasant. He's a hard man but a generous employer. Then I managed to raise the money to buy it. Ah, here he is.'

Leonizio returned and now they were able to settle down together for the evening. Ellie was fascinated. She was seeing new sides to Leonizio and he intrigued her more every moment.

As they left the building he said in a cheerful voice, 'I guess I don't have any reputation left.'

'Why should you think that?'

'I overheard some of what Nico said, especially *libertino.*'

She laughed. 'Well, you never pretended to be a man of strict virtue. Actually, Nico said some very nice things about you. According to him, you're better than your uncle, who was cold, hard, indifferent to everyone but himself.'

'True enough. Growing up with him and my aunt was like growing up without any family. I used to envy the other kids who had parents who visited their school, got involved, came to see them in the school play.'

'They didn't come to see you in the—?'

'Why should they bother? They cared nothing for me.'

'But if you were your uncle's heir, mustn't he have had some feelings for you to make such a will?'

'He didn't make a will. My aunt died before him and his possessions came to me as his closest living relative. I was grateful for the lucky stroke of fate, but—well—' He shrugged.

But there had been no emotional comfort in his inheritance, she realised.

'Never mind.' He put his arm around her. 'I have a family now.'

'Yes,' she said. 'Yes, you do.'

'And it means more than money ever could.'

'As long as it makes you happy.'

'Happy? There are no words for how happy I am. I didn't believe it was possible.'

She looked down at her still flat stomach, caressing it gently.

'Do you hear that?' she asked their unseen companion. 'Your daddy is already crazy about you. Aren't you lucky?'

'I'm the one who's lucky,' Leonizio said. He addressed her belly. 'Are you listening? I'll always come to your school play. That's a promise.'

Ellie laughed and hugged him. In the taxi on the way home she leaned her head on his shoulder, wondering when she had ever felt such a sense of peaceful contentment.

Several pairs of shoes were delivered next morning. She tried them all on, enchanted by their beauty and comfort.

'They're lovely,' she said.

'Glad you like them.' Leonizio grinned. 'Now I know that our customers will like them.'

'Oh, I see. I'm a marketing experiment.'

'You don't mind, do you?'

'Not at all. I hope I'm a success.'

They both laughed, and he said, 'We'll drop by the factory and let them see you wearing them. They'll love it.'

He was right. The workers cheered when she arrived. Francesco took a load of photographs of her feet.

'They'll make great advertisements,' he said.

'You might end up with a modelling fee,' Leonizio teased her.

She stayed at the factory the rest of the morning and had lunch with him in the works canteen.

'Oh, I'm loving this,' she sighed. 'I don't know when I've enjoyed a holiday so much.'

'Is that what I am to you?' he asked ironically. 'A holiday?'

'No, I didn't mean— It was just—'

Words failed her. There was no way to express what they both knew, that they were getting to know each other to see how the future would work out. The more she enjoyed Rome, the more confused she became. Her life was settled, and how much Leonizio would be a part of it was something she still couldn't decide.

But she'd be wise to remember one thing. Leonizio was taking wonderful care of her, but chiefly because he wanted something. And she was hovering dangerously on the edge of being fooled.

It was time to escape.

'I really must leave Rome and get back to work,' she said uneasily.

'So soon? Can't you stay a little longer?'

'No, there are things I have to do—I can't just neglect my job. This has been lovely but—'

He shrugged. 'All right, let it go. I know what you're really telling me. We'll both go to England. I want to be there to see my divorce become final as soon as possible, and sign anything I need to sign.'

'Yes, it will all be simpler if you're there.'

'I must stay here for a few hours now and fix things so that they can manage without me while I'm away.'

'I'll get out of your way. I can go home and watch the news on television, and see if my Italian is good enough to follow it.'

'Fine. I'll see you this evening. I'll send for the car.'

'No need. I can walk back. It's not far, and I like to explore.'

She enjoyed the stroll through the streets. At home she put her feet up and watched the television, then took up a newspaper that had been delivered and began to read it. She found that she understood more than she had expected.

Perhaps I should try reading a book, she thought. *Let's see.*

She began to browse, remembering seeing Leonizio glancing through a large volume about Rome, which he had finally put away on a tall shelf. Searching, she found it easily and reached up to take it down. But her movements dislodged other books on either side. She grabbed them quickly, but one fell to the floor. She dropped down beside it, suddenly tense at what she could see. The book had fallen open at a page that contained a photograph of a man and a woman, dressed for a wedding.

Only half believing what her eyes told her, Ellie studied the man's face and realised that it was Leonizio. He was looking at his bride—this must be Harriet—with an expression of love. She looked up at him, not with love but with a teasing expression.

Had there really been so much difference between them? Ellie wondered. She could easily believe it. The story of their marriage and Harriet's deception suggested that she had seen him as a man she could use.

There were more pictures in the album. Absorbed, Ellie went through it, watching the couple enjoying each other's company in many different ways. One picture of them relaxing on a beach showed Leonizio in a pair of swim shorts that showed off his shape: slim but muscular, perfectly proportioned.

Could any woman look at that body without wanting to take it to bed? Ellie wondered. The memories it revived in her were achingly beautiful.

There was a brief letter enclosed, from the friend who had taken the pictures.

Thought you'd like to see how they came out. Nice to see you and Harriet so happy. Here's to your future.

Browsing through the rest of the album, Ellie grew very still when she came to another picture. The couple were sitting together with his hand on her stomach. Again he wore a look of adoration, but this time it was clearly for the baby, and the happiness he was sure would soon be his.

The sight of his face hurt her. It was so vulnerable in his belief that his dreams had come true. Ellie had always known that the truth had hurt him, but now she could sense how brutally his heart had been broken.

And so he now clung to her, she mused. Because in her he sensed a chance to revive his hopes. She couldn't blame him, despite the ache of regret that this was the only reason he valued her.

At last something in the silence made her look up to find Leonizio standing there, his eyes fixed on her.

'I'm sorry,' she said hastily. 'I didn't mean to pry. I just came across this accidentally.'

'Don't worry,' he said. 'I guess you know about that part of my life.'

'Yes, and I'm glad to understand you a little better.'

'How do you mean?'

'I've heard you talk about Harriet with something like hate in your voice. I hadn't realised how deeply you once felt about her.'

'You don't think love can turn into hate? On the contrary. The deeper the love, the deeper the hate.'

He spoke quietly but there was a violence of feeling in his eyes. This was a man who had not merely felt a mild affection. He had loved with an intensity that had put his life on the line.

She wondered how it would feel to inspire such feelings.

'What about you?' he asked. 'Don't you know how it feels to hate?'

'No. Nobody has ever mattered that much.'

'What about the guy you told me about, who left you for another woman?'

'I put him behind me. When I decided that he no longer existed—that's when he ceased to exist.'

'You make it sound so easy.'

'It can be, if you really want it to be.'

As she watched, the intensity vanished from his face, leaving it blank.

'It will happen to you one day,' he said quietly. 'Someone will become your life to such an extent that when they betray you there's nothing left.'

She shivered. He had driven all feeling out, leaving only emptiness inside himself, and somehow he troubled her more this way.

'Nothing?' she asked.

'Nothing.'

Suddenly she heard her cell phone ringing from another room. She headed out but turned in the doorway, meaning to speak to him. But what she saw held her silent.

Leonizio was looking at a picture of Harriet, and Ellie thought she had never seen so much sadness in anyone's face. He didn't move, but sat with his eyes fixed on the woman who had illuminated his life, then destroyed it. Only a moment ago his face had been blank and empty. Now it was haunted by despair.

She hesitated, longing to speak to him but fearful lest any word from her would be ill-chosen. While she tried to decide, the telephone shrilled again and she hurried away to her room.

It was her boss on the phone.

'OK,' he said. 'We've got the final papers.'

She drew a sharp breath. 'Everything?'

'Everything. Best get back here fast, both of you.'

'Yes. I'll call you back when I've spoken to him.' She hung up.

Leonizio appeared in the doorway.

'Has something happened?' he asked tensely.

'That was Alex. You were right about coming to England. We're in the final stage.'

'Great. Let's be on our way.'

'I'll check some good London hotels, although I'm sure you already know the best.'

'Hotels?' he said. 'That's a very unkind suggestion. I'd hoped you were going to invite me to stay with you.' He gave a brief laugh. 'If you could see your face! I guess I know what you think of that suggestion.'

'It's only that my place is small. I don't have another bed.'

'Do you have a sofa?'

'Well, yes, but—'

'Then I'll sleep on the sofa. And I'll do my share of tidying up. Don't argue. It's settled.'

A combination of exasperation and amusement made her say, 'There's really no getting rid of you, is there?'

'That depends how much you want to get rid of me.'

She gave him a teasing look. 'Perhaps I haven't quite made up my mind.'

'Let me help you.'

Dropping his hands on her shoulders, he drew her close enough to lay his mouth against hers. It wasn't a passionate kiss, but a gentle assertion of possession, lasting just long enough to make his point.

'Does that make it any easier?' he asked.

She considered. 'Not really. Some things are hard to decide.'

'I could try again—with your permission, of course.'

Oh, he was a cunning so-and-so, she reckoned: putting the decision on her.

'All right,' she said, 'but try to do better this time.'

That would provoke him, she thought. His next kiss would be fiercer, more determined.

But his lips only brushed her mouth even more softly than before.

'Get rid of me later,' he murmured. 'For the moment I'm coming with you to England.'

Without waiting for her reply, he turned away to the telephone and called the airport.

Ellie clenched her fists, alarmed at her own reaction. She'd been ready for the second kiss to be passionate, and its restraint had left her heart beating fiercely with disappointment.

She stepped back, annoyed with him for disappointing her, but even more annoyed with herself for caring.

'The plane leaves this afternoon at four o'clock,' Leonizio said, hanging up. 'I've bought us tickets.'

'How much do I owe you?'

'Nothing. I'll pay for your ticket.'

'Thank you, but no. I pay for my own ticket. I don't ask you to support me.'

He seemed about to argue, but changed his mind, muttering, 'I'll go and pack.'

'Me too.'

She left him quickly, lest he see how disturbed she was. The touch of his lips had aroused an eagerness for another, deeper kiss. She had resisted it, but was dismayed at herself for feeling it at all.

And why had he picked that particular moment to kiss her? Just a few minutes ago Harriet had intruded on his consciousness, reviving thoughts and feelings that disturbed him. Had he turned to her in genuine desire? Or was it an act of defiance against the past, against Harriet?

Whatever the answer, she must struggle harder to be in control of the situation. She had promised herself that control. But it wasn't working as she'd planned.

Was there any way of coping with this infuriating man?

There was no chance to brood further. Now the time was taken up with practical matters: packing, getting to the airport, boarding the plane.

'The flight will be two and a half hours,' he said, 'and it will be late by the time we reach your place. So let's eat plenty on the plane.'

He was right. By the time they landed and left the airport the light was fading. It took another hour for the taxi to reach London and start the journey to her home. At first they travelled through the expensive part of town, but gradually the streets grew shabbier.

At last they pulled up near a five-storey block of flats. Leonizio looked up high.

'You live there?'

'Yes, I'm in one of the top apartments.'

Inside, they headed for the elevator, but got no further. A notice announced that it was out of order.

'Oh, no!' Ellie groaned. 'It was supposed to be mended by now. Oh, well, up we go.'

She headed for the stairs, followed by Leonizio, who took her suitcase as well as his own.

'You can't carry them both,' she protested. 'They'll be much too heavy.'

He grinned. 'Nonsense. Superman can carry any weight. Lead on.'

She began to climb the stairs, going slowly. About halfway up she paused, taking deep breaths.

'You shouldn't be doing a climb like this,' he said. 'It's taking too much out of you.'

'Nonsense, I'm Superwoman.'

'But Superwoman needs Superman.'

They had reached a corner where the stairs flattened out into a wide ledge. Leonizio dumped the suitcases and reached out to her.

'Come here,' he said. And the next moment she was lifted high in his arms.

'Direct me,' he demanded.

'Two more flights and then we're at my front door.'

He mastered the two flights quickly, setting her down by the door while he went back for the cases. She hurried inside, wondering what would happen now.

The way he'd lifted her without checking her feelings left her in two minds.

Chivalrous? she mused. Or controlling? Or perhaps they were two halves of the same.

But she had to admit she didn't mind being saved the effort of climbing the last stairs.

He appeared with the cases and looked around. She wondered how he would regard her plain little apartment after the glamorous luxury of his own home. He'd chosen to sleep on the sofa, but that was before he'd seen how narrow and hard it was.

'You'd really better go to a hotel,' she said. 'You can't sleep on that sofa.'

'I'll be fine. I'm staying here. No arguments. My mind is made up.'

'All right, I'll get you some blankets.'

She did her best to make him comfortable, fetching some blankets and a pillow, then arranging them on the sofa.

'Can I have that?' he asked, pointing to a small table. 'And a lamp? I like to read at night.'

She put the table where he indicated, near his head, and set a small metal lamp on it.

'So what's the next step?' he asked. 'When do I sign the papers?'

'I'll call my boss. Luckily, I've got his home number.'

Alex Dallon answered the phone at once.

'We're here,' she said.

'You don't mean you actually managed to make Fellani see sense? Well done, Ellie. You've got a great career in front of you.'

Leonizio glanced up and she realised with dismay that Dallon's voice was loud and sharp enough to carry beyond the phone.

'Shut up!' she said desperately.

'Get him in here tomorrow,' Dallon continued. 'Drag him if you have to.'

'Goodnight,' she said desperately and hung up before he could say more.

To her relief, Leonizio was grinning.

'You won't have to drag me,' he assured her.

'I'm sorry. He had no right to speak of you like that.'

'Especially when I'm near enough to overhear him. Don't worry, it's not your fault. And in a way he was right. You have helped me to see sense about some things.' His tone became ironic. 'You might say there are things I'm trying to get you to see sense about. Except that so far I'm not doing well.'

'I'll ignore that remark,' she said lightly.

'Very wise. We both have to sort out our brains before anything more happens. The problem is that we don't agree what "seeing sense" means.'

'We'll have to wait and discover how things turn out. We don't know each other very well yet.'

'Don't we? Wasn't there one moment when we knew each other very well indeed?'

'No,' she said softly. 'We thought we did, but—well—it was…'

'An illusion,' he sighed.

'I think so.'

'The trouble is, there are some illusions you want to cling to.'

'But it isn't always a good idea,' she said.

'True. Or it can be a wonderful idea.'

'But if it's only an illusion—'

'Then we could work to make it reality. What is an illusion, what is reality? Is there really a difference?'

It could be so tempting to follow him along this path, she thought. But it was a temptation she must resist, and it would be better to escape him now.

'Can I get you anything before you settle for the night?' she asked politely.

'No, thank you. Just don't vanish without warning.'

'Promise.'

She left him and hurried to her own room. It felt like taking refuge, so troublesome did she find him these days. There she could enjoy the sensation of relaxing, free from the world. Poor and shabby her apartment might be, but to her it was home in a way that nowhere else ever had been. She had found it when she went to work for Alex Dallon, knowing that she had defeated four other applicants for the job. It was her independence, her success, her right to be herself, think her own thoughts, travel her own path.

She knew Leonizio had seen only its disadvantages. He would never understand her thoughts or dreams, and perhaps for that reason they would never be truly close.

CHAPTER SEVEN

ELLIE SETTLED CONTENTEDLY in bed and managed to get to sleep quickly, but awoke after a while with the night only partly over.

She wondered how Leonizio was managing next door. She could hear some faint creaking which went on for several minutes, suggesting that he was tossing and turning restlessly. She understood that very well. What was happening to them now was disturbing.

Suddenly there came a loud clatter and the sound of crashing. Hurriedly, she jumped up and dashed into the other room.

Leonizio was lying on the floor, looking stunned. Beside him lay the metal lamp.

'I fell off,' he growled. 'And I knocked your lamp down. Sorry.'

For a moment she couldn't respond. He had removed all clothes but for a pair of boxers. The sight of him almost naked made her draw a sharp breath.

He tried to hoist himself back onto the sofa, but gave up.

'My arm,' he growled. 'I landed on it. Ouch!'

'Let me help you,' she said. 'Put your other arm around me.'

He did so. She wrapped her arms about him and together they managed to lift him the few inches onto the sofa.

'Thanks,' he growled, dropping his head and beginning to rub it.

'Is your head injured?' she asked anxiously.

'No, just a little bump. I'll be all right in a moment.'

'Can I get you something?'

'No, I'll just go back to sleep.'

'Not here. This sofa is too small for you. You must sleep in my bed.'

'You mean—?'

'I'll sleep on the sofa. I'm small enough to fit on there. Come along. Don't argue.'

'Yes, ma'am.'

Leaning on her, he rose to his feet and let her support him into the bedroom and onto the bed, where he stretched out with a sigh of relief.

'I'm supposed to be here looking after you,' he sighed. 'You could say I'm making a mess of it.'

'No, you couldn't. Stop making a drama out of a little accident.'

He regarded her wryly. 'Well, you did warn me the sofa was too small. I should have listened.'

'You? Listen to advice? Don't make me laugh.'

'All right, all right. I give in.'

'That's what I like to hear.' She pulled the covers up over him. 'Now, go to sleep.'

He snuggled down and closed his eyes. After a moment she retreated into the other room. There she lay down on the sofa and tried to go back to sleep.

But sleep eluded her. Her mind was filled with visions she didn't want to see, and thoughts she didn't want to indulge.

She had made love with this man, but until tonight she hadn't seen him nearly naked. His smooth, muscular torso, narrow hips and long elegant legs had come as a shock. Even more stunning had been the sudden urgent desire to wrap her arms about his naked flesh, holding it against her, enjoying the sensation.

But it was a losing battle. The feel of his body had been so thrilling that it haunted her still, inflaming her anger and defiance.

She had vowed to fend off his attempts to take control of her, and she could manage that where it concerned him giving her orders. But there was no protection against the surges of temptation that he could inspire against her will. She could only determine not to let him suspect.

She was up early the next morning, preparing breakfast, wondering how Leonizio would cope with everything that was to happen that day. When he appeared she was shocked at the bruise on his forehead.

'I hit the lamp a bit harder than I thought,' he said, reading her expression. 'But it's all right. Your colleagues will think you've started beating me up already.'

She didn't query 'already', guessing that it was a hint about the marriage he was still trying to talk her into.

'I'll pick my own moment for that,' she said lightly. 'Eat up, then we'll get going.'

When they reached her office Alex Dallon was engaged with another client. While they waited for him, Leonizio stood by the window, gazing out at a row of shops over the road.

'That department store over the street stocks Fellani shoes.'

Ellie looked up at him and smiled. 'Your shoes are very desirable to the UK market.'

He nodded. 'Some of my best sales are in England. It's worth thinking about.'

'Sorry to keep you waiting,' came a voice from behind them.

They turned to see Alex, holding a sheaf of papers.

'I expect Ellie's told you how close we are to the finish,' he said. 'Your wife applied to the court for what's known as a 'quickie divorce' and a few brief formalities will tie up all the loose ends.'

He handed Leonizio the papers, which he sat down to read. Ellie went to sit beside him.

'You'd better go through them for me,' Leonizio said. 'I'm not sure my English is up to it.'

She did her duty, explaining as she went, making sure he knew how completely final this was. Remembering how the picture of Harriet had affected him, Ellie wondered how this would make him feel, but he listened with a blank, unresponsive face.

'And when I sign these papers, that's it?' he said.

'There will be no barriers to divorce,' Alex said. 'And it will be granted in a few days. You'll be completely free.'

'Thank you,' Leonizio said in a toneless voice. 'Now I must go. Send me your bill and I'll pay it at once.'

He headed for the door. Alex indicated for her to follow him and she did so, gladly. Something told her that Leonizio shouldn't be alone just now.

They found a restaurant with tables in a small garden. Leonizio ordered coffee for her and whisky for himself.

'I need a drink,' he said. 'So that's tied up all the ends. Now Harriet has her divorce it leaves her free to marry her lover before they have their child.'

'Don't,' Ellie pleaded. 'I know it's hard for you, but let her go. Let the baby go. Don't grieve for the rest of your life.'

'But what am I supposed to do? Forget grief because it's inconvenient?'

'No, I suppose not,' she sighed.

It hurt her to see his air of defeat. It was as though all life and hope had ended for him.

'That's it,' he said. 'All done. All over.'

'Not over,' she said. 'You haven't lost everything.' She took his hand and laid it on her stomach. 'You still have this.'

'Do I?'

'Yes. This baby is yours and nothing will ever change that.'

'Does that mean you'll marry me now that I'm a free man?'

'It means it doesn't matter whether we marry or not. You'll have a relationship with your child whatever happens. Marriage isn't everything. I can give you a great deal without that.'

He made a wry face and took a sip of whisky.

'I'll be going now,' he said. 'I mustn't keep you from your work. I'll see you at home tonight.'

'You'd better have your key,' she said, reaching into her purse. 'I got you a spare before we left this morning, so you can come and go without me.'

'Thanks. And thank you for—for everything.' He departed so quickly that she sensed he desperately needed to get away.

For the rest of the day she tried to concentrate on work, but it was hard when she couldn't help thinking of Leonizio, wandering alone, brooding bitterly on the feeling that his life was over.

Unless I agree to marry him, she thought. *It would be so easy to say yes, but I just can't. He has no feelings for me. Only for our baby and his other life. Could I bear to live with that?*

No. She couldn't face it. It would be easy to develop

feelings for Leonizio, and that was a reason for not marrying him. It would mean a life of misery and jealousy.

At last the day was over and she could return home.

'I'm here,' she called as she entered.

Silence.

'Hello, Leonizio. I'm home.'

But there was no reply. She wandered through the rooms, seeking him, finding only emptiness, while her heart sank.

Where was he? What was he doing that had taken him so long? Now she recalled that when he had left her in the café he'd had an air of purpose.

But what could his purpose be?

Was it possible that he had gone to seek Harriet, determined to have one more meeting with her?

Was his love for her really as dead as he thought? Had he discovered renewed feelings that made it vital for him to see her again? He had spoken of the link between love and hate. Had his hate taken a new direction?

No, she told herself. That was absurd fantasy. He would return soon.

But an hour passed without any sign of Leonizio. Glancing out of the window, she saw an empty street.

Now she knew she had no choice but to accept the truth. She could only go to bed, not on the sofa, as she had previously decided, but in her own bedroom, since he would not be coming back. There she lay in silent desperation until at last she fell asleep.

She awoke in the early hours to find the apartment still silent. She knew at once that he had not returned. He was out there, making the plans that suited him, ignoring her wishes, thinking only of his own.

And what are his wishes? she wondered. *If I give in and do whatever he wants, what happens then? He doesn't care for me. I'm useful to him, that's all.*

She had sensed a growing warmth between them, but it had all been an illusion. She had deceived herself, ignoring the warning signs that had brought her to the edge of reacting to him with dangerous intensity.

'Fool,' she muttered. 'The truth was always there before you, but you wouldn't see it. Fool!'

She lay motionless for an hour, finally drifting back into sleep. She was awoken suddenly by a noise from next door. Rising quickly, she went out into the main room, switching on the light.

'Have a heart!' said a voice.

He was there on the sofa, covering his eyes against the light.

'I'd only just gone to bed,' he complained. 'And you had to do that.'

'I'm sorry—I didn't know you were here. You weren't here an hour ago.'

'I came in quietly, so as not to wake you. I fell asleep almost instantly. It's been a heavy day.'

'Why? Has something happened?'

'In a way. Things don't always turn out the way we expect. I've had a lot of thinking to do—decisions to make.'

'Hard decisions?' she asked, as lightly as she could manage. It wasn't easy.

'Some of them.' He made a wry face, full of self-mockery. 'I'm not one of the most original thinkers in the world. I can handle business fine, but when it comes to people I tend to make a mess of it.'

'Don't be so hard on yourself. Why must you take such a gloomy view of life?'

'Is that how I seem? Well, maybe—it's just that things don't seem to work out as I hoped. I've had ideas we need to discuss before we—' He checked himself sharply, as though continuing would be a problem. 'You couldn't get me a drink, could you?'

'Tea?'

'I was thinking of something a bit stronger.'

Wine, she thought. Men always chose alcohol when they needed all their courage for a tough conversation.

She could almost hear him saying, *Ellie, I'm leaving you. I still want to see my child, but there's nothing else between us.*

How much wine would he need for that?

She poured him a glass of red, thrust it into his hand and stood waiting, silently preparing herself for the worst.

'All right,' she said at last. 'Let's hear it.'

He hesitated. 'Some things aren't easy to say.'

The words seemed to confirm her worst apprehensions.

'I'm sure you're good at them,' she said, forcing herself to speak casually.

'Sure, I've had some practice at that. More than I'd like. But we need to talk about how things are now.' He waved his hand around the room. 'This isn't working. We're getting on each other's nerves here, so I thought about it and—well—'

'Decided to get out,' she said quietly. Her heart was quivering.

'Yes. That's where I've been this afternoon—looking for somewhere. I think I've found the perfect place.'

'When are you leaving?'

'That's up to you. I'll take you to see it later on today. I think you'll like it, and then we'll move in as soon as possible.'

'*We?* Did you say *we*?'

'Of course. You can't go on living here with those rickety stairs and the lifts that don't always work.'

She stared at him. Now her heart was thundering.

'And that's what this is all about?' she whispered.

'Look, don't be offended that I went searching without you. I wanted to see what was available. I know what you're thinking.'

'I really don't think you do.'

'Yes, I can follow your mind by now. You believe I should have discussed it with you first, that I take too much on myself. But I just wanted to look at some nice places and see if any were likely to appeal to you.'

She had been wrong. He wasn't leaving her. Her relief was so fierce that she almost lost control.

'Ellie, are you all right?'

'I'm fine—fine.'

'You don't look fine. You look as though something has knocked you sideways. I didn't mean to upset you.'

'I'm not upset. Just confused. You've been looking at apartments?'

'I've seen several, and there's one in particular that I think would be right for you. The sooner you see it the better, so why don't we go today?'

'You mean you've already made an appointment?' she guessed.

'Yes, I felt I should. Sorry about not consulting you first but I didn't want it to slip through our fingers, so I've arranged for us to see it.'

'But I have to go to work.'

'Can't you slip out for an hour at lunchtime? I don't want you to miss this.'

She didn't want to miss it either. She was alive with curiosity to see the place he had chosen as right for her.

'All right, I'll come at lunchtime.'

'It's a date. I promise you, this place will make your head spin.'

Her head was already spinning, but in ways he must not be allowed to know.

'I'll see you in the morning,' she said, and left him quickly.

* * *

Alex Dallon was waiting for her when she reached work, full of praise for her skill in looking after a wealthy client.

'I heard what Signor Fellani was saying about his English sales yesterday,' he said. 'It would be good for his business to have a branch over here. And it would certainly be good for our business to handle his profitable stuff. So try to keep him in a cheerful mood.'

'I'm having lunch with him today.'

'Good work. Take as long as you need. Call him now and tell him to collect you early.'

She did so, and was ready when Leonizio arrived at midday. Alex gave her a thumbs-up sign and waved them off.

'You're doing my career a mass of good,' she teased when they were settled in the back of a taxi. 'Alex thinks you're planning to expand into an English branch, and he's tasked me with making sure that you do.'

'Sensible man. So is that why you're with me now?'

'Officially, yes.'

'It's all going to be very interesting. But let's get this apartment sorted first.'

'Yes. I'm really looking forward to seeing it. Is it far?'

He gave her a scrap of paper on which he'd written the address, and her eyebrows rose. It was only a short distance away, which meant it was in the expensive part of town. At last they drew up outside an elegant building, and made their way inside to an apartment on the ground floor.

It was large and well furnished, with three bedrooms, plus a well-equipped bathroom and kitchen. She liked it at once, but she guessed the cost would be beyond her.

'What do you think?' he asked.

'It's lovely but I doubt if I could afford it.'

'You won't have to. I'm paying. Yes, I know what you're

thinking. You reckon this is me being controlling again. But I'm doing it for practical reasons. This place is much nearer your office, so that will be easier for you.' He added wryly, 'Unless you've decided to marry me and just forgotten to mention it.'

'No, I haven't changed my mind about that.'

'So you'll continue working, and living close will be useful. But that's not my real reason for wanting you to live here. You can't stay in that dump where you're living now. You'll have an accident on those stairs any day. Here there are no stairs and you're much safer.'

'I can see that, but—'

He laid his hand on her stomach. 'You wouldn't take risks just for the pleasure of telling me to go to the devil, would you?'

He was right, she knew. Here the baby would be far safer than in her present home.

'I guess I wouldn't,' she admitted with a smile. 'All right. You win.'

He gave a grunt of ironic laughter. 'I can only guess what it cost you to say that. You can thump me if it makes you feel better.'

'I'll save that pleasure for another time. This looks like a nice place but—isn't it really too expensive?'

'You have two options. You tell Alex how successful you've been in persuading me to open a branch here. He's impressed by your skill and gives you a huge rise. Or you could just accept that I'll pay. I'll be spending some time here when I need somewhere to stay.'

'Well—' she paused, seeming to consider '—I guess I'll end up doing it your way, as usual.'

'That's what I like to hear.'

She touched his cheek. 'And you are taking good care of me—of both of us.'

'Yes. We're a family now.'

She wasn't sure how she should answer, but he saved her from having to.

'There are different kinds of families,' he said. 'We'll have to wait and see about us. Now, let's go and make sure you can rent this place.'

'Wait,' she said quickly. 'Isn't it better if you rent it?'

'But it'll be your home.'

'Not yet. Don't hurry me.'

'All right,' he said reluctantly. 'It will be mine—until you say otherwise.'

A short journey brought them to the estate agent's office that handled the arrangements. Leonizio organised everything with his usual stern efficiency and in a short time the key was his.

When they returned to the new apartment she had to admit that it would be a pleasant place to live. Leonizio showed her into the main bedroom, which contained a double bed. But he made no attempt to join her there, retreating into the second bedroom.

Ellie studied everywhere carefully, lingering in the doorway of a third smaller bedroom.

'This is just what I need,' she murmured.

'For the baby, when it's born?'

'No, for the help that I'll have to hire. I want to keep my job, which means I'll have to employ a nanny to live in and care for my child.'

'You mean our child, don't you?' he asked quietly.

'Yes, our child.'

He touched her cheek gently. 'Don't shut me out, Ellie.'

'I didn't mean to. But we won't be living together all the time.'

'We would if you married me.'

'But I can't.'

'Can't or won't?'

'It's just not a step I feel I can take, and I have to make

plans for when you're not here. But I won't shut you out, I promise.'

'You *are* shutting me out.'

'I'm sorry. I wish I could do what you want but it's not so easy. There's something in me that just can't— I guess I'm just awkward.' She gave a brief laugh. 'Just like you. Well, you know that by now. But I'm not spiteful, and I want you to be happy with your child.'

She spoke warmly, and he returned her smile. The moment passed and all seemed well between them, but she could sense the tension that had briefly possessed him. It was a reminder, if she needed it, that only one thing really mattered to him. And it wasn't herself.

'Now tell me,' he said, 'do you like this place?'

'Yes, it's lovely.'

'You're not thinking of me as a controlling fiend any more?'

'I never said that.'

'Not out loud, but admit it, when we arranged to come here you were thinking the worst of me.'

'How do you know that?'

'Because you always think the worst of me. It's your default position.'

'Well, I don't like you paying for everything,' she agreed.

'Too late. You've already agreed to accept it.'

'In a sense, but I must tell you—I'm not going to give up my own apartment.'

'You what? But you don't need that place any more.'

'But I do. Please try to understand—it's mine. When I'm there I'm myself, completely myself. It's like my own little kingdom.'

'But, Ellie, we're a couple now. This will be our home.'

She clenched her hands desperately. 'No, we're not a couple. Maybe one day we will be but there's a lot we still need to know. And it's too soon to call it our home. I still need my own place.'

He gave her a look of wry bitterness. 'So that if I annoy you, you can walk out, tell me to go to blazes and escape into your kingdom. That's letting me know where I stand, isn't it?'

'It's telling you that there are still question marks hanging over us. We need to give it a little time. Please, Leonizio, don't let's argue any more. Let's just wait and see how things work out.'

Reluctantly he shrugged.

'I guess I have no choice. You win.'

'Good.' Having scored a victory, she felt her mood soften. She was going to enjoy the next few moments. 'And now I have some news for you. I'm planning something that will annoy you, but you'll just have to accept it.'

He looked uneasy. 'What's this? You're annoyed with me and you're going to make me suffer?'

She gave him a teasing smile. 'Terribly.'

'You're going to thump me, kick me in the shins, lock me in the cellar?'

'No, that would be boring. I'm planning something that you'll object to a lot more. But you have no choice. I simply won't accept a refusal.'

'You're scaring me.'

'Good. You're going to do what I say without argument.'

'I can't wait to hear this.'

'Tonight we're going out for a celebratory meal. And I shall pay for it, whatever it costs. I want no arguments. However much you dislike it, you'll just have to put up with it. *I'll* pay, not you. Do you understand that?'

His face brightened as he understood her jokey mood.

'Yes, ma'am, no, ma'am. Three bags full, ma'am.'

She burst out laughing and he joined in, wrapping his arms about her and hugging her tightly.

'I mean it,' she cried. 'Don't you dare try to pay. Don't even mention money or my revenge will be terrible. Now, let me finish settling in here, then I'll sort out the details for tonight.'

CHAPTER EIGHT

ELLIE CHOSE THE restaurant carefully. It served Italian food, luxuriously presented, and was one of the best in London. Also one of the most expensive. In this too she was making a point to Leonizio. He might have more money but she had enough to cope, and she would show him that she couldn't be bought and sold.

She called, booked the best table and gave a happy sigh of anticipation. She was really looking forward to this.

When the time came she put on the glamorous dress he'd bought her for the opera.

'Very nice,' he said, nodding approval.

'Is it?' she asked, turning around in front of a floor-length mirror. 'I shan't be able to wear it when I start putting on weight.'

'But just now it's perfect. The only thing you need to change is to let your hair hang loose.'

She let it fall, and at once her other self confronted her from the mirror.

'I'm not sure,' she said, pushing it back a little.

'Let's see.' He took over, brushing his fingers against her face until they became wreathed in hair. 'Like that? No, perhaps this way.' He drew her tresses forward again. 'I like it like this.'

'But drawn back makes me look more sensible. Which I am, although you don't want to believe it.'

'Perish the thought. I prefer the girl who seduced me.'

She gave him a teasing smile. 'Oh, yes? Are you sure who seduced who?'

He grinned. 'Well, I can't quite make up my mind. My partly conceited side tells me I was the seducer. My totally conceited side says it was you who wanted me. My hopeful side says it was mutual.'

He was still smiling as though his words were humorous. But there was something in his eyes that made her heart beat a little faster.

'I guess your hopeful side—is very knowing,' she said, a touch breathlessly.

He nodded. 'I like to think so. After all, you could always have socked me on the jaw.'

'Yes, but it wouldn't have been very polite. And I'm a polite person.'

He kissed her cheek. 'I'm glad of that. Let me get dressed and it'll be time to go.'

He vanished. Not until he was gone did Ellie yield to the temptation to touch her cheek where his lips had brushed it.

When he reappeared, dressed in elegant evening clothes, she had to admit that his conceited side had a point. He was the most attractive man she had ever seen, and his hopeful side was right. Their lovemaking had been mutual.

But she concealed these thoughts beneath an efficient manner, and they set off.

As they reached the restaurant she had the satisfaction of seeing him gape with astonishment at the luxurious place.

'Ellie, you can't mean here. You'll never be able to afford it.'

She met his eyes, her own full of teasing, to reassure him that their battle was light-hearted, although she meant every word.

'You don't know that,' she told him. 'In fact, you don't know the first thing about me, except that I've always given in and let you have your own way. Now I'm asserting myself because it's time for a change.'

'I guess it is.'

'So come along, our table is waiting.'

A waiter greeted them, checked her booking and led them to a table in an alcove by a window. There they studied the menu.

'Great food,' Leonizio observed. 'But did you really think the prices would be so high when you made me this offer?'

'It wasn't an offer, it was a command,' Ellie reminded him.

'But perhaps you'd like to have second thoughts.'

'Don't even mention it. I've made my own choice.'

She indicated two of the most expensive dishes on the menu and he followed her lead, occasionally pausing to give her a questioning glance. She met it with a smile.

'Here's the waiter,' she said. 'You give him the order for the food and wine. And mineral water for me.'

He did so, but he had a surprise for her. When it came to the drink he simply ordered mineral water for both of them.

'Did you do that for the sake of my purse?' she demanded when the waiter had gone.

'No, I did it because we're in this together. Can't you understand that?'

'Yes, I guess I can,' she said, pleased. 'All right, one up to you.'

'One up to me? That makes a change. Normally you enjoy wrong-footing me, don't you?'

'However did you guess?'

'I'm getting used to it. I'm even beginning to enjoy it.' He gave a brief laugh. 'I've got to say this for you; you're never dull.'

'So you'd like a few more threats as entertainment?'

'Why not? I'm sure you've got plenty up your sleeve.'

'You'll find out—gradually. You might find me a very interesting enemy.'

His face softened. 'Joking apart, you're not my enemy. You're my best friend. And you always will be.'

'Friend?' she echoed, instinctively touching her stomach.

'Yes, I know it sounds a little strange, considering our history. But in a way it's our success. We have a lot of arguments, but we've spent some valuable time trying to get to know each other. You said I don't know the first thing about you, but I think I know the things that matter.'

'I wonder what they are,' she mused, giving him a speculative glance. 'We might have different ideas about that.'

'We know how to make each other laugh. And, let's face it, I also know how to make you good and mad.'

'And that's important?'

'Considering how mad you can make me, I think it's vital. When I think of our future I see some of the most entertaining rows there have ever been.'

'Hmm. I wonder who'll win,' she mused.

'My money's on you. You know more of my weak spots than I know of yours.'

'Weak spots?' she echoed. 'You have weak spots?'

'Don't pretend you don't know by now. It's you who can knock me into a corner.'

'Very tactfully said, but I think it's just about even.'

'We'll have to wait and see.'

At last the meal arrived, everything was set out on the table and all was ready.

'Here's to you,' Leonizio said, raising his glass in salute.

'No, here's to us,' she said, raising her own. 'It's all going well, and we're a great success.'

He clinked glasses with her.

'I'm not sure I can claim to be a great success. You said that you always let me have my own way, but that's not true. I don't see any wedding ring on your finger.'

'Weddings aren't the only things that matter,' she hedged.

'They are if you're having a child. But let's leave it for the moment. In time you may come to feel differently. At least I hope so.' For a moment he paused, seeming to consider, as though trying to make a decision. At last he said heavily, 'I don't want to lose that special feeling you give me. It means more than I can say.'

She could hardly believe her ears. A special feeling. Had he really said that?

'Couldn't you try to say it?' she murmured.

'It's hard because I'm not sure of the right words to describe it.'

But it's called love, whispered a voice in her heart. *Why is it so hard to say?*

If only he would speak of love, then perhaps she might be able to marry him. Somewhere deep inside her was the hint of an emotion that longed to respond to him, but could never do so while he kept his distance.

'The fact is—I want to tell you about how I've felt since that first day we made love,' he said. 'You inspired me with a feeling of—' He paused again.

'A feeling of what?' she asked softly.

'A feeling of—safety.'

'"Safety"?' she echoed, only half believing.

'It goes back to that time we spent together. Do you remember it?'

How could he ask her? she thought desperately. That wonderful hour had lived in her mind ever since, never banished for long, always returning.

'Yes, I remember,' she said quietly.

'So do I. I'll never forget how it felt when we were talking and I looked into your eyes and saw there a sympathy and understanding unlike anything I'd ever known. I knew then that you were different from all other women, with a generosity and kindness that I had to reach out to, hoping it would reach out to me. And you did.

'Since that day nothing has been the same. I don't just mean because of the baby. I mean because of you, because of your strength. You're the one person I've ever met that I know I could trust with my life, and with everything that's in my life. I've been betrayed so often—'

By Harriet, she thought, who had seemed to offer him new hope, then snatched it away, leaving him desolate.

'But you make me feel that there's someone in the world who can be relied on,' he said. 'With you I know I'm safe.'

Suddenly he checked himself and spoke self-consciously. 'Oh, heavens, listen to me. Why am I talking like this? Admitting that I cling to you for safety.'

'Isn't it true?'

'Yes, it's true, but there are some things a man shouldn't admit. It's not exactly macho, is it?'

'Do you have to be macho?' she asked.

'I'm supposed to be. Ask anyone who's done business with me. Hard, cold, grim, unyielding, unforgiving. That's my reputation.'

'And with them you should keep it up. But not with me.'

'No, because I trust you as I thought I'd never trust anyone again.'

He took her hand in his and raised it to his lips.

'Thank you,' he whispered.

'I'm glad if I've given you something.'

'You've given me everything. And when our child is born you'll give me everything again. A future, a reason to live. I even think—'

He stopped suddenly, his face filled with dismay and tension. Following his gaze, Ellie saw a man and a woman entering the restaurant. The woman was young, beautiful and heavily pregnant.

'Oh, goodness…' she breathed. 'Isn't that—?'

'Yes,' Leonizio said softly. 'It's her.'

Ellie could just recognise her as Harriet, the woman in the pictures in his possession. She was filled with shock at suddenly finding her here, and Leonizio's expression told her that he felt the same.

Harriet and her companion had not noticed them, being totally absorbed in each other. Harriet's eyes were fixed adoringly on her lover's face, and his attention was riveted on the swell of her pregnancy.

Leonizio turned his head away sharply, as though unable to bear the sight.

'Is that really her?' Ellie asked.

He turned his gaze on her and she was astounded at the change in him. The gentle affection of a moment ago was gone, replaced by harsh suspicion.

'Yes, it's really her,' he said. 'You knew, didn't you?'

'What?'

'You knew they would be here. That's why you chose this place. How could you?'

She stared at him in outraged disbelief. 'You think I knew she was coming? You actually think I brought you here on purpose? How could I even know that she would be here?'

'You chose this place. Am I supposed to believe that it's coincidence?'

'Yes, because it is. I didn't know. I chose this because it's the best Italian restaurant in London. If I'd known she would be here I'd have found somewhere on the other side of town. Leonizio, you've got to trust me. I would never play such a trick on you. How could you imagine I'd ever be so spiteful?'

'I don't know. But it's enough to make a man believe in a malign fate.'

'Let's hope it teaches you not to make meaningless speeches,' she said bitterly. 'It's only a minute ago you were saying how much you trusted me. I'm telling you I didn't know she would be here, and if you can't bring yourself to believe me then your so-called trust means nothing.'

She braced herself for a vitriolic response but he didn't reply. Instead, his shoulders sagged and he sighed.

'I'm sorry,' he muttered. 'I should have known better than to blame you, but I'm in such a state, I don't know if I'm coming or going.'

'If you ever treat me like that again you'll be going. A long way away. And for ever. I won't have it, do you understand? I deserve better from you than that. Now, let's get out of here.'

'No!' His tone was quiet but forceful. 'I'm not going to run away as though I was scared of her.'

On the last words his voice faded as though something had stunned him. Following his look, Ellie saw that Harriet was holding out her hand for the man to put a ring on it.

'Their engagement,' Leonizio said bitterly. 'Now our divorce is almost finalised she's a free woman, they can marry and acknowledge that her child is his. I've played right into her hands.'

'No,' Ellie said fiercely. 'You've claimed the right to live your own life and to hell with her.' She took his face between her hands and said, 'Forget her. She doesn't exist any more.'

'You're right—you're right—'

'And we are leaving. Waiter, my bill, please.'

Leonizio made no protest, seeming content to follow her lead. In a few moments they were on their way out.

'That was a great meal,' he said. 'Thank you.'

'Yes, it was good to celebrate,' she agreed. 'Now, it's time to go home.'

'Home,' he echoed. 'That sounds nice.'

'Yes, doesn't it?' She took his hand. 'Let's go.'

Outside the restaurant there were several taxis waiting. She hailed one and headed towards it. But suddenly her foot seemed to turn and she felt herself falling. The next moment Leonizio had seized hold of her.

'I've got you,' he said. 'Just hold onto me.'

She did so. 'I'm all right, honestly.'

'Better be on the safe side,' he said, lifting her in his arms and heading for the taxi.

As he turned to set her down she glanced over his shoulder and gasped at what she saw. There was a woman looking out at them through the restaurant's window. Her face was disconcertingly like Harriet's.

Perhaps Harriet *had* noticed Leonizio in the restaurant and tracked them as they left, curious about his companion. Now she was watching them as they clung together.

Surely not, Ellie thought.

She tried to look back again, but the face had vanished from the window. The next moment she was in the taxi.

I'm just imagining things, she thought. *At least I hope I am*. She didn't need any more complications.

They didn't speak again until they reached the apartment.

'Shall we celebrate a fine evening with another drink? Even if it's only a cup of tea?' Leonizio attempted to lift the dark mood that had descended between them.

'Thank you but I'm very tired,' she said quickly. 'I can hardly keep my eyes open.'

'Goodnight then.'

She departed for her own room, undressed and got into bed quickly, feeling a strange need to escape him. The evening's events had left her in a turmoil. Leonizio had spoken with such fervent emotion that she had been sure it was a declaration of love. The truth, when it came, had been startling.

The one time he had made love to her, it had not been out of passion but out of a need to cling to her.

She knew that many women would have entered eagerly into such a marriage, glad of a husband who needed his wife so intensely. She thought of her own mother, shut out of her husband's needs and emotions, devastated by the isolation.

But there's more than one kind of isolation, she thought. Leonizio wanted her, but not in the right way. He didn't love her and that mattered. She wished it didn't, but she couldn't deceive herself. They could never have a happy marriage.

But there was something else that tormented her. How quickly his faith in her had turned to suspicion.

One moment he was saying that he trusted her as he'd thought he would never trust anyone again. The next moment he'd accused her of playing the most appalling, spiteful trick on him.

How bitterly he'd asked, *'How could you?'*

True, he'd recovered himself at once and apologised, but she couldn't forget the burning suspicion in his eyes. Instinct told her that he'd asked her forgiveness with his brain, not his heart.

He didn't really mean that apology, she thought. He just wanted to keep her on side for the sake of their child. But that suspicion would always be there. He might think he trusted her, but at the back of his mind there would always be a doubt. And that doubt would come between them.

She kept her eyes closed, hoping to vanish into the safety of sleep. But was there anywhere that was really safe?

* * *

In his own room, Leonizio stripped off his clothes and lay down, but almost at once he rose to his feet again, knowing that it was useless trying to sleep. Tonight, things had happened that both gladdened and confused him. The moment when he'd suspected Ellie of treachery had burned into him with terrifying pain. If she could not be trusted then nothing and nobody in the world could be trusted.

He'd pulled himself together, fighting off the sensation that the world had collapsed about him. But it had left him weakened and fearful. He needed to explore and understand his feelings, yet something warned him to keep a safe distance, lest exploring only confused him with more mysteries.

For half an hour he managed a kind of restraint, but then he couldn't stand it any more and slipped out of his room, heading for hers, two doors away.

Quietly he entered, going closer to the bed where she lay motionless, her breathing soft and steady. Slowly he dropped to one knee, leaning close to her until he could feel her breath on his face.

'Ellie,' he whispered, 'can you hear me? I hope you can. I so much need to tell you everything I feel. When I said you were my friend, and you made me feel safe, I meant that you're the most important person in the world. I thought you'd know everything I meant because we once talked about friendship and how much it matters in marriage. Do you remember that? I thought we'd understand each other at last.

'I know that's not easy. Sometimes I think we'll never understand each other. At other times I believe we'll find a way. Don't you think so?'

She didn't answer. He waited, holding his breath, while she began to twist restlessly, her arms flailing until one hand brushed his bare chest. But it fell away at once, and he knew she hadn't meant to touch him. She didn't even know he was there.

'You're not awake, are you?' he whispered, drawing back. 'You haven't heard a word I've said.' He gave a sigh. 'But, since everything I say seems to annoy you, perhaps that's just as well.'

He rose, backing out of the room, keeping his gaze on her until the last moment.

Only when she heard the door close did Ellie open her eyes. For a while she lay staring into the darkness while the sounds and sensations whirled in her.

The most important person in the world. He'd said it, but then been glad that she couldn't hear him. Hadn't he? Or had he meant—something else?

He'd said they might never understand each other. Or perhaps they might find a way.

Don't you think so? he'd asked in a voice that sounded like a plea.

But she didn't know what to think. And perhaps she never would.

Rising next morning, Ellie dressed and went out into the main room.

'Are you up?' she called.

Silence.

'Leonizio. Are you there?'

Silence.

Flinging open the door of his room, she found it empty. There was no sign of him anywhere in the apartment, and her heart sank.

He'd gone. The events of last night had disillusioned him. How quickly he'd mistrusted her. How fearful he was of life with her. Even the hope of their child wasn't enough to bring him back. The voice she'd heard in the night had been no more than a dream.

A fantasy, she told herself bitterly. *You heard what you wanted to hear because you need to believe you're growing closer. But the reality is he's gone and left you in a desert.*

But then a sound from the front door made her turn her head to see something she could hardly believe. There was Leonizio, entering with his arms filled with newspapers.

'I went out to the newsagent,' he said. 'I ordered us a delivery every morning, and bought several papers. Ellie? Ellie, are you all right?'

'Yes, I'm fine.'

'Sure? It seems that whenever we meet you look as though you've had a nasty shock. Do I have that effect? Do you want to get rid of me?'

She pulled herself together, managing to say in a teasing voice, 'Suppose I said yes. Would you vanish?'

'I might try to persuade you I'm not as terrible as you think. But I doubt I'd succeed.'

She laughed, almost dizzy with the pleasure of having him back when she'd seemed to lose him for ever.

'I'll leave you to think about that,' she said. 'Time I made the breakfast.'

Over breakfast they scanned the newspapers until she said, 'Aha! Look what I've found.' She showed him a column of text. 'If you really want a factory in England there's a building in this area that might be ideal. Apparently the owners have big financial problems.'

He studied the paper eagerly. 'So I might get it at a knock-down price. Well done! I'll get onto this today. But first I'll call Alex Dallon and tell him what a brilliant job you're doing as my right hand. Then he'll be only too glad to give you the time off.'

'You really know how to move the pieces to your own advantage, don't you?' she laughed.

'Of course. To gain control, that's what you've got to do,' he replied. 'One thing I've learned in business is that power is everything. If you're not in charge you have no control over your fate.'

'Control over fate,' she mused. 'But who in the world has that, ever?'

'We're going to have it if we do things properly.'

'Will we? Or are we hoping for too much?'

'Stop looking on the dark side, Ellie. We're going to make things happen as we want them to.'

'You make it sound so easy.'

'If you're determined enough it can be easy.'

'All right. Let's stop nattering and get out and view that building.'

'That's my girl!'

CHAPTER NINE

LATER THAT MORNING Ellie contacted the estate agent to arrange for them both to look over the building. She was about to call Leonizio when Rita, her secretary, appeared in the doorway.

'There's someone to see you,' she said. She lowered her voice to add, 'It's *her*.'

'Who is *her*?' Ellie queried, but fell silent when she saw Harriet standing behind Rita.

Now she realised that she had always known this would happen. Two women at war with each other were always bound to meet.

'Please come in, Signora Fellani,' Ellie said calmly.

Up closer, Harriet was a beautiful woman, but her face was sharp, her eyes hard.

Her pregnancy was nearing its final moments. Ellie pulled out a chair for her and Harriet edged carefully into it.

'I don't call myself Signora Fellani any more,' she said. 'I stopped being Leonizio Fellani's wife months ago, when I couldn't stand him any longer.'

'Are you saying he ill-treated you?' Ellie said, speaking with difficulty.

'That depends what you call ill-treatment. He didn't knock me about. He didn't have other women. The world would have said he was a good husband, except when you got close to him, tried to look into his heart and found that there was nothing there.'

'I really don't think—' Ellie began carefully.

'You don't think I should be telling you the truth about what a cold, hard man he is because you don't want to know it. Oh, yes, I know all about you and Leonizio. I've heard the rumours but I didn't believe them until last night when I saw you together.'

'You saw a lawyer dining with her client—'

'So I thought until I saw how you were with each other at the table. And then you ended up in his arms.'

'So it was you watching us through the window. But what you saw was an accident. I fell over.'

'Don't try to fool me. You're in love with him. I recognise the signs because I was in love with him once. It was the biggest mistake I ever made. Oh, he's pleasant enough until he gets his own way, but that's all that matters to him. And if he doesn't get it—heaven help you!'

'You didn't love him,' Ellie said passionately. 'If you did, you could never have gone with another man.'

'I found a man who truly valued me, put me first, treated me as though I mattered. You know what Leonizio cares about? His business, his ambitions, his power, *himself.* And people fall for it. They all jump to do his bidding. But you'll learn. He'll break your heart as he broke mine.'

'As you broke his,' Ellie raged.

'He's hurt because of the child, not because of me.' She leaned closer to Ellie. 'I'm really sorry for you. On the outside you're all businesslike efficiency. Who could suspect that you could let emotion get the better of you? But I think you have. You won't admit it to yourself, but it's true. And he'll make you pay for it.'

'Get out,' Ellie said furiously. 'Get out of here *now.*'

A jeering smile illuminated Harriet's face. 'Don't worry, I'm going. You've told me all I need to know.'

In the doorway she paused, looking back. 'I tried to warn you. Never forget that.'

Then she was gone.

For a moment Ellie was too shocked to move. At last she managed to make her way to the door and look out into the corridor. It was empty. There was no sign of Harriet. It was as though she had never been there, except for the legacy of dread and dismay she'd left behind in Ellie.

Businesslike efficiency. That was what Harriet had said, and at this moment she must cling to it, doing her job, refusing to let herself be disturbed by what she had heard.

The phone rang. She snatched it up and heard Leonizio's voice.

'Did you call the estate agent?' he asked.

'Yes. He's expecting you this afternoon.'

'Can you come with me?'

'Yes, I've no appointments.'

As she'd expected, Alex was ready to give her the time off to indulge such a client. It brought back the uneasy memory of Harriet saying that people jumped to do Leonizio's bidding.

Leonizio arrived to find her waiting for him outside her office.

'Are you OK?' he asked. 'You look a bit shaken.'

'No, everything's fine.'

She wondered if she should tell him about Harriet's visit, but just now she couldn't bring herself to do it.

Together they inspected the building. It was a large, bleak-looking place that had been built nearly fifty years ago. As far as Ellie could tell it was in good condition, but she could be sure of little else.

She found it hard to know if Leonizio was pleased with

what he saw. He allowed very little satisfaction to be revealed to their guide.

'It's not quite what I expected,' he observed at last.

'There's more I could show you,' the agent said in a pleading voice.

'No need. I'll take another look around before finally deciding against it. I'll see you before I go.'

When the agent had hurried away Ellie said, 'So you really don't like it?'

'Whatever gave you that idea?'

'You told him—'

'I said what was necessary to knock the price down. In fact it's ideal for me. I can see exactly where I'll put all the machinery. Let me show you.' He led her to a nearby wall. 'The toe-laster will go at this end.'

'Toe-laster?'

'It's the machine that shapes the front point of the shoes. And over there I'd put the heel-attacher, which makes sure the heel is straight with the toe. A little further on there's the perfect place for the finishing room.'

'You've got it all worked out,' she said, dazed. 'However did you do it so fast?'

'It was obvious to me the moment we came in. Not that I said so to the agent. If I'd told him how much I really like this place it would have cost me a fortune.'

'You conniving so-and-so!' she exclaimed.

'I'll take that as a compliment. It's just another name for a good businessman. I do it my way and I won't yield more than I have to.'

She looked at him with interest. 'But you don't just mean that in business, do you? That's how you live as well.'

He seemed to consider.

'Mostly,' he said at last. 'Sometimes I achieve my victory, sometimes I'm defeated.' His tone changed, became more thoughtful. 'But the thing to be really wary of is that occasionally a victory turns out to be meaningless. You think you've won everything you want, but something you hadn't anticipated undermines it. There's no way to predict in advance what it's going to be.'

'That's true,' she said quietly. 'You can make me quite nervous that way.'

He shook his head. 'Let's be clear about one thing. I don't make you anything like as nervous as you make me.'

'Oh, surely—'

'You're the one with all the power, Ellie. We both know that.'

'And you hate it, don't you? It makes you furious with me.'

'It's not that simple.' He hesitated before saying quietly, 'I have angry moments, but there are also other moments when you make me think—'

'Think what?'

'Think all sorts of things that I don't want to think, but I have to because I'm afraid they're true. And think about how I have to change myself to—'

'Hello! Are you there?'

The voice of the agent a few yards away made them both tense. Leonizio checked himself and looked away from her.

'Yes, we're here,' he called back.

Before her eyes he became his other self, confronting the agent with a wry, dismissive manner.

'This place isn't bad,' he said grudgingly. 'But it's not worth the price that's being asked.'

'It's a very fine building,' the agent protested. 'Well built, well designed, and in good condition.'

'So I should hope. But my best offer is—'

The price he named made the other man gulp then attempt an unconvincing laugh.

Ellie regarded the ensuing discussion with fascination. Leonizio had described his business self as hard and unyielding. Now she saw that it was true.

Eventually the agent telephoned the head of the company that owned the building. A sharp conversation followed, after which he hung up and told Leonizio, 'He'll call you tonight.'

'Fine. Tell him not to keep me waiting too long. Now, I'll be going.'

She thought wryly that if he was trying to win her admiration he was succeeding. His ruthless manner might have seemed chilling, but she'd heard enough about the previous owners to know that they had brought their financial problems on themselves by bad management. Leonizio was merely proving his skill.

As they left the building she said, 'Do you think they'll give in?'

'Not a doubt. I recognise the signs.'

Of course he did, she thought. Making the other side give in came naturally to him.

But his other words haunted her. He'd spoken of having to make changes in himself. That suggested a different Leonizio, one who could be self-critical. It was a side of him she hadn't suspected, and which warmed her to him.

On the way home he said, 'I've got some investigating to do before I conclude this. Okay if I use your computer?'

'Go ahead. You need all the backup you can get. Let me know if I can help.'

When they arrived she expected him to head straight for the computer, but he picked up the phone.

'Alex? It's Leonizio. I just want to thank you for letting me have Ellie's services. She's the best. I've found the place I want to buy and she's been a great help. I'll rely on her to handle the purchase, and I hope you'll let her hang around to help me. What's that? You will? Great! You want to talk to her? Here.'

He handed over the phone and vanished.

'Ellie?' Alex sounded full of eagerness. 'Congratulations. You're doing a fantastic job. He wants you to stick with him and I've told him you can. Well done. We won't have many customers rolling in as much money as him. Bye now.'

She found Leonizio sitting at her computer, using the Internet to connect to his firm in Italy, his professional contacts and his bank accounts.

'Great,' he said at last. 'Whatever the price, I can handle it.'

He sent a few messages, then gave the thumbs-up sign. Ellie returned it in a mutual salute.

'What's that noise?' he asked, turning in the direction of the front door.

'Maybe the postman. I think something landed on the carpet.'

She was right. A letter with her name lay there. Opening it, she found a note from a friend who lived in the same building that she had left.

The postman was about to put this through your door. I stopped him so that I could send it on to your new address.

It contained a letter that made Ellie draw a sharp breath of delight. 'They want to set a date for my first pregnancy scan,' she said.

'Great. We'll go together.' He gave her a quick sideways glance. 'Unless you object.'

'Of course I don't. How can you think that?'

'I'm not usually part of your plans.'

'Nonsense. Just because I won't marry you doesn't

mean I'm shutting you out. You're this baby's father, and nothing's going to change that.'

'Thank you,' he said. 'And you're right. Nothing will change that. And I'm going to be there, part of our child's life. Always. Give them a call and set the date for us to go.'

She called the hospital, but received an offer that made her hesitate.

'It could be tomorrow,' she murmured to Leonizio.

'Excellent.'

'But won't you be busy tomorrow, making all the business arrangements? That building is important.'

He shook his head. 'Not as important as this,' he said, pointing to her belly. 'Nothing in the world is as important as this.'

Joyfully, she turned back to the phone and made the arrangements.

'Ten o'clock tomorrow morning,' she told Leonizio.

He nodded, smiling in a way that touched her heart. It had a warmth and eagerness that was unlike anything she had seen in him before. He was happy, she thought. Involvement with the baby gave him a pleasure that nothing else could offer.

That evening he insisted on cooking supper for both of them.

'You shouldn't exert yourself tonight,' he said. 'I'll even do the washing-up, while you have an early night. No arguments.'

'No arguments,' she promised.

It was lovely to be so well looked after, even if she knew that she wasn't really the object of his loving concern.

He was the same next morning when he cooked breakfast and served her carefully. When it was time to leave for the hospital he took her in his arms, drawing her close for a hug.

'Look at me,' he said at last.

She looked up and found him gazing at her tenderly.

'Are you all right?' he asked.

'I'm fine, looking forward to what we're going to find out.'

'Yes, it'll be wonderful.'

He dropped his head and she felt the soft touch of his mouth against her own, lingering for the briefest possible moment.

'We're in this together,' he whispered. 'Now, let's hurry.'

She nodded and backed out of his arms, knowing that she must escape before he sensed the reaction she could barely control. Another second and she would have yielded to the temptation to return his kiss.

Perhaps it was better that she hadn't, she thought. Her own lips might have revealed too much of the reaction she could barely control.

They reached the hospital in good time and were directed to the department where scans took place. There they were greeted by the sonographer.

'It's not a long process,' she said. 'Maybe twenty minutes. I'd like you to lie down on this couch and remove all covering from your stomach.' She smiled at Leonizio. 'Are you staying with us?'

'Definitely,' he replied.

He assisted Ellie in removing some of her clothes and took her to the couch, where she lay down.

'What actually will the scan reveal?' Ellie asked.

'Several things,' the sonographer said. 'It will give us some idea of exactly how far along in the pregnancy you are and when you're likely to give birth. That's why it's called a "dating scan", because it makes it easier to plan dates. Can you remember the date of your last period?'

'Yes, but I can also tell you exactly when the pregnancy started. It was—' She gave the date of their love-making.

'As precise as that?' the sonographer queried.

Ellie met Leonizio's eyes. 'Yes,' she said, smiling. 'That date and no other.'

'You didn't need to tell me that,' he said softly.

'That would mean you're about twelve weeks pregnant,' said the sonographer. 'So the baby should be about five or six centimetres. Let's see.'

She began work, smoothing some gel over Ellie's stomach, then began to move a small handheld device over it. Leonizio sat beside Ellie, taking her hand in a comforting hold. She squeezed and felt him squeeze gently back.

At last a picture began to appear on a screen just above Ellie. Astounded, she saw the shape of a little head, viewed sideways.

'Is that—?' she gasped.

'That's your baby,' the sonographer agreed. 'And it seems to be the right size.'

Ellie felt Leonizio's hand tighten. She looked up, meaning to meet his eyes but his gaze was fixed on the screen. The sonographer continued moving the device over the gel and gradually more details came into view.

'You can even see some features,' Ellie murmured.

'That's a real personality coming out,' Leonizio agreed. 'Our child. *Our child.*'

'And it seems to be a very healthy child,' said the sonographer. 'All the signs are good.'

'Perfect,' Leonizio murmured.

He put his arms around Ellie and drew her close to him, looking down into her face, his eyes shining with delight.

'Thank you,' he whispered. 'Thank you with all my heart.'

'You can get dressed now,' the sonographer said.

She went to the other side of the room, leaving them

alone while she put something into a computer. Tenderly Leonizio supported Ellie as she eased down from the couch, and helped her to dress.

'Do you feel all right?' he asked anxiously. 'Did you suffer at all?'

'No, I'm well. Isn't it wonderful?'

'It's the most wonderful thing that's ever happened,' he said with intensity.

Over his shoulder she saw the sonographer signalling for her to approach, but also making a slight gesture indicating that she was to come alone.

'I'll be back in a moment,' she said, and slipped away.

The sonographer greeted her with a smile, murmuring, 'Are you completely certain when the pregnancy started?'

'Absolutely.'

'And the information from the scan confirms it. So we know when you can expect the birth. Here.' She gave Ellie a printout from the computer. 'This is a report of everything we've discovered today, and it makes cheerful reading for you and your partner.'

'I can't believe that we actually saw our baby,' she said.

'It was an excellent picture, and you can keep it. Here.'

She held up a paper for Ellie to see. It was a printout of the picture that had appeared on the screen.

'Oh, lovely!' Ellie gasped, seizing it. 'Thank you, thank you!'

She tucked it away. Showing it to Leonizio was a treat to be enjoyed later.

As they left the hospital he said, 'Let's find somewhere to celebrate.'

When they were settled in a restaurant he ordered sparkling water for them both.

'But aren't you having champagne?' she asked.

'Are you?'

'No, we agreed I couldn't drink alcohol.'

'And neither will I.'

'Thank you. That's nice of you, but I really don't mind. Have champagne if you want to.'

'But I don't want to.'

The waiter arrived with the sparkling water. Leonizio filled their glasses and raised his to her, saying, as he had often said before, 'We're in this together. Isn't that true?'

'Oh, yes.'

'Here's to our baby. Here's to the future. Here's to the best day of our lives. At least—' he checked himself '—the best day of my life. I hope you feel the same.'

'I feel wonderful but—' she sought for the right words '—I'm cautious, superstitious maybe. Just when things seem most hopeful, that's when they can often go wrong. You told me yourself that a victory can sometimes turn out to be meaningless.'

'And I have reason to know it,' he agreed wryly. 'This isn't the first pregnancy scan I've been to.'

'You went with Harriet?'

'Yes, although she tried to persuade me not to. Idiot that I was, I didn't realise that she might have a suspicious reason. But of course I wasn't part of her life any more.'

'But could she have known for certain that you weren't the father?'

'I suppose not. She must have slept with another man while she was still sleeping with me, so she must have known it was possible but she couldn't be sure. I guess she didn't want to risk me finding out at that moment. It was only later that she decided to leave me.'

'So you went to her scan. What was it like?'

His face became bitter. 'The cruel irony is that it was pretty much like today. A perfectly formed baby, the right size, everything happening as it should. It felt marvellous, both then and subsequently. But it was an illusion, and I should have known it.'

'But how could you have known it at that moment?'

'Because I knew her, the kind of person she was. I knew she told lies when it suited her, but I told myself they were only little lies about unimportant things, so it didn't matter. She'd buy an expensive dress and pretend that it had cost less than it really had, so I just shrugged. In fact, I believed what I wanted to believe.'

'The way people do when they're in love,' Ellie ventured.

'Whatever being in love means,' he grunted.

'It means what you felt about Harriet. You ignored the truth about her because you didn't want to know it.'

'Because I'm a coward who couldn't face it.'

'Love can make people weak,' she mused.

'Is that experience talking?' When she didn't answer he said, 'I can't believe that a woman like you has never been in love.'

'A woman like me?' She gave a little laugh. 'Awkward, stubborn, recklessly stupid, opinionated—'

'Of course. Those are the things I like best about you.'

'That's lucky, because that's the only side of me you'll ever see. It tends to get in the way of the sentimental stuff.'

Without looking directly at her, he poured himself another glass of water.

'But surely there's been some sentimental stuff in your life? What about after your ex-boyfriend left you?'

'What happened with him taught me a lesson about survival, but it doesn't haunt me. Why should it?'

'If it really meant anything to you, it would never completely go away.'

Like Harriet has never really gone away from you, she thought.

Still, Leonizio was curious about her love life. What she had told him on their first night together had made it easier for him to confide in her about his wife. Her warmth and kindness had made him reach out to her, with results that once he would never have expected.

She'd implied that a man had left her because her looks weren't up to standard, and certainly she was no conventional beauty. But she wasn't plain. There was a beauty in her face that had little to do with the shape of her features. It was the light that sometimes shone in her eyes. There was warmth in that light, also a shrewd intelligence that could make a man want to know and understand her better.

She could intrigue him, charm him, but also make him want to fight and overcome her. The one thing she never did was bore him.

He reckoned the man who'd abandoned her because she wasn't pretty enough was a fool.

He glanced up, intending to meet her eyes, but found he'd lost her attention. She was looking around her urgently.

'Is something the matter, Ellie?'

'I'm trying to find the waiter. I'd like a little snack. Ah, there he is, but he's not looking this way. I'll go and talk to him.'

She vanished before Leonizio could protest that this was his job. For a moment he sat brooding about the events of the morning. Then he noticed where she had left the large envelope that contained the details of the scan. Eagerly he reached out to open it. There was the picture of his unborn child. He studied it, remembering the other time that had seemed full of hope, until the hope died. But this hope would not die. He would cling to that belief. He raised his head, closing his eyes, withdrawing into another world where there was only himself and his determination.

On the other side of the restaurant Ellie caught up with the waiter, asked him to attend and turned back to the table.

What she saw made her pause. Leonizio was holding

the baby picture, his face full of an emotion she could not understand. Was it happiness or sad remembrance? Sometimes, when he laughed and joked with her as he often did in their relationship, he seemed like a man who hadn't a care in the world. But for him laughter was a protective shield. Beneath it there was always the sadness and vulnerability that he was determined the world would never discover.

As she watched he raised his head, closing his eyes, seeming to retreat to a place where he was alone.

Ellie had sworn to protect herself against love, but in that moment her heart went out to him. She wanted to console him, reassure him that he wasn't alone, that she was there, that she would do anything for him if only it would bring him joy and confidence.

She returned to him slowly. At first he didn't seem aware of her and she sat opposite him, staying silent until he looked down.

'Are you all right?' she asked.

'I'm fine.'

'You don't look fine.'

'It's just that—when I think I'm managing all right certain thoughts come over me and catch me unprepared.' He made a wry face. 'I don't come out of this well, do I?'

'You come out looking vulnerable, the way people do when their feelings are more than they can cope with.'

He frowned ironically. 'I don't think I can agree with that. I'm a businessman. I don't have feelings.'

'You'd really like to believe that, wouldn't you? Even though you know it's not true.'

He sighed and shrugged. 'I guess you're right. You know, I could get scared at how well you understand me.'

'Nonsense. We're best friends, remember?'

He nodded. 'The best friend I'll ever have in my life.

I've begun to realise that I've never talked to anyone the way I can talk to you.'

'Not even Harriet?'

'I could never be completely frank with her, certainly not about my failings. She'd have used them against me.'

'And you think I won't?'

He gave her a warm smile. 'No, you'll just laugh at them.'

'One of the great pleasures in life,' she said with a soft chuckle. 'A man you can laugh at.'

'Let's hope I don't disappoint you.'

She had a sense of delightful warmth. They were growing closer, drawing her nearer to the moment she longed for.

'I'll let you know if you do,' she said.

'So I needn't kid myself that I'm the boss.'

'Well, I might let you kid yourself, now and then.'

'I'm sure you will. We have a saying in Italy. In any relationship the man is the head. But the woman is the neck, and the neck controls the head.'

'I must remember that. It could be useful.'

'Now you've really got me scared.'

But he smiled as he said it, and again she had the sensation of being engulfed in warmth and pleasure. Every instinct told her she was where she belonged, with the man she belonged to and who belonged to her.

If only he would admit that he did.

Briefly Harriet appeared in her mind, warning her.

But Ellie shooed her away. Harriet had admitted defeat, something she herself would never do.

The waiter appeared, apologising because he could not supply the cakes she had ordered.

'Never mind, I'm happy to go home,' she said. She wanted to be alone with Leonizio.

'Me too,' he agreed. 'It's time you had a rest.'

'I don't think I need one. I'm stronger than you think.'

'Let's not take chances on that. We've already agreed that we don't know what the future holds. Come along. Home.'

CHAPTER TEN

HE TURNED OUT to be right. On the journey home Ellie began to feel a little queasy. She was glad to lie down while Leonizio sat at the computer. She needed to think of many things, for which she needed to be alone.

As she relived the afternoon in her mind certain moments stood out. The way he'd taken her in his arms, holding her close as he might have held a treasure he wanted never to lose. The warmth in his embrace and the even greater warmth in his eyes as they met hers.

We were together, she thought joyfully. *Together as we've never been before, even when we made love. Only it wasn't love that we made. There was passion, but not the feeling that now—*

She stopped, reluctant to face what lay in wait for her, although she knew now that it could no longer be avoided.

Love, she thought. *It's been there all the time but I was afraid to admit it. I want him. I want him in every way, but all he feels for me is kindness and need because of the baby. If Harriet hadn't betrayed him he'd still be with her. That night he saw her in the restaurant with the other man, it hurt him more than he could bear.*

But there was always hope. With every day they were growing closer and surely soon they would reach the moment when he reached out to her as a man to a woman?

She knew from their night together that she could inflame his desire, and perhaps with a little tenderness and encouragement she could make everything else happen.

I can make him realise he's mine, she thought. *Surely I can.*

There was a click as the door opened.

'Are you all right?' he asked. 'I didn't wake you, did I?'

'No, I'm awake.'

He came in and sat on the bed.

'I thought today must have been a strain on you.'

'It was better because you were with me. You make everything better.'

'Do I really? Sometimes I think I just drive you mad.'

She smiled. 'I don't mind being driven mad, as long as it's you.'

'Nice of you.' He laid a gentle hand on her stomach. 'It's too soon to know if we have a son or a daughter.'

'Do you prefer one to the other?'

'Not really. A man wants a son that he can raise in his own way, teach him his own ideals. But if I could have a daughter who was like her mother, with the same wicked sense of humour, the same lovely blue eyes with the hint of something mysterious behind them—I think I might prefer that.'

The emotion in his voice almost made her weep. The moment she longed for was drawing closer. He loved her, he was hers and soon he would declare it.

'You might not like it at all,' she mused. 'A daughter like that can be exasperating. That's what my father used to say.'

'He obviously didn't know how to appreciate such a daughter. But I may manage better. With you to help me.'

Her heart began to beat a little faster as her hope grew. It was happening, everything she longed for.

'Tell me,' she said softly. 'Do you think—?'

But she was interrupted by the sound of his cell phone.

'Damn!' he muttered. 'Why do people always ring at the wrong times?'

He answered the phone with a grunted, '*Sì? Sono* Leonizio.' Then he glanced up at her. 'It's my assistant in Rome. *Ciao*, Francesco.'

As he listened Ellie saw him grow still, frowning with displeasure. She could follow enough of the Italian words to know that there was a problem. Leonizio became annoyed, and he hung up suddenly.

'He's got rocks in his head,' he growled. 'A tiny difficulty with one of our customers, and he's confused. He wants me to go back fast, actually get on the next plane.'

Her heart nearly stopped. 'Oh, no, surely not?' she whispered.

'Of course not. I told him I can't even think of it, not when there are so many things here that matter.'

She knew a leap of pleasure at his refusal to leave her.

'No,' she said softly. 'You can't go back. Not now, when there's so much happening.'

'So much happening,' he repeated. 'And so much that's going to happen that we have to be ready for.'

'But we will be ready,' she said happily.

'Oh, yes, we will. How could they imagine I'd go back to Rome when I have to be here to finish buying the factory?'

'What? The factory? You mean—?'

'There's a mass of things to do, and I'm not leaving until it's all finished.'

Her head was spinning, and she could hardly believe she'd heard correctly.

'Yes, of course. The factory is a big development. We mustn't lose sight of what's important.'

She didn't know how she'd forced herself to speak so casually when her heart was thumping with disappointment. She'd convinced herself that he would stay for her sake, that he was beginning to love her, but it was only a stupid illusion.

Fool, she thought. *He's made his feelings plain enough. Just accept it. You can always marry him.*

But she knew she could never do that. Marriage would mean a life full of the aching desolation that pervaded her at this moment.

'Perhaps you should get back onto the Internet,' she said. 'Send Francesco an email with a lot of information about the business you're engaged in here. That should make him more realistic.'

'You don't know Francesco or you wouldn't talk about him being realistic.'

'No, but I do know that realism is vital,' she whispered.

'You're right. Of course it is. And I'm going to do what you said—get onto the Internet and contact Francesco with things he needs to know. Thanks for that. What would I do without my lawyer friend?'

'Hire another lawyer?' she ventured.

'No, thank you. You've got a terrific brain, and I don't want anyone else. Come on, let's get online.'

'You want me there too?'

'You're part of the firm that's handling the purchase for me. How can I manage without you?'

He led her into the next room and started the computer. Ellie's head was reeling from his words.

You've got a terrific brain. That was his idea of a compliment. She would just have to be satisfied with it.

She performed her duties with rigorous efficiency. He was grateful, hugging her warmly, declaring that he was lucky to have found her.

She managed to follow the emails he sent to Francesco, saying that he must remain in England. She drew comfort from that. He wasn't staying to be with her, as she would have wished, but it would buy her time to draw him closer to her.

She would cling to that hope. It was all she had.

After that she forced her efficient side to take over. Returning to work, she had a good meeting with Alex Dallon, who praised her skill in securing Leonizio and assigned her the task of handling his purchase.

'There's an interesting conference coming up in a few months,' he observed. 'You might like to attend with me.'

'I'm afraid not,' she said. 'I've been meaning to tell you that I'm pregnant, and I'll be on maternity leave by then.'

'Pregnant! I never suspected. Who—?'

'Leonizio.'

'So that's it. Will we be hearing wedding bells soon?'

'No.'

'You mean the wretch won't marry you?'

'Don't blame him,' she said quickly. 'I'm the wretch who won't agree to marry.'

'What? You'd turn down a man with his money? That security? Are you out of your mind?'

'No, but I'm a woman who prefers to live her own life, make her own decisions. We can do that now. This isn't the nineteenth century.'

'But surely—you could gain so much. A rich husband, an established place in the world—'

'There's more than one way to have a place in the world,' she said. 'And marrying a rich man isn't necessarily the way to do it.'

Now her work was even more concerned with Leonizio's business as she handled the purchase of the factory. He was greatly appreciative of her efforts, and often complimented her. Soon, she thought, he would speak some loving words. Just a few. And after that she could tell him that she agreed to marriage.

One night she returned home to find the apartment empty. There was a brief note from Leonizio letting her know that he was visiting some clients.

She had supper, then an early night. But there was no sleep. His unexpected absence had revived the old fears, making her recent hopes seem foolish fantasies. Restlessness grew in her. It was intolerable to be lying here, doing nothing when so much was happening that she longed to control. But the truth was that she had no control. There was the brutal fact she must face. She could do nothing while life whirled past, spinning her in directions she couldn't see or understand.

An ironic memory came back to her: Leonizio saying, 'Power is everything. If you're not in charge you're not in control of your fate.'

He'd been talking about business but she realised his words could apply to anything. From the start they had been engaged in a power game. They smiled, laughed, teased and flirted, but the underlying tension between them had always been a battle, never completely resolved.

Where will it end? she wondered. *How will it end? Or will it ever end?*

She rose and went to the window, gazing down into the street below, which was deserted. The street lamps were out and only the moonlight broke the darkness.

He could have gone anywhere in the dark, she reckoned. What was to stop him seeking the company of a woman who satisfied him more than herself? Restlessly, she paced the floor, but stopped as she saw her door opening.

'I got back half an hour ago,' he said. 'I tried to be quiet so as not to disturb you. Then I heard you moving about. I was worried about you. Are you all right?'

The relief of seeing him there was so great that she gasped. 'Yes, yes, I'm fine.'

He came further in and closed the door. 'Why aren't

you getting the sleep you need? Are you worrying about anything?'

'Worrying? Well, a little. There's a lot to worry about, for both of us.'

'You won't believe this, but when I heard movements coming from in here I got a bit scared,' he said. 'I thought you might have decided to slip away from me in the night, and I could hear you getting ready to go.'

'That's funny,' she said. 'I thought you'd vanished too.'

'Don't be silly. The only thing that bothers me is the thought of losing you. I'd do anything to prevent that.' His voice became gently humorous. 'Lock you up, bolt the door, bar the windows.'

'In other words, keep me a prisoner?' she asked lightly.

'I'll do what I have to.' He wrapped his arms about her. 'Don't forget I'm ruthless in pursuit of my ends.'

She rested her head against him. 'So am I,' she said.

His arms tightened a little. 'You might be shocked to know just how terrible I can be.'

'I could say the same.'

'Are you warning me to beware of you?'

She raised her head to look him in the eye.

'You already know that,' she whispered.

'I guess I do. But it might be interesting to find out the rest.'

He drew her closer, letting his mouth rest on hers in a way that made her heart beat faster. But suddenly he tensed and drew away.

'I'm sorry,' he said. 'I should have more self-restraint.'

'You mean you shouldn't kiss me?'

'If we went any further I couldn't stop at kissing you. I want to make love to you but—well, I know I mustn't. Not now.'

'Leonizio—'

'When our child is born and it's safe again, then we'll

make love urgently. We'll have a wonderful night. But now I could do harm to you and the baby. I'm just concerned for you both.'

No, she thought. *You're concerned for the child. Not me.* Besides, it simply wasn't true that making love would hurt their baby. The medical advice she'd received had reassured her that there was no danger of that at all. But it hurt that Leonizio seemed to be using her pregnancy as an excuse to keep her at arm's length.

She was still tormented by the flood of desire that had risen in her, and which now turned into agonising emotion. She tried to control it but it overcame her and suddenly she began to cry. Tears poured down her face, defeating her efforts to stop.

'Ellie, please—'

'Go away,' she choked.

'I'm sorry I made you cry. I should have remembered that it happens easily in pregnancy. Harriet used to cry over nothing at all.'

'Yes, and you didn't care for her feelings.'

'Don't say that. How could you possibly know?'

'Because she told me what you were like.'

She spoke without thinking, and knew at once that she had done something disastrous. Leonizio's hand on her shoulder grew tense and his voice was harsh.

'What did you say? Have you and Harriet been talking?' His hands gripped her painfully. 'You told me you and she weren't in cahoots, but you were lying, weren't you?'

'No, I wasn't. She turned up in my office the other day. I didn't invite her and I threw her out.'

'But that night in the restaurant—'

'I hadn't met her then. I didn't meet her until she arrived in my office. She saw us together and wanted to come prying. She said things about you that I couldn't bear.'

'What did she say about me? Tell me.'

'I didn't mean to talk to her—'

'Tell me!'

'She said she wanted to warn me that you were a hard man with an empty heart; pleasant enough until you got your own way, but that was all you cared about. She said everyone jumped to do your bidding, and you'd break my heart as you broke hers.'

'And you believed that nonsense?' Leonizio exploded. 'I never broke her heart. If anything, it was the other way round. But you know that. I've told you things I'd die before telling anyone else.' He broke off and a frozen look came over his face. 'Now I'm beginning to wish I'd died before I told you. You swore I could trust you.'

'But you can,' she said desperately. 'I told you I didn't know Harriet was going to be in the restaurant that night and it was true. But she saw us there and came to find me at work. I couldn't stop her, and I told you I threw her out.'

'But not before you'd put your heads together and had a sneering talk about me.'

'Why do you find it so easy to believe the worst of me?' she demanded furiously. 'Or is it just that you believe the worst of everyone?'

'I don't want to. I guess sometimes I can't help it. After all, you might have told me she'd met you before this, but you chose not to. Am I supposed to trust you after that? Sometimes the worst is true.'

'Yes, I suppose it is,' she agreed quietly. 'That's something we have to decide. I think I'll go to bed now. No, don't come with me. I want to be alone.'

He didn't try to dissuade her, but stared blankly until she had left the room. Then he turned and left the apartment, slamming the door violently behind him.

Ellie heard the slam, feeling the sound go through her.

It was like listening to the world end. Whatever she had hoped might happen between them, it wouldn't happen now.

Maybe they never had a chance, right from the start. Perhaps she should have told him about meeting Harriet but she'd thought she was doing the right thing. Sometimes the right thing was the wrong thing. But it had proved that they could never have a life together.

She lay down and tried to sleep. But sleep wouldn't come. There was something she had to do. She got to work.

Leonizio returned hours later to find Ellie sitting at the computer. She rose to confront him.

'Look, we have to talk,' he said.

'I don't think so. Everything's been said and we understand each other.'

'But earlier I said things I didn't mean—'

'I know what you meant. I understand far more than you think. Now, I have something to say to you.'

He was very pale. 'What is it?'

'I've been reading Francesco's emails. I don't understand the Italian perfectly, but I can follow enough to understand that he needs you out there urgently. I think you should go.'

Silence. Leonizio looked at her closely, as though trying to read in her face the things she refused to say.

'I've told him how to handle the situation,' he said. 'If I advise him some more I'm sure he can manage.'

'No, I think you should go back there at once. Francesco obviously feels he needs you.'

'Yes, but—don't you need me to look after you?'

'Thank you but I can look after myself.'

'In some things, yes, but—'

'I don't work too hard, take too much exercise, eat the wrong food.'

'Yes, the practical things, but is everything practical? Haven't there been nights when you awoke from bad dreams and came into my arms for me to comfort you?'

Yes, she thought bitterly. *But that was a mistake, and one I regret.*

'Don't you care about things we share?' he asked.

'I care about a lot of things you never even think of,' she said.

'That's not my fault. I don't know what it's like for you to be pregnant, and what you could be going through. I try to imagine, but I'm sure I get it wrong. You should tell me more about it. Can you feel the baby moving? That sort of thing.'

'No, not yet.'

'But when you do, won't it be a wonderful moment for us to share?'

'Of course, but—there are lots of things we can't predict. It might not happen until you come back from Rome.'

'So you really think I should go?'

'Your business needs you. Don't leave Francesco fumbling on his own.' She managed to put a teasing note in her voice. 'After all, what kind of father lets himself go bankrupt?'

'Well, I suppose if you put it like that—'

'We can stay in touch.'

'Of course. We must.'

'I'll continue handling the factory purchase according to your instructions.'

'Oh, yes—I see.'

His expression showed that he'd finally understood that she was putting a distance between them.

'I guess I'd better go then,' he said.

His voice was blank and emotionless. Try as she might, there was no way she could be sure what he was thinking and feeling. And that was how he wanted it, she realised.

He telephoned Francesco for half an hour, then hung up to say he would leave that afternoon.

'It sounds serious,' he said in a low voice.

'Then you'll be gone for some time.'

'I guess so. I'd better start packing.'

She accompanied him to the airport, waiting in silent patience while he went through the formalities. For the last few minutes they went to a small café.

'Let me know when you arrive safely,' she said.

'Yes. And we must stay in touch. Let me know when you have appointments, and what the doctors tell you.'

'Of course I will.'

'How are you feeling now?'

She pointed down to her stomach.

'All is well,' she said. 'We're fine, both of us.'

He looked closely. 'You're just beginning to show a slight bump.'

'Is it really beginning to show? Oh, good! It makes everything more real, especially now I have that picture.'

'Yes, there's a new person on the way,' he said softly. 'Something to look forward to.'

Before she could reply, the loudspeaker proclaimed the start of boarding.

'Time to say goodbye,' Leonizio said. He laid his hand gently on her bump. 'Goodbye to you too, little one.'

'Goodbye, Daddy,' Ellie said.

He grinned. 'Thanks. That's lovely.' Laying a hand on her shoulder, he drew her forward and laid his lips on hers. It wasn't a passionate kiss, but it was affectionate and she returned it with pleasure.

She went with him as far as the check-in gate.

'Here's to the next meeting,' he said. 'Whenever it is.'

'I guess that's not in our control,' she said. 'We'll just have to hope for a kindly fate.'

He made a wry face. 'Don't count on fate being kind.

It's more likely to be spiteful. The best fate is the one we make for ourselves. I wish—'

He hesitated, as though uncertain what to say next.

'What?' she asked.

'I wish—it's hard to explain, but I wish—if only we—'

Final call for Flight—

The crowd was moving about them, making further talk impossible.

'Goodbye,' she said.

'Goodbye—goodbye.'

She kept her eyes on him until the last moment. She had a feeling that he'd turned back for a last look at her but with so many people milling around him it was hard to be sure.

Then he was gone.

CHAPTER ELEVEN

ELLIE KNEW THAT the sensible thing would be to return home at once, but these days she found it hard to be sensible. Instead she lingered in the airport, seeking a place where she might be able to see his plane begin to move slowly towards the take-off point

As she went out to the taxi rank she heard a sound overhead and looked up to see the plane soaring into the sky. She watched until it vanished into the clouds. Then she turned away and walked back to the taxi rank.

She could sense herself moving like a robot, and even thinking like one. Leonizio was gone. Life was over. Why was she bothering to return home? What was home? Did she have any such place?

At the end of the day he emailed her to say that he'd arrived safely. She already knew, having checked the plane's arrival online. But she was glad to hear from him, even though his tone was efficient and unemotional.

But perhaps that was only to be expected, she thought. She had urged him to leave, making it plain that he was no longer welcome. And now that he had gone there was no indication when she would see him again. Or if she would ever see him again.

She returned to work at the office, seeking comfort in her career, which was reaching a high point. Alex was proud of her, assigned more cases to her care and expressed his pleasure at the way she dealt with them.

Her thoughts of Leonizio grew more confused every day. He had turned against her in a way that seemed to freeze her out. But, to her amazement, she discovered that he had taken practical steps to protect her.

Two days after his departure she received a letter from the bank saying that every month a large sum of money was to be deposited into her account, from Leonizio.

She emailed him.

Why didn't you tell me?

He emailed back.

Why are you surprised? It's my job to look after both of you.

She surveyed the words with bitter irony. In her job she often talked to mothers frantically fending for themselves because the men who'd fathered their children had abandoned them, ignoring their responsibilities.

How those women would have envied her, thinking her lucky to have a man who attended so rigorously to his financial duties.

Lucky, she thought. *That's what they'd say I am. If only they knew.*

As promised, Leonizio stayed in touch. His business dealings were troublesome, but he seemed able to get control. At her end the formalities of the factory purchase were also going well.

In this way time passed. Any hope she might have had that he would seize the first chance to hurry back proved empty. Often she relived the moment at the airport when he had said, 'I wish—it's hard to explain, but I wish—if only we—'

What had he wished? What was the meaning of 'if only'? She longed to understand but she could gain no whisper of hope.

Many times she asked herself why she had not simply taken the easy option of marrying him and enjoying whatever closeness could unite them. But she knew she couldn't have done it. The pain would have been too great. She could never have deceived herself that he loved her. If she'd had any hope his casual acceptance of their parting would have forced her to face the truth.

Gradually the time passed, more time than she had ever imagined when she'd first urged him to go. At last came something she had longed for and dreaded equally: the feeling of her baby moving in the womb.

It was what Leonizio had wanted. 'A wonderful moment for us to share', he'd said. But he wasn't here to share it. And that was her fault, she reflected sadly. She had sent him away.

She emailed him.

The baby's moving. I can feel it.

It took two days for him to reply.

Sorry to be so long but I've had to be away for a few days dealing with someone who's trying to ruin my business. Dealt with him, but got behind with my mail. Wonderful news about the baby moving. Glad everything's going well. Take care of yourself.

She was lucky enough to feel well most of the time; the morning sickness had abated now, and so she was able to bury herself in work. Alex was pleased with her success and she could sense her career climbing as never before. How she was going to combine it with motherhood was something she still hadn't worked out. But she had no doubt it could be done.

Often she would brood over the different choices that faced her. It was hard to sort them out when she didn't know how large a part Leonizio would be playing. But she didn't regret her decision not to marry him. She was her own woman, independent, able to stand alone whatever happened. And she wasn't going to let that change.

Days passed relentlessly. Her pregnancy was now nearly twenty-four weeks along and it was time for another scan. The first one had shown everything was normal, which was likely to be the case with this one. She was in a confident mood as she entered the hospital and headed for the department.

The sonographer was the same one who had scanned her before. She greeted her cheerfully, indicating the couch. Ellie settled herself on it, then pushed down her skirt to her hips and raised her top high up, leaving a bare space for the scan.

They started work. Again the sonographer adjusted the screen in a position where they could both see it easily. She spread gel over Ellie's stomach, then began to move a handheld device over it. As before, the baby appeared on the screen.

Ellie drew in her breath in delight at the picture, larger than before. There was her child. Its head was at a slight angle, but her impression was that it was facing her, sending a silent message of love and need.

If only Leonizio could have been here now to see this new picture. How happy it would have made him. She smiled at the picture, sending back her own message of love.

'Isn't he gorgeous?' she breathed. 'Or she.'

'One moment,' the sonographer said. 'I need another look.'

After a few more tense moments she said, 'I'm afraid we'll have to do another scan soon. The baby is a little smaller than I'd expect at twenty-four weeks. It might not be serious, but we need to discover a little more.'

'Discover what?' Ellie asked in a shaking voice. 'What will you be looking for?'

'It's too soon to say—'

'But what could the worst be? Tell me. I must know.'

'There is the possibility of foetal abnormalities. It's not certain, but there's just a chance that we have to look into.'

'Abnormalities. Oh, heavens.'

The sonographer uttered more comforting words but Ellie barely heard them. The word 'abnormalities' thundered in her head. Filled with confusion, she left the building and made her way home in a daze.

Once safely shut inside, she found a silence that descended on her like thunder. Everything she had believed in, hoped for, was suddenly snatched away, leaving her in a nightmarish desert.

For hours she remained there, sometimes walking about from room to room, sometimes sitting with deadly stillness.

At last she knew what she must do. There was only one person she could tell about this disaster. He had a right to know and he was the only person she could trust to understand. She checked the time. It was late afternoon but she might just catch Leonizio at work. She seized the phone and dialled the number of his office. The call was answered by his secretary, who fortunately spoke English.

'I'm sorry, Signor Fellani is not here,' she said.

'Where is he? I must speak to him. It's desperately important.'

'He isn't in this country. He had to go to Paris to attend a business conference. There is much depending on it.'

'When will he be back?'

'Maybe next week.'

'Oh, heavens!' she whispered through the tears that were beginning to choke her. 'Ask him to call me then. Goodbye.'

She slammed down the phone, then dived into her diary, seeking his cell phone number. Wherever he was, she would find him now. But when she had dialled she received only a recorded message saying that the number was unobtainable. She fired off an email, not giving details but urging him to call her as soon as possible. Surely he would be checking his email, even if he was away from Rome and his office at the factory?

With all her heart she longed to reach out to Leonizio, but now she felt it was hopeless. It was surely not a coincidence that she couldn't reach him. He'd switched off his cell phone and instructed his employees to shut her out.

Bitterly, she reckoned that she had only herself to blame. She had banished him from her life, and he'd accepted her decision. She couldn't hope that he would call her.

He didn't. Hours passed, darkness descended and there was no sound from the phone. She knew she was clinging to false hope. Even if he finally called, would things be any better? He valued her only because of the baby, and would he still value their child when he learned of the disaster that threatened them?

There was no escape from the despair that had descended on her. There was only desert loneliness, and perhaps that was all there would be for the rest of her life.

Suddenly the silence was broken by the sound of the doorbell, ringing urgently. She stumbled out of bed, made her way to the door and pulled it open, too dazed even to put on the light. She could barely even see who was there until she felt herself seized in his arms.

'Ellie—Ellie—'

'Leonizio—it's you?'

But it couldn't be him, said a voice inside her. Dreams didn't come true like that.

'Yes, it's me—I'm here—hold onto me.'

She did so, clinging to him frantically, desperate to believe this was really happening.

'Leonizio! But you're in Paris.'

'I was, but when I got your message I came at once.'

'Your business conference—she said there was much depending on it.'

'To hell with that. Do you think it matters beside you? What's happened?'

'Oh, Leonizio—'

'Ellie, what is it? Why did you call? What's happened?'

Suddenly tears overwhelmed her and she collapsed against him. He lifted her, carried her to the bed and sat down, still holding her.

'Tell me,' he said.

'It's the baby—there's something not right. I had another scan today and there might be abnormalities.'

'What do they mean by that? What kind of abnormalities?'

'They don't know yet. They still have to find out. They say they can't be certain. It might still be all right or…or maybe not.'

His arms tightened about her and she felt him draw her down so that they were both lying on the bed.

'Hold onto me,' he said.

'Oh, thank heavens you're here.'

'I've always been here for you, even if you didn't know it. And I always will be.'

She clutched him, burying her face against his shoulder

while her tears flowed. He held her in silence, letting her weep while she needed to. He waited until she'd calmed down a little before speaking.

'Try to talk. Try to tell me everything that happened today.'

In a shaking voice she described the scan, the results.

'They'll need to do more tests,' she said, 'to find out how bad it is.'

'Of course. I have to see the medical report about the test you had today. So that I can show it to the doctors in Rome when we go over there for the tests.'

'Rome? You mean—?'

'Trust me, Ellie. I'm going to keep you with me all the time. If a disaster happens I'll be there, on the spot, to care for you.

'If you knew what my journey here was like today, terrified what might have happened, whether I'd find you alive…I can't endure another separation, so—' He hesitated before saying with a touch of nervousness, 'You have to come home with me, because I couldn't stand anything else. I'm sorry if you don't want to—'

'Yes—yes—I do want to.'

'You're sure? I know I'm giving you orders and that annoys you but—'

'You can give me all the orders you like. We're a family, all three of us.'

'Are we?' he asked. 'Do you mean that? I've never been sure that you actually felt that way.'

'But I do. You were right. There's nobody I need as much as you. *We're in this together.*'

'Yes,' he breathed joyfully. *'Yes, we are!'*

He lay down beside her. 'Go to sleep,' he whispered. 'We'll worry about the rest tomorrow. Tonight, it only matters that we're together.'

He couldn't have said anything more true. He was here.

He had put her first. It was like a dream come true. She lay in his arms, holding him with love and tenderness, while some of his words echoed in her brain.

He had said, 'You have to come home with me.'

Home. Wherever he was, that was home. And never had it been truer than now.

She awoke in the dawn to find herself still in his arms. He was regarding her tenderly. He looked down at her bulge, now much bigger, and touched it with tentative fingers. His eyes were alight with pride.

'It's about time you two reconnected,' she said. 'It's been a long time.'

'Yes, too long. The way you told me to go—I had a feeling you might be throwing me out for good.'

'I could never do that. But it seemed—we've never really understood each other.'

'That's true. But the time is coming when everything is going to be different.' He looked a little anxious. 'Don't you feel that?'

'Yes, I do. But we don't know how—'

'Hush!' He kissed her forehead. 'We must make it the right way, for the sake of—' He touched her bump. 'Come now. We have much to do.'

He helped her up, and remained at her service while she dressed. Over breakfast he studied the scan report. She watched his face, frowning, troubled, but then smiling as he glanced up at her, as though determined not to worry her.

At last he returned it to her, saying, 'The sooner we're gone the better. I've checked the times of the trains.'

'We're going by train?'

'It's better that way. I know flying in pregnancy is mostly safe, but if there are any fears about the baby it's better not to fly. It'll be a long journey, but I'll make sure you're comfortable all the way.'

He took her to the station and helped her into the first class carriage he'd booked for them both. At last they started the journey from London to the coast, through the tunnel beneath the sea and on their way to Paris. There they had to change trains for the final part of the journey to Rome.

She had an uneasy journey. For much of the way she felt queasy and had a headache. Leonizio cared for her every moment and when night came and she fell asleep she awoke to find him leaning anxiously over her.

'We're nearly there,' he said. 'Did you sleep well?'

'Oh, yes,' she whispered.

She'd had a lovely night, safe and contented in the feeling that she was going home. She reached up to him and they held each other close as the train headed for the last lap to Rome.

Ellie was only vaguely aware of the next few hours. A taxi was waiting for them at the station, and soon they were on their way home.

A doctor called the same evening. He talked to her at length and studied the information from the scans.

'I will make a referral. He's the best obstetrician there is.'

He arranged the appointment for the very next morning. Leonizio accompanied her and sat in tense silence while more tests were made.

'Is the baby really too small?' Ellie asked nervously.

'A little smaller than I'd expect, but it isn't necessarily serious.'

'But when will we know if there are any abnormalities?'

'When we get the test results. Don't assume the worst. Things could still go well.'

'And if they don't?' she wept. 'How badly could our child be hurt?'

'It's much too soon to say.'

'Could it be my fault? Have I done something wrong?'

'Stop it,' Leonizio told her. 'Don't look for reasons to blame yourself.'

'I'm afraid it's what mothers tend to do,' the doctor said. 'But sometimes things just happen for no apparent reason. I'll be in touch as soon as we know more.'

'Don't you have any idea now?' Ellie begged.

'I couldn't possibly speculate.'

His words seemed to threaten the worst. She dropped her head, feeling as though the world was crashing around her. Only the support of Leonizio's arms prevented her from crying out in despair. While he held her she could feel safe.

'Come along,' he murmured. 'Let's go home.'

They were silent on the journey home. When they reached the apartment he made her some coffee and sat beside her, sad and serious.

'I want you to stay here now,' he said. 'I have to look after you. I couldn't bear it any other way.'

'Nor could I,' she said. 'As long as we have you—'

'You do have me. Both of you.'

For the next few days Ellie tried to think as little as possible. She functioned mechanically, fulfilled her domestic duties, and did whatever Leonizio asked. But she kept her brain silent as much as possible. Brooding about what might be about to happen only brought pain.

She sensed that Leonizio was going through exactly the same thing. They didn't talk about it, but his fear was in his eyes. Whenever the phone rang he would answer it tensely, always expecting the crucial news. But it didn't come, and when he'd hung up he would shake his head and pat her on the shoulder.

At last, after three tense, agonising days, it happened.

The phone rang again. Ellie's eyes were fixed on

Leonizio's face as he snatched up the receiver, grating, *'Sì?'* in a harsh voice.

Then he didn't speak for several seconds, while her heart thumped with fear. But suddenly his face brightened, his eyes lit up and he made her a thumbs-up gesture.

'Yes!' he cried. *'Yes, yes!'*

He slammed down the phone and seized her in his arms.

'Good news!' he yelled. 'Everything's fine.'

'You mean the baby—?'

'Our baby is perfectly healthy. The tests say there's nothing wrong.'

'Oh, thank heavens!' She burst into sobs against him and for several moments they clung tightly, as if protecting each other from the world.

She could feel him shaking. Looking up, she saw that his face was as wet as her own, as though he too had been weeping tears of joy.

'I don't dare believe it,' she said. 'Can it really be true?'

'We're going to see them tomorrow,' he said huskily. 'And they'll show us everything. That call was just to alert us in advance.'

They saw the doctor next day and received a mass of communication that eased their minds. Also included was the estimated date of the birth, over three months ahead.

'And until then I strongly advise you to avoid all stress,' the doctor said. 'You've been lucky so far, but you're to take no chances.'

'We're going back to England,' Leonizio said.

'That's all right, as long as you go by train. No stress.'

'She'll be resting from now on,' Leonizio said. 'I'll see to that.'

'That's good to know. It's a relief to be able to leave her in your care.'

When they were alone Leonizio said, 'Aren't you going to say it?'

'Say what?'

'How dare I make decisions without consulting you? How dare I say that I'll make sure you rest when you have a job to go back to?'

She gave him a warm smile. 'I guess I know you too well by now to say any of that. I guess you've made all my decisions.'

He eyed her with a wry smile. 'Am I allowed to make your decisions?'

'I suppose I'll have to give you my permission. So tell me what I'm going to do.'

'We're returning to England because I think you'll feel happier there, and feeling happy will make you safer. You've done a great job buying the new factory, and I'm going to base myself there until our child is born.

'We settle back into our apartment and you stay there, where I can protect you and our baby, because nothing else matters but your safety.' A sudden thought seemed to trouble him. 'You did really give me your permission, didn't you? I didn't imagine that?'

'Don't worry. I'm not going to fight you about this.'

'What will Alex Dallon say when we tell him you're taking a long maternity leave?'

'He'll understand. I know it's what I must do.'

'Then everything's going well and we can stop worrying.'

'Hush, don't talk like that,' she said, urgently putting her fingers over his mouth. 'Never be too sure that things are going well. It's bad luck.'

'All right, I'll be cautious.' He gave a small wry laugh. 'I used to think that we made our own luck, that control was important. But now it's you who makes my luck, and I lost control a while back.'

'Are you saying that I have control?' she teased. 'You

don't really mean that. Tomorrow you'll say just the opposite.'

'You have some control. But our little unborn friend has most of it. Since the day we knew about him he's given the orders and somehow I find myself dancing attendance.'

'He? You want a son?'

'No, I'll be happy with a girl or a boy, as long as it's mine.'

'I've promised you it's yours. Don't you believe me?'

'Yes, I believe you. When I said "mine" I didn't mean like that. I meant that he or she will call me Daddy, ask me questions, tell me what they're thinking and hoping for, give me birthday and Christmas cards. If they get into trouble I want to be the one they send for. I want to know that nothing can ever take me out of their life.'

The emotion in his voice affected her painfully. His child meant everything to him. More than she ever would.

'You can be sure of that,' she said, speaking with difficulty. 'I won't come between you.'

'Does that mean you'll marry me?'

'Don't. I can't talk about that now.'

'But why—?'

'You don't understand. There are so many things we have to—let's talk later. I'm carrying your baby. Can't that be enough for the moment?'

'Except that you could run out on me whenever you like.'

'And you think if I was your wife I'd be your prisoner? Marriage certificates and formalities don't make it work,' she persisted. '*We* have to make it work.'

'And you don't think we can? All right, don't answer that. Your refusal is an answer in itself. Let it go. I promise not to trouble you again.'

So that was it. He'd bowed to her wishes and would no longer annoy her with marriage proposals. She guessed she should feel satisfied and triumphant.

But she only felt sad and defeated.

CHAPTER TWELVE

THE TRAIN JOURNEY back to England was peaceful, and life settled down quietly. As the weeks passed Leonizio behaved perfectly. He cared for Ellie like a dutiful protective father, anticipating her needs, ensuring that she was never under strain. And, true to his promise, he never uttered a word about marriage.

Ellie supposed she should be glad of that. It made her life easier and more relaxed. And if she occasionally had moments of desolation she told herself firmly to ignore them.

Gradually she grew bigger. The time was coming when they would know everything about the future. One night Leonizio helped her undress for bed. As her bump came into view he touched it reverently.

'I'm a lucky man,' he said. 'So much happiness now, and so much more in store for us. I can hardly wait. Do we really have to wait another month?'

'So the doctors say. But it moves so much I get the feeling of a real personality in there, almost as though our child was with us already.'

'In a way it is. Hey there!' he addressed her stomach. 'Be careful of your *mamma*. Don't give her a hard time.'

'I can always hope he or she will listen to you,' Ellie chuckled. 'But I don't think I can count on it.'

'True.' He grinned, saying, 'After all, its mother never listens to me.'

'Well, that might change—ah!' She checked herself with a gasp as a sharp pain attacked her stomach.

'What is it?' Leonizio demanded. 'Ellie, what's the matter?'

'I'm not sure. I just—something happened—' She clasped her bump and gasped again.

'Is it starting?' he asked in an alarmed voice.

'It's too soon for that but—yes, I think it is. Oh, heavens, I can feel such—*ah!*'

Now there could be no mistake. The pain that went through her was fierce and threatening.

'It's happening,' she groaned.

'Happening?' he echoed in alarm. 'You mean the baby—?'

'Yes, but—oh, no—please, this mustn't happen. It's too soon.'

'I'll call the ambulance,' Leonizio said through gritted teeth.

He seized the phone, made a tense call, then gathered her in his arms.

'Hold on to me. It's going to be all right.'

Desperately she clung to him as the pain ripped through her again, warning her of possible tragedy to come. The birth wasn't due for another month, yet now—

'It can't happen yet,' she groaned. 'It can't, it can't.'

But it could. In the despairing depths of her heart she knew that fate could be against them, snatching their child away in the last few moments before life began.

Her heart broke for Leonizio. She had promised him so much, longed so fiercely to make him happy. But in a few cruel minutes it might all be snatched from him again, banishing him back into the same bleak desert from which she had vowed to rescue him.

'They'll be here soon,' he said. 'We'll go to the hospital and they'll make everything right.'

But he sounded too firm, too determined, as though he was trying to convince himself as well as her. Looking at his face, she saw fear as well as hope.

'I'll do everything I can,' she choked. 'Truly—I'll try—I'll try—I don't know why this is happening—'

'It's not your fault,' he said fiercely. 'Don't even think like that.'

They clung together until the sound of the doorbell made him go and look out of the window.

'They're here,' he said, and hurried away.

A few moments later a stretcher was wheeled into the room. Leonizio lifted her in his arms, laying her gently upon it then taking her hand, which he held for the whole journey.

She was only vaguely aware of what was happening around her. There was the hum of the vehicle, and she could hear voices as Leonizio asked fearful questions, but she could understand little. The greater reality was the surge of pain that went through her again and again.

The ambulance stopped. They had reached the hospital. Through her spinning senses she could feel herself being wheeled inside. Faces appeared, full of concern. Hands touched her gently. She heard Leonizio talking to the doctor, explaining what had happened, exactly when the pain had started.

'The baby isn't due for another month,' he said. 'That's what we were told. It can't be coming now, can it?'

'We'll have to see,' the doctor said quietly.

Again pain flooded her, making her scream. 'Leonizio—*Leonizio.*'

Hardly aware of what she was doing, she reached out blindly and felt him take hold of her hands.

'I'm here, *cara,*' he vowed.

'Don't leave me.'

'It's all right if I stay, isn't it?' he demanded of the doctor. 'I can't leave her.'

'If she needs you it may be best for you to stay,' the doctor agreed. 'But please—'

'I won't interfere or get in your way,' Leonizio promised at once.

'Excellent.'

Again Ellie cried out. Now there could be no more doubt. Her body was possessed by contractions that told her things were moving fast. She clung fiercely to Leonizio, looking up so that her eyes met his.

'Soon,' he whispered. 'Soon we will have everything.'

If only, he thought desperately, her suffering could end now. It tortured him to see her terrible pain and know that he couldn't help her bear it.

Useless, he thought. *That's all I am. Useless!*

Time passed slowly. Sometimes she seemed able to relax, but then another contraction would seize her, leaving her seemingly exhausted.

'How long can this go on?' Leonizio asked wretchedly.

'It's coming,' said the doctor. 'Any moment now—'

Then he was reaching forward to help the baby out into the world. Leonizio had a slight vision of a tiny body, but it did not seem to move and he held his breath, silently praying in hope.

Suddenly it happened. The air was split by a wail that grew in vigour until everyone was smiling with relief.

'That's it,' exclaimed the doctor in delight. He examined the baby closely. 'It's a girl. She's a little small and she'll need extra care at first, but the signs are good.'

Leonizio leaned close to Ellie. 'Did you hear that, *carissima*? We have a daughter, and we're a family. Isn't that wonderful?'

But her eyes stayed closed and she only murmured, 'Mmm?'

'Ellie—Ellie—'

'I'm sorry but you'll have to leave now,' the doctor said grimly. 'She's losing a lot of blood and it needs urgent action.'

'Or what?' he demanded. 'If she loses too much blood—what will happen?'

'Then we'll have a tragedy, which we're fighting to prevent. Please, you must go now.'

Leonizio felt like tearing his hair out. He knew he must go but he couldn't bear to leave Ellie. Her eyes were still closed and he didn't know how much she heard. Leaning down, he kissed her forehead, her cheeks, her mouth.

'I'll be back,' he whispered. 'Just promise to be here, waiting for me.'

He went out into the corridor and found a seat just a short distance from the door. From here he could return in a moment if she needed him.

But he couldn't banish the thought that she didn't need him and would never need him again. She was disappearing into another world.

He had the strangest sensation of watching a parade. Everyone he had ever cared about was there, reminding him how little warmth and love there had been in his life and how cruelly it had vanished. The uncle and aunt who had raised him had merely done their duty, without giving him anything he could feel as affection. With Harriet there had been love, or so he'd thought until she'd betrayed him. And the child he'd believed his, who'd inspired his love while still in the womb. That love too had been snatched from him, abandoning him in what would have been a desert but for Ellie.

With Ellie there had finally been hope, but now she too was slipping away, leaving him the baby he wanted so much, but which he now realised could never console him for her loss.

He tensed as the door to the delivery room opened and a nurse emerged pushing a small trolley. She came over to him.

'I'm taking your daughter to the Special Care Unit,' she said. 'She won't have to be there long. Being a month early, she doesn't have full strength, but apart from that she's doing well. Once she's through this she can have a wonderful life.'

He looked at the tiny creature who lay with her eyes closed, clearly unaware of the world she had entered.

'My little girl,' he whispered. 'Mine. And Ellie's.' He leaned closer. 'Your mother and I are going to be so happy with you. She'll be well soon, and she'll hold you in her arms.'

The doctor appeared in the doorway. 'Would you like to come back in now?' he asked.

'Is she—what's happening?'

'She's still losing blood. We're doing our best but it may not be enough.'

'Not enough?' he echoed wildly. 'She can't die—she mustn't—'

'We'll keep her alive if we can,' the doctor assured him.

'But *can* you?'

'I hope so, but I can't give you a promise just now. Please come in.'

He returned to the delivery room. Ellie lay there, still and quiet.

'Ellie,' he whispered. 'Ellie, can you hear me?'

'Yes—yes.'

She hardly made a sound, but the movement of her lips encouraged him.

'It's me, Leonizio. I'm here. I'll always be here for you. And you must always be here for me. I can't lose you. I couldn't bear it. Promise not to leave me. Promise. Promise.'

At last she opened her eyes. He moved his face closer, desperately seeking some sign that she understood him. But she looked at him in confusion.

'Promise me,' he repeated frantically. 'I couldn't endure life without you. I love you.'

'Me?' she whispered. 'Love me?'

'Of course. You must always have known—'

'No—no—'

'But you know now. Tell me that you understand, please? *Please.*'

There was no response. Her eyes had closed again and for a terrifying moment he thought the worst had happened. But then he saw that she was breathing. She was still alive, but she had slipped away into another dimension and he must somehow find the strength to wait patiently for her to return to him.

But perhaps she would never return. She was close to death and he had a despairing feeling that his pleas to her had gone unheard. Perhaps for ever.

He leaned down so that his face was against hers.

'Wherever you are,' he whispered, 'come back to me. Please come back. *Please, Ellie, don't leave me.*'

Ellie had the sensation of wandering through a corridor of shadows. She was in a place where she had never been before, not knowing what lay ahead, able only to hear mysterious voices. One of them sounded like Leonizio's.

'Ellie, can you hear me?'

She whispered, 'Yes,' but she couldn't be really sure what she heard. Leonizio's voice was speaking of love, saying he couldn't live without her.

She opened her eyes, hoping that he was there, but she could see nothing clearly.

'I couldn't endure life without you. I love you.'

'Me?' she whispered in disbelief. 'Love me?'

He spoke again but she couldn't make out the words. She knew now that it was a delusion. She believed in his love because she longed for it, but the mists were swirling her away and unconsciousness was claiming her again.

Now only one sound reached her. A desperate voice, whispering—

Wherever you are, come back to me. Please come back. *Ellie, come back!*

She turned, reaching out with her hands and her heart. But there was only the mist swirling about her until everything else vanished.

She didn't know how long she was unconscious, but when she awoke her mind was clear.

'Ah, good, you're back with us,' said the nurse.

'My baby—?'

'She's fine. A little small but she looks good.'

'She?'

'Yes, you've got a lovely little daughter. Her father's enchanted with her.'

'He's here?'

'He brought you into the hospital.'

'Oh, yes, I think I remember. But it's so confused. I can't be sure of anything.'

'He was with you during the birth. He left to spend a little time with your baby, but he came back a few minutes later. We were getting worried in case you didn't survive, and he just had to be with you. When we told him the danger was past he nearly collapsed. He's with your little girl now, telling her she's lucky to still have a *mamma*.'

'Oh—goodness!'

'Hey, don't cry. Everything's going to be all right.'

Everything all right, she thought wistfully as memories of her dream haunted her.

It had been an impossible fantasy, with Leonizio reaching out to her, declaring love in words she could never hope to hear in real life.

She was vaguely aware that the nurse had gone away, but she wasn't alone. She thought Leonizio stood there, watching her with anxious eyes. She held her breath, fearful that this too was a fantasy.

He came to sit by the bed, leaning close enough to talk softly.

'Thank you,' he said. 'Thank you for coming back to me. I dared to hope you couldn't leave me after I begged you to stay.'

'You—begged me—?'

'Don't you remember?'

'I'm not sure. Did we—talk?'

'Ellie, what do you mean? How can you ask if we talked? We said things we've never said before, perhaps because the moment was never right before. I told you that I loved you. You didn't seem to believe me, but it's the truth. Don't you remember?'

'I was in a strange place. I was walking through a dark mist and heard your voice, calling me.'

He hesitated, then asked quietly, 'Did you know the place you were heading for?'

'No, but I think now—that if you hadn't made me come back—' she trembled '—I would never have returned.'

'That's what I was afraid of,' he said. 'You were so close to—' He paused, unwilling to say the word. 'I couldn't have endured it. How could you go away from me when I love you so?'

'Do you really—love me? Truly?'

'Why can't you believe me? Haven't I begged you to marry me all this time?'

'Only because of the baby. You wanted to love someone who would always be there for you, a child who would return your love because it was yours. After what Harriet did, you needed your own child even more. And I could give you one. That was all I meant to you. I was sure of it.'

'Perhaps that was true once, but the longer we were together the more you came to mean to me. And that scared me.'

'Scared? You?'

'It takes a lot to scare me, but you managed it as nothing else ever could. I think my love for you began our first night together, when I discovered your warmth and kindness, and I was so glad to fall into your arms. It was a sweet feeling but it took me time to realise how it had taken me over. And then I was horrified to realise the love was all on my side.'

'But it wasn't. It isn't. I do love you. I've loved you for a long time.'

'How can you say that when you've always refused to marry me?'

'Because I couldn't bear the thought of an unequal marriage, loving you but knowing that you didn't love me.'

'I did love you, all the time. When you refused to marry me it hurt, and not just because of the baby. I wanted you. Nobody but you. But I thought you despised me, and I must work hard to overcome your scorn.'

'How strange that you should say that,' she murmured.

'Why?'

'Because sometimes I've felt that it was you who felt scorn for me.'

'Ellie, no, you can't have felt that.'

'I've longed for some sign that you cared for me, not

just the baby. It never came. You minded about the baby, but never me.'

'That's not how it was. I minded about you so much I was afraid to face it. But even then—I knew I loved you, but until today I didn't fully understand how deep my love is. When I thought you were dying I couldn't bear to think of what my life would be without you. A blank desert with no hope of any kind.'

'But if that had happened—if I wasn't with you any more—you'd still have our child.'

'And I'd treasure her, for her own sake and in memory of you. I'd have called her Ellie, after you, because I can't survive without an Ellie in my life. Now I'd like to call her Cosima. It means order and beauty, which is what you both mean to me.

'You must promise to stay with me. Nothing and nobody could ever console me for losing you. Please, Ellie, tell me that I can hope. I'll do all I can to win your love, however long it takes.'

'But I've already told you that I love you. Don't you believe me?'

'I'm almost afraid to. If you believe in good news too easily, it can get snatched away. You warned me of that once yourself.'

'It won't be snatched away, I promise you, Leonizio. You are my love, now and for ever.'

'Do you love me enough to marry me?'

'I always have.'

'Say yes,' he begged. 'Just that one word. Let me hear it.'

'Yes. Yes, I'll marry you. Yes.'

For a moment he didn't move. His eyes met hers, full of happiness and adoration. Then he lowered his head, resting it against her breast like a man who'd finally found the way home to a safe haven. It was a feeling that Ellie completely understood because it was her own.

'Yes,' she repeated. 'We took too long to find each other, but now we have and nothing will separate us. We're together—all three of us.'

'All three of us,' he repeated. 'Marry me, and I ask for nothing else.'

He glanced up as the doctor appeared.

'We're going to be married as soon as she's out of here,' he said. 'When will that be?'

'I'm afraid I can't tell you,' the doctor said uneasily. 'The danger isn't over yet.'

'But we thought—when she came round—'

'That was hopeful, but not final.'

'You mean she might still die?' Leonizio was aghast.

'I'm afraid it's possible.'

Leonizio dropped his head, putting a hand over his eyes. Ellie reached out to touch his face.

'Then we must marry now,' she whispered.

'Ellie—'

'If I'm going to die,' she said urgently, 'I want to die as your wife.'

He dropped to his knees beside the bed and she felt his tears against her skin.

She looked up at the doctor. 'Will you arrange it?'

'Yes,' he said, and hurried away.

Ellie stroked Leonizio's face, saying softly, 'If I do die, it's better for you if we're married. You'll find it easier to claim our baby.'

'That's not why I'm marrying you,' he said fiercely. 'I want you. No one but *you.*'

'I'll be there. Even if I'm not alive—I'll always be there with you.'

'And you will be alive. You simply must be because to lose you would break my heart for ever.'

'Together,' she whispered. 'Always together.'

The doctor appeared again.

'It has to be a civil ceremony,' he said. 'That's all we can arrange under these circumstances. Of course you can have a religious ceremony later.'

He didn't add, *if you're alive*, but they both understood.

'How quickly can we do this?' Ellie asked.

'Yes, we've waited too long,' Leonizio said, looking at her.

'I'm sorry,' she whispered. 'I should have understood before—'

'Don't blame yourself,' he said, leaning close. 'It's my fault that you didn't understand—I did everything wrong. But at last we've found the way and can marry now.'

'There are some formalities that have to be gone through first,' said the doctor. 'The law requires us to establish that the patient is in her right mind and acting of her own free will.'

'But I am,' Ellie said urgently. 'I'm doing what I want more than anything in the world. Please, please, sign anything you need, to confirm that.'

Fear was rising in her. Only a few minutes ago she had seemed to be slipping away into the darkness and Leonizio had drawn her back with his love. But, despite the power of her heart, her body was still weak and the darkness beckoned again.

For months she had loved him and longed to be his wife, despite the problems that made her refuse him. Now her moment had come, but perhaps it had come too late. In a few minutes they would have lost each other. When he raised his head and met her eyes she knew that he too understood everything.

The doctor returned with a middle-aged man that he introduced as Mr Dale, an official who could perform the ceremony.

'There are two kinds of vows,' he said. 'First, the traditional ones that everyone speaks. But then there are some more vows that you create for yourselves, that express your own true feelings. Do you think you can manage them?'

'Oh, yes,' Ellie said fervently.

Leonizio nodded. 'Yes,' he said softly.

Mr Dale handed them papers with the official vows, and looked around to check that the doctor and a nurse were present as witnesses. 'Now we can begin,' he said. He uttered the introductory words, then glanced at Leonizio, who took a deep breath as though trying to control his nerves, and began to speak.

'I, Leonizio, take you, Ellie, to be my wedded wife.'

Mr Dale nodded, then looked at Ellie.

She tightened her grasp on Leonizio's hand and said fervently, 'I, Ellie, take you, Leonizio, to be my wedded husband.'

Watching his face, she thought she saw the gleam of tears upon his cheeks, and felt her own tears begin to flow. To her horror, she could feel her strength fading and knew that they had only a little time left to belong to each other.

But she would make the most of that time, for Leonizio's sake. It was the only thing she could do for him before their terrible parting.

'What personal vows do you wish to make?' Mr Dale asked.

Gently Leonizio laid her hand against his lips.

'I promise that nobody in the world will ever matter more to me than you,' he said in a gentle voice. 'I belong to you now and for ever. You are my life, and that is what you will always be. Only promise me the same, and I will have all I'll ever want.'

There was an urgent question in his eyes, fixed on her, pleading.

'I can promise you the same,' she said. 'And I do. I am yours. I have been yours from the first moment, and I will always be yours.'

'Always?' he whispered.

'Always—and for ever.'

She saw joy come into his eyes as she said 'for ever' and hoped that he could see the same joy in her eyes as they committed themselves to each other.

At last came the declaration. *You are now man and wife.*

'We're married,' he whispered. 'You belong to me and I belong to you.'

'Yes. I'm going to stay with you always. Even if I should—'

'Don't say it,' he said urgently. 'That mustn't happen. You've got to live because I can't endure life without you.'

'Then I will,' she said.

'Swear it.'

'I swear by everything I hold sacred.'

She had given her word and she knew she must keep it at all costs. To lose her would devastate him in a way she had never imagined. Feeling sleep overtaking her, she struggled to fight it off.

Watching her, Leonizio was suddenly terrified. 'Ellie—Ellie—'

'It's all right,' the doctor said, feeling her pulse. 'She's stronger already.'

'Already? How can you tell so soon?'

'Because the tide has turned. Something—or someone—has given her the strength to fight for life much more strongly than before.'

Something or someone? Looking down at her in his arms, he wondered if their marriage could really have provided her with a reason for living. Was he hoping for too much?

As the minutes passed he felt the dawn of hope. Holding her in his arms, he murmured, 'Stay with me, Ellie. You promised—you promised—'

Gradually he sensed her breathing grow stronger until at last she opened her eyes again and he could see in them everything he longed for.

'You're better,' he breathed. 'You're going to live. Can't you feel that?'

She smiled. 'Of course I am. I promised. And I'll never break a promise to you for as long as I live.'

Now they were legally married, but when Ellie was released from hospital they both wanted another ceremony to proclaim their love to the world.

On their wedding morning he awoke to find her sitting on the bed beside him, with Cosima in her arms. The sight flooded him with peace and happiness, which was how it would always be, he realised.

They'd travelled to Rome for the ceremony. Many of Leonizio's employees were there, anxious not to miss the sight of the woman who had transformed their employer. Some of her friends, including Alex, came over from England.

When Ellie appeared in her bridal gown there was a murmur of astonishment, for she was carrying little Cosima in her arms. Leonizio's eyes were fixed on them with joy, and a whisper went around that he was marrying both of them.

Then it was time to answer questions. The preacher asked, 'Do you take this woman to be your wedded wife?'

Leonizio's eyes met Ellie's. 'A thousand times over,' he said quietly.

The preacher looked uneasily at the bride. 'That's not the answer you're supposed to give.'

'Don't worry,' Ellie said. 'To me it's the perfect answer.'

A little gulp came from Cosima. Both her parents smiled at her in delight.

'We're agreed,' Leonizio said. 'All three of us.'

'Yes,' Ellie said. 'All three of us.'

And that, they both knew, was how it would always be.

* * * * *

ENEMIES AT THE ALTAR

MELANIE MILBURNE

To my niece Angie Fouche, who is a beautiful and brave young woman.

Love you.

P.S. EEEE!!!!

CHAPTER ONE

ANDREAS got the call from his younger sister Miette in the early hours of the morning.

'Papà is dead.'

Three words that under normal circumstances should have evoked a maelstrom of emotion, but to Andreas they meant nothing other than he was now free from having to play happy families on the extremely rare occasions his path crossed with his father. 'When is the funeral?' he asked.

'Thursday,' Miette said. 'Will you come?'

Andreas glanced at the sleeping woman lying beside him in the king-sized hotel bed. He rubbed at his stubbled jaw and let out a frustrated sigh. It was just typical of his father to choose the most inconvenient time to die. This coming weekend in Washington DC was where he had planned to ask Portia Briscoe to marry him once his business here was complete. He even had the ring in his briefcase. Now he would have to wait for another opportunity to propose. There was no way he wanted his engagement and marriage to be forever associated with anything to do with his father, even his demise.

'Andreas?' Miette's voice pierced his reverie and his conscience. 'It would be good if you could be there, for me even if not for Papà. You know how much I hate funerals, especially after Mamma's.'

Andreas felt a claw of anger clench at his insides at the thought of their beautiful mother and how cruelly she had been betrayed. He was sure *that* had been what had finally killed her, not the cancer. The shame of finding out her husband was sleeping with the hired help while she was battling gruelling rounds of chemotherapy had broken her spirit *and* her heart.

And then, to add insult to injury, the brazenness of that witch Nell Baker and her trashy little sleep-around slut of a daughter Sienna had turned his mother's final farewell into a cheap and tawdry soap opera.

'I'll be there,' he said.

But that little hot-headed harlot Sienna Baker had better not.

The first person Sienna saw when she arrived at the funeral in Rome was Andreas Ferrante. At least her eyes registered it was him, but she had *felt* him seconds earlier in her body. As soon as she had stepped over the portal she had felt a shiver run up her spine and her heart had started a crazy little pitter-patter beat that was nothing like its normal, healthy, steady rhythm.

She hadn't seen him in years and yet she had *known* he was there.

He was sitting in one of the pews at the front of the cathedral. Even though he had his back towards her she could see he was as staggeringly gorgeous as ever. His aristocratic bearing was like an aura that surrounded him. He exuded wealth and power and status. His glossy raven-black head was several inches higher than any of the other black-suited men sitting nearby, his thick, slightly wavy hair neither long nor short, but cut and styled so it brushed against the collar of his shirt.

He turned his head and leaned down to say something to the young woman seated beside him. Just seeing the profile of his face made Sienna want to put a hand to her chest where her heart was flapping like a frantic fish suddenly flung out of its fish tank. For years she had dismissed his features from her mind. She had dared not think of him. He was a part of her past she was ashamed of—*deeply* ashamed. She had been so young and foolish, so immature and insecure. She hadn't thought through the consequences of twisting the truth. But then, who did at the age of seventeen?

And then, as if Andreas sensed her looking at him, he twisted his head and locked gazes with her. It was like a lightning strike when those hazel eyes hit hers. They narrowed and glared, pinning her to the spot like a bug on a corkboard.

Sienna pasted an indifferent smile on her face and, giving her silver-blonde head a toss, sashayed up the aisle and shimmied her way into a pew on the left hand side a few rows back from his.

She *felt* his anger.

She *felt* his rage.

She *felt* his fury.

It made her skin shiver. It made her vertebrae rattle like ice cubes in a glass. It made her blood race. It made her knees feel weak, as if someone had removed all of her strong stabilising ligaments and put overcooked noodles in their place.

But she showed none of that. Instead, she affected a cool poise that her teenage self, eight years ago, would have sorely envied.

The woman seated beside him was his latest mistress, or so Sienna had gathered from a recent press article. Portia Briscoe had lasted longer than any of his other lovers, which made Sienna wonder if the faint whisper she had heard of an impending engagement had any truth to it.

Not that she had ever thought of Andreas Ferrante as the falling in love type. To her he had always been the playboy prince of prosperity and privilege. When the time came he would choose a bride to suit his Old Money heritage. Just like his father and grandfather before him, love would not come into it at all.

Although, going on appearances alone, Portia Briscoe looked like the perfect candidate to be the next generation Ferrante bride. She was classically beautiful in a carefully constructed way. The sort of woman who never went anywhere without perfectly coiffed hair and expertly applied make-up. She was the type of woman who wouldn't dream of turning up at a funeral on a whim, in faded jeans with ragged hems and soiled trainers or, God forbid, a T-shirt that had suffered a food spill.

Portia Briscoe *only* wore exquisitely tailored designer couture. She even had toothpaste commercial teeth and porcelain skin that looked as if it had never suffered a blemish on it.

Unlike Sienna, who'd had to endure the torture of braces for two years and had only that morning had to reach for her concealer to cover a spot on her chin.

Andreas Ferrante would make sure his bride never put a designer-clad foot out of place. His bride wouldn't have a history of bad choices and reckless behaviour that had caused more pain and shame than she cared to think about.

No, his bride would be Perfect Portia, not shameful, scandalous Sienna.

Good luck to him.

As soon as the service was drawing to a close, Sienna slipped out of the church. She still wasn't exactly sure why she had felt compelled to pay her respects to a man in death she hadn't even liked in life. But she had seen the news in the press about his death from a heart attack and immediately thought of her mother.

Her mother Nell had *loved* Guido Ferrante.

Nell had worked for the Ferrante family for years, but not once had Guido acknowledged her as anything but his housekeeper. Sienna remembered all too well the scandal her mother had caused at Evaline Ferrante's funeral. The press had gone wild with it, like a pack of hyenas over a carcass. It had been one of the most humiliating experiences of her life. To see her mother vilified, to see her shamed in the most appalling way, was something Sienna still carried with her. She had sworn that day she would never be at the mercy of a powerful man. *She* would be the one in control. She would be the agent of her own destiny, not have her life dictated to by others who had been better born or had more money than her.

She would *never* fall in love.

'Excuse me, Miss Baker?' A well-dressed man in his late fifties approached. 'Sienna Louise Baker?'

Sienna set her shoulders squarely. 'Who wants to know?' she asked.

The man held out a hand. 'Allow me to introduce myself,' he said. 'I am Lorenzo Di Salle, Guido Ferrante's lawyer.'

Sienna took his hand briefly. 'Nice to meet you. Now, if you'll excuse me, I have to go.'

She had barely moved a step before the lawyer's words stopped her in her tracks. 'You are invited to be at the reading of Guido Ferrante's will.'

Sienna turned back around and stared at him with her mouth open. 'Pardon?'

'As a beneficiary to Signor Ferrante's estate you are—'

'A *beneficiary*?' she gasped. 'But why?'

The lawyer gave her a smile Sienna didn't much care for. 'Signor Ferrante has left some property to you,' he said.

'Property?' she said blankly. 'What property?'

'The Chateau de Chalvy in Provence,' he said.

Sienna's heart did a double shuffle. 'There must be some mistake,' she said. 'That was Evaline Ferrante's family home. Surely it should go to Andreas or Miette?'

'Signor Ferrante insisted it be left to you,' he said. 'There are, however, some conditions attached.'

Sienna narrowed her eyes. 'Conditions?'

Lorenzo Di Salle gave her a serpentine smile. 'The reading of the will is in the library at the Ferrante villa at three p.m. tomorrow. I look forward to seeing you there.'

Andreas prowled the length and breadth of the library feeling like a lion in a cat carrier. He hadn't been to his family home in years, not since the night Sienna had been found all but naked in his bedroom at the age of seventeen. The little she-devil had lied her way out of it, making him out to be some sort of lecher while she had maintained the act of innocent victim, a role she played all too well. Why else had his father included her in his will? She wasn't a blood relative. She was the housekeeper's daughter. She was nothing but a little gold-digging slut who had already married once for money. She had obviously inveigled her way into his ailing father's affections to get her greedy little hands on what she could, now that her elderly husband had died, leaving her practically penniless. His mother's estate in Provence was the one thing Andreas would do anything to keep out of Sienna's possession.

And he meant *anything.*

The door opened and Sienna Baker came breezing in as if she owned the place. At least today she had dressed a little more appropriately, but not by much. Her short denim skirt showed off the long slim length of her coltish sun-kissed legs and her white blouse was tied at her impossibly slender waist, showing a glimpse of the toned flesh of her abdomen. She didn't have a scrap of make-up on her face and her silver-blonde hair was loose around her shoulders, but even so she looked as if she had just stepped off a photo shoot.

The whole room seemed to suck in a breath and hold it. Andreas had seen it happen so many times. Her totally natural beauty was like a punch to the solar plexus. He had worked hard over the years to disguise his reaction, but even now he could feel the effect she had on him. He had felt it yesterday in the church. He had known the very minute she had arrived.

He had *sensed* it.

He glanced at his watch before throwing her a contemptuous glare. 'You're late.'

She gave him a pert look as she flipped her hair over one shoulder. 'It's two minutes past three, Rich Boy,' she said. 'Don't be so anal.'

The lawyer rustled his papers on the desk. 'Could we get started?' he asked. 'There's a lot to go through. Let's start with Miette…'

Andreas remained standing as the will was read out. He was glad his younger sister was well provided for, not that she needed it as she and her husband had a very successful investment business based in London, but it was a relief to know she hadn't been elbowed out by that brazen little blow-in. Miette had inherited the family villa in Rome and assets worth millions set in trust for her two young children. It was a satisfying result given that Miette—like Andreas—hadn't been all that close to their father over the last years of his life.

'And now we come to Andreas and Sienna,' Lorenzo Di Salle said. 'I think we should conduct this part of the reading in private. Just the two of you, if the others don't mind.'

Andreas felt his spine tighten. He didn't want his name bracketed with that little wildcat. It made him feel edgy. It had always made him feel that way. She was a tearaway who rocked his world in ways he didn't want.

Had *never* wanted.

He had stayed away from the family home because of her. For years he hadn't stepped over the threshold, not even to spend those few precious weeks with his mother before she died. Sienna's outrageous deceit had destroyed any chance of a working relationship with his father for the last eight years. Andreas blamed her for it all. She was a sly little vixen intent on her own gain.

He hated her with a vengeance.

The lawyer waited for the others to leave the library before he opened the folder in front of him. 'The Chateau de Chalvy in Provence is entailed to you both but on the proviso that you live together legally as man and wife for the minimum of six months.'

Andreas heard the lawyer's words but it took a moment for them to register. He felt a shockwave go through him. It was like being shoved backwards by a toppling bookcase. He couldn't get his throat unlocked to speak. He stood staring at the lawyer, wondering if he had imagined what he had just heard.

Sienna and him...married.

Legally tied.

Stuck together for six months.

It was a joke.

'This has got to be a joke,' Andreas said, raking a hand through his hair.

'It's no joke,' Lorenzo Di Salle said. 'Your father changed his will in the last month of his life. He was adamant about it. If you don't agree to marry each other within the time frame, the property will be handed over to a distant relative.'

Andreas knew exactly which distant relative the lawyer was referring to. He also knew how quickly his mother's ancestral home would be sold to feed the second cousin's gambling addiction. His father had laid the perfect trap. He had thought of everything, every get out clause and every escape route. He had made it impossible for Andreas to do anything but obey his orders.

'I'm not marrying him!' Sienna shot to her feet, her grey-blue eyes flaring in outrage.

Andreas flicked her a disparaging glance. 'Sit down and shut up, for God's sake.'

She pushed her chin up, her bottom lip going forward in a pout. 'I'm not marrying you.'

'I'm very glad to hear it,' Andreas said dryly and turned to the lawyer. 'There's got to be a way out of this. I'm about to become engaged. You have to make this go away.'

The lawyer lifted his hands in a gesture of defeat. 'The will is iron-clad,' he said. 'If either of you refuses to cooperate, the other automatically inherits everything.'

'What?' Andreas and Sienna spoke at once.

Andreas threw her a look before he addressed the lawyer. 'You mean if I don't agree to marry her she inherits Chateau de Chalvy, plus all the other assets?'

Lorenzo nodded. 'And if you do marry and one of you walks out before the six months is up, the one who stays inherits everything by default,' he said. 'Signor Ferrante set it up so neither of you have a choice but to marry each other and stay married for six months.'

'Why six months?' Sienna asked.

Andreas rolled his eyes as he muttered, 'Because any longer than that he knew I would probably end up on a murder charge.'

Sienna sent him a withering look. 'Only if you got in first.'

Andreas dismissed her comment by turning back to the lawyer. 'What happens at the end of six months if we do decide to stick it out?' he asked.

'You get the chateau and Sienna gets a pay-out,' the lawyer said.

'How big a pay-out?' Sienna asked.

Lorenzo named a sum that sent Andreas's brows sky-high. 'She gets that much for doing what exactly?' he asked. 'Flouncing around pretending to be the lady of the manor for six months? That's outrageous!'

Sienna curled her lip at him. 'I'd say it was pretty fair compensation for having to put up with you for six days, let alone six months.'

Andreas narrowed his eyes to paper-thin slits. 'You put him up to this, didn't you?' he said through clenched teeth. 'You got him to write this crazy will so you could get your greedy little hands on whatever you could.'

Her grey-blue eyes held his defiantly. 'I haven't seen or spoken to your father for five years,' she said. 'He didn't even have the decency to send me a card or flowers when my mother died, let alone attend her funeral.'

Andreas stared her down. 'Why did you come to his funeral if you hated him so much?'

Her chin stayed at a pugnacious height. 'Don't think I would've made a special trip because I damn well wouldn't,' she said. 'I was here for a dress fitting for my sister's wedding next month.'

'I heard about your long lost twin,' Andreas said. 'I read about it in the paper.' He curled his lip and added, 'God help us all if she's anything like you.'

She glared at him furiously. 'I came to your father's funeral out of respect for my mother,' she said. 'She would've come if she was still alive. Nothing on this earth would have stopped her.'

Andreas gave her a mocking look. 'No, not even common decency, it seems.'

She shot to her feet with a hand raised to slap him. He only managed to stop it from connecting with his jaw by grasping her wrist in mid-air. The shock of her soft silky skin against his fingers was like a power surge going through his body. He saw the sudden flare of her eyes as if she had felt it too.

A nanosecond passed.

Something entered the air between them, a primal, dangerous thing that had no name, no shape or form—*it was just there.*

Andreas dropped her wrist and stepped back from her, surreptitiously opening and closing his fingers to see if they were still able to function. 'You'll have to excuse Miss Baker—' he spoke to the lawyer again '—she has a reputation for histrionics.'

Sienna threw Andreas a filthy look. 'Bastard.'

The lawyer closed the folder and got to his feet. 'You have a week to come to a decision,' he said. 'I suggest you think about this carefully. There's a lot to lose on both sides if you don't cooperate.'

'I've already decided,' Sienna said, folding her arms across her chest. 'I'm not marrying him.'

Andreas laughed. 'Nice try, Sienna,' he said. 'There's no way you'd turn your back on that amount of money.'

She came and stood right in his body space, her chin up, her eyes flashing, her hands on her slim hips, her beautiful breasts heaving. He had never felt such raw sexual energy coming towards him in his life. His whole body jolted with it. It was like being zapped with a Taser gun. He felt it rush through every vein like a flood of roaring fire. His groin pulsated as she leaned in closer, close enough for him to smell the sweet honey scent of her breath as it danced over his face. 'You just watch me, Rich Boy,' she said and then she swivelled on her trainer-clad feet and left.

CHAPTER TWO

'It says here that Andreas Ferrante and his mistress have broken up,' Kate Henley, Sienna's flatmate, said a couple of days later. She looked up over the newspaper and frowned. 'Hey, I thought you said they were about to get engaged?'

Sienna turned her back to wash a perfectly clean cup in the sink. 'What Andreas Ferrante does or doesn't do is of no interest to me whatsoever.'

'Hang on a minute…' The paper rustled as Kate spread it out over the clutter of the breakfast table. 'Oh, my God! Is it true?'

Sienna turned to see her flatmate's eyes were as big as the saucer she had just put on the draining rack. 'Is what true?' she asked warily.

'It says you're the other woman,' Kate said, gaping at her like a fish. 'It says *you're* the reason they broke up.'

'Let me see that.' Sienna frowned as she snatched up the paper. She scanned the article, her heart galloping like a spooked thoroughbred.

Mega-rich French-Italian furniture designer Andreas Ferrante admits his secret involvement with former housekeeper's daughter Sienna Baker destroyed his relationship with heiress Portia Briscoe.

'That's a downright lie!' Sienna slammed the paper down, knocking over the milk carton in the process. *'Oh, shoot!'* She grabbed a tea towel and mopped ineffectually at the mess while her mind ran on with fury.

'Why would he say something like that?' Kate asked with a wrinkled brow.

Sienna ground her teeth as she rinsed the cloth at the sink, splashing water everywhere in the process. 'He wants me to marry him, that's why.'

'Erm…did I hear you correctly?' Kate asked. 'I *think* you said he wants to marry you. Did you actually *say* that?'

Sienna flung the milk-sodden tea towel in the sink. 'I did but I'm not marrying him,' she said with a scowl.

Kate clutched a hand to her chest theatrically. 'Be still my heart,' she said. 'Andreas Ferrante—Florence-based millionaire, no, make that *billionaire* playboy—the most gorgeous-looking man on this planet—if not the entire universe—wants you to marry him and you said *no*?'

Sienna gave Kate an irritated look as she reached past her to wipe the milk off the bottom of the peanut butter jar. 'He's not that handsome.'

'Not handsome?' Kate gaped at her. 'What about his bank account?'

'I'm not interested in his bank account,' Sienna said. 'I married once for money. I'm not doing it again.'

'But I thought you really loved Brian Littlemore,' Kate said. 'You cried buckets at his funeral.'

Sienna thought of her late husband and how close she had become to him in the few months before he died. She had married him for protection and security, not love. It had been a knee-jerk reaction when her life had spun out of control soon after the death of her mother. After a horrifying incident in which she found herself in bed with a complete stranger after one too many drinks, Brian Littlemore had offered her security and respectability at a time in her life when she had neither. Like her, he had been forced to live a lie for most of his life, but during their marriage he had been honest with her in a way few people ever were. She had come to love him for it. As far as she was concerned, his secret had died with him. She would never betray his trust in her.

'Brian was a good man,' she said. 'He put his family before himself right to the day he died.'

'It's a pity he didn't leave you better provided for,' Kate said, reaching for the dishcloth. 'I guess you could always ask your rich twin sister to help you out with the rent if you don't manage to get a job in the next week or two.'

It still felt a little strange to Sienna to think of having a sister, let alone an identical twin. Gisele and she had been separated at birth when Sienna's mother had accepted a pay-out from the high profile Australian married man who had got her pregnant. Nell had taken Sienna and handed over Gisele to the childless couple, Hilary and Richard Carter, who had subsequently raised Gisele as their own. Nell had taken the secret to her grave. Sienna had found out quite by accident about Gisele's existence when she had been travelling in Australia a couple of months ago. She had only taken the trip on a whim when she'd seen a budget air fare online. She had always longed to go to Australia and, after Brian's death, it seemed a good opportunity to help her clear her head a bit before she made a decision about her future. A chance encounter in a department store had brought about her reunion with her twin.

Although Sienna loved Gisele dearly, she was still finding her feet with the relationship. Gisele had suffered a very bitter and painful breakup because of the sex tape scandal Sienna had been caught up in. Finding herself in that man's bed with no real memory of how she had got there had been such a shameful experience she had immediately left the country, thus having no idea of the fallout it had created for her sister. How that damning footage had got on the Internet and been wrongly linked to Gisele was something Sienna knew she would always feel dreadful about.

Gisele's fiancé Emilio had believed Gisele had betrayed him, and it had only been the discovery of the truth about Sienna's existence that had finally set things right. Their upcoming marriage in Rome was something she was looking forward to with bittersweet feelings. Her behaviour had almost wrecked Gisele and Emilio's lives. They had lost two precious years together and a baby. What could she ever do to make it up to them?

But Kate had made a very good point. She had to find a source of income and find it soon. Before he had become ill, Sienna had worked in the office of Brian's antiques business, but the family had stepped in after he had died and promptly sacked her. The trust fund Brian had left her had been just about gobbled up by the ongoing instability of the economy. Her dream of purchasing a home of her own had slipped out of her grasp, and there was no way—short of a miracle—for her to get it back.

Or was there?

Sienna thought of the money Guido Ferrante had bequeathed her. It was more than enough to buy a decent piece of real estate. The rest of it, invested sensibly, would set her up for life. She would be able to pursue her hobby of photography, perhaps even take it a step further and make a proper career out of it. How wonderful to be known for her talent instead of her mistakes and social blunders. How wonderful to be on the other side of the lens for a change, to be the one taking the pictures instead of being the subject.

She chewed at her lip as she thought of the conditions put on the will. Six months married to her worst enemy. It was a high price to pay, but then the reward at the end surely compensated for it?

It wasn't as if it had to be a *real* marriage.

An involuntary shiver rippled over her skin at the thought of lying in Andreas's strongly muscled arms, with his long hair-roughened legs entangled with hers, with his…

Sienna dried her hands on a fresh tea towel before she picked up her bag and keys. 'I'm going away,' she said. 'I'm not sure when I'll be back. I'll send you the money for the rent.'

Kate swung around with the empty milk carton in one hand and a wet dishcloth in the other. 'Away where?'

'To Florence.'

Kate's eyes bulged. 'You're going to say yes?'

Sienna gave her a grim look. 'This could turn out to be the longest six months of my life.'

'Six months?' Kate frowned in confusion. 'Isn't marriage meant to be until death us do part?'

'Not this one,' Sienna said.

'Aren't you going to pack?' Kate asked, eyes still out on stalks. 'You can't just turn up dressed in torn jeans and a T-shirt. You'll need clothes, lots and lots of clothes and shoes and make-up and stuff.'

Sienna flung her handbag strap over her shoulder. 'If Andreas Ferrante wants me to dress like one of his mistresses he can damn well pay for it. Ciao.'

'Signor Ferrante is in a design team meeting and cannot be disturbed,' the receptionist informed Sienna.

'Tell him his fiancée is here,' Sienna said with a guileless smile.

The receptionist's eyes widened as they took in Sienna's travel-worn appearance. 'I'm not sure...' she began uncertainly.

'Tell him if he doesn't see me right now the wedding won't go ahead,' Sienna said with a don't-mess-with-me look.

The receptionist reached for the intercom and spoke in Italian to Andreas. 'There's a young woman here who claims to be your fiancée. Do you want me to call Security?'

Andreas's deep mellifluous voice sounded over the system. 'Tell her to wait in Reception.'

Sienna leaned over the desk and swung the speaker her way. 'Get your butt out here, Andreas. We have things to discuss.'

'The boardroom,' he said. 'Ten minutes.'

'Out here *now*,' Sienna said through gritted teeth.

'Cara,' he drawled, 'such impatience fires my blood. Have you missed me terribly?'

Sienna pasted a false smile on her face for the sake of the receptionist. 'Darling, you can't imagine how *awful* it's been without your arms around me. I'm going crazy for you. It's been absolute torture to be without your kisses, your touch and your body doing all those wonderful things to—'

'Let's keep some things private, shall we?' he interjected coolly.

Sienna smiled at the now goggle-eyed receptionist. 'You wouldn't know it to look at him, but he has the most amazingly huge—'

'Sienna,' Andreas clipped out, 'get in here right *now*.'

Sienna slipped off the desk and gave the receptionist a fingertip wave. 'Isn't he adorable?'

The boardroom was empty by the time Sienna arrived. Andreas had a face like thunder and the air was crackling with palpable tension.

'What the hell do you think you're doing?' he asked even before she had closed the door.

Sienna threw him a contemptuous glare. 'Apparently we're engaged,' she said, clicking the door shut with considerable force. 'I read about it in the press.'

His mouth went to a flat line. 'I'm not the one who leaked that to the media.' He raked a hand through his hair. 'You know what they say about a woman scorned.'

Sienna raised her brows. 'Perfect Portia did that? Wow, I bet she didn't read that in the Good Girl's Guide to Avoiding Social Slip-Ups.'

His brows snapped together. 'I was about to ask her to marry me,' he said. 'She has a right to be upset.'

'My heart bleeds,' Sienna said on an exaggerated sigh.

He threw her a flinty look. 'Bitch.'

She smiled at him sweetly. 'Bastard.'

The air crackled some more.

Andreas paced the floor, his hand tracking another ragged pathway through the thick pelt of his hair. 'We have to find a way to manage this,' he said. 'Six months and we'll be free of this. I've looked at it from every angle. There's no way out of it. We just have to do what's expected. We can both win.'

Sienna pulled out one of the ergonomic chairs and sat down, swinging it from side to side as she watched him work the floor. 'What's in it for me?' she asked.

He stopped pacing to look at her, his frown deepening. 'What do you mean what's in it for you? You get a truckload of money at the end of it.'

She held his hazel gaze. 'I want more.'

His mouth tightened even further. 'How much more?'

'How about double?'

His jaw worked for a moment. 'A quarter.'

'A third,' she said, holding his look.

He slammed his hands on the table right in front of her, his face so close to hers she could smell the good quality coffee on his breath. 'Damn you to hell and back, you're not getting any more,' he said. 'The deal stands as it stands. I'm not negotiating on it.'

Sienna rolled her chair back and rose to her feet in one fluid movement. 'I guess that's it then,' she said. 'If you want me to marry you then you'll have to pay for the privilege.'

She was at the door when he finally spoke. 'All right,' he said on a heavily expelled breath. 'I'll give you a third on top of what my father bequeathed to you.'

Sienna turned to face him. 'You want that chateau real bad, don't you?'

His expression was rigid with tension. 'It belonged to my mother,' he said. 'I will do anything it takes to keep it out of the hands of my greedy, profligate second cousin.'

'Even marry me?'

He gave a humourless chuckle. 'I can't believe I'm saying this, but yes, I can actually think of worse things than marrying you.'

'Your imagination is streets ahead of mine because I *can't* think of anything worse than being married to you,' she said as she resumed her seat.

The air tightened like a steel cable.

Sienna felt his gaze run over her. It felt like a hot caress on her skin. His eyes seemed to sear the flesh off her bones. She felt naked under his scrutiny.

But then he *had* seen her naked, or almost.

She cringed at the memory. She had wanted him to be her first lover. She had dreamt about it for months. She had fantasised about him rescuing her from the life of drudgery she and her mother had been forced to live. All those years of never knowing what house they would be living in next. Not knowing what school or suburb she would be residing in. Her childhood had been a patchwork of packing up and leaving, of trying to fit in a new place, of trying to make friends with people who already had enough friends. She had always felt the odd one out. She didn't belong upstairs or downstairs.

But everything had changed when her mother had got the position as housekeeper at the Ferrante villa in Rome. It was the most stunning property, with fabulous gardens and a massive swimming pool and tennis court. It had felt like paradise after years of living in a variety of cramped and mouldy inner city flats.

It had been the first time in her life Sienna had seen her mother truly happy and settled. She hadn't wanted it to end. In her immature mind she'd had it all planned. Andreas, the son and heir of the Ferrante fortune, would fall in love with her and marry her. He was the handsome playboy prince, she was the pretty but penniless pauper, but their love and desire for each other would overcome that. She had been determined that he would notice her for once instead of treating her like an annoying puppy that hadn't been properly housetrained. To him, she had always been the cleaning lady's brat. He had even called her *enfant terrible*.

But this night it would be different. He hadn't been home in months. This time he would see the change in her. He would see her for the sexually mature young woman she had believed herself to be.

She had seen his hazel eyes follow her all evening when she had helped bring in the family's meal. She had sensed his male appraisal as she brought in the coffee and liqueurs to the *salone*. His nostrils had flared when she had leant down to place his cup beside him, as if he was breathing in her fragrance. Her hair had brushed against his arm and she had felt the electric current of awareness shoot through her body. He had looked at her then with those green and brown-flecked eyes of his and she had known he wanted her.

She had *felt* it.

She had waited for him in his bedroom, draping herself alluringly across his bed, dressed only in her knickers and bra, nervous but excited at the same time. Her body had tingled all over in anticipation.

The door had opened and Andreas had stood there for a moment, his eyes drinking in the sight of her. But then he seemed to give himself a mental shake and his expression immediately locked down, becoming stony, marble-like. 'What the hell do you think you're playing at?' he growled. 'Get dressed and get out.'

Sienna had been crushed. She had been so certain he wanted her. She had seen it. She had felt it. She had sensed it in the air. The heavily charged atmosphere had practically exploded with erotic tension. The same tension she could see in his body even though he had done his best to hide it. 'I want you to make love to me,' she said. 'I know you want me. I've known it for ages.'

His mouth had been so tight it looked as if it had been drawn there with a thin felt tip pen. 'You're mistaken, Sienna,' he said. 'I have no interest in you whatsoever.'

Sienna had got off the bed and approached him. It had been brazen of her and impulsive but she had wanted to prove to him that what she felt was not just a figment of her youthful imagination. 'I want you, Andreas,' she said in a sultry tone as she reached for him.

Andreas had grasped her by the upper arms just as the door opened…

Sienna blinked herself out of the past. She didn't want to remember that dreadful scene between Andreas and his father. She didn't want to remember the unforgivable lies she had told. She had been desperate, terrified that her mother would lose the job she loved so much. The words had come tumbling out, a river of nonsense that she had regretted ever since. Andreas had never come home again, not even when his mother lay dying.

When Sienna looked up Andreas was standing behind the boardroom table, his steely gaze focused on her. 'There are some practicalities we need to sort out,' he said.

She resisted the urge to moisten her bark-dry lips. 'Practicalities?'

'The will states we have to live together as man and wife,' he said. 'That means you will have to sleep wherever I sleep.'

Sienna shot to her feet so fast the chair toppled over behind her. 'I'm not sleeping with you!'

He rolled his eyes as if dealing with an imbecile. 'Not in the same bed, Sienna, but under the same roof,' he said. 'We have to put on a show for the public.'

She blinked at him. 'You mean we have to act as if we really wanted to be married to each other?'

He continued to look at her with that unwavering hazel gaze. 'As much as it pains me to say this, yes, we will have to act as if we're in love.'

'Are you out of your mind?' she gasped. 'I can't do that! Everyone knows how much I hate you.'

'Likewise,' he said dryly, 'but it's only for six months and it's only when we're in public. We can wrestle each other to the ground when we're alone.'

Sienna felt her cheeks flame with colour as the images his words conjured up flooded her brain. 'I haven't the faintest clue how to wrestle.'

'Perhaps I could teach you,' he said with a slanting smile that contained a hint of mockery and something else she didn't even want to think about identifying. 'The only thing you have to remember is the winner is the one who finishes on top.'

Sienna turned away so he couldn't see how hot and bothered she felt. Her body felt as if it were on fire. Her skin was prickling all over as she thought of his strong lean body pinning hers beneath his. 'How soon do we have to…you know…make things official?'

'As soon as possible,' he said. 'I've applied for a special licence. It should come through any day now.'

'And what sort of wedding do you have in mind?' she asked, turning to look at him again.

'You're surely not hankering for a white wedding?' he said with a mocking arch of one of his eyebrows.

She gave him a flippant look in return. 'It's supposed to be the bride's day.'

'You've already been a bride.' He held her gaze for a microsecond before adding in disgust, 'To a man old enough to be your grandfather.'

Sienna raised her chin at him. 'At least I loved him.'

His lip curled. 'You loved his money, you trashy little gold-digger,' he said. 'Did he make you earn every penny by opening your legs on command?'

She gave him her wild-child smile, the one the press had documented time and time again—the one that painted her as a sleep-around-slut on the make. 'Wouldn't you like to know?' she asked.

He flung himself away from the table, thrusting his hands deep in his trouser pockets as if he didn't trust himself not to shake her till her teeth rattled.

Sienna found it exhilarating to know she had yanked his chain. He was always so cool and in control, but there was a side to him only she brought out. It was his primitive side, the raw male side that wanted to dominate and subdue her. The thought of him making her submit to him made her skin lift in a shiver.

She would fight him tooth and nail.

* * *

Andreas took some steadying breaths. She was doing it deliberately, of course. Trying her best to get under his skin, to prove nothing had changed in spite of the passage of time. How could one woman have such an effect on him?

He was *not* a slave to lust.

He had abhorred that in his father, how he had betrayed his wife of more than thirty years to bed a common tart.

Andreas prided himself on his self-control. He had the normal urges of any full-blooded male, but he always chose his partners with discretion. The women he slept with had class and poise. They were not headstrong harpies. They did not stir in him such unbridled passion.

He *never* lost his head.

But something about Sienna inflamed him and he had no control over it. He wanted to drive himself in her as hard and deeply as he could. He wanted to rut her like a wild animal did a random mate. He wanted to tame her, to have her submit to him in every way possible. His body ached and burned for her feverishly.

She was the forbidden fruit he had always prided himself he *could* resist.

That was no doubt why his father had set things up the way he had. He had known the temptation Sienna had always been for him. His father could not have thought of a worse punishment than tying her to him, dangling her under his nose, day in and day out. What had he been thinking? Had his father really hated him that much?

Andreas turned back to face Sienna. She was sitting down again, her jeans-clad legs propped up on the desk, her arms folded across her chest, which pushed her beautiful breasts upwards, looking every bit the impudent schoolgirl called into the headmaster's office. She had a lamentable disrespect for authority. She was wilful and defiant. She didn't know the meaning of the word respect. She could be surly and then sunny in the blink of an eye. She could be a sultry siren one second and an innocent waif the next.

He didn't have a clue how he was going to manage this farcical arrangement, but manage it he would, even if it meant sleeping with her to get her out of his system once and for all.

Every drop of his blood sizzled at the thought.

'Where are you staying?' he asked.

'I haven't found a place yet,' she said. 'I only just flew in.'

'Where are your things?'

'I didn't bring anything with me,' she said. 'I thought I'd leave the wardrobe arrangements up to you. I figured the stuff I normally wear won't suit.'

He stared at her incredulously. 'You came here with nothing but the clothes you're wearing?'

She gave him a feisty look. 'If I'm going to act the part, I need to dress for it. But you can pay for it, not me.'

'I have no problem with footing the bill,' Andreas said. 'It just seems a little unconventional, if not impetuous, for a young woman of your age to fly about the globe with nothing but jeans and a T-shirt and a handbag. Most of the women I know carry enough make-up and toiletries to sink a ship.'

'I'm very low maintenance,' she said.

'I very much doubt it,' he muttered.

She lowered her slim legs to the floor with a movement that was both coltish and graceful. 'I'll need a place to stay until we make things official,' she said. 'A five-star hotel will do nicely.'

'You can stay at my villa.' He scribbled the address on a sheet of paper and pushed it across the desk to her. 'I want you right under my nose where I can keep an eye on you.'

'You think I'll spill my guts to the press like your ex-fiancée did?' she asked with an insolent smile as she popped the folded paper inside her bra.

'Technically, she wasn't my fiancée,' he said, tearing his gaze away from the tempting sight of her pert breasts. 'I hadn't got that far. I had bought a ring, however. You can borrow it if you like.'

She gave him a slitted-eye glare. 'Don't even think about it, Rich Boy,' she said. 'I want my own ring, not someone else's.'

Andreas came over to where she was standing. He could feel the force field of her as soon as he crossed that invisible line. Her summery fragrance assaulted his nostrils, a combination of flowers and feminine warmth that was as heady as any mind-altering drug. This close, he could see the tiny dusting of freckles over the bridge of her retroussé nose and the tiniest of chickenpox scars above her left eyebrow.

Almost of its own volition, his gaze flicked down to her mouth.

Lust gave him a knockout punch in the gut when he saw the way the tip of her tongue darted out to leave a glistening layer of moisture on those plump, ripe lips.

He fought his leaping pulse back under control, dragging his gaze back to her glittering one. 'This is all a game to you, isn't it?' he said.

Her top lip curled at him and her grey-blue eyes glittered. 'You were going to kiss me, weren't you?'

Andreas ground his teeth until he thought he'd have to eat jelly for the rest of his life. 'I want to throttle you, not kiss you,' he said.

'You put one finger on me and see what happens,' she said, matching him stare for stare.

Andreas already knew what would happen. He could feel it in his body. It was thundering through his veins like a torpedo. He couldn't think of a time when he had felt such forceful, uncontrollable desire. It was like being a hormone-driven teenager all over again. Dynamite couldn't do more damage than Sienna in temptress mode. 'Get out of my sight,' he ground out savagely.

She put up her chin. 'Say please.'

He strode over to the door, holding it open pointedly. 'Out.'

She tossed the silver-blonde curtain of her hair back behind her shoulders. 'If I'm going to stay at your place I'll need a key,' she said.

'The housekeeper will let you in,' Andreas said. 'I'll call her now and tell her to expect you.'

'What will you tell her and the rest of your staff about us?' she asked.

'I don't make a habit of exchanging confidences with the household staff at any of my residences,' he said. 'They will assume it's a normal marriage, just like everyone else.'

A little frown appeared over her grey-blue eyes. 'Even though we won't be sharing a room?'

Andreas felt that punch to his gut again. He could think of nothing more tempting than rolling around his bed with her legs wrapped around his waist, his body buried to the hilt in hers. His blood thickened and pulsed as he thought of how it would feel to finally satiate this need he had harboured so long. He would have his fill of her once and for all. In six months he would walk away. He would finally be immune. Free. In control.

'It's very common for people with villas the size of mine to occupy different suites,' he said. 'It doesn't make sense to cram into one room when there are thirty others to choose from.'

Her eyes went wide. 'That big, huh?'

'It's bigger than my father's.'

A little smile played about the corners of her mouth. 'I just bet it is,' she said.

Andreas took out his wallet and handed her a credit card. 'Here,' he said, handing it to her. 'Go shopping. Get your hair and nails done. Have coffee. Have a meal. I won't be back till late. Don't wait up.'

She took the card from him without touching his fingers and popped it in her bag. She moved past him in the doorway, not touching but close enough for every hair on his body to stand to attention and for every blood vessel to expand and throb. He was about to let out the breath he was holding when she suddenly stopped and turned back to look at him. 'Do you have any idea why your father did this?' she asked.

'No idea at all.'

She chewed at her lower lip for a moment, a shadow passing like a cloud over her face. 'He must have really hated me…'

'What makes you think that?' he asked, frowning at

her. 'This is about me, not you. My father hated me as much as I hated him.'

A little beat of silence passed.

'I'd better get going,' she said with an overly bright smile. 'So many things to buy, so little time. Ciao.'

Andreas closed the door once she had left and leant back against it heavily, a frown tugging at his forehead. Half an hour with Sienna was like being in the middle of a hurricane with nothing but a paper parasol for protection.

How was he going to get through six months?

CHAPTER THREE

SIENNA took a taxi to Andreas's Tuscan estate once she had finished shopping. The Renaissance-style villa was a few kilometres outside Florence, set amongst acres of olive groves and vineyards in the Chianti region of Tuscany, made famous for its wine. The fading afternoon sunshine cast a spectacular light over the fresh growth on the vines. Flowers in an array of bright colours tumbled from baskets hanging near the entrance to the villa. It was breathtakingly beautiful and a jolting reminder of the wealth Andreas had been born into and had never questioned. Sure, he had forged his own way with his furniture designs, but he had never had to worry about bills not being paid or where the next meal was coming from. It was hard not to feel a teensy bit jealous. Why did he even want his mother's wretched chateau in Provence when he had all of this?

The thought of owning a property like the chateau made Sienna wonder if she should set about making him default on the will by making it impossible to live with her. It was a tempting thought: a chateau of her own, her own patch of paradise. It wasn't as if Andreas would be left homeless or anything. He had homes everywhere. The one in Florence was his base, but she knew for a fact he had a villa in Barbados as well as one somewhere in Spain.

The door of the villa opened and a motherly-looking woman who introduced herself as Elena smiled as she ushered Sienna in. 'Signor Ferrante told me you would be arriving this evening,' she said. 'I have made up the Rose Suite for you.' She winked knowingly. 'It is right next to his.'

Sienna forced a smile. 'That was very thoughtful of you.'

'It is no trouble,' Elena said. 'I was young and madly in love once. I met my husband and within a month we were married. I knew Signor Ferrante would change his mind about that one.'

Sienna frowned slightly. 'Erm…"That one"?'

Elena made a noise that sounded something like a snort. 'Princess Portia. She was never happy. I had to fetch and carry. She did not like red meat. She did not like cheese. She only ate this. She only ate that. I nearly went crazy.'

'Maybe she was thinking of her figure,' Sienna offered generously.

The housekeeper gave another snort of disapproval. 'She is not the right one for Signor Ferrante,' she said. 'He needs a woman who is as passionate as he is.'

Sienna couldn't help wondering exactly what Andreas had told his housekeeper about their relationship or whether Elena had assumed their whirlwind courtship had come about because they had suddenly fallen deeply in love. Or, even more worryingly, could the housekeeper see something in Sienna that she desperately wanted to keep hidden? It wasn't as if she still had a crush on Andreas or anything. She didn't love him. She hated him. But that didn't mean his physical presence didn't disturb her. It did, and way too much. 'You seem to know him very well,' she said.

Elena smiled. 'He's a good man. He's very generous and hard-working, too. He helps in the vineyard whenever he can, and the orchards. You knew him before? I read about it in the paper. Your *mamma* used to work for his family, *sì*?'

'Sì,' Sienna said. 'My mother took up the position as head housekeeper when I was fourteen. Andreas wasn't living at home then, of course, but we ran into each other from time to time.'

'Friends to lovers, *sì*?' Elena said, smiling broadly.

'Erm…something like that.'

'I can see the fire in your eyes,' Elena said. 'He will be happy with you. I can tell these things. You will make good babies with him, *sì*?'

Sienna felt her face grow hot. 'We haven't talked about kids. It's been a bit of a whirlwind affair, actually.'

'The best ones are,' Elena said with matronly authority. 'Come, I'll show you your new home. You'll want to settle in before Signor Ferrante gets back.'

Sienna followed the cheery housekeeper on a tour of the villa. It was even bigger than she had expected. Room after room, suite after suite, all beautifully and tastefully decorated. It occurred to her that in a villa this size she could pass six months without even running into Andreas, or anyone else for that matter.

'I'll leave you to shower and change,' Elena said. 'I will set up the dinner before I leave.'

'You don't live here?' Sienna asked.

'I live in the farmhouse next to the olive grove,' Elena said. 'My husband, Franco, works for Signor

Ferrante too. If you want anything we are only a phone call away. I will be back in the morning around ten. Signor Ferrante likes a bit of privacy. He has lived with servants all his life. I understand he wants his space.'

Sienna hadn't factored in actually being alone with Andreas. Alone with servants was a whole lot different than *alone.* It put a completely different spin on things. Could she trust him to keep his distance? The chemistry between them was volatile, to say the least. She knew it wouldn't take much to set things off. If that tense little moment in his boardroom was anything to go by, things could get pretty intense in a flash and what would she be able to do about it? It wasn't as if she had any immunity, not really. She put on a good front but how long was that going to last? He had only to look at her a certain way and her insides coiled with lust.

It was ironic because sex was something she had never really taken to with any great enthusiasm. Although she had partied, and partied hard after Andreas's rejection, it had been months and months before she had even thought about dating, and even when she had finally gone out with a couple of young men her age, the intimate encounters had left her cold. She had felt nothing for either of her partners and they clearly had felt nothing for her. And then, after the shameful night that had found her in a stranger's bed, she had locked herself away in a sex-less and safe marriage of convenience. Before that night, whenever the press had portrayed her as a sleep-around-slut, she had laughed it off, pleased that she was getting some attention, even if it wasn't positive. *She* had known the truth about herself and that had been all that mattered. But now the label had a ring of truth to it she dearly wished she could remove.

After she had unpacked and showered and changed, Sienna came downstairs. The villa seemed rather empty without the warm and friendly chatter of the housekeeper. She picked at some food and poured herself a glass of wine, feeling restless and irritable.

Maybe she should have thought about this a little more before she went any further. It wasn't the first time her impulsive nature had got her into trouble. Was it too late to back out?

The money stopped her thoughts of escape in their tracks. What was she thinking? It was like any other unpleasant job that had to be done. A six-month contract that would be over before she knew it. She would receive a handsome pay-out for her trouble.

There was that T word again. Trouble.

She had a habit of attracting it, no matter what she did. Was she forever destined to be at the mercy of circumstances she couldn't control? Was it her fault her mother had kept her and given away her sister?

Jealousy was something Sienna didn't want to feel around her twin, but she couldn't help feeling a little cheated by how things had panned out. Gisele had grown up well provided for. She'd had a private education and gone on fabulous exotic holidays. She had lived in the same gorgeous house all of her childhood. She hadn't had to pack up her things every few months or so when someone got tired of her mother's laziness or cheek. She'd had a father to watch out for her, to provide for her and protect her from those who preyed upon the vulnerable.

Sienna, on the other hand, had grown up a whole lot

faster than her peers. She'd learnt early on that there were few people you could trust. Everyone was out for his or her own gain.

And now she was no different.

She would get what she could out of this and move on. She would milk Andreas for every penny she could before she walked out of his life.

For good.

Sienna was on to her second glass of wine when she heard Andreas's car. The deep throaty roar of the engine made her stomach clench unexpectedly. His fast car, fast-living lifestyle was something that had always attracted her even as it annoyed her. He had probably never had to push start a car in his life. He had never had to make his own bed or butter his own toast. He hadn't been born with just a silver spoon in his mouth, but an entire dinner service. He ate from fine bone china and drank from crystal glasses. He had everything that money could buy and then some.

How she hated him for it.

Andreas came in to find Sienna lying on her stomach on his leather sofa with a half drunk glass of wine in her hand and the remote control to his big screen television in the other. Her hair was pulled back in a high ponytail and she was wearing close-fitting black yoga pants and a loose hot-pink top that had slipped off one of her sun-kissed shoulders. Her feet were bare as she swung her lower legs back and forth in a slow motion kicking action. She looked young and nubile and so damned sexy he felt a tight ache deep in his groin.

'Hard day at the office?' she asked without even looking his way as she flicked through the channels.

He tugged at his tie to loosen it. 'You could say that.' He shrugged off his jacket and tossed it over the end of the other sofa. 'Making ourselves at home, are we?'

She took a sip of her wine before she answered. 'Having a blast,' she said. 'You make great wine, by the way. I like your housekeeper too. We're already best friends.'

'You're not supposed to make friends with the servants,' he said, frowning.

She muted the television and swung her legs down to sit up. 'Why's that?' she asked. 'Because they might forget their place and get too close to you?'

Andreas let out a carefully controlled breath. 'They're employees, not friends,' he said. 'They do the work and they get paid. There's nothing else that's required of them.'

She got off the sofa and padded over to where he was standing with her loose-limbed sensual gait. She looked up at him with those big sparkling-with-mischief grey-blue eyes of hers and he felt his groin tighten another excruciating notch. It was all he could do to stand there without hauling her against him to show her how much he lusted after her. But he had decided he would have her when *he* said so, not because she thought she could manipulate him at will.

'Have you eaten?' she asked.

'What is this?' he asked with a mocking look. 'Wifely duties 101?'

She lifted that deliciously bare shoulder of hers in a little shrug, her mouth going to a resentful pout. 'Just trying to be helpful,' she said. 'I thought you looked tired.'

'Maybe that's because I haven't slept a wink since I

heard about my father's will,' Andreas said, rubbing a hand over his face, which was in need of a shave.

He walked over to the bar and poured himself a glass of the wine Sienna had opened. He took a couple of sips before swinging his gaze back to her. 'I've got the licence. I pulled a few strings. We can get married next Friday.'

Her eyes widened a fraction but her voice when she spoke was all sass. 'You move fast when you want something, don't you, Rich Boy?'

'No point in dragging things out,' he said. 'The sooner we marry, the sooner we can get a divorce.'

'Sounds like a plan.'

Andreas narrowed his gaze in sharp focus. 'What's that supposed to mean?'

Her slim brows lifted archly. 'Exactly what I said,' she said. 'You seem to have it all figured out.'

'I do,' he said. 'We marry and then at the end of six months we end it. Simple.'

'What did you tell Elena about us?' she asked.

'Nothing, other than we're getting married as soon as possible.'

'You must have said more than that,' she said, toying with the end of her ponytail.

'Why do you think that?' he asked.

She lifted her golden shoulder up and down again. 'She seems to think we're madly in love,' she said.

'Most people are when they marry,' Andreas said, taking another mouthful of wine.

A beat of silence ticked past.

'Were you in love with Portia Briscoe?' Sienna asked.

Andreas's brows shot together. 'What sort of question is that?' he asked.

She tilted her head on one side, her finger tapping against her lips. 'No, I don't think you loved her,' she said. 'I think you liked her well enough. She ticked all the boxes for you. She comes from money, she knows what cutlery to use and she dresses well and never has a hair out of place. She never says the wrong thing or rubs people up the wrong way. But grab-you-in-the-guts love? Nope. I don't think so.'

'You're a fine one to harp on about true love,' he said. 'You weren't in love with Brian Littlemore. You barely knew him when you waltzed him down the aisle before his wife was even cold in her grave.'

'Actually, I did know him,' she said with an imperious air. 'I'd met him well before his wife died.'

Andreas gave her a disgusted look. 'And no doubt you opened your legs for him then too. Did he pay you? Or did you give him one for free to get him so hot and hungry the poor old fool couldn't help himself?'

Sienna's eyes flashed at him with undiluted venom. 'You have a mind like a sewer,' she said. 'You sit up there in your diamond-encrusted, gold-inlaid ivory tower of yours, passing judgement on people you don't even know from a bar of soap. Brian was a decent man with a big heart. You haven't even got a heart. All you've got inside your chest is a lump of cold, hard stone.'

Andreas took a measured sip of his wine. 'Your loyalty to your late husband is touching, *ma chérie*,' he said. 'But I wonder if you would be so loyal if you knew he had another lover the whole time he was with you.'

Her eyes flickered before moving away from his. He watched as she moved back to where she had left her glass of wine. She picked it up and cradled it in her hands without drinking any of it. 'We had an open marriage,' she said, still not looking at him. 'It gave us both the freedom to do what we wanted as long as we were both discreet about it.'

Andreas wondered if he should have been quite so blunt with her. There had been nothing in the press about her late husband's affair. He had heard it second-hand and not from a particularly reliable source. But if she was hurt or upset by the news she was doing a good job of concealing it. Admittedly, she was standing stiffly, almost guardedly, but neither her expression nor her tone showed any sign of emotional carnage.

'You knew about his mistress?' he asked.

She turned to look at him, a little puzzled frown pulling at her brow. 'His…mistress?'

'The woman he was seeing,' he said. 'His lover.'

She gave a little laugh that seemed totally out of place. It sounded almost…relieved. 'Oh, *her…*' she said. 'Yes, I knew about her right from the start.'

'And you married Littlemore anyway?' he asked, frowning deeply.

She met his gaze with a directness he found jarring. 'I did it for the money,' she said. 'The same reason I'm marrying you. It's only for the money.'

Andreas felt his jaw clamp down in anger. She was so brazen about her gold-digging motives. Had she no shame? No self-respect? What sort of laughing stock would she try and make of him during their six-month marriage? She had no sense of propriety. She was as selfish and self-serving as she had been as a teenager. She would do anything to get as much out of this situation as she could. He could practically see the dollar signs flashing in her eyes. 'While we're on the subject of money,' he said, 'I want to make a few things clear, right from the start. Throughout the duration of our marriage, I will not tolerate any behaviour on your part that leads to speculation in the press that this is not a normal relationship. If you don't behave yourself there will be consequences. Do I make myself clear?'

She gave him one of her insolent schoolgirl looks. 'Perfectly.'

He drew in a breath for patience and slowly released it. 'Secondly, I will not be made a fool of by your practice of leaping in and out of bed with a host of unsavoury men,' he said. 'That means no boudoir photos and no seedy little sex tapes uploaded to the Internet or social networking sites. Got it?'

Her cheeks turned a cherry-red, he presumed from anger at being reminded of the sex tape incident that had occurred a little over two years ago, for which her twin sister had inadvertently taken the rap. He'd missed the scandal as he had been abroad at the time, but, after reading about her twin's recent reconciliation with her fiancé, the thing that had struck him most was that Sienna hadn't come forward at the time. To be fair, she hadn't known she even had a twin then, but it was just typical of Sienna's inability or unwillingness to take responsibility for her actions. She didn't give a toss what anyone else suffered because of her reprehensible behaviour. She just barrelled her way through life with no thought or care for what anyone else was feeling.

'There won't be any slip-ups,' she said stiffly.

'There had better not be,' he warned.

She turned away from him and drained her glass,

putting it down with a little rattle against the coffee table. 'Will that be all?' she asked.

Andreas pressed his lips together. Her subdued tone was a new one. He hadn't heard her use it before. How did she do it? How did she switch things so deftly to make him feel as if *he* had overstepped the mark? 'If it is any consolation to you, I will also refrain from any behaviour that could compromise our arrangement,' he said, ploughing a hand through his hair. 'It's only for six months. A bout of celibacy is supposed to re-energise the soul and sharpen the intellect, or so I've heard.'

She gave him a little smile, that old familiar spark back in her gaze. 'Do you think you'll last the distance?' she asked.

Andreas wasn't prepared to put any money on it. Not with her looking so damned hot and gorgeous without even trying. 'I'll take it one day at a time,' he said, deliberately running his gaze over her from head to toe and back again.

She held his look but he noticed one of her shoulders rolling as if she suddenly found her clothes prickly against her skin. 'Good luck with that,' she said in an airy tone.

He refilled his wine glass and took a couple of mouthfuls before he turned to look at her again. 'By the way, I'd appreciate you making an effort to buy something suitable to wear to the wedding. I'm not sure yoga pants or tattered jeans are going to set a new trend in bridal gear, no matter how good you look in them.'

Sienna raised her brows at him. 'My, oh, my, a compliment from the impossible-to-impress Signor Ferrante,' she said. 'Wonders will never cease.'

Andreas frowned at her in irritation. 'What are you talking about? I've complimented you plenty of times.'

'Remind me of one,' she said, folding her arms across her chest as she tilted one hip forwards in a pose of youthful scepticism. 'My memory seems to have completely failed me.'

He rubbed at the back of his neck. 'What about the time you were going to that school dance when you were sixteen or thereabouts,' he said. 'You were wearing a crinkly candy-pink and white dress. I said you looked pretty.'

She gave him a resentful look. 'You said I looked like a cupcake.'

Andreas felt a smile tug at his mouth. 'Did I really say that?'

'You did.'

'Well, then, what I probably meant to say was you looked good enough to eat,' he said.

The air seemed to thicken in the ensuing silence.

'You probably should take a little more care with your diet,' Sienna said. 'Too much sugar is bad for you.'

'Yes, but once in a while it's good to have a little of what you fancy, don't you think?' Andreas said.

'Only if you can keep control,' she said, holding his look with a haughty air he found incredibly arousing. 'For some people, one taste is never going to be enough. They can't just have one square of chocolate. They have to have the whole bar.'

His gaze swept over her slim figure again. 'You're obviously not speaking from personal experience,' he said. 'I could just about span your waist with my hands.'

'Lucky genes, I guess.'

Andreas saw a flicker of something move through

her gaze. 'What are you going to tell your sister about this arrangement between us?' he asked.

She rolled her lips together for a moment. 'I feel uncomfortable about lying to her, but I don't want her to worry about me either,' she said. 'I think it's best if I stick to the script for now.'

'We should probably tidy up a few details then,' Andreas said. 'Like how we came to fall in love so quickly.'

Sienna gave him one of her worldly looks. 'Do you really think people are going to believe you fell in love with me? We have nothing in common. I'm a cleaning lady's kid from the wrong side of the tracks. You've had more silver spoons in your mouth than most people have had hot dinners. Men with your sort of heritage don't marry trailer trash. It's just in fairy tales where that sort of thing happens. Not in real life.'

Andreas frowned. 'That's rather a harsh way to speak of your background,' he said. 'I have never once referred to you as trailer trash.'

'You don't have to,' she said. 'I see it in your eyes every time you look at me.'

He felt a little stab of guilt. He had called her plenty of other things in the past and none of them were any less disparaging. 'Look, Sienna,' he said. 'I realise we have some ill feeling because of our history. But I'm prepared to put that aside for the moment in order to get through this period.'

She chewed at her lower lip in a childlike manner he found at odds with what he knew of her. 'Are you saying you forgive me?' she asked.

'I wouldn't go as far as saying that,' he said. 'What you did was unforgivable.'

'Yes,' she said, biting down on her lip again. 'I know…'

Andreas ratcheted up his resolve. She was toying with him, trying to appeal to his better side to get herself off the hook. He wasn't buying it for a moment. Behind that forgive-me-I-was-too-young-to-know-what-I-was-doing façade was a conniving little social-climbing trollop who was on a mission to land herself a fortune. She might have fooled his father into writing her into the will, but it wasn't going to work on him.

He scooped up his jacket from the sofa. 'I'm going to be tied up for the next few days,' he said. 'I hope you can stay out of mischief until Friday.'

'It'll be a piece of cake,' she said.

He gave her a droll look before he left. 'Just stick to one slice, OK?'

CHAPTER FOUR

WHEN Sienna came down after a shower the next morning there was no sign of Andreas. Elena hadn't yet arrived so it gave her some time to wander about and get her bearings. She made a cup of tea and took it out onto a wisteria-covered terrace. She felt the heat of the sun-warmed flagstones through the bare soles of her feet as she walked towards one of the wrought iron chairs. She sat and looked out at the expansive view. There were a hundred shades of green and a thousand fragrant smells and sounds to dazzle her senses.

She put her cup down and went back inside to get her camera from her handbag. It was compact but high-tech enough to allow her to capture images that took her fancy. She went back down to the terrace and beyond, snapping away in bliss, losing track of time as she explored the gardens.

She was aiming for a shot of a bird on a shrub when she caught sight of a dog skulking in the distance. She lowered the camera and, shading her eyes with one of her hands, peered to see if anyone was with it. It seemed to be alone and, by the look of its sunken-in sides, half starving.

Sienna looped her camera strap around her wrist and

walked towards the dog. 'Here, boy,' she called when she got a little closer. 'Come here and say hello.'

The dog looked at her warily, the back of its neck going up in stiff bristles.

Sienna was undaunted. She crouched down and crooned to the dog softly, holding out her hand for it to smell. The dog crept closer, its body low to the ground, the hackles going down and its tail giving the tiniest of wags. 'Good boy,' she said. 'That's right; I won't hurt you. Good dog.'

Just as she was about to see if the dog's worn collar had an identifying tag on it, there was a sound behind her and the dog tore off, disappearing into the nearby woods with its tail tucked between its legs.

'You little fool,' Andreas said. 'You'll get yourself bitten. That dog is a stray. Franco was supposed to shoot it days ago.'

Sienna rose from her crouching position but, even so, he seemed to tower over her. 'But it's wearing a collar!' she said. 'It must belong to someone. Maybe it's just lost and can't find its way home.'

'It's a flea-bitten mongrel,' he said. 'Any fool can see that.'

Sienna scowled at him. 'I suppose you only allow pure-bred dogs with pedigree papers the thickness of three phone books on your precious property.' She brushed past him to go back to the villa. 'What a stuck-up jerk.'

He caught her arm on the way past, swinging her round to face him. 'You shouldn't be wandering around down here without shoes,' he said. 'Are you completely without sense?'

Sienna tugged at his hold but it tightened like a vice.

She felt the sexy rasp of his callused fingers on her wrist and her stomach gave a little fluttery flip-flop. She met his hard hazel eyes and something shifted in the atmosphere. Her gaze slipped to his mouth. He hadn't yet shaved and the sexy pepper of his stubble sent another shockwave of awareness through her. He smelt of man and heat and hard work, a potent smell that stirred her feminine senses into a mad frenzy. Could he tell how much he got under her skin? Could he sense it? Was that why he kept looking at her with those smouldering eyes? 'What would you care?' she said. 'I'd be better off to you dead, wouldn't I?'

His brooding frown cut deeper into his tanned forehead. 'That's a crazy thing to say,' he said. 'Why would I want you dead?'

'Because you'd automatically inherit the chateau,' she said. 'You wouldn't have to go through a marriage you didn't want to a woman you hate more than anyone else in the world.'

'You hate me just as much as I hate you, so we're pretty square on that,' he said. 'Or are you hiding a secret affection for me, hmm?'

She gave him a withering look. 'You have got to be joking.'

He tugged her closer, flush against his rock-hard body. The heat of his arousal was like a brand against her belly. 'You like to tease and tantalise, don't you, *cara*?' he said. 'You like the power. It's like a drug to you, to have men falling over themselves to possess you. I see it in your eyes. They dance with sensual intent. You can't wait to have me fall at your feet. But I won't do it. I won't let you play your seductress games with me. I will have you on my terms, not yours.'

Sienna pushed against his chest with the flat of her hands but, while it put some distance between their upper bodies, it made their lower connection all the more intense. She felt the thundering roar of his blood against her, the rigid length of him taking her breath clean away.

The air sizzled with sexual electricity.

She felt the force of it like waves of searing heat rippling over her skin. She felt her heart rate pick up and her inner core clenched and released, clenched and released, in a primitive rhythm of need.

She wondered if he was going to kiss her. His eyes had dropped to her mouth in an infinitesimal moment of sensual suspense that made her heart beat all the faster. She sent her tongue out over her lips, wondering what he would taste like. Would he be rough or smooth? Forceful or gentle?

'Damn you,' Andreas ground out as he put her from him roughly. 'Damn you to hell.'

Sienna let out a ragged breath as she watched him stride back the way he had come. She put a hand to her chest where her heart was beating like a maniacal metronome. She felt light-headed and shaky on her feet, her body still tingling from the hard male contact of his. That primitive pulse of longing was still thrumming deep inside her and she couldn't seem to turn it off.

She looked down at her wrist where her camera was swinging from its strap. The imprint of his fingers was almost visible on her skin. She touched the tender area with the fingertips of her other hand, her stomach slipping like a skater who had mistimed a manoeuvre.

She was in trouble with a capital T.

* * *

Sienna didn't see Andreas until the evening before the wedding. Elena told her he had been called away to some important business in Milan but Sienna wondered if he was keeping his distance for as long as possible before they were thrust together as man and wife.

The days flashed past as she fielded phone calls from Gisele and her flatmate Kate in London. Somehow she managed to convince her twin she was madly and blissfully in love with Andreas and couldn't wait to get married. As Gisele's wedding was in a few weeks' time and the guest list had blown out considerably, Gisele was nothing but supportive of Sienna's plan for a simple witnesses-only ceremony so she and Andreas could be left alone by the press.

Kate didn't buy into the 'we suddenly fell in love' story but, as a hopeless romantic herself, she was convinced Andreas would finally come to his senses and want Sienna to stay with him for ever.

Sienna didn't like to disabuse her friend of the impossibility of such an outcome. His refusal to forgive her was not the only stumbling block to their relationship. She had long ago given up her foolish dream of him falling in love with her. And, as for her falling in love with him, well, that was *not* going to happen.

Sienna went shopping a couple of times under the escort of a very willing Franco, who faithfully carried her bags and waited patiently in the car while she had her hair and beauty treatments done.

There was also a visit to a lawyer's office where Andreas had set up the signing of a prenuptial agreement. Sienna understood it was part and parcel of many modern marriages, and she totally understood Andreas's motivations given the wealth he had at his disposal, but even so it rankled that he didn't trust her to walk away without a legal tussle when the time was up on their marriage.

The rest of the time Sienna spent working on befriending the dog, whom she called Scraps. He had built up enough confidence to take titbits of food from her hand, but he wouldn't allow her to touch him as yet. She was prepared to be patient, however. And she had made Franco promise he wouldn't shoot him, no matter what orders Andreas gave to the contrary.

Sienna had not long fed the dog and settled him in one of the buildings close to the villa when she heard the roar of Andreas's car come up the driveway that curved through the property, fields of vines on one side, olive groves on the other. A church bell calling the faithful to Mass sounded in the distance, a peaceful sound that was totally at odds with the tension she could feel building in her body as soon as Andreas came into view.

She watched as he unfolded his long, lean length from the low-slung vehicle. He had loosened his tie and his shirtsleeves were rolled up past his strongly muscled wrists. His suit jacket was hooked through one of his fingers and was slung over his shoulder, his briefcase in his other hand.

His eyes ran over her shorts and T-shirt, resting a heart-stopping moment on the upthrust of her breasts, before meshing with her gaze. 'Isn't it supposed to be bad luck to see the bride before the wedding?' he asked.

'That's the morning of the wedding,' she said. 'I don't think the night before counts.'

He gave a slight movement of his lips that could only be very loosely described as a smile, and a half one at that. 'Glad to hear it,' he said. His footsteps crunched over the gravel as he came to where she was standing. 'Elena tells me you have a new conquest.'

'That would be Scraps,' Sienna said, rocking on her feet. 'I've just tucked him in for the night.'

One brow curved in an arch over his eye. 'Scraps?' he said.

'It's what he likes to eat,' she said. 'Plus it's sort of a tribute to his mixed heritage.'

His mouth quirked upwards in that almost smile again. 'Original.'

'I thought so.'

He indicated for her to go ahead of him into the villa. 'How has your week been?' he asked.

'I've shopped myself silly,' Sienna said. 'Thanks for the use of the car, by the way. Franco quite fancies himself as a chauffeur. I think you should get him fitted for a uniform.'

Andreas closed the door and placed his car keys on a marble table in the foyer. 'I've ordered a car for you,' he said. 'It should be here some time next week.'

'I hope it's an Italian sports car,' Sienna said, just to needle him. 'I'll be the envy of all my friends. It's the ultimate status symbol.'

He gave her a derisive look. 'It will get you from A to B without mishap, that is if you drive with any sense of responsibility. But, judging by what you do in your personal life, I'm not holding my breath.'

'I'll have you know I'm a very safe driver,' Sienna said, following him into the *salone*. 'I've never had an accident or even copped a speeding fine. Parking tickets, well, now, that's another thing.'

'So you have a history of outstaying your welcome,

do you?' he asked as he poured himself a drink. 'I'll have to make a note of that.'

Sienna threw him a haughty look. 'If you think I'll stay even a minute over the six months, then you are seriously deluded,' she said.

He looked at her with his unwavering hazel gaze. It seemed more brown than green in the subdued lighting of the *salone*. But then she had noticed lately that his eyes seemed to change with his mood. 'Just as long as we're both clear on the terms of this arrangement,' he said. 'I don't want any complications. And you, *cara,* are nothing if not a magnet for complications.'

Only Andreas could make a term of endearment sound like an insult, Sienna thought. But she had to concede that he was right about the complications. Other people had such simple, uncomplicated lives. She seemed to go from one stuff-up to another. It was as if she had been cursed since birth. But then, maybe she had. Born out of wedlock to a man who had used her mother and then tossed her aside when he was done with her, taking one of her babies for a sum of money to pay for her silence.

It didn't get more complicated or cursed than that.

Sienna suddenly realised Andreas was still watching her with that slightly narrowed focused gaze of his. 'Are you going to offer me a drink or should I just help myself?' she asked.

'Pardon my oversight,' he said. 'What would you like?'

'White wine,' she said. 'The one from your vineyard. It's my favourite.'

He handed her a chilled glass of wine but, just as she reached for it, his brows moved together as he saw the fading marks on her arm. 'What happened to your wrist?' he asked.

Sienna put her hand back down by her side. 'Nothing.'

He put the wine aside and reached for her hand, gently turning over her wrist to look at the full set of his fingerprints there. She saw his face flinch with shock. 'Did I do this to you?' he asked.

'It's nothing,' she said. 'I bruise easily, that's all.'

Her stomach folded over as the pad of his thumb gently moved across the purple stain of his touch. 'Forgive me,' he said in a voice so deep it felt as if it had come from beneath the floor at their feet.

She swallowed as his eyes meshed with hers. 'Really, Andreas, it's nothing…'

'Does it hurt?' he asked, still gently cradling her wrist in the warmth of his hand.

Sienna wasn't used to this tender, more considerate side of him. It made something inside her melt like molasses under the blaze of a hot summer sun. A dangerous melting that she should not allow, but somehow she couldn't prevent it. It flowed through her like a slow-moving tide, all the way through the circuitry of her veins, loosening her spine and all of her ligaments until she felt as if she would end up in a pool of longing at his feet. Her swiftly indrawn breath hitched against something in her throat. 'No…'

He brought her wrist up to his mouth, his lips barely touching the sensitive skin, but it set off a shower of sensations that travelled all the way up her arm and shoulder, making every hair on her head lift away from her scalp.

His eyes were the darkest she had ever seen them. 'It won't happen again,' he said. 'I can assure you of that.

You have no reason to fear for your safety while living under my protection.'

'Thanks for the reassurance,' Sienna said, pulling her hand out of his with a sassy little smile to hide her vulnerability, 'but I've never been scared of you.'

'No, you haven't, have you?' he said, still studying her intently.

Sienna picked up the wine he had poured for her earlier. 'So, I take it we're not going on a honeymoon?' she said before taking a sip.

'On the contrary,' he said, 'I thought we should go to Provence. It's a perfect opportunity to pretend we are taking some time together. I want to see how the Chateau de Chalvy estate is being run. My father appointed a husband and wife team to manage it quite a few years back. I'd like to reacquaint myself with them.'

'Why don't you go on your own?' Sienna said. 'It's not as if you really need me to tag along. I'll only get in the way or say something I shouldn't or dress inappropriately.'

'Sienna, we are getting married tomorrow,' he said with an expressive roll of his eyes. 'People will think it highly unusual if within hours of the ceremony we go our separate ways. That's not how newly married couples behave.'

'But what about Scraps?' she asked. 'I can't just leave him. I've only just got him to trust me. He probably won't take food off Franco or Elena. He might starve or run away again.' She narrowed her gaze at him pointedly and added, 'Or get shot.'

Andreas let out a breath. 'Is that mangy-looking mongrel really that important to you?'

'Yes,' Sienna said. 'I've never had a pet before. I was

never allowed to have one because we always lived in a flat or other people's houses. I've always wanted my own dog. Dogs don't judge you. They love you no matter how little or much money you have and they don't give a toss about whether or not you come from a posh suburb or a trailer park. I've always wanted to be…' She suddenly checked herself. God, how embarrassing. What was she thinking, blurting out all those heartfelt longings as if she was a soppy fool?

Andreas was looking at her quizzically. It was the sort of look that suggested he was seeing much more than she wanted him to see.

Sienna lifted a shoulder in an indifferent shrug as she took another sip of her wine. 'Now that I think of it, maybe Elena could toss him a bone or two,' she said. 'I won't be able to take him with me when I leave in six months, anyway. Best not to get too attached.'

'Why won't you be able to take him with you?' Andreas asked, frowning slightly.

'I want to travel,' Sienna said. 'I don't want to be tied down. I'll have enough money by then to go where I want when I want. It's what I've always dreamed of doing. Having no responsibilities other than to please myself. That's what I'd call the perfect life.'

'It sounds rather pointless and shallow to me,' he said. 'Don't you want more for your life than a never ending holiday?'

'Nope,' Sienna said. 'Give me nine to five partying any day, as long as someone else is paying for it.'

A muscle worked like a hammer at the side of his mouth, while his eyes had gone all hard and glittery. 'You really are a piece of work, aren't you?'

'That's me,' Sienna said, draining her wine glass

before holding it out to him. 'Can you pour me another one?'

Andreas threw her a disgusted look. 'Get it yourself,' he said and strode out of the *salone*, snapping the door shut behind him.

The following morning Elena arrived earlier than usual to help Sienna prepare for the ceremony. She bustled about like a mother hen, gushing about how beautiful Sienna looked as she dressed in a slim-fitting cream dress, the purchase of which had hit Andreas's credit card a little more heavily than Sienna cared to think about.

'Signor Ferrante is going to be…how you say?' Elena said. 'Knocked out by you, *sì*?'

Sienna gave the housekeeper what she hoped passed for a convincing smile. 'I'll be glad when this bit is over,' she said, smoothing a hand over her abdomen. 'My stomach feels like a hive of bees.'

'Wedding jitters,' Elena said reassuringly. 'It happens to every bride.'

Sienna didn't feel like a bride. She felt like a fraud. She thought of her twin sister preparing for her big day with Emilio and she felt a twinge of something that felt very much like pain. When she was a little girl she had dreamed of a white wedding with all the trimmings: a church filled with fragrant flowers, with bridesmaids and flower girls and a cute little ring-bearer. She had envisaged a horse-drawn carriage and footmen just like Cinderella. She had imagined a handsome husband who would look down at her as he lifted back her veil with such love and adoration that her heart would swell like a balloon.

But then her dreams and reality had always had a problem socialising.

'Come,' Elena said. 'Franco has brought the car around. It's time to leave.'

Andreas was waiting at the foot of the stairs when Sienna came down. He hadn't been sure what to expect. He had wondered if she would appear in her signature torn denim or a ridiculously short skirt or even bare feet. He hadn't been expecting a vision in designer cream satin that was so stylish and yet so elegantly simple it quite literally took his breath away.

Her silver-blonde hair was up in a classic French roll that showed off her swan-like neck to perfection. Her make-up was understated but somehow it worked brilliantly to showcase the luminosity of her flawless skin. Her grey-blue eyes had a hint of eye shadow and her lashes were long and lustrous with mascara. Her model-like cheekbones were defined by a subtle sweep of bronzer and her lips adorned with a glisten of pink-tinted lipgloss.

The only thing she lacked was jewellery.

An elbow of remorse nudged him in the ribs. He should have thought to buy her something but he had assumed she would spend up big all by herself since he had given her carte blanche on the credit card he had issued her with.

'You look magnificent,' he said. 'I don't think I've ever seen you look quite so beautiful.'

'Amazing what a bit of money splashed around can do,' she said in a flippant tone. 'You don't want to know what this dress cost. And don't get me started on the shoes.'

He took her hand as she stepped from the last stair, a smile tugging at the corners of his mouth. 'At least you're wearing them,' he said. 'I was wondering if you might go without.'

'Watch this space,' she said with a wry twist of her mouth. 'These are what I call car-to-the-bar shoes. They're not meant for walking unless you want to end up with seriously deformed toes.'

Andreas was aware of Elena and Franco hovering in the background, looking suspiciously like the proud parents of the bride. In the space of a week Sienna had charmed them, along with the feral dog. She certainly had a way about her that was unlike any other woman he had associated with before. But then she was very good at fooling people into believing she was all sweetness and light, when underneath that friendly façade was a cold and calculating little madam who—like her mangy dog—could lash out and bite when you were least expecting it.

Andreas turned to Franco. 'Give us a few minutes, there's something I have to give Sienna before we leave.'

'Sì, signor.'

'Come,' Andreas said to Sienna, leading her by the hand towards his study. 'I have something for you.'

'God, my feet are already killing me,' Sienna said, click-clacking beside him.

'This won't take long,' Andreas said, closing the door once they were inside the study.

'Have you bought me a present?' she asked with bright interest in her eyes.

Another sharp elbow of guilt nudged him. 'No,' he said. He opened the safe and took out the box that contained a pearl and diamond necklace and matching droplet earrings. 'These are just on loan.'

'They're beautiful,' Sienna said, peering at them for a moment before straightening. 'But if you bought them for your ex, then forget about it. I'd rather go without.'

Andreas lifted the necklace off its bed of maroon velvet. 'These belonged to my mother,' he said. 'She wore them on her wedding day.'

She looked at the jewels without touching them. 'I'm not sure your mother would appreciate me wearing her jewellery.' She raised her eyes to his. 'It seems a bit… tacky, given the circumstances, don't you think?'

Andreas rolled his thumb over one of the pearls as he looked at her. 'Every Ferrante bride has worn them,' he said. 'They are a family heirloom.'

'Oh…well, then,' she said, turning her back to him. 'That's different. I wouldn't want to break with tradition or anything.'

Andreas fastened the necklace around her neck, his fingers fumbling over the catch as his skin came into contact with the silk of hers. 'You smell nice,' he said. 'Is that a new perfume?'

'If you wanted me to stick to a budget then you should have said so,' she said, turning around to scowl at him.

Andreas handed her the earrings. 'I think you've shown remarkable restraint,' he said. 'But then it's early days yet.'

She clipped on the earrings, still giving him the evil eye as she did so. 'There,' she said once she was done. 'How do I look?'

'Breathtaking,' he said.

'Good,' she said. 'It's not every day a girl like me

gets to marry a billionaire. I want to make the most of every single minute of it.'

Andreas held open the door, his jaw set in a tight line. *Not if I can help it*, he said beneath his breath as she sashayed past him.

Sienna had thought her marriage ceremony to Brian Littlemore had been a bit on the sterile and impersonal side but it had nothing on the clinical detachment of the service Andreas had organised. The vows were nothing like the ones she had composed in her girlish dreams. They were stilted and formal and she'd even been forced to say the O word. Obey.

She was fuming by the time it was almost over. Her lips felt as if they'd been stitched in place. Her teeth were half a centimetre down from grinding and her back was rigid with tension.

'You may kiss the bride.'

The words jolted her out of her simmering fury. 'I don't think—'

Andreas drew her closer, one of his hands in the small of her back, the other holding the hand that had not long ago received the slim gold band that now bound her to him as his wife. 'Relax, *ma chèrie*,' he said in an undertone. 'This one is for the cameras.'

'What cam—?'

A flash went off but it wasn't from any lurking cameras. It was a flare inside Sienna's brain that almost took the top of her head off. As soon as Andreas's lips touched down on hers she felt a tectonic shift of her equilibrium. The world seemed to tilt on its axis.

His lips were firm and yet soft.

Warm and yet dry.

He tasted of…she wasn't quite sure. It was something she had never tasted before and yet it was incredibly addictive.

She wanted more.

She *craved* more.

Her hands went to the front of his chest. She could feel his heart thudding beneath her palm. It mimicked the erratic rhythm of hers. He felt warm and male and vital. He felt strong and capable and arrantly potent.

His tongue stroked along the seam of her lips, a bold and commanding stroke that didn't ask permission for entry, but rather *demanded* it.

She opened to him on a soft little whimper, her stomach dropping in delight as his tongue deftly found hers. She felt the stirring of his arousal, the hot, hard length of him swelling against her as his mouth wreaked sensual havoc on hers. She moved closer, an instinctive, almost involuntary shift against him that evoked a husky-sounding groan from his throat as he deepened the kiss even further.

'Ahem…' The celebrant cleared his throat. 'I have another ceremony in five minutes.'

Sienna stepped out of Andreas's hold, her heart still galloping like a racehorse on steroids. Her mouth was tingling, every nerve alive with feeling, her lips swollen and sensitive from the pressure of his. She ran the tip of her tongue over them and tasted his hot male potency. Her stomach gave another tripping movement as she looked up at his darkly hooded gaze…

A flash went off but this time it was the surge of the paparazzi.

'Looks like it's show time,' Andreas said grimly and,

taking her hand in his, led her towards the pack of journalists and photographers.

Sienna's emotions were in such turmoil she didn't want to examine them too closely. She had responded with such wantonness to Andreas. She had forgotten everything but the feel of his mouth on hers. The whole world had ceased to exist in that heart-stopping moment when he had kissed her with such fiery passion and intent. She had felt the primal rhythm of his blood through the surface of his lips. She hadn't wanted the kiss to end. Her insides were still trembling from the sensual onslaught of being in his arms.

It was at least an hour before they could escape. Her face felt stiff from all the fake smiling. Her head was aching and her feet were throbbing by the time they got back to where Franco was waiting for them in the car.

'That went remarkably well,' Andreas said once the partition between the driver and the passenger section was closed.

'You think?' Sienna bent down to prise off her shoes. 'Ouch! I've got blisters.'

'Elena will probably have an intimate dinner set up for us back at the villa,' he said. 'She's a hopeless romantic so just go along with it.'

'She reminds me of my flatmate Kate back in London,' Sienna said, closing her eyes and flinging her head back against the headrest in bone-aching fatigue. 'She thinks you're going to fall in love with me before the end of this and beg me to stay with you for ever.'

'I hope you put her straight on that.'

'I did,' she said flatly. 'She forgot to factor in the fact that I wouldn't stay on even if you paid me.'

Andreas gave a mocking laugh. 'If the price was right you'd stay.'

Sienna turned her head on the headrest to glare at him. 'Even you don't have enough money to buy me, Rich Boy,' she said. 'And, just for the record, I am *not* going to obey you.'

He gave her a supercilious smile. 'You just promised to do so in front of a legally appointed celebrant.'

'I don't care,' she said, throwing her head back and closing her eyes again. 'I am *not* going to bend to your will.'

'So what was that kiss all about?' he asked.

Sienna jerked upright in her seat to glower at him. 'That was your doing, not mine,' she said. 'I was all geared up for the hands-off clinical deal we'd agreed on and then you sideswipe me with a wedding kiss. That was low. That was *really* low.'

His look was smouldering, and it centred on her mouth just long enough to set her lips tingling all over again. 'It was a good kiss,' he said. 'I can see why you have the reputation you have. I was starting to think how it would feel to have those lips of yours on my—'

'Will you stop it, for God's sake?' Sienna hissed at him. 'My lips are going nowhere near your…your whatever. We're meant to be keeping this strictly to the terms.'

He was still looking at her mouth with that hooded dark gaze. 'We could always adjust the goalposts a little to suit our needs,' he said. 'After all, six months is a long time to be celibate.'

'It's not a long time for me.'

The words seemed to hang suspended in the air for a moment.

'How long is a long time for you?' Andreas asked.

Sienna felt the weight of his gaze but resolutely kept her head facing forward. 'How long is a piece of string?' she asked.

She heard him give a snort of derision. 'You have no idea, do you?' he said. 'Do you even know the names of some of the men you've slept with?'

'Not all of them,' Sienna answered with ironic truthfulness. 'Some men don't require a personal introduction before they sleep with you.'

Andreas let out a breath of disgust. 'You are such a shameless gold-digging whore,' he said. 'Don't you have any self-respect?'

'Plenty,' Sienna said, lifting her chin. 'I could've settled for the deal your father set up, but I know you'll pay more to have what you want. And you want it. You want it so badly you'll do anything to stop me from taking it from you.'

His hands went to white-knuckled fists on the armrests each side of him. 'You'd better believe it,' he said. 'Don't say you weren't warned.'

CHAPTER FIVE

As soon as the car pulled up in front of his villa, Andreas wanted to head to the furthest reaches of the property to put as much distance as he could between him and Sienna. He wanted to regroup before she made him lose control completely. But for the sake of Franco and Elena's presence he was forced to play the role of devoted husband, which included carrying his new bride over the threshold of the villa. He could already feel his blood simmering at the thought of holding her against his body.

Sienna gave a little gasp as he scooped her up in his arms. 'What are you doing?' she asked.

'It's considered bad luck not to carry one's bride over the threshold,' he said and strode to the door being held open by his housekeeper, who was smiling broadly.

Andreas felt his skin grow hot and tight where Sienna's arms had looped around his neck. Her right breast was pressed against his thumping heart and the fragrance of her alluring perfume teased his nostrils. She was lighter than he had expected and she fitted against him like a glove. He tried not to look at her mouth. Tried not to remember how it had felt to taste her moist hot sweetness. The taste of her lingered on his tongue; it was a potent potion as addictive as a drug. One taste was not going to be enough. It was never going to be enough. But then he had always known that. He had fought it for so long. This raw need to have her as his had been a part of his life for so long he had no idea how to subdue it. It was an ache that resided deep within him. It would not go away, no matter how much he distracted or disciplined himself.

He wanted her.

He lowered her to the floor by sliding her down the length of his body, his blood roaring in response to her curves as they brushed against him.

He wanted her and he would have her.

He heard the soft intake of her breath and saw the flare of her pupils as her eyes meshed with his. The barrier of their clothes was no barrier at all. They might as well have been standing there naked.

Sienna glowered up at him. 'Was that really necessary?'

'But of course,' Andreas said. 'Elena and Franco were watching.'

'Yeah, well, no one's watching now,' she said. 'Let's just step back into our true characters and tear strips off each other again.'

He gave a soft deep chuckle and pressed her even closer with his hand on the shapely curve of her bottom. 'Why the hurry, *ma petite*?' he said. 'I'm getting to like the feel of you against me. You like it too, *sì*?'

Her eyes were pools of stormy grey and blue. 'This is not part of the plan,' she said, but she didn't do anything to push him away. If anything her body shifted closer, a subtle movement that sent another hot lightning rod of lust straight to his groin.

'Is it not?' he asked with a mocking smile. 'You've planned this from the start. You want me to think twice about ending this marriage when the time is up.' He captured one of her hands and pressed his lips to each and every fingertip, watching as her eyes darkened with desire. 'And what better way than to entice me into your bed as soon as you can?'

Her gaze flicked to his mouth, her tongue sweeping over her lips. 'That's not what I'm planning at all,' she said in a breathless voice. 'I don't want to be married to you any longer than I have to be.'

Andreas's fingers tightened on hers. Her hand was dainty and small in the grasp of his. He could have broken her fingers with just the slightest pressure. He was so close to her he could feel her body warmth radiating through him. She smelt of summer, of jasmine and honeysuckle and red-hot temptation. The skin of her hand was soft against the roughness of his. He felt her fingers move experimentally against the cup of his palm, whether to test his hold or tease him, he wasn't quite sure. It shouldn't have had anywhere near the sensual impact it had. It felt as if she had dipped her hand down the front of his trousers and touched him flesh on flesh.

He brought his mouth down to hers for the second time that day, and for the second time in his life a seismic shift knocked him sideways.

She tasted of sweet, hot, forbidden longings. He couldn't get enough of her delicious moistness. He fed off her with a greed he hadn't known existed. He savaged her mouth like a hungry beast on a rampage.

It was rapacious. It was primitive. It was raw male lust let off the leash. He hadn't realised how out of control a kiss could get until he thrust through the seam of her lips in search of her tongue.

Hers was hot and moist and brazen. It danced with his in a tango that was as sexy as anything he had ever experienced. It shot fireworks off in his head. Desire filled him so tightly he thought he would explode. His teeth scraped against hers. She bit him and he bit her back. It only made him want her more.

He thrust a hand at the back of her head, his fingers burying deep into her scalp as he explored her mouth with a thoroughness that left both of them breathless. His hand found her breast. It filled his palm with sensual heat, the tight bud of her nipple pressing against him. She felt so damn good, so feminine and soft. His need pulsed and pounded against her belly.

He wanted her naked.

He wanted to see her silky skin, every gorgeous inch of it. He wanted to taste her feminine heat, to move his lips and tongue against her to make her scream with ecstasy. He wanted to drive himself deep within her honeyed warmth, to feel the tight grip of her body contracting around him as she came.

He started to lift up the skirt of her dress but she suddenly stepped back, turning away from him with her arms going across her body as if she were suffering a chill. 'I'm sorry, Andreas,' she said. 'I don't want to continue with this.'

'Is this part of your technique?' Andreas asked. 'To tempt and to tease?'

Her cheeks flushed with delicate colour. 'It was unfair of me to give you the wrong impression,' she said. 'I didn't mean to mislead you.'

'The impression you gave me is that you want me just as much as I want you,' he said.

'Yes, well, I'm sorry about that but I had no idea that was going to happen every time you kiss me,' she said with a return to her haughty air. 'Maybe you should keep your mouth to yourself for the rest of the time we have together.'

'Ah, but that would not be half as much fun, would it, *ma belle*?' he asked. 'I quite like kissing you. I am developing rather a hunger for it, actually.'

She challenged him with those incredible grey-blue eyes and that stubborn little uptilted chin. 'Then you'll have to satisfy your appetite elsewhere. I'm not going to be a rich man's mistress.'

'You're not my mistress,' he said. 'You're my wife.'

'Same difference, as far as I can see,' she threw back.

Andreas fought down his frustration and anger. She had been toying with him all along and he had been fool enough to fall for it. She knew how much he wanted her. It wasn't as if he could hide it. She had sensed it. Damn it, she had *felt* it.

And she wanted him. He'd have to be blind not to see it. He felt it in her kiss, in her touch and in the way she had pressed herself closer as if she had wanted to climb into his skin.

He would not rest until he had her where he wanted her.

Where he had always wanted her.

Sienna was the one woman who could make him lose all sense of control. He had sensed it all those years ago and had fought it determinedly.

But now was different.

Now there was nothing to stop them exploring the

heat and passion that was flaring between them every time they were in the same room.

He could hardly wait.

Sienna closed her bedroom door and leant back against it, her heart thumping like a jackhammer. Her breathing was still out of control and her insides quivered with a longing so intense she could barely stand up. They had been married only a matter of a couple of hours and already things were spinning dangerously out of control. She didn't want to feel this level of attraction, not to Andreas Ferrante, not to a man who hated her as much as he desired her. But what was she to do? Her mind said *no* but her body kept saying a resounding *yes*. It completely disregarded her common sense. Instead, it was set on a pathway to sensual hedonism that she could not control. She didn't want to end up like her mother, madly in love with a man who only saw her as a convenient outlet for his lust. Unrequited love for Andreas's father had destroyed her mother. After Guido Ferrante had rejected her so publicly, Nell had sunk into an alcohol and prescriptions drugs binge that had eventually killed her.

Sienna wasn't prepared to go down the same path of destruction. She was determined to keep her heart well guarded. Andreas was by far the most attractive man she had ever met and his kisses were a temptation she couldn't seem to resist, but that didn't mean she had to fall in love with him. She had thought herself in love with him as a teenager, but that had just been a youthful crush, an infatuation that had got totally out of hand. She was no longer that foolish star-struck teenager caught up in the fantasy of thinking a well-born rich and powerful man was the answer to all of her problems.

Things would be different this time.

She would do what other young women her age did and what men had been doing for centuries. She would separate her emotions from her physical needs. Sex would be just sex. Love would not come into it at all.

Sienna joined Andreas in the *salone* for the intimate celebration Elena had taken such delight in setting up for them. The housekeeper was clearly in her element, a beaming smile was spread across her face as she brought in an ice bucket and a bottle of vintage champagne.

'I have left everything ready for you in the dining room,' she said. 'You will prefer to be alone, *sì*? It will be much more romantic.'

'*Grazie*, Elena,' Andreas said. 'I'm sure it will be delightful.'

'Thank you for going to so much trouble,' Sienna chimed in. 'I saw the dining room on my way past. It looks fabulous with all the candles and the food smells absolutely delicious.'

'Enjoy,' Elena said and bustled out, closing the door softly as she left.

Sienna went over to where Andreas was standing and handed him his mother's pearl necklace and earrings. 'I thought I'd better hand these back before I get too attached to them,' she said. 'I'm sure your next bride will appreciate the chance to carry on the tradition.'

He took them from her with an unreadable expression on his face. 'Thank you,' he said.

'So,' she said with forced brightness. 'Champagne, huh?'

'Yes,' he said. 'Would you like some?'

'Why not?'

Sienna watched as he unpeeled the foil cover and unwound the wire before he popped the cork. A soft flutter like wings passed over the floor of her belly as she thought of those hands on her breasts and other parts of her anatomy. He had beautiful hands. Not soft and unused to hard work, but strong and capable.

She took the bubbling glass of champagne from him and was about to take a sip when his voice stalled her.

'Shouldn't we make a toast?'

'Sure,' she said, holding her glass up. 'What shall we drink to?'

He clinked his glass against hers, his eyes holding hers in a steely little lockdown that made her spine tingle. 'To making love, not war.'

She looked at him archly. '*Love*, Andreas?' she said. 'Don't you mean sex?'

His eyes glinted smoulderingly as he gave her a half-smile. 'You want it as much as I do,' he said. 'There's no point pretending otherwise.'

Sienna gave a little indifferent shrug. 'I admit the thought of seeing what you're like in bed holds a certain fascination,' she said. 'But I don't want you getting any ideas that *if* we conduct an intimate relationship it will mean anything to me other than the satiation of physical lust.'

He held her gaze for a pulsing moment. 'If?'

She gave him a defiant look. 'If.'

He took a leisurely sip of his champagne. 'I think we both know this thing between us is not going to go away,' he said. 'The thing is, it can only last as long as six months. By that time we will both have achieved what we want and will be free to move on with our lives.'

Sienna toyed with the champagne flute with her fingers, determined to rattle his chain as much as she could. It was an impish urge in her she couldn't quite control. 'What if you want me to stay a little longer?' she asked. 'What if you get so used to having me around you don't want to let me go?'

His hazel eyes drilled into hers with burning intensity. 'I will let you go, Sienna,' he said. 'Make no mistake about that. You are not the woman I want to be my wife or the future mother of my children.'

Sienna wasn't expecting his cutting response to hurt, but it had and deeply. Having children of her own was a subject she had put to the back of her mind. It was one of those things she didn't want to think about. Her childhood had been so unsettled and chaotic, and her mother's example of mothering so poor, she had always felt worried she might not be a good mother herself. But to hear Andreas say she was a totally unsuitable candidate as the mother of his children made her feel crushed in that closely guarded centre of her being. No woman wanted to hear that sort of insult. It felt as if she had been stabbed in the heart. The pain was so acute and so raw it momentarily took her breath away. She was annoyed at herself for feeling so upset. It wasn't like her to be so emotionally ambushed by a throwaway comment.

She quickly disguised her feelings by pasting an insolent smile on her face. 'Just as well, because I'm not planning on ruining my figure any time soon for a brood of obnoxious brats,' she said. 'Even a billionaire's ones.'

Andreas's eyes hardened. 'Is your twin sister as selfish and shallow as you?' he asked.

Sienna took a sip of her champagne. 'You can find out for yourself when you meet her in a few weeks,' she said. 'I'm going to be her bridesmaid. You'll be expected to attend the wedding with me in Rome. Won't that be fun?'

'I can hardly wait,' he said dryly.

Sienna sat down and flung one leg over the other, idly swinging her ankle up and down. 'So, this proposed honeymoon,' she said. 'When do we leave?'

'Tomorrow morning,' he said. 'I can only be away a couple of days, three at the most. I have a lot of work on at the moment.'

'Is it absolutely necessary I come with you?' she asked.

'We've already had this discussion, Sienna,' he said a little impatiently. 'I'm sure your dog will survive the separation from you. I have already spoken to Franco about making sure it is taken care of.'

She gave him a narrow-eyed look. 'You're not going to get rid of him while my back is turned, are you?'

'While I don't share your enthusiasm for the mutt, I can see you've taken him on as some type of project,' he said. 'I just hope you won't be disappointed when he fails to live up to your expectations. He's half wild and quite possibly dangerous. You shouldn't let your guard down around him in case he reverts to form.'

'You sound as if you care about my welfare, Andreas,' Sienna said giving him a teasing smile. 'How touching.'

Andreas put his barely touched drink down. 'We should go and eat,' he said. 'I don't want the food to be spoiled.'

While the wedding ceremony had not been in line with Sienna's dreams, the wedding breakfast Andreas's housekeeper had prepared certainly was. Dish after delectable dish of local produce had been laid out in the dining room. There were hot dishes and cold ones, main ones and gorgeous desserts. Elena had even made a wedding cake. It was only a small one but it had been decorated with marzipan and white royal icing with fresh flowers as decoration. It even had a bride and groom on the top, and a silver knife with a satin ribbon tied around the handle lay ready.

It was a jarring reminder that none of this was for real.

'Gosh, will you check this out,' Sienna said. 'Elena's made us a wedding cake. Isn't that sweet?' She leaned down to peer at the plastic figures standing together. 'And the groom even looks like you, see? He looks all stiff and formal.'

Andreas gave her an irritated look. 'She shouldn't have gone to so much trouble.'

'No point complaining,' Sienna said as she picked up a plate. 'You're the one who insisted on telling everyone this is the real deal.'

'And what would you have done in my place?' he asked in an embittered tone. 'Told everyone you know—including the world's media—that you've been manipulated by your father into marrying a sleep-around gold-digging slut? I would be laughed out of town, if not the country.'

The words echoed in the silence.

Sienna put the plate she was holding down on the sideboard with calculated precision in case she was tempted to throw it at his face. Then, turning to face him, she gave him the coldest look she could muster. 'Enjoy your dinner,' she said. 'I hope it damn well chokes you.'

She moved past him to leave but he blocked her with his body. 'Sienna,' he said.

Sienna refused to even look at him. 'Get out of my way,' she said through tight lips. 'I don't want to talk to you.'

He put a hand on the top of her nearest shoulder but she jerked back out of his grasp. 'Don't you dare touch me,' she said, glaring at him furiously. 'I can't bear it when you touch me.'

His green and brown-flecked eyes challenged hers. 'We both know that's not true.'

'It *is* true,' she said. 'I hate you. I hate the way you think you can just crook your little finger and get what you want just because you're rich and powerful. You can't have me.'

'I *can* have you,' Andreas said with steely conviction. 'I can have you any time I want. That's what you're frightened of, isn't it, Sienna? You don't like it that you want me. You like it when you're in the driver's seat, but you can't be with me. You can't call the shots with me, *ma chérie*, because I'm not playing by your rules.'

Sienna tried to get past him again but he made a roadblock with his arm. Her belly tingled when she came into contact with those strongly corded muscles and she immediately sprang back as if he had burned her. 'Move out of my way or I'll hit you,' she warned.

His mouth curled upwards mockingly. 'Go on, I dare you,' he said. 'Show me what a little guttersnipe you really are.'

The hair trigger on her temper suddenly snapped. Sienna flung herself at him. She felt the tornado of her anger and frustration propel her forwards with such force she surprised even herself. Her fist landed a punch to his abdomen but it bounced off as if she had struck a slab of stone.

She slapped at his face but his hand came up and deflected it with a deftness that was as swift as it was effective.

She tried to kick him in the shins but somehow his thighs were so close to hers all she could do was make little shuffling movements with her feet that did nothing other than remind her how seriously outmatched she was.

There was only one avenue left and it wasn't one she normally used. She couldn't even understand why she was using it now. It bubbled up from nowhere, catching her off guard. Emotions she normally hid under layers of sass and cheek suddenly rose to the surface. She burst into tears but, thank God, it worked like a charm.

Andreas dropped his hold as if she were on fire. 'What the hell?' he said.

Sienna knew she wasn't the prettiest crier on the planet. Not only did her nose go bright red but it streamed as well, and her eyes got pink and swollen, and if she really got going she couldn't speak past the hiccups.

'Sienna,' he said, taking her by the upper arms. 'Stop it. Stop crying. Stop it right now.'

'I...I can't,' she blubbered.

He let out a whooshing breath. 'I'm sorry,' he said. 'I pushed you too far. I can't seem to help myself.' He pulled her into the cradle of his arms, one of his hands pressing against the back of her head. 'Come on, *ma petite*. Don't cry, please. I didn't meant to upset you like this.'

Sienna should have pushed back from him at that point but something about the warm, strong protective circle of his arms struck a chord inside her that insisted she stay right where she was. It felt good to have his heart beating right against her cheek. It felt amazing to have his hand pressed against her head in such a gentle and tender manner. It felt wonderful to have his other arm around her in a band of iron that made her feel safe in a way she had never felt before. His body felt so warm and solid. So dependable, so fortress-like she wanted to stay there for ever.

The breeze of his warm breath ruffled her hair when he spoke. 'This is not like you, *ma belle*. Has today been too much for you? I should have realised. You've had a lot to do to prepare. Leaving your flat and your friends in London, moving in with me and handling the press's interest in us. It's a lot to cope with in a very short time.'

Sienna gave a big noisy sniff and he dug in his pocket for a handkerchief. 'Here,' he said. 'Dry your eyes, *cara*.'

She buried her nose in the clean linen and pulled herself together with an effort. 'Sorry,' she said. 'I don't know what came over me. I don't do this normally.'

He brushed her hair out of her eyes with a gentle hand. 'I've been a brute to you,' he said. 'It's not helping anything, is it? We're stuck together and we have to make the most of it. It won't make the time go any faster by trading insults.'

Sienna rolled his handkerchief into a soggy ball in her hand. 'I'm sorry about hitting you.'

He gave a wry smile. 'I didn't feel a thing.'

She pressed her lips together, feeling a little more exposed and vulnerable than she cared for. 'Would you mind if I gave dinner a miss?' she asked. 'I think I'll have an early night. I have a bit of a headache.'

'Can I get you anything for it?' he asked. 'Some painkillers?'

She shook her head. 'No, I'll be fine. I always get a headache when I cry. It'll pass.'

She moved across to the door, stopping to turn to face him before she left. 'I'm really sorry, Andreas,' she said.

'You don't have to apologise,' he said. 'I was the one who was out of line.'

She chewed at her bottom lip for a moment. 'I'm not only talking about just now…'

His whole body stilled, as if every muscle and cell inside him had come to a sudden halt. His expression was like a mask, not even his eyes gave anything away.

It seemed a very long time before he spoke. 'Go to bed, Sienna,' he said. 'I will see you in the morning.'

Sienna slipped out of the room, closing the door softly behind her and, with a heart that felt like a dumbbell inside her chest, quietly made her way upstairs.

CHAPTER SIX

DURING the journey to Provence Sienna could sense Andreas was making an effort to be polite and solicitous towards her. Whether it was for the benefit of any lurking press, or whether it was because he had taken on board her attempt to apologise for her behaviour all those years ago was still open to question.

Andreas had explained on the way in the car from Marseille that the chateau had been in his mother, Evaline's, family for generations, but since his uncle Jules had died some years ago without leaving an heir, the place had been left to Andreas's father in Evaline's will.

Although he didn't say anything specific, Sienna could tell Andreas was intensely frustrated that his mother hadn't changed her will before she'd died. Sienna knew for a fact that Evaline had found out about Guido's affair with Sienna's mother Nell several weeks before her death, but she had been desperately ill with aggressive rounds of chemotherapy. Sienna suspected Evaline hadn't had the energy or wherewithal to correct things before it was too late. She also suspected Evaline had been hopeful that her husband's affair was just a one-off thing that would soon pass.

As Andreas drove up the long entrance to the chateau, Sienna drew in a breath of wonder. She had seen pictures of the Chateau de Chalvy in the past, but it was completely different witnessing the exquisite beauty of the centuries-old chateau face to face.

Lavender fields lay in front of the chateau, while rolling green hills and pastures and the mountains beyond were its backdrop. A distant field of bright red poppies danced in the warm summer breeze. The air was fresh and fragrant and the birdsong from the shrubbery in the chateau's gardens was such a delight to hear after the bustle and busyness of the airport.

The tempting thought of actually owning this piece of paradise came back, but stronger this time. It dangled like an irresistible lure in front of her. If Andreas left her before the six months was up, all of this would be hers. Every hectare of fertile land, every ancient stone of the chateau and its surrounding buildings, every bloom of every fragrant flower and every blade of grass would be legally hers.

It made her heart thump excitedly. Was it mercenary of her to want a place like this? No one would be able to kick her out. No one would be hammering on the door for unpaid rent. She would feel secure for the first time in her life. She would have a roof over her head that no one could take away. It would be hers and hers alone.

But it could only be hers if Andreas called an early end to their marriage.

As Andreas was helping her from the car, the estate manager Jean-Claude Perrault and his wife Simone greeted them. The French couple were obviously keen to show Andreas that they were worthy caretakers of his mother's beloved estate, although their formality with Sienna was annoying. According to the Perraults, Sienna might be Andreas's wife, but she was a foreigner, and a British one at that.

After refreshments were served, Jean-Claude suggested he take Andreas on a quick tour of the property while Simone helped Sienna to settle in.

Sienna followed the Frenchwoman upstairs to where a suite had been specially prepared for their stay. Heirloom linen had been taken out of storage and washed and ironed, and the big walnut bed dusted and polished. Sienna didn't like to tell Simone that she and Andreas weren't actually sharing a room, so she just smiled and complimented Simone on the lovely décor and the fresh flowers sitting on the antique dressing table and on a chest of drawers.

'This has always been the bridal suite,' Simone said. 'For centuries, Chalvy brides have started their married life here. It has the best view of the lavender fields. It is a pity you can't stay longer. It is a very short honeymoon, but then Monsieur Ferrante is a very busy man, no?'

'Very busy,' Sienna agreed.

'I'll leave you to rest,' Simone said, some of her earlier formality softening slightly. 'Dinner will be served at eight-thirty. I have organised a chef from the village to prepare a celebratory meal for you both.'

'That was very kind of you,' Sienna said.

'Not at all,' Simone said. 'This is the first time in many years that Monsieur Ferrante has been to the Chateau de Chalvy estate. It is a time to celebrate both that and your marriage. Jean-Claude and I are happy he is finally settled. For a time we wondered if he would be like his uncle and never marry.'

'You mean Andreas's uncle Jules?'

Simone nodded as she smoothed the perfectly neat bedcover. 'He was very much a playboy,' she said. 'Definitely not a one-woman man, if you know what I mean. His sister Evaline, on the other hand, only ever had eyes for Andreas's father. She fell in love with him as a teenager. It was a happy marriage until…' She gave a discomfited smile, two spots of colour pooling high on her cheekbones. 'I should not be gossiping like one of the village girls. Forgive me. I forgot your connection to the family. I did not mean to offend you.'

'It's all right,' Sienna said. 'I understand my mother's involvement with Andreas's father caused a lot of pain for a lot of people.'

'I suppose no one really knows what goes on in a marriage other than the two people involved,' Simone said with a little sigh. 'Evaline loved Guido to the day she died, but I suspect he might not have loved her at all. Some men are like that, especially rich men. They can have anyone they want and they know it.'

Sienna couldn't have agreed more. Didn't her marriage to Andreas prove it?

'I have a problem,' Sienna said as soon as she found Andreas in the garden of the chateau. She had spied him from the window of their suite and had immediately come down to speak to him. He was standing on some flagstones next to a fishpond where some frogs were croaking volubly. Water lilies floated on the surface of the pond and every now and again a flash of bright orange came to the top as a goldfish came in search of food.

'Let me guess,' Andreas said with a flicker of his signature mocking smile. 'You forgot your hair straighteners?'

She gave him a speaking glance. 'I am *not* sharing a room with you,' she said, 'especially the bridal suite. Do you have any idea of the trouble Simone has gone to? It's like she was expecting royalty to arrive. There are flowers on just about every surface and the linen your great-great-great-grandparents slept in has been brought out of storage and is on the bed, for God's sake!'

He took her arm and looped it through one of his and led her away from the fishpond to a long avenue of yew trees that led to a magnificent fountain. 'There are workers about, *ma chérie*,' he said. 'Keep your voice down.'

Sienna felt her breast brush against his arm and suppressed a shiver of forbidden delight. 'You have to do something, Andreas,' she insisted.

'There's no need to get all het up about it,' he said. 'It's only for a couple of nights. Besides, we can't break with the Chalvy tradition. Every new bride spends her first night there with her husband. It's been that way for hundreds of years.'

She stopped in her tracks and glared up at him. 'You knew about this all along, didn't you?' she said. 'You knew it and didn't warn me.'

'To be quite honest, I'd forgotten about the tradition until you mentioned the linen,' he said. 'My grandmother was the last Chalvy bride, as my mother married my father in Italy and only came back for occasional visits well into their marriage. And my uncle never married, so you are the first new bride to stay here since.'

'Aren't you forgetting a minor detail here?' Sienna asked. 'I'm not a Chalvy bride. I'm a Ferrante bride.'

Something moved at the back of his eyes as they held hers, something dark and pulsing. 'According to the tradition, a bride is a bride no matter who she belongs to,' he said.

Sienna narrowed her eyes at him. 'I don't belong to you, Andreas,' she said. 'And you'd better not forget it.'

His lips curved upwards as he captured both of her hands in his and brought her closer. 'Stop scowling and start smiling like a blushing bride, *cara*,' he said. 'There's a gardener clipping a hedge about twenty metres away.'

Sienna felt the brush of Andreas's hard male body against her stomach and a flare of heat rushed through her. Her gaze went to his mouth, that beautiful, sinfully sculpted mouth that had already done so much damage to her equilibrium. It was impossible to ignore the way her body reacted to his. His proximity, his touch, even his hazel gaze sent an electric jolt of awareness through her. Her breasts rose to sensitive peaks against his chest as he brought her a little bit closer, and then her stomach plunged when he lowered his mouth to hers.

His lips were firm but gentle as they played with hers: a soft press, a lift-off, another soft press and then a slightly firmer, more insistent one. Then his tongue stroked over her bottom lip, making it tingle and fizz with sensation. She opened to him on a soft gasp and her stomach plummeted even further when his tongue masterfully took control of hers. He cajoled it into an erotic duel, leaving her in no doubt who was going to win the sensual war in the end. He'd had her at his mercy from the first moment his lips touched hers. She was boneless within seconds, leaning into him, desperate to feel more of his magical touch…to feel the urgency of his need against hers…to feel the potency of his raw male desire. It made her feel dizzy with longing. The need crept through her like a stealthy opponent on a covert mission. She didn't want to feel so out of control but her body was hungry for every erotic feeling he was tempting her with.

He drove a splayed hand through her hair, tilting her head so he could kiss her deeper and longer, the rough stubble of his jaw scraping along her softer skin. She lost herself in the frenzied fever of his kiss. It was urgent, it was boldly insistent and, with that captivating edge of taboo about it, it made her forget about the past or the future. She was totally in the moment and the moment was all about him and how he made her feel.

His hand went from her head to slide down to the dip in her spine, pulling her against the jut of his erection. It was shockingly, shamelessly intimate. It made every sensible thought fly out of her head. She was suddenly and totally reduced to raw physical need.

His mouth lifted off hers as his gaze drilled smoulderingly into hers. 'Still want separate bedrooms?' he asked.

Sienna drew in a sharp little breath that was connected to something deep in the pit of her belly. 'I'm starting to see there could be some benefits to airing that musty old linen,' she conceded wryly.

He gave a spine-tingling chuckle as he cupped her face in his hands. 'I like how you make me laugh, *ma petite*,' he said. 'You don't kowtow to me like a lot of women do. I like that you are spirited and feisty. You always stand your ground with me.'

Sienna wished she could find some ground to stand on, but right now she was on the rockiest platform she had ever occupied. She was teetering on the edge of throwing caution to the wind and diving head first into a passionate affair with Andreas, no matter what the cost to her ultimately. She looked into his gaze and felt another layer of her resolve peel away like a slough of old useless skin.

She wanted him.

She had *always* wanted him.

She could have him for six months.

The thought was more than a temptation. It was a statement of intent. The rationalisations began in her head. It was a finite time. She would be able to walk away when it was over. She knew the rules from the outset and so did he. It was a convenient arrangement, a no-strings affair that had benefits for them both. She wouldn't fall in love with him and he wouldn't fall in love with her. It would be an exciting erotic interlude to pass the time while they were shackled together in marriage. God knew she could do with the experience of a red-hot affair. Her body was craving an outlet for the sensuality denied her for so long.

Andreas stroked the broad pad of his thumb over Sienna's bottom lip, his hazel eyes meshing with hers in simmering heat. 'You know how much I want you,' he said. 'You've known it from the start. I think my father must have known it too, otherwise why would he have orchestrated this?'

Sienna salved her tingling lips with a quick darting sweep of her tongue. 'I meant what I said last night,' she said. 'I'm sorry I acted the way I did when I was seventeen. I panicked when your father came in. I didn't want my mother to lose her job. It was the first time I'd seen her really happy. I didn't want to be the one who wrecked everything for her. I didn't think things would get so out of hand. I didn't think you would leave and never come back.'

'There were lots of reasons I didn't come back,' he said, dropping his hands from her face to walk with her back towards the chateau. 'My father and I always had a difficult relationship. We locked horns on many things. He didn't want me to pursue my furniture design work. But I wanted to work for my wealth, not simply inherit it from him and his father and grandfather before him. I wanted to make my own way, not stand on anyone's shoulders. My father took that as a slight. He liked to have control, but I refused to play by his rules.'

Sienna walked alongside him, wondering if he would ever forgive her for her shameless behaviour. She had made his already strained relationship with his father so much worse. No wonder he hated her so much. She had ruined any chance of him making peace before his father had died. How could she expect him to overlook that as just a bit of immaturity on her part? 'I didn't realise the reason my mother was so happy was because she was having an affair with your father,' she said after a little silence. 'I think I would've acted differently if I'd known about that at the time.'

He stopped walking and turned to look down at her, an embittered frown slicing between his dark brows. 'Your mother wanted a quick leg up in life,' he said. 'She ruthlessly set her sights on my father. He was to be her next meal ticket. To this day I don't understand why he was so foolish to get involved with a shameless slut like her.'

'My mother loved him,' Sienna said, glaring at him for painting such a tawdry picture of her mother. 'He was the only man she had ever loved. She told me a few days before she died. Her life before that had been a litany of meaningless affairs. But once she met your father she fell deeply in love. She was devastated when he refused to acknowledge her publicly. I think she thought after your mother passed away that he would marry her.'

Andreas's expression was cynical. 'Are you sure it was him she loved or the lifestyle he could give her?' he asked.

Sienna gave him another flinty glare. 'I don't expect you to understand what love feels like,' she said. 'You're exactly like your father in that sense. You take what you want from people and give nothing back. Emotion doesn't come into it. Your life is a series of cold, hard business deals conducted one after the other.'

'Ah, but is that not just like you?' Andreas asked with a sardonic slant to his mouth. 'You married Brian Littlemore for money. You have married me for exactly the same reason. Is that not rather cold and businesslike? You want money in exchange for your body, but you will not give your heart.'

'Do you *want* my heart, Andreas?' she asked with a deliberately taunting look.

His gaze ran over her like the scorching stroke of a naked flame. 'I think you know what I want,' he said. 'It's what we both want. And tonight there is nothing to stop us from having it.'

She lifted her chin at him. 'I haven't said I'll sleep with you.'

He bent his head and pressed a brief but searing kiss to her mouth. 'Not yet, but you will,' he said, flashing one of his satirical smiles. 'You won't be able to help yourself.'

'Let's see about that, shall we?' she said.

He touched her cheek with a soft brushstroke of one of his fingers, his eyes burning hers with the glinting fire of his. 'I can hardly wait,' he said and, with another mocking smile, he left.

CHAPTER SEVEN

SIENNA felt in an edgy mood by the time she joined Andreas for pre-dinner drinks downstairs. She had successfully managed to avoid him since their meeting in the garden but she had been aware of him all the same. She had heard him come upstairs to shower and change for dinner. She had imagined him standing under the showerhead as she had done only minutes before, his body lean and tanned, all rippling muscles and toned naked male flesh. Her stomach had triple somersaulted at the thought of standing there with him, of feeling his hard body dividing the softness of hers to claim her as his. Her body seemed to be intent on having what her mind tried so valiantly to resist. Her traitorous body was clamouring for more of his touch, for more of his kisses, for more flesh on flesh contact—for everything.

And Andreas—damn him—knew it.

Sienna entered the large *salon* overlooking the chateau's formal garden with her nerves jangling in irritation. 'Where are Jean-Claude and Simone?' she asked. 'Aren't they joining us?'

Andreas gave her a crooked smile that made his eyes glint. 'It's our honeymoon, *ma chérie*,' he said. 'Four's a crowd, don't you think?'

She averted her gaze and reached for the champagne he had poured for her. 'I can see why you wanted to secure this place,' she said to change the subject. 'It's very beautiful.'

'My mother loved it here,' he said. 'She wanted her grandchildren to grow up like Miette and I did, with both French and Italian cultural experiences.'

Sienna looked at the bubbles in her glass, trying not to think of Andreas's future children running about the chateau and its gardens. It was unsettling to think of him with some other faceless woman on his arm, a woman he had selected as prime wife material. Or maybe he would take Portia Briscoe back once his brief marriage to Sienna was over. But that thought was even more upsetting. The more she knew of Andreas, the less suited Portia seemed to be for him. Couldn't *he* see that?

'Was Miette upset that the chateau was left to you and not to her?' Sienna asked after a little silence.

'My sister was more upset it was co-inherited by you,' he said. 'She is worried you will do everything in your power to make me default.'

Sienna could see why his sister would feel the way she did about her. Their relationship during the time she had lived with the family had been fraught with tension. Many a petty or bitchy argument had broken out between them, which, to be fair, Sienna knew she was largely responsible for. She had been insanely jealous of Miette as the only daughter of the Ferrante dynasty. To Sienna, Miette was everything she was not. Miette had two parents who adored her, an older brother who was loving and protective towards her, and she had grown up with the sort of wealth that meant she never had to worry about anything other than what designer brand to choose over another. Like Andreas, Miette had been to the best schools and university. Miette had even spent a year at a Swiss finishing school before she'd moved to London, where she had met her now equally well-heeled husband. Miette's life was the dream life Sienna had always wanted for herself. 'What did you say to her?' she asked before taking a sip of her drink.

'I told her not to worry,' he said. 'I am well aware of the tricks you might feel compelled to play.'

Sienna shrugged off his comment. 'Well, you can assure her I only want the money,' she said. 'The chateau is nice and all that, but what would I do with a place this size? I'd have to sell it. I could never afford to maintain it. The heating bills in winter must be crucifying.'

Andreas took a sip of his drink, still watching her with his hazel eyes. 'Just so you know, Sienna,' he said. 'I will not be tricked out of inheriting this property. You can do the time the nice way or the hard way but, either way, I am not leaving until I inherit what rightly belongs to my family.'

'Fine,' Sienna said, throwing him a testy look. 'But the same goes for you. I'm not going to be forced out by your brooding, boorish behaviour or your bad moods.'

Andreas gave an ironic chuckle. 'You're a fine one to talk of bad moods,' he said. 'You've been spoiling for a fight from the moment you stepped in the room. I can see it in your eyes. They've been flashing like sheet lightning for the last five minutes.'

Sienna glared at him. 'Maybe that has something to do with your own chicanery in making sure I have no choice but to sleep in your bed,' she said.

'What is the problem with sharing a bed that is large

enough to house a family of five?' Andreas asked. 'I bet I won't even notice you're there.'

She set her mouth. 'Just another nameless woman lying beside you, eh? Nice one, Andreas. You have such class.'

'Are you jealous?' he asked.

'Of course not!' Sienna gave her head a toss. 'It's just that I don't like the thought of you suddenly forgetting who's lying beside you. You might take liberties that I'm not comfortable with.'

'Take liberties?' He gave a little snort of amusement. 'You sound like someone out of a Regency period drama. What, are you worried I might see one of your naked ankles or wrists, are you? I've seen a lot more of you than that, Sienna, and you know it. So, too, did most of the cyber world when your little bedroom peccadillo was aired, so don't play the outraged virgin card with me. It just won't wash.'

Sienna turned away so he couldn't see the way her cheeks coloured up. She concentrated on drinking her champagne, desperately trying to appear cool and collected when inside she was anything but. She hated him for reminding her of that wretched event. How like him to needle her with her past, the past she wanted to forget about, the past she wished had never happened. She pretended it didn't hurt but it did. Every time she saw a photo or snippet about herself in the press she cringed in shame. How could her life have come to that?

'Dinner will be waiting for us,' Andreas said after a moment. 'I hope you're hungry?'

Sienna gave him one of her arch looks. 'It sure beats making small talk, doesn't it?' she said and sashayed past him to the dining room.

* * *

Dinner was a tense affair. Sienna knew she wasn't helping things by being prickly but she resented the way Andreas always saw the worst in her. He assumed she would try to wangle him out of his inheritance, but if it weren't for the money she needed to kick-start her life she would have already defaulted so he could have the chateau. She wanted to be free of him just as much as he wanted to be free of her.

Well, maybe that wasn't quite true, she thought as she toyed with her glass. The physical fascination she felt for him was something that drew her to him irrespective of the ill feeling between them. She could feel the tension of it brewing in the air. It was an atmospheric change that occurred every time they were on their own.

Knowing he wanted her made her need for him all the harder to ignore. She could feel the traitorous pulse of it in her blood, the way her insides clenched every time his gaze encountered hers. Those tense little eyelocks unfurled something deep inside her until she had to look away or betray herself completely.

'More wine?' Andreas offered.

Sienna covered her glass with her hand. 'I think I've had enough, thank you.'

There was a ghost of a smile in his eyes. 'Always wise to know when to stop, *sì*?' he said.

She gave him a direct look. 'Do you know when to stop, Andreas?' she asked. 'Or do you keep going just because you can?'

He sat back and surveyed her for a moment before he answered. 'I don't believe in losing control in any area of my life.'

She raised a questioning brow at him. 'Not even during sex?'

He continued to hold her gaze with an intensity she found both thrilling and unsettling. 'It depends on what you mean by losing control,' he said. 'If you mean do I lose myself in the moment of orgasm, then yes, that is exactly what happens.'

Sienna knew her face was hot. She could feel it. So too was her body. Just the thought of him losing control—*having an orgasm*—with her was enough to send her senses spinning all over the place.

'You're blushing, *ma belle*,' he said with a slanting smile.

'I'm not blushing,' she retorted. 'It's hot in here.'

He rose from the table and opened one of the windows, letting in the fragrant night air. 'Better?' he asked, turning back to face her.

Sienna felt the caress of his gaze. It touched her from head to foot, lingering on the upthrust of her breasts just long enough for the fiery combustion of her need to engulf her.

She felt the tingle of her flesh as he came towards her, his eyes still doing that erotic little tussle with hers, as if he was already making love with her in his mind, running through the images of their naked limbs entangled, their bodies joined in the most intimate way possible.

Her body shivered involuntarily. She could almost feel his hard male presence inside her. It started as a tiny flicker and then it became a pulse that was like a distant drumbeat inside her, growing in intensity as each sensually charged second passed.

Sienna swallowed as he came towards her with slow but purposeful strides. Her heart gave a stumble as he stood right beside her chair, the tip of his index finger lifting her chin to face him. 'What are we going to do about this tricky little situation between us, hmm?' he asked.

She rose to her feet as if he had drawn her up by tugging on invisible puppet strings. Her body was within a hair's breadth of his, her insides coiling tightly with lust. 'I don't know,' she said a little too huskily. 'Ignore it?'

His mouth tilted in that sexy smile again as his thumb brushed over her bottom lip. 'Sounds like a good idea in theory,' he said. 'How do you propose we do that in practice?'

Sienna swept her tongue over her lip where his thumb had just been and tasted the salt of him. A shockwave of longing rippled through her. She felt the rush of her blood and the hot tingle of feminine want darted like an expertly aimed arrow deep inside her. 'I don't know,' she said, trying to keep her tone light and unaffected. 'Do you have any suggestions?'

His hazel eyes pulsed as they held hers. 'Just the one,' he said in a deep gravel-rough voice.

Her gaze drifted to his mouth and her heart gave another little tripping movement. 'I sure hope it's a good one,' she said so softly it was barely audible.

'It is,' he said and, taking her by the upper arms and pulling her against him, chest pressed to chest, he bent his head and covered her mouth with his.

His lips were neither soft nor hard but somewhere right in between. They moved with mesmerising magic on the surface of hers before he took things to another blistering level with the bold and commanding thrust of his tongue.

It was like a flame let loose amongst bone-dry tinder. The kiss was suddenly hot and hard and urgent, just as hot and hard and as feverishly urgent as his body pressed against hers.

His hands went from their grip on her upper arms to slide down to her waist, one hand slipping behind her to press in the small of her back to hold her against the heated trajectory of his body. She moved against him, an instinctive and utterly primal movement that signalled her rapidly escalating need for him.

His mouth explored hers with spine-tingling expertise. His tongue played with hers, teasing and flirting at first, but then with increasing demand as his desire to mate took hold. She felt it in his body, the way he hardened and throbbed against her. Her body responded automatically. It softened and melted against him, her desperate need to get closer taking over whatever objections her scrambled mind tried to put up.

One of his hands skimmed over her breast in a teasing motion that set every nerve beneath her skin on fire. She whimpered against his mouth, pushing closer, desperate to have him hold her, to caress her, to touch her, to brand her with his lips and tongue.

He continued to kiss her deeply as his hand came back, firmer this time, cupping her, caressing her through the thin barrier of her dress and lacy bra. It was like torture not to have him as close as she wanted him. But then, as if he read her mind, or her body, or indeed both, he slid the shoulder of her dress aside. His warm dry hand on the skin of her neck and shoulder made her flesh sing with delight. He pushed the strap of her bra aside and then lowered his mouth to her skin. She shuddered in response when his tongue grazed the soft skin stretched tightly over her collarbone.

She snatched in a breath when he pushed the lace cup

of her bra away. Her belly clenched with a hard fist of desire as his warm breath skated over her naked breast before his mouth closed over her achingly tight nipple. Thousands of fiery explosions went off beneath her skin at that toe-curling caress. His teeth and tongue teased her into a frenzy of want she had never imagined possible. The sensation of having his mouth suck on her made the hair on her head tingle at the roots.

Sienna slid her hands up his chest to work on his buttons; one by one she released them, kissing each section of his hot salty skin as she exposed it.

He made a deep sound at the back of his throat as she went lower, his hands fisting in her hair as she got to his waistband. The jut of his erection tented his trousers and she boldly touched him, caressing the length of him, delighting in the feel of him as he shuddered in response.

He made another deep guttural sound and pulled her down with him to the floor, his mouth slamming back down on hers as he pinned her with his weight. It was a bruising kiss but she was with him all the way, nipping at his lower lip, her teeth tugging and pulling at him in a desperate urge for satiation. His tongue thrust and stroked, cajoled and teased and finally tamed hers. In between hot searing kisses he got her dress off and her bra and knickers in a wild tangle of fabric and limbs that made Sienna's heart race with excitement. She only got his shirt off and his belt. There was barely time for the application of a condom before her head snapped back on the carpeted floor as he drove into her with a thick, hard thrust that made her cry out in sharp and sudden discomfort.

He froze above her. 'What's wrong?'

'Nothing,' Sienna said, quickly averting her eyes from his. 'It's been a long time, that's all.'

He captured her chin and made her look at him. 'How long?' he asked.

Sienna caught her bottom lip with her teeth. 'A while…'

His frown deepened, making a criss-cross of lines over his forehead and between his eyes. 'How long is a while?' he asked.

She gave a little shrug, secretly holding her breath. 'I can't really remember.'

His eyes were narrowed in focus. 'You mean it is a while since you slept with your husband?' he said.

Sienna found it hard to lie to him when she was facing him eye to eye. 'I never slept with Brian,' she said.

His face blanched, his eyes shrinking back in their sockets as if she had struck him across the face. 'What?' he asked.

'It was a marriage of convenience,' she said. 'Brian wanted a wife in name only. I wanted the respectability of marrying well. It was a mutually satisfying agreement.'

Andreas pulled away from her and got to his feet in an agitated manner. He zipped up his trousers and then snatched up his discarded shirt and handed it to her. 'Here,' he said in a gruff tone. 'Put this on while I get your things.'

Sienna slipped her arms through the long sleeves and wrapped herself in his warmth and smell. His shirt didn't offer the same dignity as her clothes would have done but at least it covered her nakedness.

She watched as he gathered up her clothes from the floor, his hands folding them with meticulous care when only minutes ago he had been all but ripping them from her body. His brow was furrowed with a preoccupied frown as if he was having trouble processing what she had told him.

He came back over and handed the tidy pile to her, his eyes meshing with hers. 'I hurt you,' he said, his voice grave. 'I'm sorry.'

'You didn't hurt me…not really,' Sienna said.

'Why didn't you tell me?' he asked, still frowning.

'Tell you what?' she said. 'That I haven't had sex in ages? You wouldn't have believed me. The press make it pretty clear I'm up for it with anyone any time. Why would you take my word over theirs?'

'Why do you let them write that stuff without defending yourself?' he asked.

She gave an indifferent shrug. 'I don't care what people think. I know what's true. That's all that matters.'

'Why didn't you have a normal marriage with Brian Littlemore?' he asked. 'He paraded you about enough times. You were always at some gala event hanging off his arm like a trophy. Was it really all an act?'

Sienna wished she'd kept her mouth shut. What was *with* her tonight? Such honesty and openness was totally out of character. Before she knew it she'd be spilling the beans on Brian's 'mistress', the male lover he had adored even before he had married his wife Ruth and fathered three children with her. It wasn't her secret to tell. She had promised Brian on his deathbed she would honour his decision to protect his children from the knowledge of his true sexual orientation. But she realised she would have to be a little more careful around Andreas. He wasn't the sort to be fobbed off and lied to. His sharp intelligent gaze saw too much as it was.

'I'd rather not talk about it,' she said, hugging her pile of clothes close to her body. 'Brian was good to me. I don't regret being married to him. He looked after me.'

Andreas screwed up his face. 'He had a mistress, for God's sake,' he said. 'How could you have so little self-respect to allow that to continue right under your nose?'

Sienna squeezed her clothes even tighter against her body. 'I told you I don't want to talk about it.'

He studied her for a long moment, his gaze narrowing slightly. 'You married him soon after the sex tape scandal, didn't you?' he asked. 'It was only a few weeks or so, wasn't it?'

She kept her expression closed. 'What of it?'

'What happened that night?' he asked. 'What happened that made you suddenly run off and marry a man nearly forty years older than yourself?'

Sienna couldn't hold his penetrating gaze. She stared at the middle of his chest instead. Her chest felt tight and heavy with all the regret she carried inside. She had made such a mess of her life and her sister's. Maybe it was time to air some of her guilt. To confess how awful she felt about what had happened. Why she felt compelled to confess it to Andreas was something she would have to think about later.

'I was out drinking with friends,' she said. 'The girls I hung around with were regular binge drinkers but I never let myself get totally wasted. But that night…I must have had more than I realised or not drunk enough water or something. I don't remember much other than waking up in some guy's hotel room. I didn't know who he was. He was naked. I was naked. I was so ashamed of myself. For the first time I started to feel like the slut the press had always painted me. Before, I used to laugh it off when they wrote something about me being a bed-hopper because I'd only had sex twice.' She gave a little humourless laugh. 'By today's standards, I'm practically still a virgin. But after that night I felt like I deserved it for not taking responsibility for my actions.'

'Did you ever consider you might have been the victim of a drink spike?' Andreas asked, frowning.

Sienna tried to shrug it off. 'I did wonder about that but, even so, it was still my fault for being so careless,' she said. 'I should've chosen my friends a little more carefully. I think they enjoyed seeing me pulled down a peg or two. I was always the one who kept her head. That night certainly put an end to that.'

'Sienna,' he said heavily, 'you were a victim of a crime. Why didn't you report it to the police?'

'Who would have believed me?' she asked. 'Like mother, like daughter, everyone would've said. Anyway, I didn't know if a crime *had* been committed. The tape showed me kissing that guy and him kissing me and his arms and hands all over me, but there was no way of knowing if anything else had happened.'

Andreas let out a stiff curse, his hand dragging over his face again. 'I can't get my head around this,' he said. 'Why didn't you say something when the press named your sister as the woman in that tape?'

Sienna shifted her gaze from his. 'I didn't know about any of that,' she said. 'As soon as I woke up in that hotel room I caught the next flight out of the country. I wanted to get as far away from it as I could. That's when Brian stepped in. I rang him in a bit of a state from the airport. We'd met at a function a few years before and really hit it off in a friends-only way. He was like a father to me, the father I'd never had. He offered me a safe haven. I didn't think twice when he suggested we marry as soon as possible. I wanted the respectability. I wanted to feel safe.'

Andreas lifted her chin up so her gaze met his. 'Why have you let everyone believe such scurrilous lies about you?' he asked.

Sienna could feel her carefully constructed composure cracking. She was used to acting all tough and resilient but it was hard to keep that façade in place when Andreas seemed so tender and concerned. 'Can we drop this topic?' she said. 'It's in the past. I'd like to leave it there.'

'Sienna, you can't just brush something like this aside,' he said. 'You've let everyone—including me—believe you're a gold-digging slut when you're no such thing.'

She raised her chin away from the pressure of his fingertip. 'I might not be a slut but I still want the money,' she said. 'That makes me a gold-digger, doesn't it?'

He stared her down. 'That's what you want everyone to believe,' he said. 'Why do you do that? What do you hope to achieve by making everyone hate you?'

'People hate a lot more easily than they love,' she said. 'It's just the way things are. I do it too. I'm good at it. Look at just now, for example. I was prepared to sleep with you, even though I hate your guts.'

He continued to look at her for a lengthy moment, those hazel eyes searching hers until her heart jumped and thumped behind the wall of her chest. He touched her cheek with his fingertip; it was hardly more than a brushstroke but it made every pore of her skin reach up on tiptoe to feel more of his touch. 'If you didn't hate me before, then you surely do so now,' he said with a touch of ruefulness. 'I was rough with you.'

Sienna swallowed a tight tangled knot inside her throat. 'It wasn't that bad,' she said, affecting what she hoped was a casual tone. 'Anyway, I probably should've said something.'

He gave a self-deprecating grunt. 'Do you think I would've believed you?'

She acknowledged that with a wry on-off smile. 'Probably not.'

'Do you know the man's name?' Andreas asked.

Sienna felt a ripple of panic roll through her. 'Leave it, Andreas, please. I don't want Gisele to be reminded of it all again. She's about to get married. I know what the press would do if you went looking for justice on my behalf. There's enough CCTV footage of me coming in and out of nightclubs to make me look like the biggest lush out. You know how lawyers can twist things to build a case for the defence. I just want to forget about it.'

'You can't keep running away from unpleasant stuff, Sienna,' he said.

She hoisted her chin. 'I'm not running away,' she said. 'I'm moving forward, for my sake as well as Gisele's.'

He held her gaze for a moment before he tucked a strand of her hair behind her ear, as one would do to a small child. Sienna didn't feel like a child, however. His touch against the sensitive skin of her ear made her shiver with womanly want and need. She felt him inside her still, a tender ache where her flesh had been stretched by his hot, hard presence.

What would it feel like to have him totally possess

her? To have him move inside her in the throes of passion? To have him lose control in the soft, moist cocoon of her body? To feel her own body respond to his in a rhythm as old as time?

The silence throbbed with the erotic tension Sienna could feel in her body. She saw it in the dark heat of his eyes. It smouldered there in the black ink spill pools of his pupils. She felt the slow burn of his gaze move over her face like a lighted taper, scorching her like a blowtorch when it came to rest for a tantalising moment on her mouth.

Her heart gave a swift hard kick against her ribcage. Her tongue came out to moisten the arid landscape of her lips. Her stomach lifted and fell a thousand feet as he brushed that same gentle fingertip he had used on her cheek over the surface of her lips, a faint movement that sent every nerve into a frenzy of want.

His hand suddenly dropped from her face and just as swiftly a shutter came down on his features. 'I think it's best for the time being if we keep our distance from each other,' he said. 'I'll sleep in one of the spare rooms.'

Sienna hid behind the screen of her sarcasm. 'Frightened you might get too attached now I'm not the bed-hopping harlot you once thought I was?' she asked.

He held her look with cool but implacable determination. 'I want this chateau, Sienna,' he said. 'I am prepared to do whatever is required to obtain it. Neither of us needs the complication of a relationship that to all intents and purposes has been thrust upon us for reasons as yet unclear. If it hadn't been for my father's will, I would never have considered you as a temporary partner, let alone a life one. I suspect you would not have considered me either.'

'You're spot on there,' she said. 'You're the last person I would consider spending the rest of my life with. Can you imagine the fights we'd have? You're so anal you get antsy when the tea towels aren't aligned.'

'And you're so chaotic you're like a whirlwind,' he said, but he softened it with a wry smile. 'I still find it hard to believe you came from the womb of a woman who made a living out of being tidy.'

'Yeah, well, she might have been good at tidying up other people's messes, but she wasn't so crash hot at sorting out her own,' Sienna said with a little slump of her shoulders. 'I spent most of my childhood wondering where we'd be living the next week. Mum would say or do something she shouldn't and the next thing I'd be packing all my things. I lost count of how many schools I attended over the years. The time with your family was the longest we'd stayed anywhere. I didn't want it to end.'

Andreas took one of her hands in his, toying with her fingers, one by one. 'I had no idea things were so difficult for you,' he said. 'I always thought you were a bit of a brat, but now I can see why you flounced around with such an attitude all the time. You felt terribly insecure.'

'I shouldn't complain,' Sienna said, trying to ignore the sensations firing up her arms from the warm stroke of his fingers against hers. 'Plenty of people have it so much worse.'

He brought her hand up to his mouth and gently kissed her bent knuckles. 'I should let you get to bed,' he said, giving her hand one last gentle squeeze before releasing it. 'Is there anything I can get or do for you? Perhaps run a hot bath for you?'

Sienna could see the concern in his eyes. It made

her feel delicate and feminine, a startling and somewhat unsettling change from having to act tough and streetwise around him. 'No, I think I can manage to turn on the taps for myself,' she said with a crooked smile. 'Thanks all the same.'

He continued to study her for a long pulsing moment. Sienna suspected those green and brown-flecked eyes could see right through her shabbily erected façade. That brief moment of physical intimacy had changed the dynamic between them and she wasn't sure how it could be changed back. The air was thick with the sensual energy their brief but passionate encounter had unleashed. It swirled like a current, a wild vortex that could so easily carry her way out of her depth if she wasn't careful.

'What happened here tonight…' He frowned as if searching for the right words. 'I don't know how to make it up to you. I've misjudged you, misunderstood you and insulted you. I hope you will find it in your heart to forgive me.'

'Wow, I really like this nice guy thing you've got going,' Sienna said. 'Maybe I won't hate you quite so much if you keep that up for the next six months.'

His eyes pulsed with something dark and intense as they held hers. 'You don't hate me, *ma petite*,' he said. 'In fact, I have a feeling you have never hated me.'

She challenged him with another lift of her chin. 'You surely don't think I'm still harbouring that silly little teenage crush on you, do you?' she said. 'That was a long time ago, Andreas. I might not have as much experience as other women my age, but I can assure you I haven't been saving myself for you.'

'Why haven't you got involved with anyone?' he

asked. 'It can't have been for lack of opportunity. Men fall over themselves to be with you. I've seen it with my own eyes. You can stop a speeding train with your looks.'

'I saw my mother move from one shallow hook-up after the other,' Sienna said. 'I saw what it did to her self-esteem. I was always picking up the emotional pieces. I felt like the parent a lot of the time. I guess it turned me off the thought of allowing someone that close who could turn around and hurt you. Besides, I want to be appreciated for more than my looks. I have dreams and aspirations. I'm not a narcissistic airhead. Unfortunately, a lot of men can't see past the physical stuff, or maybe they don't want to.'

He moved his fingertips across the sensitive skin on the slope of her lower jaw in a soft-as-air caress that set her nerves into a frenzied dance. 'You're a complex little thing, aren't you, *cara*?' he said.

'No more complex than the next person,' she said, shooting him a look from beneath her lashes. 'And not half as complex as you.'

A wry smile tipped up the corners of his mouth. 'Perhaps we are more alike than we are different, *sì*?'

'I don't think we have much in common at all,' Sienna said, barely able to breathe with his fingers tracing back and forth along the line of her jaw.

He trailed a fingertip over her bottom lip before dropping his hand back down by his side. 'Perhaps you're right,' he said as he moved over to open the door for her. 'Call me if you need anything during the night. I'll only be a few doors down the hall.'

She gave a vague nod and moved past him in the

doorway, trying not to notice his warm body so close she could have touched it. 'Goodnight.'

The only answer she got was the soft, but no less definite, closing of the door.

CHAPTER EIGHT

ANDREAS paced the floor for hours after Sienna had left. Her perfume lingered in the air. He could even smell it on his skin. He could still taste the sweetness of her in his mouth in spite of the three stiff drinks he had consumed since.

The shock of finding out she had never had a sexual relationship with her late husband had left him more than a little dumbfounded. Just about everything he had believed about her was wrong. He had thought she had prostituted herself by marrying for money. To find the marriage had been nothing more than a paper arrangement had completely stunned him.

And that wasn't even half of it. He couldn't get his head around the fact that she had so little experience. She'd only had two sexual partners and she was twenty-five years old. For all these years she had played the role of a hardened tart. The press had constantly portrayed her as an easily picked up party girl and she had done nothing to discourage that view. The circumstances of the sex tape scandal had obviously affected her deeply, as indeed they would most young women. Andreas suspected she had hidden behind the label of gold-digger because that was Sienna's way of hiding her hurt, by toughing it out and pretending it didn't matter one jot, when of course it did.

Guilt gnawed at his conscience. He had pulled her to the floor like a common whore. Desire and lust had got the better of him. It had got the better of both of them. She had been just as willing, but it didn't make him feel any less responsible.

He had physically hurt her.

He groaned out loud and paced some more. He had acted *exactly* like his father. He had been intent on slaking his lust with no thought to the consequences. He dragged a hand through his hair. Was this what his father had wanted to teach him? To show him how hard it was to resist the lure of lust?

Had his desire for Sienna been so obvious? He had done his best to hide it. He had disciplined himself to ignore her on his visits or, at the very least, treat her as if she was just a kid. He had watched her bloom into young womanhood. From visit to visit she had morphed from a pimply fourteen-year-old to a sultry siren of ripe sensuality at seventeen. His rejection of her had been the honourable thing to do, and yet he wondered if that and not her mother's antics had caused her to hit the party scene in a defiant attempt to save face.

By the time she was eighteen or so she had a reputation as a wild party girl. A 'nightclub nymphet', some journalist in London had labelled her. Night after night she had teetered out of clubs and hotels with her gaggle of giggling girlfriends.

And then at the age of twenty-two she had suddenly married a man old enough to be her grandfather. Everyone had called her a greedy little gold-digger. He had done it himself. He had thrown the newspaper aside in disgust when he had read about it on one of his visits to England. He had sworn and cursed and called her every filthy name under the sun.

His chest tightened and cramped with its weight of guilt.

Sienna was nothing like the person he'd thought she was. For years she had hidden behind a façade to protect herself from being hurt. Behind that tough smart-mouth exterior was a vulnerable young woman, a young woman who had never felt safe and secure. He had made the mistake of assuming she was just like her mother, on the take for whatever she could get.

But Sienna was nothing like Nell Baker. She wasn't a social climbing harlot with no sense of propriety. Sienna had more pride than he had given her credit for.

Every insult he had flung at her came back to haunt him. She had thrown back her own insults with a feistiness of spirit he had always secretly admired. Defiance had glittered from her sparkling grey-blue eyes in every one of their exchanges. He had found it invigorating to spar with her. She always gave as good as she got. It was verbal foreplay. A little game they had played for as long as he could remember.

He closed his eyes as he thought of how she had felt wrapped so tightly around him. The silky warmth of her had engulfed him. His body still ached and pulsed with the burden of desire. It was a pounding ache that reverberated through his flesh.

He wanted her.

That desire was nothing new to him, but somehow now it was stronger than ever. He had tasted the sweet pleasure of her; it was like a drug he could no longer resist.

He drew in a breath and slowly released it as he

looked out at the moonlit fields of the estate. Six months and all of this would be his. Sienna would get her pay-out and he would inherit what was rightly his.

He knew she wanted the money. She was currently out of work and the funds her late husband had left her were just about gone. He was confident it was enough to keep her by his side for the allotted time. An affair between them would be an added bonus.

He closed the curtains with a flick of his hand.

He had a feeling that keeping her with him was not going to be the problem. Letting her go at the end of the six months might very well prove to be the biggest hurdle he had yet to face.

Sienna woke the next morning to a knock on the bed-room door. She pushed the hair out of her eyes and sat upright. 'Come in.'

Andreas came in with a tray with fresh croissants and a pot of fragrant steaming coffee. 'I thought you might like breakfast in bed,' he said.

'Is this another Chalvy bridal tradition?' she asked.

His lips moved in the semblance of a smile as he set the tray down over her knees. 'One of many,' he said.

'Well, as much as I'd like to keep the ghosts of this place happy, I'm afraid there's no way I can drink cof-fee at this time of the morning,' she said. 'I'm a tea girl. Call me British if you must but, in spite of living all those years in Italy, I can't quite get used to starting the day without my cup of tea.'

He gave a little eye roll as he whipped the coffee pot off the tray. 'I should've guessed,' he said. 'Give me five minutes and I'll be back with your tea.'

Sienna tilted her head at him. 'You wouldn't last five

minutes as a servant, Andreas,' she said. 'You have to accept all commands and requests with grace and poise.'

'Perhaps you could give me some lessons,' he said.

'You already know I'm absolute rubbish at following orders,' she said. 'As soon as someone tells me to do something I always want to do the opposite. I think it's a personality flaw or something.'

'I'll have to make sure I say the opposite of what I want you to do then,' he said. 'It's called reverse psychology, *sì*?'

'Something like that,' she said.

Sienna picked at one of the croissants once he had gone, licking the buttery crumbs off her fingers. She had slept fitfully last night. Her body had thrummed with need for hours, and then, when she had finally drifted off to sleep, she had dreamed of Andreas. She had dreamed of his mouth and hands pleasuring her, touching her, caressing her, of him making her body sing with delight.

She squeezed her legs together and felt that tiny intimate ache where he had been. It made her belly feel all fluttery, like a thousand moth wings moving inside her. She put a hand over her stomach, trying to stop the sensation, but if anything it intensified.

The door opened after a few minutes and Andreas came in bearing a pot of tea. 'Your tea, Madame,' he said with a bow.

'Way too obsequious,' Sienna said, smiling at him. 'Your employer would automatically assume you're pilfering the silver or something.'

An answering smile flickered in his eyes. 'Perhaps I do have an ulterior motive,' he said as he poured her a cup of tea.

Sienna took the cup off the tray, burying her nose in

the steam rising from its surface rather than meet his gaze. 'So I take it this breakfast in bed routine is a guilt trip, not a tradition?' she said.

'How do you expect me not to feel guilty?' he asked. 'I spent most of last night pacing the floor over what happened.'

Sienna kept staring at the steamy mist rising from her tea. 'You're making too big an issue out of it,' she said. 'Let's just forget it ever happened.'

He brushed a strand of hair away from her face. 'Look at me, Sienna,' he said.

She drew in a breath and looked into his eyes. Her belly did that moth wing thing again and her heart skipped a beat. His face was cleanly shaven. His breath smelt of mint. His eyes looked tired, however. There were thumbprint-sized shadows beneath them. Had he too spent most of last night wondering what it would have felt like to make love properly? Had his body throbbed and ached for hours as hers had done? Had he dreamt of her as she had dreamt of him? It was so hard to tell what he was thinking or feeling. He had never been one for showing much in the way of expression. She had only seen him smile a handful of times.

His fingers brushed against her cheek as his eyes held hers. 'I overstepped the mark. I take full responsibility for it. I broke the rules we set down. It was a mistake I promise won't be repeated, not unless it's what you want. If you want a six-month affair, then, of course, I would consider it.'

Of course, Sienna thought cynically. She would be a convenient plaything to pass the time, just like her mother had been for his father. He would walk away when the time was up and leave her without a flicker of regret. Within months, if not weeks, he would go on to marry some other beautiful woman with a blue blood pedigree and fill his precious villas with his gorgeous little black-haired heirs.

How would she cope with it?

The same way she coped with everything else. She would put on a brave face. She would show him she could play him at his own game. She could be just as ruthless and mercenary as him. When the time was up she would walk away without a single regret, or at least none that he could see. 'I don't think an affair between us would work out,' she said. 'I think it's best if we stick to our original agreement.'

If he was surprised or disappointed by her response he showed no sign of it on his face. 'Very well,' he said, rising from where he had perched on the edge of the bed. 'I have some business to go over with Jean-Claude. I probably won't see you until this evening.'

'I'm sure I'll find something to amuse myself with,' Sienna said. 'Maybe I'll find a wolf or a wild boar in the woods to tame.'

His lips twitched as he looked down at her. 'I noticed your camera the other day,' he said after a moment. 'I thought you liked being in front of the lens, not behind it.'

'Yes, well, that just goes to show how little you know me, doesn't it?' she said.

His eyes held hers in a beat or two of silence.

'Does anyone know the real you, *ma petite*?' he asked.

Sienna gave a little shrug. 'I have friends, if that's what you're asking.'

'A person can have hundreds of friends but it doesn't mean anyone knows who they really are when they are alone.'

She gave him an arch look. 'Who are you when you're alone, Andreas?' she asked. 'Or aren't you ever alone? I bet there's always some willing woman to keep you company or some bowing and scraping servant to cater to your every whim.'

'It is one of the burdens of being born into wealth,' he said. 'One is rarely left alone. There are people always keen to be with you, but it is never clear if they want to be with you because they genuinely like your company or because they want something from you.'

'Given a choice, I'd rather live life from your side of the tracks than mine,' Sienna said. 'Besides, who needs genuine friends when you have loads and loads of money?'

He looked at her unwaveringly for a long moment. 'Do you really believe that, Sienna?' he asked. 'Do you really think being rich will make you truly happy?'

'I'll let you know once the money drops into my account in six months' time,' she said, picking up the rest of her croissant. 'Mind you, I reckon a chateau thrown in for free would bring a smile to my face.'

His mouth flattened to a thin line. 'You are *not* getting the chateau,' he said.

'Lighten up, Andreas,' she said. 'I'm only joking. I don't want your precious chateau. It's probably haunted by all your stuffy old relatives anyway.'

'Try and stay out of trouble today,' he said, with his brooding frown still in place. 'And remember, if you speak to anyone, we're supposed to be on our honeymoon.'

She arched a brow at him. 'You're the one rushing off to work the first chance you get.'

He came back to stand next to the bed, his eyes raking over her smoulderingly. 'Changed your mind already, have you, *cara*?' he said.

Sienna felt those gossamer wings brush over her belly again as she brought her eyes up to meet his glittering ones. 'Not yet,' she said. 'You can't give me what I want.'

He cupped her cheek with his hand as his eyes held hers captive. 'What do you want, Sienna? A promise of forever?'

She forced herself not to blink. 'Of course not,' she said. 'Neither of us is the forever type.'

His thumb moved over the surface of her bottom lip. 'We could be good together for a while, *ma cherie*,' he said. 'It seems a shame not to take advantage of the situation we find ourselves in. You and me, alone and legally married. Why not explore the possibilities, *sì*?'

Sienna couldn't think when he looked at her like that. Those hazel eyes promised sensual heaven. That mouth had already tempted her beyond endurance. She wanted him even though she knew it would probably end badly. How long could she say no, especially after that deliciously hot taste of sensuality last night?

She drew in a breath as he brought his mouth inexorably closer. The feather-light brush of his lips against hers made her senses skyrocket. The gentle pressure called every nerve into play, making her lips tingle and fizz like champagne underneath her skin. He lifted his mouth away but for a microsecond her lips clung to his. It seemed her body was determined to betray her, no matter what she said to the contrary. Need pulsed inside her. Rampant hungry need that only he could satisfy. She had always known it. He was her physical nemesis. No one came close to making her feel what he did. His touch, his kisses and his caresses all made her blood race through her veins and her heart gallop in excitement. She wanted to feel his complete possession. She wanted him to satisfy this aching longing that just wouldn't go away.

He gave her cheek a light brush with his fingertip, his eyes dark and intense as they held hers. 'Have you really only had two partners?' he asked.

'Yes,' Sienna said. 'I know the press have always made me out to be a sensual hedonist but, to tell you the truth, I felt awkward and uncomfortable having sex. I just wanted to get it over with. I didn't feel anything much at all.'

'That's probably because you weren't in tune with the other person physically,' he said. 'The first few times you have sex you shouldn't rush it. You need time to get to know your body's needs and rhythm. I rushed things last night because I thought you were more experienced. It will be different the next time. I'll make sure of it.'

Sienna felt her insides tremble with anticipation. Could she risk everything to indulge in a red-hot fling with him? It would be a sensuous feast she could sustain herself with for the rest of her life. But could she keep her feelings well clear of it?

It was a gamble she felt more and more tempted to take.

'You sound pretty certain there's going to be a next time,' she said. 'Isn't that a little arrogant of you?'

'There's a difference between arrogance and confidence,' he said. 'I'm confident we're going to be dynamite together, but I'm not so arrogant to assume it's going to last.'

It wasn't quite the answer Sienna was looking for.

It seemed to suggest he had only a passing interest in her. She was more of a novelty to him than a person of any lasting value. 'Does any woman hold your interest longer than a month or two?' she asked.

'Some more than others.'

'What about Portia Briscoe?' she asked. 'You were going to marry her. What were you going to do once you got bored? Have a little affair on the side, just like your father did?'

A flicker of heat passed through his gaze. 'My father made promises to my mother he later broke,' he said. 'I made no such promises to Portia. She knew what I wanted in a wife and she was prepared to provide it.'

'She's not the right person for you, Andreas,' Sienna said. 'Your housekeeper Elena thinks so and, quite frankly, so do I.'

His top lip curled. 'I suppose you think you're a much better candidate, do you?'

'No, but obviously your father thought so,' Sienna said. 'I can't see why else he would have done this. He must've wanted you to stop and think about what you were doing. Perhaps he didn't want you to lock yourself into a loveless marriage for the rest of your life.'

Andreas's eyes clashed with hers. 'So he locked me into a hate-filled one with you?'

'Only for six months,' she reminded him.

He looked at her for a long moment. 'You know, it was a whole lot easier hating you when I thought you were a money-hungry trollop,' he said. 'Now I know more about you, it seems rather unfair to maintain such negative feelings.'

'What are you saying, Andreas?' Sienna asked with

a deliberately goading smile. 'That you're falling a tiny bit in love with me?'

'I'm no more in love with you than you are with me,' he said, his expression locking down like a shutter over a window. 'What we feel for each other is lust. There's no other fancy way of putting it. And, in my opinion, the sooner it burns itself out the better.' And, without another word, he left, clipping the door shut behind him.

Later that day Sienna was coming back from photographing the lavender fields when she saw Andreas in the distance. He was walking through the vineyard, inspecting the vines as he went along the rows.

She raised her camera and zoomed in to frame him in a series of shots. She captured him deep in thought. She captured him squinting against the late afternoon sun. She captured him picking a leaf from a vine and running it through his fingers, his brow furrowed in a frown. And then, as if he suddenly became aware of being watched, he turned and looked directly at her.

Sienna lowered the camera as he walked towards her. She watched as his long legs ate up the distance, the muscles of his thighs bunching with every step. Her belly gave an excited little quiver. He looked so arrantly male, dressed in dark blue denim jeans and a close-fitting white T-shirt. Every honed and toned muscle stretched against the fabric, reminding her of the potent power of his body. She had felt that hard male body move inside hers.

She wanted to feel it again.

He came and stood right in front of her, his towering height almost blocking the sun from her view. 'Are you going to let me see what you've been up to?' he asked.

Sienna positioned herself beside him and pressed the buttons on her camera to recall the shots. 'You make a good study when you're not aware of the camera,' she said. 'But that's like most people. It's hard to get a natural shot of someone when they know they're being watched.'

His eyes met hers. 'These are good,' he said. 'How long have you been doing this?'

Sienna shrugged dismissively as she turned off the camera. 'A while.'

He took the camera from her and turned it back on, scrolling through the archive of pictures she had loaded. 'You've got a good eye,' he said, looking at her again. 'Is this a hobby or is it what you want to do? To pursue a career in photography?'

Sienna took the camera from him, her fingers briefly coming in contact with his. 'I lost my office job when Brian died,' she said. 'His family didn't want me working in the business. It made me think about being my own boss instead of being at the mercy of other people all the time. Of course it will take me a while to build up the business, but I'd like to have a go at it. I could never afford decent equipment before. I'd need a much better camera for official portraits and wedding photography and I'd need to rent a studio. I couldn't afford to do that before. But after this six months is over… well, I'll be laughing all the way to the bank, won't I?'

His expression was deeply thoughtful. 'So why did you encourage me to think you only wanted the money for a layabout holiday and endless partying?' he asked.

She shifted her gaze from his as she put the camera back inside its vinyl case. 'I might not make it as a photographer,' she said. 'There's pretty stiff competition out there. I'm under no illusions that I'm any more talented than anyone else.'

'Where would you like to base yourself?' he asked.

'London,' Sienna said. 'But I could travel to other places on assignment. It'd be fun travelling around to take pictures all over the world. I could even do a book, you know, like one of those super-glam coffee table ones.' She flashed him a little smile. 'You could tell everyone you knew me before I was famous.'

'I'm sure you'll do very well,' he said, a small frown forming between his eyes. 'You seem to have rather a knack for falling on your feet.'

She tucked a strand of hair behind her ear that the light breeze had been playing with. 'What will you do with this place once you inherit it?' she asked. 'Are you going to base yourself here or Florence, or travel between the two?'

His eyes held hers in a brooding little lockdown. 'It is not yet certain that I will inherit it,' he said. 'It would be foolish of me to make plans at this stage. I'll take a wait and see approach.'

Sienna frowned at him. 'You don't trust me, do you?'

'This is a valuable property,' he said. 'It surely can't have escaped your notice that it's worth five or six times what you will get in the pay-out. Why should I trust you?'

'No, indeed,' she said, throwing him a blistering look. 'Why should you?'

He let out a breath of irritation. 'Sienna, I realise I've made some errors of judgement with you in the past, but I would be a fool to take it for granted that you'll abide by the terms of the will. We haven't been married a week. How do you know what you'll feel in six weeks from now, let alone six months?'

'I know exactly what I'll feel,' she said, glaring at him. 'I'll still hate you.'

'Best you keep on doing that,' he said, turning to walk back towards the vineyard. 'It will make the end much easier for both of us.'

'Why are we leaving so soon?' Sienna asked as Andreas loaded their bags in the car later that evening. He had given her very little notice. He had sent a message via Simone, telling her to pack as they were leaving to catch the next available flight. 'I thought you said we were staying for two or three days.'

'I've seen what I came here to see,' he said as he snapped the boot shut and came around to open her door for her. 'The Perraults are managing things just fine. I have other things I need to see to in Florence. I have a business to run.'

'Aren't you worried what the press will think of you cutting short your honeymoon?' she asked once they were on their way.

He sent her a brief unreadable glance. 'I thought you were desperate to get back to your feral dog?'

'So you're doing this for me?' Sienna asked with a sceptical look. 'Somehow, I don't think so.'

'I'm doing it for both of us,' he said and put his foot down on the accelerator.

Sienna didn't see much of Andreas after they got back from France. Each day he left early in the morning and returned well after she had gone to bed. It annoyed her that he had just left her to her own devices, not even having the decency to communicate with her, other than via the housekeeper or a short text. It made her feel like an uninvited guest who was being tolerated, rather than welcomed.

But then, that was exactly what she was. Andreas had planned his life with meticulous precision. She had never been a part of it. She was the last woman he would ever have considered marrying. But his father's will had changed everything. So, too, had that brief moment of intimacy. Yet ever since that night Andreas had kept his distance.

Her heart gave a funny little spasm. He could easily find someone else. He might have already recruited someone to satisfy his needs. There were hundreds of women who would do anything to be his mistress. Would she have to pretend not to notice for the rest of the time they were stuck together in this arrangement? Was he doing it to make her default on the will? After all, she was the one with the most to lose. All he had to do was wait it out and he could claim what was rightly his. Her lack of experience was probably the biggest turn-off for someone with his level of expertise. He probably couldn't wait to get rid of her now she was of no further use to him.

Sienna was sure Elena was well aware that Andreas didn't share a bed with his new wife, but the housekeeper was either too discreet or polite to mention it in any of her interactions with her.

Elena had mentioned something about a furniture design collection Andreas was working on, commissioned by a wealthy American businessman, and how it was taking up a lot of his time. 'He barely sleeps when he is working on a special project,' she said. 'He spends hours and hours at his office. Once it is finished he will be able to relax a little, *sì*? Maybe he will take you away somewhere special for a proper honeymoon. It is lonely here all day on your own.'

'I'm not lonely,' Sienna insisted. 'I have Scraps to keep me company.'

Elena gave her an indulgent smile. 'It will be easier when you have a *bambino* or two to keep you busy, *sì*?'

Sienna pushed the thought of a dark-haired hazel-eyed chubby baby out of her mind. She thought instead of a home of her own in London, a luxury home with a studio and a garden and money in the bank—lots and lots of money.

That was her goal, not marriage and babies.

When Sienna came downstairs for dinner towards the end of the week Andreas was in the *salone* sipping an aperitif. His gaze skimmed over her coffee-coloured dress before meshing with hers. 'I was expecting you to send word via Elena that you wouldn't be joining me for dinner,' he said.

Sienna held her head at an imperious angle. 'I considered it, but then I thought that would be letting you off the hook,' she said. 'I'd much rather annoy you with my presence since you seemed to be actively avoiding it for the past week.'

A half-smile kicked up one side of his mouth. 'Feeling neglected, are we?'

She took the glass of wine he had poured for her, giving him a hardened look. 'Not at all,' she said. 'I just can't help wondering what your housekeeper thinks of our relationship, with you spending every minute you can at work while I'm stuck here twiddling my thumbs.'

'She is employed to keep order in the villa, not to speculate on my private life,' he said. 'She knows she would be fired immediately if she spoke out of turn. Anyway, if you're bored, why not take the car out I bought you?'

'I'm not bored,' Sienna said. 'I've got plenty to do; it's just I don't like having to pretend things are normal between us when they're not.'

'There's one way to change that,' he said with a glinting look in his eyes. 'We can make them normal. You can move into my bed tonight.'

Sienna felt her stomach do a flip turn. 'How can you be so clinical about this?' she asked. 'We don't even like each other.'

'Liking one another has nothing to do with it,' he said. 'Physical compatibility is what matters. I've had lovers I didn't like much at all, but they were perfectly fine as sexual partners.'

'Have you ever been in love?' Sienna asked.

'No,' he said. 'It's not that I don't believe it exists. I've seen it and admire it in others. I just haven't felt that level of attachment.' He took a sip of his drink. 'What about you?'

'I think my twin got all the love genes instead of me,' she said. 'I don't think I've ever seen two people more in love than Gisele and Emilio. Their wedding is in three weeks. You haven't forgotten, have you? I called your secretary to put it in your diary. I'm going to go a couple of days before to help with things. I'll meet you at the hotel.'

'No, I haven't forgotten,' he said. 'I'm looking forward to meeting them both, particularly your sister.'

'We're nothing alike,' Sienna said. 'Well, apart from looks, I mean.'

'You must have more in common than looks,' he said.

'Not much,' she said. 'Don't get me wrong. I adore her. She's so sweet and caring I can't help but love her. But because we haven't shared the same parents, or the same experiences, we want different things for our lives. I wonder if it would have been different if we had grown up together. I guess we'll never know now.'

He studied her for a moment as if he was memorising her features in fine detail. 'I wonder if I'll be able to tell you apart.'

'I'll give you a tip-off,' Sienna said. 'My sister will be the one wearing white and she'll have a big smile on her face. Oh, and a wedding band on her finger to match the fabulous diamond engagement ring Emilio gave her.'

'That reminds me.' Andreas put his drink to one side. 'I have something for you,' he said. He took an antique ring box out of his pocket and handed it to her. 'You might recognise it. It belonged to my mother and my grandmother before her.'

Sienna opened the tiny box to find the diamond and sapphire dress ring she had often admired on Evaline Ferrante's hand, nestled in the groove of black velvet. 'I do recognise it,' she said, looking up at him with a little frown. 'But shouldn't you be keeping such an heirloom for your future bride?'

'If you don't like it then I'll get you something else,' he said.

Sienna wasn't sure what to make of his expression or his curt tone. 'Of course I like it,' she said, putting it on her finger. 'I've always thought it was a gorgeous ring. But I'll give it back to you when we get divorced. That would only be fair.'

'Fine,' he said, refilling his glass. 'But I've noticed you don't seem to have a lot of jewellery.' He took a sip of his drink. 'What happened to all the diamonds you had dripping from you when you were with Littlemore?'

'I gave them back to his family,' she said. 'I didn't feel comfortable keeping them.'

He gave her another one of his thoughtful looks. 'I got the impression from what was reported in the press that his family never accepted you,' he said. 'At times they were quite vitriolic in their comments.'

'Yes, well, they loved their mother dearly and didn't want anyone to take her place,' Sienna said. 'I totally understood where they were coming from.'

'Do you think they would have accepted his mistress any better?'

She shifted her gaze from his. 'No.'

'And yet, by all accounts, he had been involved with her a long time,' he said. 'It seems strange he didn't offer to marry her instead of you.'

She shrugged off his comment and took a sip of her wine.

He continued to study her. 'You're very loyal to Littlemore, aren't you?' he said.

Sienna forced herself to meet his gaze. 'Why wouldn't I be? He was good to me.'

'There's more to it, isn't there?' he asked. 'It's been niggling at me for days. Why didn't he marry his mistress? Why marry a woman younger than one of his daughters instead of the mistress he had kept for all those years?'

'Maybe his mistress was already married,' she said.

Andreas lifted her chin with his index finger, locking his gaze with hers. 'That's not the reason, though, is it?' he said.

Sienna remained silent. The intense scrutiny of

his hazel gaze made her heart beat faster and faster. It was harder and harder to hide anything from him. He seemed to see through the layers of her skin to the very heart of her.

'Brian Littlemore wasn't involved with a woman, was he?' Andreas said. 'His long-term lover was a man.'

Sienna swallowed tightly. 'That's not true.'

'Don't lie to me, *cara*,' he said. 'I hate being lied to. Don't you think you've told enough lies by now? Surely you can be honest with me over this. It will go no further than this room.'

She chewed at her lip. 'How did you find out?' she asked. 'No one is supposed to know. Brian didn't want his children to find out. He was worried it would hurt them. He didn't think they'd understand. If this gets out in the public arena it will hurt so many people.'

'It's not common knowledge, as far as I know,' he said. 'I came to the conclusion myself so it's likely others will do so as well. But if it goes public, I can't see how you should be blamed.'

'Brian wanted to protect his family,' Sienna said. 'He came from a very conservative background. His parents would've disowned him if they'd known. He did all the things that were expected of him. He got married and raised a family. Even after his wife died he still had to maintain the lie. Do you know how hard that was on him? He was trapped. You mustn't let anyone know about it. You mustn't, Andreas. So many people will get hurt.'

He stroked her chin with his thumb, back and forth like a slow-moving metronome. 'You care more about his family's feelings even though they've trashed you any time they could in the press?'

Sienna looked into his warm hazel eyes and felt something reposition itself in her chest. A soft little gear change of emotion that was totally unexpected and deeply unsettling. She didn't want to lose her grip on her feelings. She wanted to keep her emotions under lockdown. Falling in love with Andreas would be the biggest mistake of her life so far. She couldn't afford to let her feelings get involved. She had to be strong enough to walk away when the time was up. 'I care about what Brian wanted,' she said. 'He trusted me. I didn't want to betray that trust.'

Andreas's eyes held hers in an intimate lock that made her insides flutter. His thumb was still doing that mesmerising little caress that made her feel as if her nerves were pirouetting beneath the surface of her skin. 'So you were prepared to let me carry on thinking you were a gold-digger?' he said as his hand fell away from her face. 'Does my opinion of you mean absolutely nothing to you at all?'

Sienna swept the surface of her lips with a quick dart of her tongue. 'I figured after this six months is up it won't be relevant what you think of me,' she said. 'We don't mix in the same circles. We probably won't see each other again.'

Something passed through his gaze as it held hers. 'That will be a shame, don't you think?' he said.

'Why?'

'Because I have a feeling I'm going to miss doing this,' he said, and lowered his mouth to hers.

CHAPTER NINE

SIENNA felt the warm, gentle pressure of his lips as they met hers. It was a slow kiss, no sense of urgency or out of control passion, just his lips moving at a leisurely pace as they explored the softness of hers.

She returned the kiss in much the same way, slow and soft, touching down, lifting off, touching down again, varying the pressure ever so slightly, but not the speed.

It was a getting-to-know-you kiss. It felt like a romantic first kiss between two people who were attracted to each other, but were mindful of overstepping the boundaries too early. A kiss where the two parties were taking tentative steps to see how well they worked together intimately.

No other parts of their bodies were touching. He didn't gather her to him. He didn't put his arms on her shoulders or her waist. She didn't put her hands on his chest or around his neck. Only their lips bridged the gap between them, but, even so, Sienna felt a roar of heat go through her. Her insides melted like the wax of a candle under a powerful heat source.

After endless dreamy minutes, Andreas slowly lifted his mouth away. His expression was faintly bemused as he looked down at her. 'You have such a soft, kissable mouth,' he said. 'It's surprisingly soft given how razor-sharp your tongue can be.'

Sienna couldn't hold back a rueful smile. 'Yes, well, you do seem to bring the shrew out in me at times.'

He made a little sound of amusement, a deep and totally male sound that made her belly quiver like unset aspic. His hand came up to cup her cheek, his thumb lazily stroking her skin as his eyes made love with hers. 'You haven't always brought out the best in me either,' he said. 'But maybe, once this period of time is up, we can walk away from this as friends. Do you think that's possible, *ma petite*?'

Sienna felt her breath come out in a little flutter but she hoped he hadn't noticed. 'I'm not sure I could ever get used to thinking of you as a friend,' she said playfully. 'I guess I'll have to find someone else to sharpen my claws on, won't I?'

He stroked her cheek one last time before dropping his hand back down by his side. 'I bet it won't be half as much fun with someone else,' he said, his expression now inscrutable.

Sienna had a feeling he wasn't just talking about their verbal sparring. The crazy thing was, she couldn't imagine kissing another man now. She couldn't imagine another man holding her and caressing her and making love to her.

She only wanted Andreas.

She gave herself a swift mental slap. He wanted the chateau, not her. She was a means to an end. In six months it would all be over. He would walk away from her, just as his father had done to her mother.

This wasn't forever.

'No, perhaps not,' she said. 'But I won't know that until I try, will I?'

His eyes flickered as if something behind them had momentarily become unstuck. 'We should have dinner,' he said, putting his glass down as if it had suddenly turned into a poisoned chalice. 'I still have some work to see to afterwards.'

'Do you ever take time to relax?' Sienna asked. 'You can't possibly go at this pace for weeks on end. It's not healthy.'

'I have a lot of people depending on me for their incomes and their futures,' Andreas said, scraping a hand through his hair. 'My father's death couldn't have come at a worse time.'

'I'm quite sure he didn't plan to die just then to personally inconvenience you,' Sienna said in a dry tone.

'Don't bet on it,' he said with an embittered scowl.

'You didn't really hate him, did you, Andreas?' she asked.

He held her look for a moment before he let out a long breath. 'I used to look up to him when I was a young child,' he said. 'I wanted to be just like him when I grew up: successful and wealthy. But as I got older I started to see that, like most people, he had a dark side. He was driven by his emotions. He was selfish and at times outrageously ruthless in getting what he wanted. He exploited the love my mother felt for him. I don't think he ever truly loved her. I think he only married her because he knew she would never challenge him. She would just accept whatever he did without question. She could've left him over his affair with your mother but she didn't. She stayed until the bitter end.'

'Sounds like your father didn't want you to make

the same mistake in your choice of a bride, don't you think?' Sienna asked.

His gaze narrowed. 'What do you mean?'

'Perfect Portia,' she said. 'The wife who would never do or say the wrong thing. The wife who would meekly turn a blind eye when her handsome, charming, virile husband took up with someone else every now and again. That was the sort of marriage you had planned, was it not?'

His frown closed the space between his brows. 'You don't know what the hell you're talking about.'

'Don't I?' she asked with an arch of one brow.

He threw her an irritated look as he wrenched open the door. 'I've changed my mind about dinner,' he said. 'I'm going back to the office. I'll see you when I see you.'

Andreas came home the following evening to find Sienna wasn't home. The villa felt completely different without her in it. The air didn't have that intoxicating trace of her perfume lingering in it, and the scatter cushions on the sofas were all neatly propped in place. There were no half empty cups or glasses littered about, and the television wasn't blaring with some inane reality show or the sound system shuddering with noise that he wouldn't even go as far as calling music.

It was quiet and peaceful, ordered and neat, but sterile.

A bit like his life.

He quickly dismissed the thought and snatched up his phone and rapidly dialled her number. 'Where are you?' he asked as soon as she answered.

'I'm on my way back now,' she said. 'I'm about ten minutes away.'

'Back from where?'

'I've been…erm…at the doctor's,' she said.

His heart gave a sudden lurch. 'The doctor?' he said. 'Why? What's wrong? Are you sick?'

'Not really…'

He heard the hesitancy in her tone. 'What's going on?' he asked.

'I had a bit of an accident,' she said. 'I had to have a couple of stitches in my hand. Nothing serious, however.'

'An accident?' His heart jerked again. 'What happened? Are you all right?'

'I'm fine but you have to promise you won't get rid of Scraps.'

Andreas frowned as he clutched the phone until his knuckles whitened. 'Did that mongrel attack you?'

'It was my fault,' she said. 'I tried to get too close to him. I tried to put some ointment on his sore leg but he wouldn't let me. He snapped at me in pain, not spite.'

'I told you to keep away from that dog,' Andreas said. 'Are you all right to drive? Why didn't you get Franco to take you? Pull over and I'll come and get you. Where are you?'

'Stop fussing, Andreas,' she said. 'You're really starting to scare me. You sound just like a doting husband.'

Andreas drew in a sharp breath and strode over to the windows to scan the driveway of the estate to see if he could see her in the distance. 'That's an expensive and very powerful car you're driving,' he said. 'It needs two hands on the wheel, not one.'

'I won't hurt your precious car,' she said and hung up on him.

* * *

Sienna pulled up in front of the villa but didn't even get time to turn the engine off before Andreas had the driver's door open.

'You silly little fool,' he railed at her as he helped her out. 'Why didn't you call me as soon as it happened?'

'I didn't want you to overreact,' she said. 'It's just a scratch.'

He gently picked up her thickly bandaged hand. 'How many stitches?' he asked.

Sienna considered fibbing but decided against it. 'Five,' she mumbled.

'Five?' His eyes flared in alarm. 'That's not a scratch. You could have lost a finger or even your hand.'

'Well, I didn't so everything's all right, isn't it?' she said.

'That dog has to go,' he said trenchantly. 'I will see that Franco destroys it first thing in the morning. And if he won't do it, then I'll do it myself.'

Sienna glared at him as she cradled her hand against her stomach. 'You do that and I swear to God I'll never speak to you again.'

His hazel eyes collided with hers. 'Why are you so determined to rescue a dog that clearly doesn't want to be rescued?' he asked.

She raised her chin at him. 'He does want to be rescued,' she said. 'He just doesn't know who to trust. He'll get there in the end. I just have to be patient.'

Andreas let out a curt swear word as he cupped her by the elbow to lead her into the villa. 'You're going to give me a heart attack one day, *ma petite*,' he said. 'I didn't realise one small woman could cause such chaos.'

Sienna threw him a pert look. 'Just as well I won't be around any longer than a few months, isn't it?' she said. 'Once this is over you can settle back into your boringly ordered life and forget all about me.'

He shouldered open the heavy front door of the villa as she stalked past. 'I can hardly wait,' he muttered darkly.

CHAPTER TEN

SIENNA woke during the night and had trouble going back to sleep as the local anaesthetic had worn off. The painkillers the doctor had given her were still in her handbag in the car. With all the fuss Andreas had made, she had forgotten to bring it with her into the villa. She tossed off the covers and padded downstairs, turning on the minimum of lights as she went.

She walked past Andreas's study and saw the thin line of light shining from beneath the door. She heard the tapping of his computer keyboard and the squeak of leather as he shifted in his chair. There was a pause in the tapping as she heard him mutter a very rude word, and then the tapping resumed.

She tiptoed past in her bare feet, but one of the floorboards protested volubly and suddenly Andreas's study door was flung open and he stood there towering over her. 'What are you doing?' he said.

'I'm going out to the car.'

His brows slammed together over his eyes. 'Whatever for?'

'I forgot to bring in my bag,' she said. 'The painkillers the doctor gave me are inside it.'

'Why didn't you ask me to get it for you?'

'I didn't think of it till now.'

'Go back upstairs,' he said, rubbing a hand over his weary-looking features. 'I'll bring it up to you.'

Sienna went back to her room and sat propped up against the pillows. Within a few minutes Andreas came in, carrying her bag as well as a glass of water. She took the pills and he set the glass on the bedside table.

'Does it hurt much?' he asked.

'A little,' Sienna said. 'Just a dull throb.'

A little silence passed.

Sienna felt the drumbeat of her heart as his gaze meshed with hers. One of his hands was resting on the bed within a hair's breadth of hers. She felt the magnetic pull of his body, the sensual tug on her flesh, as if all of the organs and cells inside her body wanted to shift to be perfectly aligned with his.

His thumb moved just a fraction and stroked against the little finger of her undamaged hand. It was such a tiny touch and yet it made a tumultuous storm of feeling erupt inside her. Her skin tingled all the way up her arm. Her heart picked up speed and her insides flexed and coiled with unbridled need.

His hooded gaze slipped to her mouth. It felt as if he had physically kissed her. Her lips burned and fizzed and she had to sweep her tongue out over them to dampen down the sensation.

He raised a hand to her face, his touch so gentle it felt as if he were wearing kid gloves. He traced the pad of his finger over the cushion of her bottom lip. It was such an achingly intimate caress—the moisture of her lips and the dryness of his fingertip meeting in an erotic moment that stirred something deeply primal in the core of her being.

'I want you,' Sienna said on a whisper of sound.

Andreas's eyes locked on hers, dark, intense and serious. 'Is that the painkillers talking or you?' he asked.

'It's me,' she said, touching her hand to the stubbly skin of his jaw. 'I want you to make love to me.'

He covered her hand with his and, lifting it from his face, pressed a kiss to the middle of her palm, his tongue moving against the sensitive flesh in an erotic stroke that sent her senses into a tailspin. 'I want you too,' he said. 'It's driving me crazy. *You've* been driving me crazy, do you know that?'

Sienna shivered as he leaned in to kiss the skin of her neck just below her ear. 'We're both a little crazy, don't you think?' she said. 'Hating each other and yet wanting each other.'

His mouth brushed over hers, a light-as-air, teasing kiss that made her want to scream out loud for more. 'Total craziness, that's what it is,' he said, sliding one of his hands underneath the curtain of her hair as he gently drew her closer.

Sienna closed her eyes as his mouth came back down on hers. His lips moved with gentle urgency against hers. The undercurrent of lust that flowed between them made her blood race like high-octane fuel through her veins. Every thudding heartbeat made her longing for him rise to a feverish level. She could feel it building inside her body. A tug and release sensation that resided deep in her womb, making her hot and moist and restless for the full possession of his body.

His tongue commanded entry to her mouth and with a soft sigh of pleasure she opened to him. He played with her tongue, dancing with it, cavorting and teasing it into submission.

Electric shocks arced down her spine when his hand moved to cover her breast. The barrier of her thin nightwear was no barrier at all. If anything, the movement of the fine fabric against her nipple intensified the sensation. But then he pushed the fabric aside and took her nipple and areola in his mouth. It was an explosion of feeling that made her flesh sizzle and shiver with delight. His tongue teased her nipple by rolling over it and circling it, making all the tiny super-sensitive nerves dance in excitement. He uncovered her other breast and subjected it to a similar heart-stopping sensual assault, making her breathing and heart rate go into a frenzied mismatched rhythm.

His mouth came back to her as he gently eased her back on the bed, his weight supported by one of his elbows. 'Let's get rid of this, shall we?' he said, peeling away her nightwear.

Sienna shucked herself out of it, feeling strangely at ease with him without the covering of her clothes. His gaze devoured her hungrily. It made her flesh sing with delight as his eyes took in every curve and contour of her body.

'You're incredibly beautiful,' he said, sliding a hand down over the jut of her hipbone. 'So slender and your skin is like silk.'

'I want to touch your skin,' Sienna said, starting to work on the buttons of his shirt, but she didn't get very far with only one hand.

'Hold that thought,' he said. He lifted himself off the bed and stood there, looking down at her as he undid each button of his shirt, shrugging it off his shoulders before unfastening the waistband of his trousers.

Sienna's eyes followed his every movement with

breathless anticipation. Seeing him totally naked for the first time made her breath stall like a misfiring engine. He was all strongly corded muscles and lean and tanned planes. Masculine hair was lightly sprinkled over his chest in a T shape, arrowing down to his groin, where his erection jutted boldly.

He fished a condom out of his wallet and joined her on the bed again. 'Are you sure about this?' he asked. 'It's not too late to stop. I don't want to hurt your hand.'

'It *is* too late, and I've forgotten all about my hand,' Sienna said. 'I want this. I want you.'

His mouth came down and sealed hers with a long passionate kiss that set her flesh alight. He took his time caressing every inch of her body, making her aware of herself in a way she had never been before. She hadn't realised the pleasure spots she possessed. She hadn't known how delicious it felt to have his mouth on the undersides of her breasts, or the way it felt to have his hands stroke the silky skin of her inner thighs. She hadn't known how it would feel to have him gently separate her feminine folds with his fingers and then with the stroke and flicker of his tongue. Her body responded with a sensual energy that took her completely by surprise. It was like a giant wave of sensation that she could not stop even if she tried. It snatched her up in its powerful surge of momentum, tossed her about and flung her out the other side, spent, limbless, breathless and dazed.

Sienna blinked her eyes open and looked at Andreas. 'Wow…' she said.

His hazel eyes glittered. 'It gets better.'

'You can top that?' she said with an incredulous look.

He gave her a smile that made her insides quiver all

over again. 'I'll take it slowly,' he said. 'You're tiny and I don't want to hurt you. Just relax, try not to clamp up. You're meant to stretch to accommodate me.'

Sienna sighed with pleasure as he positioned himself so as not to crush her with his weight. She loved the feel of his hair-roughened thighs and the way his hands were so gentle, almost worshipful, as they caressed her. Tasting the feminine essence of her body on his mouth was a new experience, but a totally erotic one. He kissed her lingeringly while his fingers played with her, making sure she was moist and relaxed before he eased into her slowly, pausing as her body got used to his thickness, before going deeper. She felt her inner walls wrap around him; the sensation of him moving inside her made her spine instantly melt. She moved against him experimentally and her belly somersaulted as she heard him give a deep groan of pleasure. 'Am I wowing you?' she asked, sliding her uninjured hand up and down his strongly muscled back.

He swept a strand of her hair away from her face with a tender movement of his hand. 'Most definitely,' he said and, with a spasm of pleasure passing over his face, he took her with him to paradise.

Andreas lay on his side, watching as Sienna slept. She was curled up on her side facing him, her little bandaged hand resting in the space between them. Her hair was a tousled cloud over the pillow. The scent of her was on his skin, the taste of her both sweet and salty on his tongue.

He had made love many times with many women. It was a physical union that he enjoyed. But somehow, making love with Sienna was something else, something infinitely more pleasurable, more deeply satisfying—a mind-blowing experience that touched him where no one else had been able to reach before.

But then she constantly surprised him. That was part of her alluring charm. He never knew what to expect from her. She was totally, and yet somehow delightfully, unpredictable.

She suddenly opened her eyes and gave him one of her breath-snatching smiles. 'I had this amazing dream,' she said. 'This amazingly gorgeous-looking and disgustingly rich guy made love to me. I hate his guts in real life, but in my dream we made magic together. Wasn't that a weird dream?'

Andreas smiled crookedly as he stroked a lazy finger down her cheek. 'Are you sure you hate him so much in real life?' he asked.

She pretended to think about it. 'Mmm, maybe not as much as I did before, but I'm not in love with him or anything.'

'So what's the plan?' he asked. 'A short affair to get him out of your system?'

She tiptoed her fingers up his sternum, making his heart leap like a mad thing behind the cage of his ribs. 'That's the plan,' she said, meshing her gaze with his. 'Five months, give or take a day or two, ought to do it, don't you think?'

Andreas studied her soft plump mouth for a moment. 'What if the amazingly gorgeous-looking, disgustingly rich guy wanted you to stay a little longer?' he asked.

Her grey-blue eyes stilled for a moment. Then she blinked and asked, 'Why would he want that?'

He slowly coiled a strand of her silver-blonde hair

around his index finger. 'Maybe he likes having you around to mess up his ordered life,' he said.

She gave a little gurgle of laughter. 'I can't quite see it, somehow,' she said, doing that sexy little tiptoe thing again. 'We'd drive each other nuts.'

Andreas felt an arrow of lust stake him in the groin when her fingers suddenly changed direction, step by exquisite step, as they made their way down to dance tantalisingly over his erection. He snatched in a breath when she boldly circled him with her hand, her soft skin like a silky glove.

She gave him a sultry little smile and bent her head to him, her hair tickling his abdomen and thighs, as she stroked her tongue over his engorged flesh. He groaned out loud as she licked him like a shy, tentative kitten. But then she suddenly turned into a wild rampaging tigress and consumed him whole. Shudders of delight rocked through him as she fed off him hungrily.

He tried to pull away but she pressed him back down with a determined hand. 'Stay,' she said.

'You don't have to do this,' he said, fighting for control.

'You did it to me.'

'That was different,' he said, breathing raggedly.

'"All's fair in love and war",' she said in a sing-song voice.

'So which is this?' he asked. 'Love or war?'

She gathered her hair in one hand before curling it over one shoulder, her eyes glinting with mischief and daring. 'This is war,' she said, and then lowered her mouth and claimed victory.

CHAPTER ELEVEN

IN the weeks leading up to her twin's wedding Sienna settled into Andreas's life as if she had always been in it. They didn't discuss the future by tacit agreement, although their affair was as blisteringly hot as ever. She had wondered if Andreas's ardour would cool over time but it hadn't any more than hers had. She had been constantly surprised by her body's capacity for pleasure. His mix of tenderness and daring as a lover repeatedly took her breath away. He would only have to look at her a certain way and she would shudder in anticipated pleasure. She had become more adventurous as her confidence grew. She delighted in catching him off guard, seducing him when he least expected it.

He had been generous to her in showering her with gifts. He had bought her a sophisticated camera and a computer of her own to store her files of pictures. He had encouraged her to have copies professionally printed and had even hung some framed ones in his office in Florence.

Sienna wondered if they would still be hanging there when their marriage came to its inevitable end.

The other project Andreas had helped her with was Scraps. With careful handling and patience, the dog was now totally at ease around them. Andreas drew the line at having the dog inside the villa, but Sienna was content that Scraps was at least healthy and happy and comfortable with the staff as well as her and Andreas.

For once in her life the press left her alone. They seemed to have accepted that she and Andreas were a happily married couple and, apart from an occasional snap of them having dinner or attending a function together, there was no hint of scandal or anything untoward.

Sienna knew it wouldn't last but she tried not to think about it. She was becoming very good at not thinking about things that troubled her. Denial had become her closest companion. As soon as a worrying or wayward thought entered her head she would immediately dismiss it, like her feelings for Andreas, for instance. She absolutely refused to think beyond the fact that she no longer hated him. What she actually felt for him was locked behind a door inside her head marked private and off-limits.

She just didn't want to go there.

As to what Andreas felt about her, she knew was equally dangerous to examine too closely. He had a goal in mind and within a few rapidly passing months he would achieve it. He would be able to claim his inheritance and move on with his life. She didn't like to presume she would continue to be a part of it.

He never spoke of his feelings. He was attentive and affectionate, and even teasing and playful at times, but occasionally she would catch him looking at her with a frown pulling at his brow. It was as if he wasn't quite sure what to do with her. She suspected she delighted and frustrated him in equal measure.

One such time was a couple of days before Sienna was due to leave for Rome to help her sister prepare for her wedding. Andreas came into the bedroom they shared just as Sienna was sorting out what to take with her. She had been determined to take a leaf from his book and become better organised. She had planned to be packed well and truly in advance—there would no longer be any last minute mad grabs or flying off without packing appropriately. The bed was strewn with clothes and the floor with shoes, but that was all under control, or it would have been if he hadn't come home earlier than she had expected. 'Hi,' she said with a bright smile. 'You're home early.'

His brooding frown looked as if it had been stitched to his brow. 'Do you have to take everything out of the wardrobe every time you get dressed?' he asked.

Sienna lifted her chin, more than a little stung by his surly mood. 'I'm packing.'

A muscle jerked at the side of his mouth. 'What?'

'I'm leaving for Rome, remember?' she said, turning to fling a pair of jeans on to the not-taking-this pile on the floor. 'I'm going to my sister's wedding. I told you about it, not that you probably listened. Of course, it's entirely up to you whether you come or not. No one is pressuring you. I can imagine going to a real wedding where the couple actually love each other will be quite an eye-opener for you.'

'What the hell is that supposed to mean?' he asked.

'Figure it out for yourself,' she said as she pushed past him to fetch a suitcase.

He shackled one of her wrists with his hand, turning her round to face him. 'What's got into you?' he asked.

'What's got into *me*?' Sienna asked. 'You're the one

who came home like a bear with a thorn in his paw.' She shoved at his chest with her free hand. 'Take your hands off me.'

A burning gleam entered his hazel gaze as it collided with hers. 'You wanted my hands on you twice last night and this morning,' he said. 'I've been getting shivers all day just thinking about what you did to me in the shower.'

She threw him a caustic glare that belied her quivering insides. 'Well, I don't want them on me now.'

He tugged her closer, his pelvis hard against hers, his desire warring with her will. 'Prove it,' he said.

'I don't have to prove anything,' she said, giving him another shove, but it was like trying to shift a skyscraper.

He put a hand at the base of her spine, holding her to the hardened probe of his erection. 'One kiss and I'll let you go,' he said.

'All right,' Sienna said, determined to show him she could resist him. She would rise to the challenge the same way she dealt with all of her traitorous thoughts. She would block it from her mind. 'Give me your best, Rich Boy.'

His mouth came down but, instead of completely covering hers, his lips teased the side of her mouth, making every nerve twitch and writhe in rapture. She fought against the desire to turn her head that tiny fraction so her mouth was right under his. She scrunched her eyes closed and tried to ignore the way her body was responding to his as if on automatic. Her spine loosened as he shifted his attention to the other side of her mouth. His stubble caught on her skin, sending a lightning bolt of desire to her core.

'You're cheating,' she said, a little shocked at how breathless she sounded.

'How am I cheating?' he asked, moving up to suck on her earlobe.

Sienna shivered. 'You said one kiss, but you haven't even kissed me.'

'I'm working my way up to it,' he said, coming back to that incredibly sensitive corner of her mouth where her top lip joined her bottom one.

She let out a wobbly breath as his tongue came out to stroke along the partially open seam of her mouth. He still hadn't pressed his lips to hers and yet she was thrumming like a tuning fork struck against a hard object.

Finally she could stand it no longer. She grabbed at his head with her hands, digging her fingers into his scalp as she pressed her mouth to his. He took immediate control by going in search of her tongue, the sensual and commanding thrust of his destroying any hope of her resisting him. She slammed her body up against his, rubbing herself against his arousal, delighting in the crackling sexual energy that fired between them at the intimate contact.

He growled against her mouth as he walked her backwards to the clothes-strewn bed. 'Get your clothes off.'

'Off the bed or off me?' she asked, tearing at his shirt, popping buttons with scant disregard for the designer label it bore.

'Let's start with you,' he said, pulling off her T-shirt as if it were nothing more than tissue paper.

Sienna landed on the mattress with a gasp as he came down on top of her. Somehow her jeans and knickers had met the same fate as her T-shirt. She was naked and sizzling with need as he parted her, thrusting into her with a groan of primal pleasure that made the skin on her arms come up in a fine sandpaper of goose bumps.

He set a rhythm that was breathtakingly fast, his strongly muscled body pumping into hers with raw urgency until she was screaming out loud her release. She wrapped her legs around his waist, desperate to hold on to the exquisite sensations for as long as she could. She sobbed as the final waves coursed through her. She had never felt such exhilarating pleasure. It racked her body with its aftershocks just as his release burst out of him. She felt every shuddering pulse of his body as he spilled. She felt the way the muscles of his back and shoulders finally relaxed under the soothing stroke of her hands.

In that quiet moment of the aftermath, she felt the carapace of her closely guarded heart fall away as if chipped at by a sharpened chisel.

It terrified her.

She could not allow this to happen.

She had to squash it before it took hold.

'Get off me,' she said, pushing against him.

Andreas frowned as he moved to let her get up. 'What's wrong, *ma petite*?'

Sienna shoved her hair back from her face. 'Why do you always switch languages?' she asked irritably. 'It totally confuses me.'

'You understand both Italian and French,' he said. 'It doesn't confuse you at all.'

'I *am* confused,' she said, snatching up a wrap to cover her nakedness.

He rose from the bed and came over to where she was standing with her back towards him. He put his hands on her shoulders, his breath skating past her ear as he drew her back towards him. 'What's confusing you, *cara*?' he asked.

Sienna turned to face him. 'I'm sorry,' she said, letting her shoulders go down in a slump. 'I think I'm letting my sister's wedding get to me. It's so…so starkly different from ours.'

His eyes searched hers. 'And that's a problem for you?'

She shifted her gaze from his. 'No,' she said, fiddling with a dress on the bed that was now in desperate need of an iron. 'Why should it be? It's not the same thing at all. We're not in love or planning a future together. We both want what we can get out of this arrangement. This little affair we've got going is all well and good for now, but I don't want to be tied to you in the long term any more than you want to be tied to me.'

A long silence ticked past, measured by the rustling of her increasingly haphazard sorting.

'Do you want some help packing?' Andreas asked. 'It looks like you need it.'

Sienna turned and faced him again. 'I can do it by myself,' she said. 'I think it's time I learned how to sort out the mess of my own making.'

'This is not your mess,' he said, frowning as he raked his hair with his fingers. 'This is my father's.'

'Is it?' she asked, giving him a world-weary look. 'Is it really?'

He held her gaze for a long moment. 'I suspect my father wanted to teach me a lesson,' he said. 'He wanted me to understand how hard it is to choose between what I think I want and what I really need.'

'So have you figured it out yet?' she asked.

He continued to hold her gaze. 'I already know what I want,' he said. 'I'm not sure, however, that it's what I need.'

'And what is it that you want, Andreas?' she asked. 'More money? More fame and notoriety?'

He took her by the upper arms and pulled her close, making her heart beat triple time as she felt his body stirring against her belly. 'I think you already know the answer to that,' he said and pressed his mouth down firmly on hers.

CHAPTER TWELVE

'YOU look absolutely amazing,' Sienna said as she made one last adjustment to Gisele's veil. 'Emilio is going to be speechless when he sees you.'

Gisele smiled as she squeezed Sienna's hands in hers. 'I think Andreas is going to have a similar reaction when he sees you,' she said. 'You look stunning.'

'Thanks…' Sienna slipped her hands out of Gisele's and moved to the dressing table so she could do a last minute touch-up of her make-up before Hilary, Gisele's mother, came back from the suite next door where the hairdresser was styling her hair. With all the bustle of getting ready, it was the first time Sienna had been alone with her sister.

'Is everything all right?' Gisele asked.

Sienna met her twin's grey-blue gaze in the mirror. It still startled her sometimes to see an identical replica of herself standing there. They were so physically alike it was uncanny, and yet they were so different. 'I'm fine,' she said, forcing a bright smile to her lips.

Gisele came over and put a gentle hand on Sienna's bare shoulder. 'You and Andreas are happy together, aren't you?' she asked. 'It was such a whirlwind courtship, I just wondered if—'

'Of course we're happy,' Sienna said, dipping the lipstick brush in a pot of lip-gloss. 'We're just peachy.'

'You don't have any regrets about having such a small wedding?' Gisele asked.

Sienna's hand trembled slightly as she painted her lips with the lipgloss. 'No, why should I?'

Gisele caught her gaze in the mirror. 'I saw you looking at me when Mum was helping me into my dress,' she said. 'You had such a sad look on your face. I realised then how difficult it must have been for you, getting married without your mother to help you. Is that why you kept things so simple?'

Sienna put the lip brush down with a little clatter on the dressing table. 'I'm not like you, Gisele,' she lied. 'A big wedding has never interested me. For one thing, I'd be rubbish at organising it. I'd probably forget to invite someone terribly important or not order the right colour flowers. Anyway, can you see me wearing white? I wouldn't make it to the church without spilling something on it or tripping over the train or something.'

Gisele smiled and tucked a wayward strand of Sienna's hair back into the elegant style the hairdresser had arranged earlier. 'You're good for Andreas,' she said, putting her hands on Sienna's shoulders and meeting her gaze in the mirror once more. 'I could tell from last night's dinner that he has a tendency to be a little formal and distant. It probably comes from his wealthy background. He doesn't feel comfortable letting people get too close until he works out whether he can trust them or not. I see the way he looks at you. It was as if he can't quite believe his luck to have found someone who loves him for who he is, not for what he can provide.'

Sienna reached for the bronzer brush, even though

she really didn't need it given that her cheeks were doing a perfectly fine job of blushing all by themselves. 'He is lucky to have me,' she said. 'We're lucky to have each other.' *Even if it's only for another few months*, she thought.

'He'll make a wonderful father,' Gisele said. 'Have you talked about when you'll start a family?'

Sienna averted her gaze. 'I'm not...He's not...We're not...ready...'

Gisele smiled. 'It's just I have some news for you,' she said. 'I wondered if that was why you and Andreas married in such a rush. I got all excited. I thought it'd be so cool if we were pregnant together.'

Sienna swung around on the stool so quickly her head spun. 'You're pregnant?' she said.

'Yes,' Gisele said, beaming radiantly. 'Emilio is beside himself with pride. We haven't told anyone, other than Mum. I wanted you to be one of the first to know. We're having twins.'

'Twins!' Sienna grabbed Gisele's hands, desperately trying to ignore the sudden pang of envy that seized her. It was wrong of her to feel jealous. It was hideous of her. It was selfish. She wasn't the one who had longed for a family since she was a young girl. Sienna had no idea of what to do with a baby. She hadn't even held one in her arms.

What right did she have to wonder what it would be like to carry a pregnancy to full term? To feel those tiny limbs growing and moving inside her? To hold that precious little bundle soon after it was born? To smell that sweet innocent smell and stroke that soft fluffy head?

A wave of longing rushed through her. It set off an ache that felt like a weight pressing down on her heart.

There would be no sweet-smelling babies for her. Andreas had already made it clear how unsuitable he thought her as a mother for his children. He had left nothing to chance. Every time they had made love he had used protection.

The ache tightened in her chest like a spanner working on a nut and bolt.

Just as Sienna couldn't imagine having someone else kiss her or make love to her, she couldn't imagine having someone else's baby. She didn't *want* anyone else's baby.

'Do you know if they're identical?' she asked, thinking of those little limbs wrapped around each other like she and Gisele had been.

'Yes,' Gisele said. 'The ultrasound showed they're sharing the same placenta.'

'And what about the sex?' Sienna asked. 'Do you know if they're boys or girls?'

'Boys,' Gisele said, placing a hand on her only very slightly rounded tummy. 'After losing Lily, I never thought I'd be able to face a pregnancy again, but this time I just know it's going to be different. It *feels* different.'

The door of the suite opened and Hilary came in, looking every inch the stylishly coiffed and very proud mother of the bride. 'Ready, darling?' she said to Gisele. 'Emilio is eagerly awaiting his beautiful bride.'

Sienna handed Gisele the bridal bouquet, forcing an I'm-so-happy-for-you-smile to her lips, while inside her heart felt as if it were being backed over by an earthmover.

She had already forfeited love.

Would she have to forfeit motherhood as well?

* * *

Andreas felt his heart do a couple of leapfrogs in his chest as Sienna walked up the aisle ahead of her twin sister. She was wearing a floor-length latte-coloured satin gown with a cream bow tied over her left hip. Her hair was up in an elegant style that gave her a distinctly regal air. She was breathtakingly beautiful, but then, so too was her twin sister.

He tore his eyes away from Sienna to look at Gisele as she floated up the aisle in an ivory satin gown and a stunning veil and diamond tiara. Before the bridal party dinner last night he had only seen photographs of her in the press. The likeness, even in print, was amazing but meeting her in the flesh had been totally surreal. It was like looking at a mirror image of Sienna.

It occurred to him then, with an unexpected twinge of guilt, that this was what Sienna would have looked like as a proper bride if he had married her under normal circumstances.

Had *she* wanted something like this?

He felt another ferocious fist of guilt grab at his gut.

Didn't most young women dream of having their day as a fairy tale princess?

As the service got underway he watched to see if any of the heartfelt vows that were being exchanged were affecting Sienna. She stood looking at her sister and the handsome groom with a smile on her lips, but Andreas wasn't sure if that glittery moisture in her eyes was from happiness or something else. She looked rather pale, he thought, and once or twice he saw her lick her lips, from nervousness or dryness, he couldn't quite tell.

Andreas was surprised to find the service so moving. He had attended weddings before and, while he had mostly enjoyed them, he had not felt a lump of emotion suddenly stick like a nut halfway down his throat when the groom promised to love and protect his bride.

Emilio Andreoni was clearly a man deeply in love. His voice cracked unashamedly as he slipped the wedding band on Gisele's finger. Gisele looked up at him with absolute devotion, tears of joy shining in her eyes.

Andreas felt ashamed of how his marriage to Sienna had been such a sterile, businesslike affair. She hadn't looked at him with her eyes full of love. Hers had glittered with hatred. Their clinical, emotionless union made a mockery of one so sacred and deeply poignant as this. How had his life become such a tawdry sideshow alley game of smoke and mirrors?

He caught Sienna's eye across the church. She smiled at him but it was a weak movement of her lips that didn't involve her eyes. She looked away again, focusing her gaze on the bride and groom as they exchanged their first kiss as a married couple.

Andreas wondered if she was thinking of *their* first kiss. Their mouths had never touched until they had exchanged those meaningless vows. He was reminded of the electric shock of that kiss every time he had kissed her since. It was a power surge in his flesh. He could feel it now just thinking about it. His body ached for her. His blood thrummed with it. He had expected the pulse of lust to wane a little by now, but if anything it had increased. Would the five months left of their marriage contract be enough to satisfy him?

Because she was part of the bridal party, Sienna was separated from Andreas for most of the reception. It made his hunger for her all the more intense. He couldn't wait until the formalities were over so he could stake his claim. His whole body prickled with annoyance when she danced with the best man as part of the bridal waltz routine. Andreas clenched and unclenched his fists under the table as he watched the best man's arms go around her and bring her up close.

Jealousy was a new experience for him. He could not remember ever feeling it before. He bristled with it. It made his teeth grind together. It made his jaw ache. It made his blood boil.

His gaze narrowed. Was Sienna *flirting* with that guy? She was smiling up at him with that dazzling smile of hers. Her left hand was on the guy's shoulder and her right encased in the grasp of his. Her body was moving in time to the music, a slow romantic waltz that had her pelvis brushing against the best man's every now and again as her feet tangled with his.

Andreas strode across the dance floor and laid a firm hand on the best man's shoulder. 'I'd like to dance with my wife,' he said.

The best man dropped his hold on Sienna and stepped back. 'Sure,' he said with an easy smile. 'She's a fabulous dancer. I have two left feet but she made me dance like a pro.'

Andreas ground his teeth behind his stiff smile. 'She is indeed an expert at executing tricky manoeuvres.'

Sienna's grey-blue gaze collided with his once the best man had gone. 'What the hell are you playing at?' she asked in a hushed voice. 'You interrupted the bridal party waltz, for God's sake.'

Andreas turned her so she wasn't facing the wedding guests. 'I had to step in before you made a complete fool of yourself,' he said. 'You were practically crawling into that guy's skin.'

She glowered up at him. 'I was not!'

He tugged her against him. 'The only man you should be getting up close and personal with is me,' he said. 'We're married, remember?'

'Only for another five months,' she said, challenging him with her haughty gaze. 'After that, I'm free to be with anyone I want and you won't be able to do a thing to stop me.'

He whipped her around as the music changed tempo, his groin alive with want as her slender thighs bumped against his. 'I wouldn't dream of trying,' he said, 'but for now you are my wife and I expect you to act accordingly.'

Her eyes flashed at him like blue lightning. 'I'm not really your wife,' she said. 'This is just an act, a stupid little game of charades. I'm surprised no one has already guessed we're not the real deal. I'm sure Gisele already suspects something.'

'What makes you think that?' Andreas said, holding her close to him as another couple glided past.

'She kept grilling me on why we got married so quickly and why I hadn't gone for a big wedding,' she said, frowning and chewing at her lip as if the conversation had somehow distressed her.

Andreas deftly led her off the dance floor to a secluded area behind a column. He kept his arms around her, his body thrumming with need with her standing thigh to thigh with him. 'Are you disappointed we didn't have a proper wedding?' he asked.

She pulled her chin back against her neck in a gesture of scorn. 'Are you joking? Of course I'm not disappointed. What we have is a sham. It was bad enough lying in front of a celebrant, let alone a priest and a huge congregation. Anyway, it's different for Gisele. She loves Emilio and he loves her. They have their whole lives to look forward to.'

Andreas held her gaze for a beat or two. A shadow had passed through her eyes and her beautiful white teeth began to nibble at her bottom lip again. He pushed against the soft pillow of her lip with the pad of his fingertip. 'What's wrong?' he asked.

She jerked her head away from his touch. 'Nothing.'

'I know you better than that, *ma petite*. You always do that to your lip when you're brooding or mulling over something.'

She drew in a breath and then let it out on a long exhalation. 'I'm being stupid and sentimental,' she said, slipping out of his hold. 'Weddings do that to me, or at least ones like this.'

'Yes, well, it was certainly a very moving service,' Andreas conceded. 'Anyone can see Emilio and Gisele belong together. I've never seen a more radiant bride.'

'Gisele's pregnant,' she said. 'She's having twins.'

'That's wonderful news,' he said. 'You must be very happy for her.'

'I am…It's just…' She bit her lip again and dropped her eyes from his.

'Just what?' he asked, cupping the side of her face to bring her gaze back in line with his.

Her eyes shimmered for a moment but then she blinked and her gaze cleared. 'Just as well you're using protection,' she said lightly as she slipped out of his hold. 'Can you imagine the snotty nosed little brats we would make? If we had twins, I bet they'd fight like demons from the moment of conception. I'd probably get stretch marks from all the punches and kicks going on inside.'

Andreas felt a primal tug deep and low in his groin. He pictured Sienna ripe with his seed, her body swelling as each week and month passed. He thought of two little baby girls with silver-blonde hair, or two little boys with jet-black hair, or one of each. He imagined seeing them born, holding them in his arms, loving and protecting and providing for them for as long as he drew breath.

He put a brake on his thoughts like a speeding driver trying to avoid a crash.

In a matter of months he would have everything sewn up the way he wanted it. He would have the chateau and Sienna would have her money. He didn't need or want the complication of being tied forever with her. Their passion would burn out. Their marriage had come about for all the wrong reasons.

He would *not* be a slave to lust.

It would burn out.

It *had* to burn out.

'We should get back to the reception,' he said. 'Everyone will be wondering what's happened to us.'

CHAPTER THIRTEEN

IT WAS late by the time they got back to their room at the hotel. Sienna kicked off her shoes and tossed her wrap on to the bed. She felt tired and overwrought. Her emotions had been building to a crescendo all evening. Andreas's brooding silence hadn't helped. He had barely spoken a word to her during the remainder of the reception. He had danced with her but it had felt as if he were just going through the motions, just like their relationship.

Their marriage was a lie.

It was a farce compared to her sister's. It made her feel like a fraud. It made her feel cheap and tainted. How could she have signed up for something so far from what she longed and yearned for?

She couldn't carry on like this, telling lie after lie after lie. How long before Andreas saw through it? How long before everyone saw through it? She would become an object of pity, just like her mother. She would be known as the woman not good enough, not beautiful enough or smart enough to hold her man.

'I'm going out,' Andreas said.

Sienna frowned. 'What? Now? It's almost one in the morning.'

'I feel like some air.'

She shrugged as if she didn't care either way. 'Don't expect me to wait up for you,' she said, pulling the pins from her hair and tossing them on to the dressing table willy-nilly.

A stiff silence passed.

'I have to fly to Washington DC for a few days,' he said. 'I've organised for Franco to collect you in the morning.'

'You don't want me to come with you?' she asked, meeting his gaze in the mirror.

His expression was unreadable. 'I'll be busy with meetings,' he said. 'The businessman I'm doing a collection for wants me to meet a colleague of his.'

Sienna loathed the feeling of being dismissed like a mistress who no longer held the same fascination and appeal. Was this how her mother had felt? Discarded? Betrayed? Unlovable? Worthless?

Her heart contracted as she looked at Andreas's stony expression. She was not important to him. How could she have let things get to this? She had betrayed every one of her values. He had used her to get what he wanted. He felt secure now she had succumbed to his seduction. After all, he had nothing to lose. If she left him now, he would still get what he wanted, what he had always wanted. He wanted a wretched old pile of bricks and mortar, not her. She had been a silly little fool to imagine otherwise.

She kept her expression cool and collected. 'Aren't you worried about what people will think of us being in separate countries when we've only been married a month?' she asked.

'I have a business to run,' he said. 'I don't want to be distracted when I'm working on such a big contract.'

'Fine,' Sienna said, throwing him a casual look to cover the wrenching pain she was feeling inside. 'I guess I'll see you when I see you.'

He didn't answer but the door closing on his exit was answer enough.

'What do you mean she's not here?' Andreas said when he got back to his villa in Tuscany a week later.

Elena lifted her hands in a don't-blame-me manner. 'She told me to tell you it's over,' she said. 'She doesn't want to be married to you any more.'

Andreas sucked in a furious breath. 'When did she leave?'

'The day after her sister's wedding,' Elena said. 'I tried to talk her out of it but she was very stubborn about it. She'd made up her mind.'

'Why didn't you call me and tell me this days ago?' he asked.

'She made me promise.'

'You are employed by me, not her,' Andreas railed at her. 'You should have informed me the minute she left.'

Elena gave him an accusing look. 'Maybe you should have called her every day like a loving husband would have done,' she said. 'Maybe then she wouldn't have run away.'

Andreas clawed a hand through his hair. 'Where the hell is she?' he asked.

'She didn't say where she was going,' Elena said. 'I don't think she wants you to know. She left this for you.' She handed him his mother's ring.

Andreas closed his fingers over the ring until it bit

into his palm. He had thought he'd had the upper hand by distancing himself for a few days but Sienna had turned the tables on him. Didn't she want the money? If she left him she would automatically default. She wouldn't get a penny. A month ago that would have pleased him no end. Now, all he could think about was getting her to come back.

He reached for his phone and rapid-dialled her but it went straight to voicemail. He shoved his phone back in his pocket and glared at Elena. 'She must have left some clue as to where she was going,' he said. 'Did she take her passport?'

'I think so,' Elena said, sighing heavily. 'Scraps is pining for her. He won't eat. I'm worried about him.'

Andreas gave a scornful grunt as he raked his fingers through his hair. 'Shows how much she cares about him.'

'She loves him,' Elena said.

'If she loved him she'd be here with him, not running off to God knows where,' he said.

'Maybe she doesn't know if he loves her back,' Elena said with a direct look.

Andreas glowered at her. 'Don't you have work to do? Some cushions to straighten or some clothes to fold and iron.'

'Sì, signor,' she said, 'but without Signora Ferrante here there is not much for me to do. She makes this place come alive, no?'

Andreas went out to the barn but Scraps barely lifted his head off his paws. His woebegone eyes followed Andreas's movements as he crouched down in front of him. 'What's this I hear about you not eating?'

The dog let out a mournful little whine.

'She won't answer her phone,' Andreas said, absently scratching behind the dog's tattered ears. 'I've left hundreds of messages. She's doing it deliberately, you know. She wants me to beg her to come back. But I'm not going to do it. If she wants to default, then that's her business. It's not as if I'm going to lose out if she pulls the plug on our relationship. I still get the chateau. That's all I ever wanted in the first place.'

Scraps gave a low growl, his tawny eyes staring unblinkingly at Andreas.

Andreas pulled his hand away and exhaled heavily. 'OK, I know what you're thinking. You're thinking I'm an idiot for lying to myself for so long.' He sent his fingers through his hair and let out another sigh. 'And you'd be right. I don't care about the chateau. I don't want to live there, not unless she's with me. I don't want to live here without her either. The place is so formal and...*tidy*.' He coughed out a humourless laugh. 'I hate the way she leaves her mess everywhere. Do you know she *always* leaves the lid off the toothpaste? It drives me crazy. But I'd give anything to have her with me driving me crazy right now. I don't know where she is or who's she's with.' His gut clenched in anguish and dread. 'I don't know if I can get her back. What am I supposed to do? Crawl on my belly and beg her to come back to me?'

Scraps gave his threadbare tail a wag against the dusty floor, his eyes still staring wisely at Andreas.

'You're right,' Andreas said, sighing heavily again. 'I'm crazy about her. I'm never going to get her out of my system, am I? We're not talking about lust here. It's never been about lust, has it? What was I thinking? She's the best thing that's ever happened to me. I love her.'

He frowned and gave his head a little shake. 'I can't believe I just said that. I don't think I've told anyone that before, apart from my mother, which is totally different. *I love her.*'

He cautiously reached out to ruffle the dog's ears again. 'What if she doesn't love me?' he asked. 'I'm going to look the biggest fool if I gush out what I feel and she just laughs in my face.'

Scraps let out a long doggy sigh and settled his head back down on his paws.

'I'm not going to tell her over the phone or in a text message,' Andreas said with steely determination. 'I'm going to track her down and talk to her face to face. She thinks she can outsmart me but she's wrong.'

He got to his feet and dusted off his hands. 'If you want to come inside I guess I could make an exception just this once,' he said. 'But no jumping up on the sofas and you are absolutely banned from any of the beds, do you understand?'

The little cottage by the sea on South Harris in Scotland was a perfect hideaway. The long, lonely windswept beaches on the island gave Sienna plenty of time to walk and think about her future—her lonely future without Andreas. She had kept her phone on for the first week, hoping he would call or at least text, but he had cut her loose like the trophy wife he had fashioned her into and, even more galling, she had allowed it to happen.

But now was different.

Now it was time for her to rebuild her life, a life that did not include him, a life without love and passion and fulfilment—a wretchedly lonely, miserable life, the opposite of the one her twin sister was living. How could two people so identical in looks have such disparate lives?

She had phoned Gisele, so as to avoid causing her sister any undue worry but she had refused to say where she was. She knew Gisele would immediately tell Andreas. She wasn't ready to talk to him yet. As far as she was concerned, he'd had his chance and he had blown it.

Sienna had since turned her phone off, only checking it once a day for messages. The second week there were literally hundreds of texts and missed calls from him each day. The messages had progressed from calm and polite pleas to get her to call him, to shouting tirades interspersed with colourful obscenities.

She deleted them all, only wishing she could delete all her memories of him so easily.

She lay awake at night as the wind howled against the shore, whipping up the waves like galloping white horses. She spent hours thinking of Andreas, of his touch, the way his hands felt against her skin, the way his mouth felt against hers, the way his body felt as it claimed hers.

Sienna had been on the island almost a fortnight without once setting eye on a newspaper. She had avoided reading anything on the web browser on her phone as well. She didn't want to know what the press were saying about her and Andreas. But while she was walking on Scarista beach that morning she had briefly turned on her phone and found a message from Gisele alerting her to an article that had come out a day or two before regarding the sex tape scandal. Apparently the man involved had given an exclusive interview to a journalist. He had seen the news of Gisele and Emilio's wedding and had obviously thought he could cash in on the situation by giving a no holds barred tell-all interview.

Sienna read the interview with a churning feeling in her stomach. It brought it all back: the shame and disgust she felt at herself. The way the man told it, she had acted like a drunken slut.

Despair clawed at her chest as she stood on the windswept beach. Was there anywhere she could run, far enough away to hide from this? Was this never going to go away?

But then she pressed on the second link Gisele had sent her.

French-Italian tycoon Andreas Ferrante is pressing charges of slander against Eric Hogan over Mr Hogan's claim that he slept with Mr Ferrante's wife Sienna Baker in London two and a half years ago. The case is likely to be long drawn-out and expensive but Andreas Ferrante says he will not stop until his wife's name is cleared. Police are making further enquiries regarding a possible drink spiking charge on Mr Hogan following the recent revelations of witnesses.

Sienna's heart was beating so fast she could barely breathe. She read the article again, her eyes prickling with tears.

Andreas had stood up for her.

He had publicly defended her. He was fighting her

battle for her, not even counting the cost in money, let alone the cost to his fiercely guarded privacy.

Sienna was heading back to the cottage to pack when a tall, imposing figure came striding towards her. She knew immediately who it was. She felt a shiver run over her flesh as soon as he came into view. The wild wind was whipping at his sooty black hair and his unshaven face looked as thunderous as the brooding sky above.

'You'd better have a damn good reason for not returning any of my calls,' he ground out. 'Do you have any idea of the trouble you've caused? I've spent tens of thousands of euros looking high and low for you. Why couldn't you have just told me? Just one phone call or text. God damn it, was that so hard?'

Sienna just stood there looking up at him. Her gaze drank in his features.

He had stood up for her.

'OK, so give me the silent treatment; see if I care,' he said. He shoved his windswept hair back with one of his hands. 'Just answer me one thing. Why did you run away like that?'

'How did you find me?' she asked.

'Gisele told me she thought she heard bagpipes in the background when you called her,' he said. 'That narrowed it down considerably. The rest I left up to a private investigator. Do you have any idea of what the press have been saying?'

Sienna peeled a strand of hair away from her mouth. 'I haven't seen anything in the press until this morning,' she said. 'I'm sorry about the embarrassment I've caused you.'

'I'm not talking about that,' he said, glaring at her fiercely. 'I've taken care of that sleaze ball. He won't be saying anything about you ever again. How could you think I wouldn't be out of my mind with worry over you? Do you realise what a fool you made me look in front of my staff when I turned up there at the villa and you'd already been gone a week?'

'I'm sorry but I didn't want you to talk me out of it,' Sienna said. 'Anyway, you could have called me. I was giving you a dose of your own medicine.'

'You realise you won't get a penny because of this,' he said still glowering at her. 'You defaulted. I get everything.'

'You've always *had* everything, Andreas,' she said. 'The irony is I've spent most of my life envying rich people like you. I wanted it all: the nice houses and the designer clothes, the jewellery and the fabulous holidays. I thought they would make me happy, that they would make me feel a sense of belonging. But I've come to realise possessions and prestige can never make up for what's most important in life. They're nothing when you don't have love.'

His eyes narrowed in anger. 'You think I don't love you?' he said, shouting above the howling wind. 'I've just spent the last fortnight without proper sleep or food. God knows what's happened to my business because I haven't put a foot inside my office or my workshop. And don't get me started on that contract I just forfeited. I've been too busy trying to track you down to do a thing about it. How dare you stand there accusing me of not loving you?'

Sienna swept her tongue over her wind-chapped lips as her heart went pitter-pat. 'You love me?' she said. 'You're not just saying it to save face and get me to come back?'

'I'm saying it because it's true, damn it!' he said. 'I love your madcap sense of humour. I love your mess. I love the way you tamed a flea-bitten mongrel dog that no one else wanted. I love your smile. I love your laugh. I love your cheekiness. I love the way you nearly always have a spark of mischief in your eyes. I love the way you feel in my arms. I love the way you say one thing and mean the total opposite.' He drew in a breath and released it in a whoosh before he added, 'Have I left anything out?'

Sienna gave him a sheepish smile. 'I think you've just about covered it,' she said.

He let out a laugh and grabbed her, hugging her close to his chest, breathing in the salty sea air that had clung to her hair. 'You little minx,' he said. 'I love you so much it hurts.'

She eased back to look up at him. 'Where does it hurt?'

'Here,' he said, placing one of her hands over his heart.

Sienna blinked back tears. 'I've been so lonely and sad since Gisele and Emilio's wedding. I couldn't live the lie any more. I didn't think it was right. Your father was wrong to set things up the way he did. It was cruel and manipulative.'

'I know, *ma petite*,' he said, gently cupping her face so he could stroke her cheeks with his thumbs. 'I felt like that too. Seeing the love Emilio has for your sister unnerved me. All of my life I have avoided emotional commitment. I've always set the agenda in my relationships. But with you it was different. I couldn't control what I felt. I refused to confront it. I don't think I really understood how much I loved you until I saw the way Scraps behaved after you left.'

'Is he OK?' Sienna asked. 'I cried like a baby when I left him. My eyes were red and swollen for days.'

Andreas smiled at her. 'He's decided that the barn is no longer suitable accommodation,' he said. 'He's taken up residence in the villa. He has a particular penchant for lying on the sofa watching mind-numbing reality TV shows.'

Sienna smiled back as she looped her arms around his neck. 'That's my boy,' she said. 'I always knew he could be tamed. I just had to be patient.'

Andreas held her close against him. 'I want us to have a proper wedding. I want you to wear one of those fairy tale dresses with a big floating veil, and even glass slippers on your feet if you want. Whatever you want, just tell me and you shall have it.'

Sienna let out a sigh of contentment as she gazed into his hazel eyes. 'What more could I want than you?' she said.

'What about babies?' he said, his expression sobering for a moment. 'You said you didn't want children.'

'Now that you mention it, maybe a baby or two would be nice,' she said.

He kissed the end of her nose. 'I quite fancy the idea of you being pregnant,' he said. 'I think we should get working on that right away. What do you say?'

'Sounds like a plan.'

He held her aloft for a moment. 'Do you realise you haven't actually told me you love me?' he said. 'Here I am shouting it from one end of the beach to the other but you haven't said it back.'

'I love you,' Sienna said, smiling up at him radiantly. 'I love you with all my heart. I think I've always loved you, even when I hated you. Does that make sense?'

He gave her an indulgent smile. 'From you, my adorable little scatterbrain, it makes absolutely perfect sense,' he said and covered her mouth with his.

* * * * *